The Shadowed Hills

He had forgotten how she was. The childish adoration. What might even be called fanatical worship, the intense, narrow-eyed determination of eleven-year-old Katherine Andrews who had formed such a passionate attachment for him she had refused to be parted from him, doing her best to clamp herself to his side, to go exactly where he went when was home five years ago.

She had been a child then, easy to elude, easy to placate and please and promise as one would a child. Now she was a woman, but Christ Almighty, it seemed her feelings toward him had not changed.

Her body met his with a force so strong it nearly had him off his feat.

'Jamie, Jamie, Jamie you're home . . . Dear God you've come home at last,' she was babbling, her rosy face pressed into his shoulder, the sweet, wholesome smell of her enveloping him, her arms a stranglehold about his neck and for the life of him he could not prevent his own from lifting to hold her, to fold her against him.

More Coronet paperbacks by Audrey Howard

The Mallow Years
Shining Threads
A Day Will Come
All the Dear Faces
There Is No Parting
Echo of Another Time
The Woman from Browhead
The Silence of Strangers
A World of Difference
Promises Lost

About the author

Audrey Howard was born in Liverpool in 1929 and it is from that once-great seaport that many of the ideas for her books came. Before she began to write she had a variety of jobs, among them hairdresser, model, shop assistant, cleaner and civil servant. In 1981, out of work and living in Australia, she wrote the first of her novels. She was fifty-two. Her fourth novel, *The Juniper Bush*, won the Romantic Novel of the Year Award in 1988. She now lives in her childhood home, St Anne's on Sea, Lancashire.

The Shadowed Hills

Audrey Howard

CORONET BOOKS
Hodder and Stoughton

First published in Great Britain in 1996
by Hodder and Stoughton
A division of Hodder Headline PLC
First published in paperback in 1997 by Hodder and Stoughton
A Coronet Paperback

10 9 8 7 6 5 4 3 2 1

British Library Cataloguing in Publication Data

Howard, Audrey
The shadowed hills
1. English fiction – 20th century
I.Title
823.9'14 [F]

ISBN 0 340 66078 3

Typeset by Hewer Text Composition Services, Edinburgh
Printed and bound in Great Britain by
Mackays of Chatham PLC, Chatham, Kent

Hodder and Stoughton
A division of Hodder Headline PLC
338 Euston Road
London NW1 3BH

If I'd known grandchildren were so
much fun I'd have had them first!
This book is for mine.
Daniel and Adam Pitt.

1

The letter was brought to Cloudberry End just as they were sitting down to lunch, conveyed by the second of the three deliveries which the postal service of the nearby town of Crossclough provided. It was brought, with others, on the silver tray by Freda, the head parlourmaid, as was the custom, and placed beside the master who was tapping his fingers in an impatient tattoo on the shining surface of the table.

He took out his watch and glared at it.

"Where in hell are they?" he demanded of his wife. "I ask very little of them except that they be on time for meals but it seems they can't even do that. At one o'clock precisely we eat lunch in this house and they bloody well know it."

Though Jack Andrews was married to a lady he did not call himself a gentleman and saw no reason to curb his own inclination to curse whenever he he felt like it. They were all used to it, his wife, his children, his servants and showed no surprise nor offence when he did.

"Jack, darling, it *is* only a little after one and I'm sure they'll be here any moment," his wife said soothingly, and, as though their children had overheard the exchange between their parents, and to their mother's evident relief, the door was flung open with a great flourish and a good-looking young couple were revealed in the doorway. A small, brown, rough-haired bitch ran ahead of them, settling herself at once in a square of sunshine which lay across the carpet where she immediately fell into a light doze.

The two youngest children of Jack and Sara Andrews did not so much enter the room as make an entrance, lounging for a moment in the doorway, sure of themselves and their privileged place in this household, their matching smiles winning, their demeanour unabashed, the son's expression at least telling them that though he was late he was sure they would forgive him since he was so irresistible.

His father evidently did not agree with him.

"And what time d'you call this then? You both know what time we eat."

"Good morning to you, sir. Good morning, Mother, or is it afternoon?" their son said sweetly, kissing his mother on the cheek before seating himself on his father's left. His sister did the same, placing her rosy lips to her father's cheek as well as her mother's, in the absolute certainty that neither of them could stay cross with her for long. She shook her bright red mop of curls which rioted in a wild explosion about her head, extended her artificially sweet smile to the maidservants to indicate that they might begin to serve and threw herself – her mother could think of no other way to describe it – into the chair opposite her brother.

Christopher Andrews shook out his napkin, placing it across his knee and nodded to Lottie, the under parlourmaid who was helping Freda to serve, indicating that he would have a little soup. "Very little, thank you," he added, wincing away from the very smell of food and his sister Katy knew, despite his cheerful manner and impeccable appearance, that her brother was suffering from a monumental hangover, even at this late hour of the day. His voice was somewhat hoarse as though he had smoked too many cigars the night before and his green eyes were narrowed against the daylight which, though muted, seemed to hurt them.

Chris Andrews was the youngest son of Jack and Sara Andrews, named for his paternal grandfather of whom it was said in the village of Woodhead where his widow, Jack's mother, still lived, that he could idle his way through the day with nothing at the end to show for it with more success than any man in the district. His grandson had the attractive auburn look of his mother, lean and graceful and with eyes the colour of woodland moss but his nature came from the man who had fathered his own father. His mouth was thin, hard, tilted by a somewhat cruel humour as though there was nothing and no one in this life who could possibly make Chris Andrews believe it was meant to be taken seriously and he was the proverbial thorn in his father's flesh. He was twenty years old and had never performed, at school or at the university where he was supposed to be studying law and from where he had just come, what his father considered a hard day's work in his life. Jack Andrews was a wealthy man and there was no necessity for Chris Andrews to work, in Chris Andrews's opinion, not one shared by his father, and the mighty bellowing which echoed about the house when Master Chris was at home was legendary in the Longdendale Valley.

His sister, Katherine, was very like him in looks apart from the colour of her eyes which were a rich, clear amber, like whisky, her father used to say; but where Chris was languid, indolent, his attitude one of anything for a quiet life, Katy Andrews was inclined towards downright and undisguised rebellion, a wilful determination to have her own way, becoming truculent, even aggressive when it was denied her. This seldom happened, at least when her father was away from home which, during her childhood, had been often, for it was easier to let her do as she pleased, within reason, of course, than face the awesome might of her hot temper.

They ate in silence for several minutes. Jack Andrews, who in his early days had eaten food his cook wouldn't care to put in a pig swill bucket, relished a decent meal. He didn't feel "right" unless he had a good breakfast inside him of bacon, kidneys, sausage, mushrooms, fried tomatoes and at least two thick slices of fried bread done just as Mrs Tiplady, his cook, knew how to do them.

He was the same at midday, stoking himself up for the afternoon's labour with Mrs Tiplady's vermicelli soup, salmon trout with parsley, butter and new potatoes, followed by gooseberry tart with custard. He did full justice to his heaped plate from which, Katy was amused to notice, her brother studiously kept his gaze averted. He himself toyed with a forkful of this and a spoonful of that, going through the motions of eating lunch with his family while her mother cast anxious glances at her father, well aware that the previous little exchange was by no means over. Jack Andrews was known throughout the world of railway building as a hard man, an authoritative man who had worked a full fourteen hours, sometimes more, out of every twenty-four and he fully expected his sons to do the same. He disliked failure and, since he himself had never failed despite the poor start he had had in life, he could see no reason why his sons, who had known every advantage he had lacked, should not achieve even greater heights in the world of business, or in any profession they chose to take up for that matter.

Unfortunately, the authority he showed in his working life did not produce the same results in his own home and his two youngest children were known for their lack of discipline and definite inclination to defy his direction, which was a pity, for his two eldest were a credit to him.

He sat back in his chair, indicating to Freda that she might remove his plate. Yes, he'd have another cup of coffee, he said, and then he'd best be off.

"And what do *you* propose to do with yourself this afternoon, lad?" he continued as he sipped his coffee, eyeing his son's sartorial splendour with evident displeasure. Chris wore a well-cut pair of doeskin breeches and a high-cut, single-breasted tweed country jacket and waistcoat in shades of brown and fawn. The jacket had a vent at the back, an outside breast pocket and a slit cuff on each sleeve. His knee-length riding boots were of the finest leather, a highly polished brown, and his small, octagonal tie sported a tiepin fashioned in gold in his initials. He looked every inch the favoured son of a wealthy father, which he indubitably was, the impish smile he cast in his mother's direction seemed to say as he lounged at his ease at his father's table.

"I have not had the pleasure of your company since you came home," his father went on, "so I assume you've been keeping out of my way which is wise of you. Where the hell you get to is a question I'd like answered, though I don't suppose you'll oblige me and why that damned university has to close its doors for weeks on end is beyond me. Hell's teeth, if they kept you at it for fifty-two weeks in the year, as every other damned working man is kept at it you'd be a bloody lawyer by now. And how much longer am I expected to support you while you skylark about in the so-called 'halls of learning', tell me that?"

Katy could see with something approaching horrified laughter that her brother was doing his best not to yawn. He failed, his jaw cracking with the strain.

"You bone-idle young pup," his father roared. "If you're

so bloody worn out with junketing about the district in the pursuit of pleasure, happen a day or two in my company wouldn't go amiss. Perhaps I'll take you with me to Manchester this afternoon. I've a bit of business to see to there, legal business which needs attention. Your training might come in handy."

"Well, sir, as it happens I was going to talk to you about that." His son did his best to look serious.

"Were you now?"

"Perhaps after lunch, before you . . . we . . . set off for Manchester we could have a chat?"

"A chat! A chat about what? I haven't time to be sitting about like one of your mother's callers, drinking tea and gossiping over the latest doings in the valley. I'm to be in Manchester by three and the train won't wait on my pleasure, lad, nor yours, so you'd best say what you've got to say right now."

The two maidservants exchanged resigned glances. They'd be here all day at this rate, if they were any judge of it, which they were for they'd worked at Cloudberry End long enough to recognise the signs; the master and his son were settling themselves for a rare old ding-dong.

"Go on then, I'm listening," the master said, signalling to Freda to refill his coffee cup.

"Well, sir . . ." His son leaned forward, smiling with that infectious humour which most thought so endearing but which was totally lost on his father. It cost him a great effort for his constitution was exceedingly fragile today. He had been up no more than half an hour, having spent the morning with his head beneath the bedclothes, shielding his eyes from the light. His head was painful and his stomach sour and as she watched him his sister was aware, for had she not heard the thunder of his horse's hooves beneath her bedroom window last night, that he had not come home until well past three. He would have been out with his wild-riding, wild-drinking and spending friends, those whose fathers were not of the industrial middle classes as his father was. Young squireens from the landed gentry beyond Hollingsworth on the Lancashire side of the Pennines. Johnny Ashwell from Ashwell Hall, Tim Warren of Dunsford Manor and others of the same breeding who had nothing to do with their time but lark about the countryside, getting themselves and any willing dairymaid they could lay their hands on into trouble while they waited to step into the shoes their pedigreed fathers would vacate in due course.

"Well, sir," Chris said again, evidently at a loss as to where he should begin since his head ached abominably and he had had very little sleep. "It occurs to me that I am not exactly cut out to be . . . a lawyer"

His father continued to sip his coffee, giving every indication that he had nothing to say on the matter though they all knew better, even the parlourmaids who drew closer together as though to prop one another up in the blast which was surely coming. They didn't know why Mr Andrews bothered, quite honestly, since there was nothing more certain than that Master Chris would do exactly as he pleased and why he had stayed so long at that university was a mystery to them.

"Oh aye," his father said at last and with amazing mildness.

"Indeed, I find I cannot make head nor tail of what is being taught me and I also find . . . well, I am not particularly interested in it in the first place. It needs a man with a . . . a . . . serious turn of mind, you see, to concern himself with legal matters and so I thought . . . well, I have my allowance."

Sara Andrews sighed so heavily and at such length they

all turned to look at her, even Lottie and Freda. She nodded at the maids to indicate that she would take more coffee and Lottie sprang forward with the pot, glad, it seemed, as they all were, of the diversion.

Sara thanked the maidservant then turned back to her husband, her softly clouded green eyes imploring. Please, be gentle with him, her eyes begged him. He is young and thoughtless and surely he is what we have made him? He is not industrious like the other two. He is not ambitious either but his good humour is so engaging how could anyone, least of all his mother, bear to see him chastised? She failed to realise that it was her own indulgence, which her husband was not able to withstand, that was the root cause of the problems her two youngest children caused him. Don't be too hard on him, her expression pleaded. He will fit in somewhere if his father would just be patient . . . and kind. A place would be found for him and until then . . .

Her husband was a man who had clawed his way to his present position, snatching what he wanted, for the past thirty or so years, from all rivals in the construction of the railways, fighting, she was certain, hard and dirty, for it was a competitive business. He had bid for contracts as far north as Scotland and as far south as Cornwall, and won them too, travelling for weeks on end and for thousands of miles, driving his men as hard as he drove himself, coming home like a whirlwind to disturb the routine of the home he had built for her at the base of the brooding peak of Black Hill in the Dark Peak district of north Derbyshire. He was a man who had laboured to get where he was, and what he wanted from life, and he expected his sons to do the same. His two eldest boys had not disappointed him but this one, this audaciously charming and far from unintelligent son of theirs seemed to possess a restlessness, a reluctance to settle to anything which smacked of time-keeping, of routine, of responsibility, in fact of what other men described as work, preferring to shoot grouse and partridge up on Bleaklow, drink brandy, play cards and spend his time in the company of low women, his mother feared.

Jack Andrews's face softened as he looked at his wife. He was still a handsome man despite his fifty-one years, massive of build with dark, curling hair only recently touched with grey. A man whose devotion to his wife was as well known in the valley as his disagreements with his youngest son. They had been married for twenty-five years and wherever they went showed an open delight in one another which was as diverting to those who found themselves in their company, as it was unusual. He loved her and was loved by her and neither of them saw any reason to hide it. Of course their family and servants were used to their utter devotion, their tendency to touch one another's hand, to smile a secret but what was very evidently a private smile at one another, which could be very disconcerting at times, particularly when it happened across the dinner table when they were dining with friends.

Sara, even at forty-five, was a vividly beautiful woman, graceful, elegant and sweet-natured, inclined to laughter and sometimes even mischief. Because of the nature of her husband's work she had often been alone bringing up their four children and she had been lenient with them, soft some called it, so that they had grown up out of hand, or at least the two youngest. The eldest boy, Richard, who was a clever engineer, had gone off a year or two back to make his fortune in the business of railway construction as his father had, and was at this moment on the other side of the world in Japan. The Tokyo to Yokohama line was to open in September and Richie Andrews, who had promised his mother most faithfully that he would write at least once a month, had also promised her he would come home when the line was completed before setting out on another adventure. China needed railways, Canada, South Africa, South America but Sara had given up so much of her life to the laying of those shining steel rails, first with her husband and now with her eldest boy, she was sometimes inclined to be tearful about it as she leaned on her husband's broad chest in the privacy of their bedroom at Cloudberry End.

Why couldn't Richie build his railways in his homeland, she had sighed, so that his mother could see more of him? But the truth of it was that the building of railways which had been so abundant in her husband's younger days was virtually finished now in Britain. In Jack's day thousands of miles of track had been laid from one end of the land to the other. A legion of navvies, her husband among them, had blasted their way through obstacles which had seemed insurmountable, until the network of rails spread north, south, east and west like the threads of a giant cobweb. The railway age, begun in Stockton exactly fifty years ago, carrying on through five decades was, but for the odd branch line here and there, effectively finished. By 1860 all the main lines were completed and Sara Andrews's son, her first-born, had been forced to look elsewhere in the profession first his father and then he had chosen.

Now they all waited for the explosion of displeasure which must surely come from the master of the house. Young Chris Andrews would not be allowed to skylark about the countryside with Johnny Ashwell and Tim Warren, surely, but to what occupation other than the seeking of pleasure was he suited? For the past year Jack Andrews had been retired from railway building, at the entreaty of his wife. His investments, his shares in the railway, in coal mining, shipping, in several cotton mills in Lancashire and woollen mills in Yorkshire brought him in great wealth, and the paper mill he had recently purchased beside Topside Reservoir kept him fully occupied, and at home, which pleased his wife. But what was to be done with his youngest son who, it seemed, did not care to go into the legal profession as his father intended, since a lawyer in the family would have come in right handy.

"So, my son, you are to give up your studies at the university, or is it that the university has given up on you? The latter seems more likely, I would say."

His son shrugged deprecatingly and grinned, though his eyes were wary.

"That's about the size of it, sir."

"Oh, Chris darling, now what have you done?" his mother wailed and Katy sighed and raised her eyes in the direction of the ceiling. Good God, hadn't they all been expecting this ever since her brother had gone, with great reluctance, to begin his training in the legal profession? He was no more suited to it than the dog who dozed, one eye opening occasionally to check on her whose dog she was, in the square of sunshine by the window. Chris was a pest, a menace, an aggravating nuisance who, as a boy, and even now, had teased her, fought her, coaxed her into wild escapades – not that she needed much coaxing, she remembered – the pair of them getting into so much trouble her father had threatened to send them both off to boarding school. Life had been, she freely admitted it, unendurably boring since he had left for the university. He was four years older than she was and had always harboured the belief that he was the best looking, the most winning of their mother's children, not only her favourite, which was probably true, but that of every maidservant in the house. He was never defeated, never dismayed, carefree and smiling when he got his way, strutting through life like the young lordling he thought himself to be.

But then wasn't she exactly the same? The thought made her smile.

"Really, Mother, does it matter what he's done?" she protested, "since it was bound to happen sooner or later. He was never cut out for the academic life, was he, so whatever it was, probably to do with a girl, or gambling, would have come about— "

"Katherine, that's enough from you," her father snapped.

"Well, it's true and you both know it. Does he ever show interest in anything other than playing the fool with those half-witted friends of his?"

"This is nothing to do with you, Katy Andrews, so I'll thank you to keep your mouth shut and your nose out of my business. This is between Father and me— "

"Be quiet, lad," his father interrupted him, "or I swear I'll take a strap to you" – which they all knew was an idle threat since it would distress his wife – "and as for you, Katherine, I fail to see— "

"Please, Jack, don't upset yourself, darling," which again meant don't upset *me*.

"Upset myself. *Upset myself!* God above, Sara, what am I to do with the pair of them? Chris is twenty and shows no aptitude for anything other than gaming and . . . and other things, and as for Katy she conducts herself with a lack of decorum which would not look out of place on a girl who has been brought up in the back streets of Liverpool. Jesus Christ . . ." His frustration contorted his face into a deep, ferocious frown. "I am forever being told that she has been seen somewhere she has no right to be. Oh, hell and damnation, Sara . . ."

Jack pushed his hand savagely through his thick hair, making it stand on end and his deep brown eyes, darker than his daughter's, were lit with fires of outrage. The splendidly cut black frock-coat he wore strained across his broad shoulders. He was very evidently doing his best to contain his thwarted anger, for the sake of his wife only, but his daughter did not see, or refused to see, the signs of danger.

"Father, you know there is always someone who delights in tattling about others. What I do is perfectly harmless."

"Oh, it is, is it?"

"Yes, and why you listen to such gossip is beyond me."

"Katy, I'm warning you."

"Why don't you tell them, whoever they are, to mind their own business?"

"Katherine, for your own safety's sake, either go to your room or be quiet until I have finished with this . . . this workshy young devil here. And when I have done so I shall have a word or two to say about your harmless behaviour."

"Surely you are to take no heed of some busybody who has seen me racing my mare up towards Bleaklow Head."

"There are dangerous bogs up there, girl, which— "

"Which I know about, Father, and so avoid them. I have been on the moors all my life, you know that."

"That's just it and from now on I insist you stay in the valley or, if that don't suit, in your mother's drawing room where you belong."

Her father, for once ignoring his wife's imploring expression, leaped to his feet, his face outraged. He had two sons who were a blessing to him, one an engineer and one up in Edinburgh training to be a medical doctor. Clever was David Andrews, like his older brother Richard, hardworking and assiduous in his studies, but these two wild ones, his son Christopher and his daughter Katherine, were a sore trial to him.

He glared at them both. His daughter had fallen into a frowning silence, her mouth set in a mutinous line, her jaw tight clenched, while his son appeared to have sunk into a light doze similar to that of the animal on the carpet.

His wife watched them all anxiously, her arched eyebrows dipping in a frown. Jack looked as though he would like nothing better than to give both his son and his daughter a good hiding, or, failing that, lock them in their rooms on bread and water, and Sara wondered why it was that either one of these two caused more trouble, more ructions, more downright aggravation than her other two put together. Their father turned, ready to explode with frustration, looking for something on which to vent it.

"And what's that bloody animal doing in here? I've told you a hundred times, Katy, to keep the thing out of the house. Are you incapable of obeying even the simplest order?"

"Yes, Father. I mean, no, Father."

"Well see to it in future."

"She's doing no harm, Father," and as though she knew she was being discussed the scruffy-looking little bitch raised her head, seeming almost to smile in supplication, thumping her short stubby tail on the carpet in an ecstasy of devotion.

"Katherine." Her father's voice had an ominous sound to it.

"Darling," his wife interrupted smoothly, "do sit down and see if there is any mail for me. It's time I had a letter from Richie."

It was a diversion and they all knew it. The only person who could calm Jack Andrews when his two youngest children threw him into a rage was his wife and though the matter of what was to be done with her youngest son was not yet dealt with, and the question of her daughter's wild riding on the moor was one which cropped up almost daily, it could all be left until another time, surely?

Her husband sat down, somewhat calmer, and his children exchanged relieved glances. He riffled through the post, still irritable, then handed a letter to his daughter.

"Aye, lass, there's one here but it's not from Richie. Pass it to your mother, Katy, and take that look off your face, for I mean to have my way in this. You should not be riding alone and especially not up on the moor. You know how dangerous it is. You are sixteen years old and if you want to ride then take Dicken with you," he was saying but a strange sound from the end of the table, a sound somewhere between a moan and a hiss of agony brought him instantly to his feet again and cut off his flow of exasperated words.

"Sara . . . darling?" he questioned, his voice aggressive, for what hurt his wife hurt Jack Andrews a hundredfold. In fact he wouldn't have it at any cost. His sole purpose in life was her happiness and whoever had written her the opened letter which was trembling in her hand had better have a bloody good reason for doing so.

His chair fell backwards with a crash. The dog leaped to her feet and began to bark and Lottie dropped the laden tray, scattering soiled dishes all over the rich pile of Mrs Andrews's beautiful sand-coloured carpet. Both Chris and Katy pushed their chairs back and stood up uncertainly, still clutching their napkins, watching as their large father scooped up their dainty little mother, holding her to him in an agony of remorse just as though whatever ailed her was his fault.

"Sweetheart, what is it? Tell me, darling, is it bad news?" Though he could think of nothing and no one who would dare upset his precious and half-fainting wife. "What is it?"

"Jack, oh Jack," she was moaning into his shirt front and both Chris and Katy exchanged appalled glances. What on earth could there be in the letter clenched in their mother's hand and who was it from? Whatever it was it had badly upset her and if their mother was upset their father would lash out at the first person who came to hand, namely them and hadn't they had enough for one day? Should they make a run for it? their eyes asked one another, since the one thing they had learned early in life was that for Jack and Sara Andrews no one existed but each other. Something that had happened in their past before their children were born, though they knew none of the details. Oh, they knew their parents cared about them and their upbringing had been safe and protected, a perfectly happy childhood, but they knew they came second in their parents' affections.

Their exchanged glances asked the same question. Did their mother and father want to be alone or should they stay in case . . . well, something might be required of them? It seemed unfeeling simply to drift away as though they were not in the least concerned about what was happening.

"Who's the letter from, my darling?" their father was pleading. "Won't you let me see it?" For their mother was still clutching it, all crumpled up, in her hand.

"It's from . . . someone called . . . Henry Taylor."

"Henry Taylor?" Their father looked bewildered.

"Henry . . . Oh God, Jack, it seems he is . . . *Alice's* husband."

Sara Andrews choked on the last two words. She burrowed like a small animal against her husband, incoherent sounds coming from her and Katy could feel the cold run through her veins and small frozen feathers of ice trail across her flesh. The hairs on the back of her neck rose stiffly, for the total disbelief and repudiation in her mother's voice were quite indescribable. She wanted to go to her, to hold her protectively in her own strong arms, for Katy Andrews was almost a head taller than her mother, but of course her father wouldn't allow it. He would let no one comfort his wife, not when he was there to do it and Katy accepted it, as they all did, even her brothers, at Cloudberry End.

"Let me see it, sweetheart," Katy's father said gently. "Let me have the letter. Don't cry, my love," for his wife had begun to weep with the inconsolable intensity of a whipped child.

"Father . . . Dear sweet Jesus . . . father." Chris's voice was ragged, his face white, his distress so great Katy moved round the table to take his hand. Fight like two cats in a sack they might, but in adversity Chris and Katy Andrews had always stood shoulder to shoulder.

"Oh, mum," Lottie moaned for she could not bear another moment of the overwhelming disaster which had come upon them all.

It must be Master Richie in that heathen land he'd gone to, or Master Davy up north in his grand medical college. One or the other of them must be dead to make the mistress carry on so, though she had no idea who Mr Taylor or Alice might be.

Freda led her away, murmuring soothingly, her own heart heavy, closing the door quietly behind them, for the family would want privacy at this moment of sorrow.

Jack and Sara might have been alone for all the notice they took of their bewildered children.

"I'm going to throw it in the fire, my darling," Jack said firmly. "That's the best place for it. I don't give a bugger what it says. Give it to me, Sara, please. I have no interest in that woman. None. After what she did to us . . ."

Chris and Katy were astonished to see their father, who had never been other than strong, contained, tempered, clutch their mother to him as though in fear, his face contorted with some emotion they could not even begin to describe. Loathing, perhaps, a revulsion so great it was ready to tear him apart with some dreadful memory, a strange reluctance to take hold of the letter and yet an urgency to have it out of his wife's hands and disposed of at the back of the fire. Clear, tawny brown eyes stared incredulously into vivid green then, mouths agape, jaws slack, returned to goggle at the scene which was being enacted at the foot of the table.

"Jack," their mother whispered, "you must read it." Her voice was muffled and yet stronger. "We can't just throw it in the fire and then . . . forget it ever came."

"Damn it to hell, Sara, why not? Why not, dammit? How can you bear to . . . she nearly killed me . . . not physically, I know that, but . . ."

Jack Andrews threw back his head and glared at the ceiling, his gaze so menacing, so perilous, Katy felt her brother start forward as though afraid for someone's safety but she held him back, for this was between their parents, whatever it was, and must not be interfered with by outsiders.

"I know, beloved." Her mother's voice was filled with infinite tenderness. "Oh, I know, and I will never forgive her myself but we . . . oh please, Jack, you must read what her husband has written."

"No, Sara, I can't. I won't let her tamper with our lives again. We have had twenty-five years of . . . of . . . and I cannot risk it. Please, darling, let me put it to the back of the fire . . . please."

"I can't, Jack, I can't. After all, Alice is my sister and her daughter is my niece."

"Daughter! Dear God, what are you talking about, Sara?

You're not making any sense. Come, won't you let me send for Matty? If you were to lie down . . ."

"No, Jack, oh no, please listen to me. Alice is dead and her husband is sending her daughter to us!"

2

Madge Andrews leaned forward in the small bow window of the cottage, relishing for a moment the warmth of the sunshine streaming through it as she watched her granddaughter gallop her little sorrel mare up the steep track which led to Madge's front door.

Madge sighed in resigned exasperation, for the girl was dressed as no girl should be. Oh, she was in the decent riding habit her mother had had made for her, and insisted she wore, a rich, blue boxcloth with a jacket bodice and a neat white cravat at the neck but under the long, trained skirt she wore trousers. Again, it was quite acceptable for a lady to wear trousers beneath her riding habit, Madge knew that, but not in the style Katy had adopted. Tight they were, clinging as though they had been painted on her shapely legs, which were clearly visible since the skirt, all five yards of it, was bunched up above her thighs. The top hat she was supposed to wear but rarely did, at least out of sight of her parents, was attached in some way to her saddle and her vivid red hair swirled about her head like a newly opened chrysanthemum. As though it had a life of its own it snapped in the wind which blew even on the mildest day in the high moorlands, snatched back from her white, strained face and Madge sighed again since she knew that face well and it boded ill for Madge's peace.

Madge, whose mother had been a Yorkshire woman and a great one for what she called "fettling", had just finished her own. Since seven thirty that morning she had been in a frenzy of polishing and deep scouring. Nothing in the cottage had escaped her watchful eye. She had yellow-stoned her front doorstep, cleaned her windows, turned out her bedrooms and banished from every nook and corner what had always offended her the most and that was muck. She had emptied the drawers in her kitchen dresser and relined them with clean paper and she had just been about to start on the cupboards, relishing the scrubbing of her already spotless crockery, when the sound of horse's hooves on the cobbles had brought her to the window.

She tutted irritably. "I'd best mash t'tea," she told the tabby cat in the chimney corner, which had raised its own irritated head at the commotion beyond the door.

Madge talked to the cat all the time for, as those who live alone do, she liked to address her remarks to someone. "An' I suppose I'd best get out t'gingerbreads an' all. She love my gingerbread, do Katy. Now don't tha' look at me like that, Tab," as the animal continued to show signs of annoyance, for where Katy went so did her dog and Tab and Muffy were old adversaries, "but I know what tha' mean," Madge went on, just as though the animal had spoken. "'Tis the end of our peace, for wherever she go she causes nowt but bother an' vexation. An' that animal of hers is no better, fetchin' muck all over my clean flags an' do the lass say 'sorry,' or even notice? No, she don't. I know she's me granddaughter, Tab and I'm right fond of 'er fer she's a good heart but she's worse than that there basket of kittens with her mischief, an' just as thoughtless."

Madge Andrews sighed deeply for the words were true. She had been uttering them to the cat and to herself for the past ten years, ever since the then six-year-old Katherine had evaded her governess, or whatever the woman who had charge of her education was called, finding her way, not along the road which ran beside the reservoirs from Crossclough to Woodhead, but riding her little pony up through the oak and rowan and birch woodlands which clustered on the lower slopes of Tintwistle Knarr, Round Hill and Butterley Moss. She had somehow leaped the tumbling waters of Crowden Brook, skirted the quarries, guided her small mount up gritstone slopes and down sliding shale, unafraid, unaware even that what she did was anything out of the ordinary.

Before that day she had travelled once a week with her mother in the carriage as far as it could be taken by the horses, struggling on foot up the last few cobbled yards to visit her grandmother.

But once a week was not enough for young Miss Katherine Andrews who loved her grandmother dearly and so, having decided she had no further use for the simple sums, the French verbs, the singing lessons, the learning of the neat copperplate handwriting her governess insisted upon, and the sewing lessons her mother insisted upon, she had simply – somehow – saddled her own pony and raced off in the direction of Woodhead, which she found without the slightest trouble and had been doing so ever since.

They had tried, or rather Sara had tried, for Jack was so often away, to curb her but it was like trying to put a halter on some legendary winged creature, a wild Arabian steed which would fade away, droop and die if it were tethered. At first, with Dicken, her father's conscientious stable lad always a few paces behind her, she had been given the freedom to go where she pleased. Or where Dicken pleased, for the young man had been born and bred in these parts and knew every clough and waterfall, every black reef of gritstone, every quaking morass of bog. He knew where to find stretches of rough moorland where the horses could safely gallop, how to cross steep ravines without breaking the horses' fragile legs, how to find his way home when the weather turned nasty and, more importantly, to recognise when it was about to, and when he had divulged all he knew to his young charge she simply discarded him, galloping off on her own.

What a hue and cry that had caused, her poor mother white and silent, her brothers frantic, for their father would kill them all if he came home to find his only daughter vanished beneath the innocent-looking sphagnum moss which covered the lethal boggy ground.

Just as it was getting dark and her mother about to get out her mourning gown, Katherine had ridden casually into the stable yard of Cloudberry End, slipped from her tired mare's back and professed herself astonished by all the fuss. Dicken knew she was perfectly well able to climb to the top of Bleaklow – or at least as far as the peat bogs allowed – on her own, she said. She had crossed the road which led between Valehouse and Torside Reservoirs where it turned at the village of Hollins, and then over the railway track which her own father had helped to lay nearly forty years ago. There were pastures and woodland by Rollick Stones and then straight up by the side of Wildboar Clough with the Shining Cloud Hills on her left until she reached the dizzy heights of Bleaklow Head. She had to walk her pony in several places, as Dicken had showed her and yes, she was aware it was an inhospitable wilderness as her brothers said, or rather shouted, ready to throttle her, over two thousand feet high, but she had been very careful, as Dicken had taught her to be. Yes, she knew lives had been lost on Bleaklow but not hers since here she was to prove it, and no, she couldn't promise her mother never to go again because that would be dishonest since she would be forced to break her word.

Yes, they had tried. Dear God, they'd tried, Madge Andrews knew that, especially her son who, in turn, found his daughter lovable, exasperating, defiant, good-humoured – if not crossed – honest, maddening, shocking and even terrifying with her complete lack of fear. She had been locked up, starved for two whole days once, her saddle hidden, her riding clothes and boots removed from her wardrobe, her father ready to flog her with his leather belt, but in the end he did the only thing he could do. Told Dicken to follow her the moment her pony was saddled, which was all well and good, said the mortified Dicken but Miss Katherine could ride rings round him, God knows how, but she could. She was trickier than a cartload of monkeys and she and her mount could vanish without a trace the minute he took his bloody eyes off her, he complained bitterly to his master, who understood and sympathised with him enormously, and Dicken didn't care if he got the bloody sack for saying so.

Now, here she was, labouring under some bitter and vexatious problem if her manner and the expression on her face were anything to go by as she flung herself vigorously out of the saddle. Not that she wasn't careful with her pretty little mare which appropriately she had named Storm. It was her mother who had suggested it, it was said, which Madge thought made sense since Sara Andrews's life was stormy with this girl of hers, not to mention the lad who had been named after Madge's own beloved husband.

Madge shrugged ruefully, her wrinkled face uneasy beneath her lace and ribbon cap. She was a strong, plain woman, born in Manchester to a comfortably-off family who were in cotton, ready to settle in a respectable marriage to a man her father approved of until handsome, merry, irresponsible Chris Andrews came into her life and swept her off her sensible, well-shod feet. That was over fifty years ago but she was still able to look after herself, thank the good Lord. She had most of her own teeth and though her once dark, glossy hair was now a pure, shining white, she was upright, in good health and as determined as it was her nature to be to remain that way. The only part of her that had let her down was her eyes and she wore wire-rimmed spectacles which clung precariously to the end of her nose.

Katy slashed her riding whip dangerously against her full skirt as she strode across the cobbles, bending her head beneath the low lintel of the cottage door and it was apparent from the tenseness in her face that her mood was just as savage as her whip.

"Come in, Katy lamb," her grandmother said mildly enough. "But should that there horse be left standin' like that? Are tha' not goin' to tie it up or summat?"

"No, she'll not go far," Katy answered absently.

"Happen she won't but she seems to 'ave tekken a fancy to Annie Lennox's primroses an' Annie'll not be best pleased to find 'er window box all eaten up."

"Oh, never mind Annie Lennox's primroses. I'll fetch her some more from Cloudberry next time I'm over."

Madge sighed deeply before lifting her cheek for her granddaughter's kiss then began to bustle about the kitchen, Katy at her heels, pouring boiling water into the teapot, warming it in readiness for the tea, swilling it round and round, for Madge was very particular about her frequent "brews" and warming the pot was an essential part of the procedure. Three heaped teaspoons of tea were placed in the pot, one for her, one for Katy and one for the pot itself, before the second lot of water was poured in and the tea was left to mash. A tray was laid with a pretty, drawn-thread tray cloth and two of Madge's best, rose-painted china cups and saucers, a sugar basin and milk jug to match, and on a plate she arranged the gingerbreads and an almond slice or two of which Katy was equally fond.

Madge liked to do a bit of baking every day, keeping her hand in, she called it, making sure her biscuit tin and her cake tin were well stocked since she had a great many grandchildren, even great-grandchildren, any or all of whom were inclined to descend on her without a moment's notice.

Stepping over the dog with an irritable "tcch-tcch", she placed the tray on the plush tablecloth which covered the kitchen table when it was not in use, poured out the tea and handed a cup to Katy who took it absently and began to sip.

"Sit thi' down, lass, an' give over frowning. There's summat up so why don't tha' tell me what it is? What's brought thi' over here at such a lick an'in such a state tha's lettin' that animal o' thine make free wi' Annie Lennox's window box? Nay, don't argue. Tha's in a flummox over summat, that's plain to see but best calm down first afore thi' fly off t'handle."

"Grandmother, I can't calm down. I'm . . ."

"Tha' can lass, an' tha' will."

"Oh, Grandmother . . ."

"Don't tha' 'oh, grandmother' me, Katy Andrews, for I'm too old for your shenanigans an' I'll not put up with 'em."

"It's not my shenanigans this time, Grandmother," but nevertheless Katy settled herself, sighing wearily, in the chair opposite her grandmother, soothed by her grandmother's refusal to be anything other than calm as she always was, watching as, her tea drunk, she took up her knitting which was always to hand. Katy had never, in all her life, seen her grandmother sit and do nothing. If it wasn't mending or darning, it was knitting for one of her innumerable grandchildren or great-grandchildren, this time a tiny matinee coat for Violet's latest. Violet was George's eldest girl and George was Madge's eldest boy and Violet already had eight little 'uns about her feet in the tiny, dark cottage along the lane. They all lived close by, Madge's sons and their wives, her grandchildren and their spouses, and to tell the truth she often wondered what on earth had possessed their Jack to bring his lovely, ladylike bride to this desolate place where nothing much grew but broom, heather, bracken and sheep.

The Dark Peak it was called, composed of gritstone, black reefs of it, wave upon wave of it as though it were a sea which had solidified; and interspersed with these seas of rock was a quaking morass of bogland. The land of the gritstone uplands was a fierce and treacherous land which soaked up the rain like a sponge and a horseman unfamiliar with the terrain, careless with it, could be sucked into it, horse and all, before he had time to say "whoa", which was why Jack was so afraid for his girl.

Below the line of the peatland there were wide patches of rough moorland covered with tussocky mat-grass, and hawthorn grew on the edges, with rowan and broom, with sessile oak and swathes of birch. Tumbling waters fled down ravines where fern clung, and grouse flapped from under the heather as men approached with guns. Sheep wandered, gnawing at the poor crop, rough, wild sheep with names such as Gritstones and Lonks, the only sort that could survive in this bitter land. The area was carved by running water as streams ran from the inexhaustible reservoirs of the grits, setting out from the crest of the peaks on their journey to the lowlands. The water cut narrow but deep gorges, joining forces with other streams, increasing its power as it excavated cloughs ranging from mere notches down the face of steep scarps to the narrow, wild and impressive valleys below, filling the reservoirs of Valehouse, Torside, Rhodeswood, Woodhead and Bottoms which provided the city of Manchester with clean water.

A rough land, a hard land where a man must be hard to endure it, and a woman harder, but when the sun shone, as it did today, the sky was filled with a pure blue light which seemed to shimmer on the edge of the horizon and it took on a rugged beauty. Skylarks, barely discernible to man's eye in the sky to the back of Madge's cottage, sang their hearts out and the hare's-tail cotton grass was covered with burgeoning fruit, the whiteness of it giving the impression of a recent snowstorm.

"Grandmother," her granddaughter began, replacing her cup and saucer on the table and helping herself to another almond slice.

"Yes, lass?" Madge answered serenely, since she believed nothing her granddaughter could say or do was likely to alarm her, not at her age.

"Did you know Mother had a sister?"

Madge felt her old heart lurch perilously and knew that her earlier belief was wrong. Her still nimble fingers became a jumble of thumbs and stiff joints and she was aware with that part of her brain which dealt with everyday, basic things that she would have to pull at least two rows back and start again since she'd dropped several stitches.

The startled expression on her face must have given her away, for Katy straightened up from her usual pose of sprawling indolence to one of sudden interest.

"You did know, didn't you?" Her tone was accusing, implying that she took it hard her grandmother had failed to confide in her.

"Aye, I did, but I never met 'er, lass."

"Did anyone? Meet her, I mean."

"Nay, not that I know of, anyroad."

"Well, it's a bit of a facer to learn you've family you didn't even know existed."

"Aye, lass, I suppose it is."

Silence fell as Katy brooded on this last, her unseeing gaze fixed on the crackling coals in the fire, the familiar objects of her grandmother's kitchen which she had known all her life, fading to the edge of her conscious mind.

Madge Andrews's boxframe cottage, which stood with a dozen or so others in the small hamlet of Woodhead, was built of local stone and had a rose-coloured clay tile roof over which, during the years, lichen had grown. There was ivy climbing the wall and partly covering the roof and in the summer it was joined by a thriving eruption of pink sweetbriar roses.

But despite its air of well-kept prettiness the walls of the cottage were poorly insulated, the upstairs windows, made of cylinder glass, were draughty and though the doors at the back and front of the cottage were sturdy and well fitted and much had been done to restore the old building, for Jack was a wealthy man and a good son, the only really warm place was before the enormous fireplace on the end wall. All the cooking was done in the fireplace, for Madge had resisted all Jack's efforts to put in one of the new-fangled cast-iron ranges which had become so popular. She liked the place just as it had been when her Chris had brought her here as a bride nearly sixty years ago, she protested sharply, and saw no reason for change. She was attached to her high-backed rocking chair, her hand-made rugs, her old dresser, and with a canary singing in a cage, with her Tab and Tab's everlasting litter of kittens which resided in a basket in the chimney corner, a water butt – her only concession to modernity since Jack said she was past plodding down the track to the stream – at her back door, she was as snug as Tab and her kittens themselves. She would be seventy-five this year, a great age for any woman but despite this she resisted fiercely any suggestion of giving up her independence.

Jack had wanted her to go and live in style and comfort at Cloudberry End but Madge, fond as she was of the sweet girl her son had married, couldn't quite picture herself in the overwhelming luxury and grandeur of Jack's brand new house which perched on the gentle lower slope of the valley looking out over the reservoir. A lovely house, to be sure, built of stone with a long, low front, standing solitary and alone, exposed to the fierce storms which swept over the moorland at its back. Five acres of garden it stood in, with terraces dug out of the sloping land, gardens full of old-fashioned flowers, with clipped hedges and paved walks sheltered from the cold winds. Laurel hedges edged the drive which led to a round gravel court for the easy turning of Jack's fine carriages and inside the house it was even grander. A wide hall three times as big as Madge's cottage, a parlour, a drawing room, a dining room, a breakfast room, all shining and glowing with lovely polished furniture; above these were bedrooms by the score and even a couple of bathrooms with flush "lavvies" and constant hot running water.

It was beautiful: the setting, the comfort, the velvet lawns all about the house, the colourful flowerbeds, rose beds filled with sweetbriar, with cabbage roses, moss roses, old white damask and maiden's blush and a fragrance too incredible to be described. Sweet Williams crowding against iris and peonies, pinks, carnations, wallflower and Canterbury bell, an invasion of the senses which was almost too much to be borne. An arbour spread with honeysuckle and roses, a terrace with steps leading down to it all, balustrades and sundials and benches under trees and at the end of her first visit Madge couldn't wait to get back to the simplicity of her own small home.

Cloudberry End was only a mile or so out of the busy little country town of Crossclough where a railway station on the Manchester to Sheffield line made it convenient for Jack to get about on business and for Sara to travel to Manchester and the splendid shops there. What had worried Madge more than anything when Jack begged her to come and live with them was the unimaginable situation of having her family, George's, Will's and Harry's families drop in on her at Cloudberry End in the easy and familar way they did at Woodhead. Jack had "got on" and it was rumoured he might even be a millionaire and George and Will and Harry had remained exactly what they had started out as, which was farm labourers. Jack had acquired polish, a "posh" way of talking, or so Harry said sneeringly, and Jack's wife, there were no two ways about it, was a lady and could no more sit and gossip with Madge's other daughters-in-law than Jack's elegant carriage horse could be put in tandem with the one which pulled old Arkwright's plough. A proper lady she was, though she never threw it in your face but it was there just the same. They might have been born in a different class and culture, George's lot, Will's lot, Harry's lot, so far apart had Jack grown from them. Jack had travelled all over the world and the furthest her other sons had been from Woodhead was to Penistone to see the fair.

As for Jack's children, they were the children of a lady and could find no common ground on which to meet their cousins.

There was already bad feeling between Chris Andrews and George's Paddy, who were the same age, and with Will's twin sons, Josh and Jake, who often hung about with Paddy. They were outspoken in their rough contempt – and envy, Madge suspected – of their fine cousins at Cloudberry End.

"Do you know anything about her, Grandmother?" Katy went on, leaning forward to peer into Madge's face. "For some reason Mother and Father have kept her existence a secret from us. She's called Alice Taylor, apparently, and all these years, twenty-five, ever since they married, they've spoken not one word about her and what I'd like to know is why? What possible reason can they have had for keeping her hidden? Not that I'm particularly concerned about that, you understand" – since I already have more relatives than I know what to do with, her expression seemed to be saying – "but it's all such a damned mystery and now Mother's shut up in her room with Matty, and Father's dashed off God knows where and nobody will tell us a thing. Chris, who's in trouble again, by the way, and should have gone to Manchester with Father, galloped off in great relief and Father didn't even notice, he's so upset. But nobody will tell us so I came to you."

The room was still but for the crackle and splutter of the fire, the plaintive mewing of the kittens whose mother had sauntered off in the direction of the open back door and the canary which was going through its repertoire in the window bottom.

"Grandmother?" Katy urged. "Do you know what's been going on?"

Madge lifted her head and looked into the flushed, intense face of her granddaughter. "The child of my child is twice my child," the old proverb went and though it was not true of her other grandchildren, it was about this one. Twenty-seven grandchildren she had had and she'd lost count of her great-grandchildren but this one, this unpredictable, self-willed, rebellious, hot-tempered daughter of her youngest son was the one special in her heart. She was strong, flaunting what she liked to call her independence in the face of anyone who tried to restrain her, which Madge could sympathise with since she herself was the same. But inside she was sweet, as the kernel of a walnut is sweet though the shell is hard. And though she was not yet seventeen, in Madge Andrews's opinion, she was ready for marriage, which meant for loving. She held her own mother and father in deep affection, of course, but who can lavish love on a couple who are obsessed only with one another? Who share a strange single-minded rapture which, because of its sad beginnings made the two involved so tightly welded together they were as close as two sides of a sovereign?

But was Jack and Sara's story hers to tell? Madge Andrews asked herself. Was it up to her to reveal to their daughter why Sara had not spoken to her own sister for twenty-five years? It was not much of a story really. Nothing dramatic or sensational though it had seemed tragic to Jack and Sara at the time, and the outcome had been a happy one. But perhaps it was now to be resolved, that strange estrangement, if Sara's sister had been in touch with her as Katherine's questions seemed to indicate.

"Aye, my lass," she said hesitantly, "I seem to remember thy pa telling me some tale years ago about a falling out."

"A falling out? Over what? I can't imagine Mother falling out with anyone."

"Well, my lamb, tha' must ask tha' ma what happened. I do know when tha' pa brought her back to live 'ere I were dumbfounded for there's nowt up here for someone like tha' ma but she made friends wi' . . . well, with her own sort. Mrs Ashwell an' the like and seemed content enough. Tha' pa did say as how he wanted to fetch her away from . . . memories what might hurt her, I suppose, and him an' all, from what I gathered. Summat happened in Liverpool . . . well," she went on briskly, "it's not for me to say but he wanted to mekk a fresh start."

"But why?"

"Nay, lass, that's for them to tell thi'. But why should tha' ma speak of her sister now?"

"She had a letter this morning from her sister's husband. He said Alice was dead."

"Eeh, never!" Madge put a hand to her mouth, inclined to be tearful, for the loss of a sister must be a terrible wrench.

"Yes, so he said and it seems he means to send Alice's daughter up here to stay with us. Damned cheek, I call it, after all this time." Katy's face became pink with indignation. "The thought of some squalling brat demanding everyone's attention from morning till night doesn't bear thinking about," meaning the disturbance of the smooth rhythm of Cloudberry End which revolved carefully around herself. "I have no intention of spending my days in the company of another girl which they will probably try to make me do." She shuddered visibly. "Can you imagine it? 'Take her with you, Katy,' they will say but I refuse absolutely to be bothered with her, Grandmother, and that is that."

Katy's golden tawny eyes snapped dangerously and her full mouth, the ripe colour of a hedgeberry, thinned to a white and mutinous line. She tossed her head and Madge was startled, as she always was by the movement of Katy's short halo of hair which swirled about her skull, reminding Madge of a field of corn when the wind ripples through it. Not that her granddaughter's hair was anything like the colour of corn, far from it. It was rich and glowing, like the leaves of a copper beech but with streaks of gold shot through it, a crop of softly bouncing curls. It had been the talk of the valley from the day Katy first brazenly displayed it, for how could Sara Andrews allow her daughter to wear it so short? It tumbled over her forehead and ears, curling against her creamy white neck, a declaration that Katy Andrews was like no other girl any of them knew. Delicately shaped copper eyebrows arched, or scowled fiercely more often than not, above slanted eyes which were fringed with long, copper lashes and her presence was so taut with tension, with a need to be about something, anything which did not smack of the tedious, of boredom and routine, it was positively painful to be in her company for longer than half an hour.

The rough-haired bitch who had been dozing in a patch of sunshine which lay across the scrubbed flags stood up and stretched her back legs, first one then the other, giving herself a good shake. She sauntered across the kitchen, grinning in that amiable way a good-natured dog has, her short tail moving in small circles. The kittens in the basket began to spit and claw, recognising an enemy which they appeared to think threatened them, defenceless as they were without their mother but they were beneath the bitch's notice as she laid a loving muzzle on Katy's knee. Katy stroked her head absently, her gaze still fixed on her grandmother.

"Chloe," she announced. "Did you ever hear the like? Biblical, Mother said. Something to do with Puritans, God help us."

"Chloe?" Madge murmured. "'Tis a right pretty name."

"D'you think so? Well, Chloe is to be here by the end of the week and if Mother thinks I am to make a little sister of her then she's sadly mistaken."

Katy was prevented from further speculation about the girl who was her lost cousin by a sharp rat-tat at the door which, without waiting for an answer from within, opened immediately, much to the consternation of Katy's dog. She began to bark frantically, for the animal which lumbered in ahead of the man who had opened the door could only be described as the worst canine nightmare any dog could have the misfortune to suffer. He was squat, a cross between a bulldog and some other breed which, though Katy could not immediately bring his antecedents to mind, had obviously been strong, broad-backed, thick-necked and vicious. He was a dirty white in colour, his legs short and splayed, his deep chest and neck supporting a huge head with a broad, square skull. His muzzle was short with an upturned lower jaw. His eyes were deep and dark, ringed with pink and in them was a venom which brought Katy to her feet since his intention was obvious. It was written in his snarling mouth and lowering brow. He meant to take hold of her own brave little dog by the scruff of her neck and snap the life out of her which he could do with a shake of his massive head.

The next two minutes were no more than a whirling, deafening blur to Madge, a blur which contained flashing images of snapping jaws and vicious teeth, of savage, furious eyes blood red with rage, of flying, crashing china as her precious cups and saucers were flung from the tray when the bigger dog crashed against the table. There were howls of animal pain and howls of human fury, of curses, both male and female, of shouted commands, of brawny male arms and dangerously fragile female hands as Katy Andrews and Paddy Andrews, who was her cousin and the owner of the mauling dog, did their best to separate him from Katy's defiant little terrier. The kittens mewed piteously but not even to defend her family would Tab venture into the fighting arena, cowering by the back door of the scullery and Madge found herself lifting the heaving basket on to her lap, for it seemed likely to her that its howling contents might be reduced to bleeding scraps of fur and flesh in the savagery of the turmoil.

At last Paddy had his dog by the collar, almost strangling the thing as he heaved him towards the door, still turning his head to snap and snarl at the terrier and even, Madge was inclined to think, at his master's hand in its bloodlust.

Somehow her grandson opened the door without help, for both Katy and her grandmother were fully occupied in calming their respective charges. He flung the animal on to the cobbled track where, instead of subsiding since his foe was out of reach, he threw himself against the closed door again and again, much to the alarm of Katy's sorrel mare who, since it seemed to her she was in mortal danger, took off at the full gallop in the direction of her stable at Cloudberry End.

"Dear God in heaven," Katy shrieked, and in her arms and pressed to her heaving breasts her dog shivered and moaned. "I hope you're bloody well satisfied, Paddy Andrews. That dog of your is a menace and should not be allowed out of your cottage yard without a chain on it. In fact I've a good mind to ask my father to see the magistrate and get an order to have him put down. It might have . . ."

Paddy only laughed. "Nay, lass, don't tha' speak ter me of vicious dogs. That thing tha've got clutched ter thi' is as lively as a bloody rat an' tha' knows what 'appens ter rats, don't tha'?" He appeared to be completely unruffled by the commotion, even finding it a source of amusement. There was no harm done, was there, except to his gran's cups and saucers so what was Katy Andrews, who really was growing into a very tasty piece of female flesh – and Paddy was a man who appreciated a pretty woman – making such a bloody fuss about? Her animal had a torn ear – he could see the blood on Katy's dress – but that was all. He admitted his dog was hard to handle where other dogs were concerned, since he had trained him to be a fighter but he was harmless, even docile in the presence of humans. Normally, when he was to go where he knew there would be other dogs he would keep him on a chain, but though he had taken note of the sorrel placidly eating her way through Annie Lennox's window box and had even known she belonged to Jack Andrews's lass, he had given no thought to what might be inside his grandmother's kitchen. Obviously his cousin Katy, but he had forgotten that bloody little excuse for a dog which trailed at her heels.

Paddy, Patrick George Andrews to give him his correct name, was the youngest son of Madge Andrews's oldest, George. Big he was and though it was not mentioned, nor even acknowledged, was the spit of his uncle Jack, Katy's father. He was broad of shoulder, narrow of waist and hip with long graceful legs which could stride out for hours on end, carrying him for miles across barren hillside and moor as he took his dog, and himself, to the fights which were arranged at the back of isolated inns and where prize money might be had. Since he was a lad of fifteen, enormous even then, he had fought in over a hundred bouts. He had never been marked and his good looks, dark and gypsy-like, ensured that he was never short of female company. A rebel was Paddy, working casually when he was in need of a bob or two – which was not very often since he won many purses in the ring – in the quarries which abounded in and above the Longdendale valley. Gritstone and sandstone and limestone quarries which the accessibility of the railway had made available to the industries of south Lancashire, Cheshire and the West Riding of Yorkshire. He had the dark curling hair and deep-set brown eyes of the Andrews men. His mouth was wide and inclined to smile more often than not since life was pleasant for Paddy Andrews, but his short temper and hard fists were legend in the valley, should any man attempt to cross him which few did. He was dressed casually in an open-necked checked shirt, corduroy breeches, gaiters and heavy working boots. The dark stubble on his sun-bronzed face and jaw testified to the fact that he had not shaved for several days and where it dipped beneath his chin to his throat it met a bloom of coarse chest hair which sprang from the open neck of his shirt.

Katy eyed it with distaste, her nostrils flaring. Her arms were wrapped protectively about Muffy's still quivering body and she breathed heavily with outrage.

"What the hell is there to smile about, you clod? That vicious brute of yours might have killed Muffy."

Paddy shouted with laughter. "Muffy! Muffy. What sort of a bloody name is that ter give a dog? Muffy."

"What's wrong with it? What, may I ask, do you call that devil which is howling outside my grandmother's door? Satan, I shouldn't wonder! You do realise that he has so terrified my sorrel that she has taken to her heels."

"Well, his name's not bloody Muffy, I can tell you. Jesus . . ." Paddy's laughter became even more pronounced as he lounged by the door with every appearance of great good humour, his hands on his hips, his teeth a startling white slash in his sun-tinted face.

"You realise that I shall have to walk home now, don't you?" Katy hissed, infuriated by his laughter. She advanced towards him, her intention of marking him in some way, as his opponents in the ring had never been able to do, very obvious. "And if my mare damages herself between here and Cloudberry End then you will have not only me but my father to answer to."

Paddy's grin widened. "Oh ho, you really must not frighten me, like that, cousin. I'll not be able ter sleep at night fer worrying about it." He was enjoying himself immensely for there was nothing he liked more than a good fight, particularly if that fight was with a woman, for who knew where it might lead? He allowed his gaze to roam admiringly over Katy, from her head to her well-polished boots, then up again to her flaming halo of glorious hair beneath which the furious pink of her face glowed. It lingered for several impudent moments at her breasts which still heaved against Muffy. Her eyes were the colour of the cat's in the doorway, a deep, golden amber, narrowed and snapping with flecks of outrage, glowing brown and her wide mouth was as red as a poppy, howling her affront. She turned and placed the dog carefully in the chair where she had been sitting before he arrived and, turning again, placed her hands on her hips and glared at him and as she did so Paddy was surprised by a sudden and quite incredible flow of something which began in his chest and travelled to the pit of his belly. A feeling very familiar but one he did not associate with girls like Katy Andrews, by God, and one which had something in it he did not recognise. She was a young girl to him, no more than sixteen or seventeen, he supposed, though her full-breasted figure, which was heaving threateningly in his direction, said otherwise. She'd need taming by some man and wouldn't he like to be the one to do it? A spitting, scratching she-cat who was asking for a bloody good hiding with that wicked mouth of hers but afterwards . . . aah . . . afterwards!

"Well, well." He grinned impertinently. "So Miss Andrews of Cloudberry End can't walk a couple o' miles wi'out gettin' a blister or two on her delicate little feet, is that it? An' as fer yer pa bein' a threat ter me, lass, well, that remains ter be seen. Can't manage 'is own lad, so the talk goes."

His smile gone, he turned away contemptuously. Paddy Andrews answered to no man, not even his own pa. He'd only called on his grandmother because he happened to be passing and she brewed a glass of ale which was to his liking, and he was fond of the old girl. So sod Katy Andrews and sod the lot of them at Cloudberry End. He despised them all and if he could do them a bad turn he would.

"I can walk as far and for as long as you can, Paddy Andrews, and still arrive without a blister. I'm not one of those pampered girls who can't go about without a parasol or their smelling salts."

She was beginning to annoy him with her persistence, her determination to have the last word, her absolute certainty that she was in the right and Paddy Andrews was no more than a lout who must be put in his place.

"Listen, lass, I don't give a damn what you, that prick of a brother of yours, nor that— "

They had both, in their strange absorption with one another, forgotten the existence of their grandmother and when she spoke they both turned to her with what looked like bewilderment.

"Patrick, that is enough, an' as fer thee, Katherine, I'd like ter remind thi' that this is my house and I'll have no more bad language in it. You'd best go, grandson, an' tekk that dratted dog with thi'. If tha' was half a gentleman . . ."

"A gentleman! Him!" Katy spluttered, almost in tears with temper.

". . . I'd ask thi' ter walk tha' cousin home."

"Ha! Walk home with him. I'd sooner walk home with his damned dog."

"Now then, Gran, she's just told us she can outwalk

anybody in't district so let her bloody do it, an' wi'out my help. An' remind me ter mekk damn sure there's none o' them fools from Cloudberry End visitin' thi' next time I'm over or there'll be skin an' hair flyin'. An' that means you, lady," glaring at Katy. "Yer nowt but a jumped-up load o' nobodies, the lot o' you. Yer pa came from workin' stock, like me an' me brothers an' cousins but the way tha' carries on yer'd think tha' were related ter't bloody queen. None of 'em, especially that son of a bitch who rides about wi't gentry, 'ad better cross my path, I'm warnin' yer."

He turned to glare, his contempt for Chris Andrews plain to see and Katy fell back before it, wondering what it was that had made Paddy Andrews, who had been good-humoured enough five minutes ago, turn so sour.

3

The train had laboured its way up the incline which had begun in Hadfield, climbing steadily as it rattled towards the Longdendale valley and the railway station at Crossclough which stood at fifteen hundred feet above sea level. On either side of the track were the lifting moorlands and craggy tops of the Dark Peak, bleak and inhospitable on this colourless day even to someone who was familiar with them as Jamie Hutchinson was. Crossclough, which was no more than a mile or two from Woodhead where the train would pass into the tunnel, was on the narrow peninsula of land which reached out through Lancashire and Derbyshire and into Yorkshire where the tunnel emerged at Dunford Bridge. Woodhead Tunnel, just over three miles long and on which so many men had been crippled or killed, was really two single-track tunnels running side by side beneath the dark, rolling moorlands, the upland deserts of peat and heather which were the hallmark of this land. High, wild moorland where, at this time of the year, indeed at most times of the year, the air was filled with the sound of the water which tumbled unceasingly down dozens of cloughs and into the reservoirs beside which the railway track ran.

The valley was wide and shallow, its lowest point defined by the narrow road which meandered on to Penistone; by the railway, and the string of reservoirs which lay along its bottom. There were fields on either side of the ruffled waters, dissected by dry stone walls. There were woodlands, and scattered cottages dropped down into a sea of bilberry, of wavy-hair grass and the strong and yet delicate grace of fern, and about them rose the multi-hued lift of new heather, bracken and crowberry. But higher still the moors were featureless, rolling on as far as the eye could see, which wasn't far today for the cloud was down.

Jamie did his best not to be too obvious about it but he just could not take his eyes off the delicately lovely creature who sat opposite him in the first-class carriage of the Manchester to Sheffield train. He himself had travelled from Liverpool, changing at Manchester and had only at the last minute decided to travel first class. He was careful with his money, particularly now when only God knew how far it was to stretch, but somehow his return to what he called "home" had seemed a special occasion and needed an appropriate precedent to mark its importance and what better way to travel, and arrive, than in style? It was the ending of his old, hard way of life and the beginning of his new, which would probably be just as hard though in a different way. The impetuous decision to spend his hard-earned money had manifested itself in a cushioned seat in the luxury and well-lit comfort of a first-class carriage instead of the tiny windows, the foetid atmosphere, the bare boards, the dingy, smoky oil lamps which barely illuminated the conditions third-class passengers must endure.

She was dressed completely in black, the lovely, drooping young woman who stared fixedly out of the window, and he was amazed that someone of her youth and quality should be travelling alone. The males of the middle and upper classes guarded their females as though they were made of jewelled gold, protecting them from other males like himself and would certainly not believe that any woman, at least of theirs, was capable of travelling from one town to another unchaperoned, and not only arrive, but arrive safely. Women, or at least ladies, were incapable of getting from their own drawing room to that of a friend without some male to guide them there, even if it was only a servant!

The young woman's clothing was very evidently of the best, even he who knew nothing of ladies' fashions could see that, and though it was drab, as mourning is meant to be, it was . . . well, he could only think of the word stylish, which sounded a bit fanciful. Her gown, revealed when her black, fringed shawl slipped from her slender shoulders, fitted her superbly, hugging her breasts and the smallness of her waist in a way which drew his eyes to them no matter how hard he tried not to. Her hands were small and white, the nails a perfect, pearly oval but they were not at ease, as she was not, twisting anxiously around one another, or clutching fiercely at the small, black reticule in her lap. Her bonnet was small in the style of the day, almost the shape and size of an inverted flowerpot, completely unadorned but for a small veil which she had turned back from her face, inadvisably he was inclined to think. The narrow brim allowed the muted daylight to touch her hair which was like nothing he had ever seen before, and yet at the back of his mind where distant memories lay he seemed to think he had seen hair that colour and texture somewhere. It had a gloss on it like silk and its hue was somewhere between gold and copper and pale chestnut and yet it was none of these since the three melted together into a living flame of glory.

Suddenly she turned her gaze from the drab scene she was studying beyond the carriage window and before he had time to look away their eyes met. Again they were an incredible colour. Blue-green, vivid, like the seas he had sailed across south of the equator, turquoise almost and fringed with long, curling brown lashes and again he had the strangest feeling of having seen them before. They were unfathomable, unreadable, deep and still and for a fraction of a second they stared, startled, into his before her lashes dropped in confusion. She bit her lip; the blood ran pink beneath her white skin and she turned her head away as though in deepest embarrassment, presenting him with the delicate arch of one copper eyebrow and the perfection of her profile.

Christ Almighty, but she was lovely, and where in hell was she going all alone on this murky May morning? The train would reach Crossclough soon, then on to Penistone before dropping down to Sheffield and when he alighted at Crossclough, as he was about to do, she would be left to the mercy of the fashionably dressed young dandy who, like himself he supposed irritably, had done nothing but stare at her ever since she had boarded the train in Manchester. She was very young, no more than sixteen or seventeen, he would have said and would she be safe from any advances the leering young gentleman might press on her?

Damnation, why in hell hadn't she got into a carriage with another woman in it, or at least several passengers so that the chances of her being left alone with some man who would think any woman travelling by herself was fair game would be lessened? Perhaps he might suggest to her that when the train reached Crossclough, which it should in the next five minutes, he himself could escort her to a first-class carriage where the protection of another female might be available.

Or would that alarm her even more? Would she shrink away and tremble as he had seen her do several times on the twelve-mile journey from Manchester; look at him with those amazing blue-green eyes, the expression in them telling him she was convinced he meant her no good?

Jamie sighed deeply, shrugging his broad shoulders more comfortably into his rough reefer jacket, working the collar more snugly up about his neck. Though it was May the temperature was more like January and even here in the enclosed carriage the damp seemed to slither inside his warm jacket and woollen gansey, feathering his flesh which was used to more tropical elements than these. God alone knew what those in third class suffered, he thought, travelling as they did in what was virtually a wooden box with only one small window which frequently would not close. He knew because he had travelled in one.

He shoved his hands more deeply into his pockets and clenched his blunt-angled jaw as the dilemma of the girl opposite gnawed at him and yet it wasn't his bloody dilemma, for God's sake, so why should he feel it was? He was coming home, if he could call it home; about to see his mother for the first time in five years, about to start a new way of life and before he'd even got off the blasted train he had taken upon himself a tricky problem which was not his problem to solve.

Jamie Hutchinson stood six feet four inches in his stockinged feet and had a frame to match his height. His shoulders strained at the seams of his navy blue reefer jacket and his thigh and calf muscles, which were clearly defined beneath the durable woollen fabric of his trousers, were as hard and tensile as a coiled spring. He was dark, his over-long hair tumbling in rough waves about his head and falling over his brow to his fiercely scowling eyebrows. His skin was as brown as his mother's prized walnut dining table, a rich, warm brown which had been achieved in more southerly climes than those of the Dark Peak. His eyes were blue, brilliant and penetrating, long-lashed, narrowed with fine lines radiating outwards from each corner as though he were accustomed to squinting over shimmering seas in which the sun's rays were caught. A strong man with a pleasant face, good-humoured, with a mouth which seemed inclined towards laughter, but there was something in the set of it which said he was not a man to be trifled with.

The train began to slow, the rhythm of its wheels altering and from the engine a piercing whistle warned those who stood on the platform ahead to beware. The young woman stared fearfully from the window, her hands knotting together in what appeared to be real fear and Jamie's face softened. She was nought but a young lass, a little bit of a thing who seemed to be trapped in some fearful predicament and could he, in all conscience, get off the train without doing something, saying something which might alleviate her alarm? Her eyes were wide, almost blank with some distress and her small teeth worried her full bottom lip.

He couldn't help himself. He leaned forward and when he spoke both the girl and the chap by the opposite window who still stared avidly in their direction jumped slightly.

"Are you all right, miss?" was all he said but he might have made some indecent remark to her the way she shrank back in her corner. Her skin paled even further, and her eyes widened even further, if that were possible, so that they were enormous and glittering in her face, but her answer, when it came, was quite composed.

She lifted her head haughtily. "I beg your pardon?" Her tone was icy and she recovered her balance as if by magic, her young face set in a mask of cool rebuff.

"I just thought you seemed . . . disturbed." He shrugged deprecatingly, letting her know he meant her no harm nor offence, sitting back again in his seat.

"Not at all, thank you." Her voice was polite, nipping any familiarity firmly in the bud, giving him the level stare young ladies gave to gentlemen who were making a nuisance of themselves.

"I'm sorry, I didn't mean to intrude." He smiled and the smile lit his face, giving it an endearing, boyish quality. He pushed his big hand through his unruly hair so that it fell in even more tumbled disarray on to his forehead and somehow the natural gesture seemed to reassure her, for she relaxed and her mouth did its best to smile back.

"The next stop is Crossclough," he went on gently. "I am to get off there," and in his voice was the message that if she did need help he would be only too glad to supply it. His blue eyes had melted from the vivid brilliance of the hot skies of India and Africa where he had journeyed to the gentle serenity of those above his own homeland and the girl sensed he was no threat to her.

"So am I," she answered in a low voice, once again turning to look fearfully out of the window.

"Really. Then perhaps I can help you with your luggage," glancing at the rack above her head.

"Thank you, that would be most kind."

"You are to be met?" he asked politely and was startled by the sudden shadow which darkened her eyes.

"I'm . . . I'm not sure. A letter was sent but . . ." She bent her head, again biting her lips. "I'm not sure."

"Then perhaps I might . . ."

"Oh no." She looked up at him hastily, that careful mask of a lady dealing with the unwanted advances of a gentleman settling again over her face. "I have the address. I . . . I shall take a cab and find my own way there."

"Of course."

There was silence again apart from the slowing clack and

clatter of the train's wheels and in his corner the young dandy cast furtive glances, fewer now he knew that the young woman was to alight at Crossclough, his own hopes in that direction dashed but reluctant to miss any further exchange.

Jamie stood up with a courteous inclination of his head towards the girl, lifting down his sea bag and several other packages from the rack above him, placing them on the seat he had just vacated. He looked down at her, an expression of smiling enquiry on his face, asking her permission to place her luggage beside his own, noticing the way she shrank away again in alarm as his size became apparent. He had that effect on people, some finding it reassuring, others threatening. It could be a drawback and an advantage, he had found, particularly the latter in his years at sea. Twelve years he had sailed before the mast, enduring great hardship at first, since he had been a lad of only fourteen on the day he set sail. Scrubbing decks, coiling ropes until his hands bled, climbing spars and the dangerous, dizzying heights of rigging to furl and unfurl sails, constantly seasick on a diet of pork, beef and maggoty biscuits. He had been at every man's beck and call in the first months, evading those wanting only to use his young boy's body as they might a woman's until, at the age of sixteen, he had suddenly grown upwards and outwards, fourteen stone of hard muscle, large, powerful, his body toughened by the physical adversity of his life on a sailing ship.

He had often wondered why he had elected to go to sea in the first place, for he had been brought up forty or so miles from its ocean-going call, and he supposed that was why. It was the unknown. It would be exciting, an adventure, a chance to see the world which a boy brought up in the shadow of the Dark Peak would never see. He had been born in Liverpool, his mother had told him, though he remembered none of it, for she and her husband, who was not Jamie's father, had moved to Crossclough with the family who employed them twenty-five years ago. So, he thought, if he were to call anywhere by that name, Crossclough was his home. He had come back to it to settle, to leave behind the wandering ways of the sailor, to find himself a wife, start a family and, if hard work was the key, to be successful in his new employment.

Having received her shy nod of thanks he lifted down the young lady's bags, then, lowering the window, leaned out to open the door. He stepped down on to the platform, placing her box and a somewhat worn carpetbag beside his own luggage before turning back to her, holding out his big hand.

She was still fixed in her seat, her eyes almost blind in her panic, or so it seemed to him, her glance flitting over his shoulder to what was beyond it. She pressed even further back into her seat and for a moment he felt a spurt of irritation. For God's sake, what was there to be afraid of in this quiet little country station which catered to barely more than a dozen or so passengers in a day? The picket fence which stood between it and the road was sheltered by hawthorn trees planted thirty years ago to cover the ravages the laying of the railway track had caused, and against the fence were white-painted, wrought-iron benches, placed there for the comfort and convenience of those who waited for a train. There was a little waiting room and a ticket office beside which a uniformed railway servant stood to collect tickets. It was as peaceful a scene as any to be found in a community the size of Crossclough, which was scarcely any larger than a village and yet it appeared to appall her.

"Will you take my hand?" he asked her encouragingly,

watching with fascination as she drew in her breath and clenched her small jaw with such savage determination it was as though she were about to be dragged into a cage of wild beasts. Putting her small, gloved hand in his, where it vanished in its vastness, she stepped down on to the platform.

"Thank you, you are most kind," she said in that automatic response she had been taught, probably by her governess, he thought and why the bloody woman wasn't here with her now was a mystery since she was so obviously not able to take care of herself. She stood uncertainly, staring about her, scarcely aware of him, he could tell that, and he stood beside her, reluctant to leave her on her own, looking like an enormous and kindly bear protecting a dainty kitten. She was so bloody helpless, he reflected exasperatedly, like a woman marooned on a strange island where the natives were bound to be savage and how was she to cope with it, and them, her manner seemed to ask. And yet she held herself bravely and as tall as she could, which was no higher than his collar button, her head erect, her chin rigid to stop its trembling, her wide, frightened eyes suddenly fixed on a small group of people who had come through the gate from the road and were hesitating by the ticket office.

At once Jamie was aware of who it was she reminded him. The same colouring. The same air of delicate loveliness, of fragile vulnerability, dainty and soft as gossamer, slender as a willow, a scrap of swansdown to be blown willy-nilly by any chance breeze; the woman who stood by the gate and whom she resembled so accurately was none other than his mother's employer, Mrs Jack Andrews.

They did not seem to see him, Mrs Jack Andrews, her daughter Katy and her youngest son Christopher, for all three pairs of eyes were fixed on the girl beside him, as hers were on them. The family likeness was striking, for in different shades of auburn, he supposed you would call it, they were all of the same colouring. Only Katy's deep brown eyes had come from her father's side of the family and as they all stood rooted to the spot, himself included, though he didn't know why, Katy's turned away from the girl and came to rest on him.

It was as though a candle had been lit at the back of her eyes. Katherine Andrews seemed to explode, to ignite with joy, to blind all those about her with her glowing excitement. She was dressed in some outfit of tawny silk, unadorned with the flounces and bows which were the rage, very rich and gleaming but simple, and a small hat of the same colour and material, the brim of which was turned up all round, something in the style of a child's sailor hat but worn on the back of her head. Again it was unadorned, but Katherine Andrews needed no embellishment with hair as vivid and wilful as hers. It burst from beneath the brim of the hat in a truly awesome cloud of springing curls, tumbling about her ears and neck and over her forehead to her eyebrows.

"It's Jamie," she shrieked for all of Crossclough to hear and though Jamie felt the urge to sigh in exasperation, for it seemed Katherine Andrews had not changed in five years, he could not help the sudden tug of his lips in a smile.

She began to run towards him, her hat flying off and bowling along the platform to the delight of boarding and alighting passengers, and those who stared from the train in surprise at the young woman who ran like a fleet-footed deer past their windows. Her skirt flew up to reveal several inches of lace-trimmed petticoat and even more of stockinged leg above her dainty kid shoes. She flung wide her arms as she ran, oblivious to the open-mouthed stares of those about her, her face ecstatic and on it was drawn the lodestar, the driving force, the mainspring, the very reason for living which coloured Katherine Andrews's existence. It was written as plain as words on a page what she felt, as it had always done and Jamie's heart, which had moved in pleasure at the sight of her, dropped like a stone.

Jesus God, he had forgotten how she was. The childish adoration. What might even be called fanatical worship, the intense, narrow-eyed determination of eleven-year-old Katherine Andrews who had formed such a passionate attachment for him she had refused to be parted from him, doing her best to clamp herself to his side, to go exactly where he went when he was home five years ago.

She had been a child then, easy to elude, easy to placate and please and promise as one would a child. Now she was a woman, but Christ Almighty, it seemed her feelings towards him had not changed.

Her body met his with a force so strong it nearly had him off his feet. She was not small, nor was she light. Though her waist was slender she was deep-bosomed and her hips were what he could only call womanly. She topped the girl beside him by at least half a head and the contrast between them, despite their similar colouring, was quite incredible.

"Jamie, Jamie, Jamie, you're home . . . Dear God, you've come home at last," she was babbling, her rosy face pressed into his shoulder, the sweet, wholesome smell of her enveloping him, her arms a stranglehold about his neck and for the life of him he could not prevent his own from lifting to hold her, to fold her against him.

"Katherine," he managed to gasp, doing his best now to put her from him, to dislodge her from round his neck, to avoid her kisses which she seemed intent on placing wherever her lips could reach, preferably on his own, while the girl beside him watched in bemusement.

"Oh, Jamie . . . Jamie, you're home . . . home."

Over her head Jamie could see the perilous, tight-lipped outrage on the face of the young man who stood by the gate. What the hell was going on, his green slitted eyes demanded and Chris Andrews, galvanised into sudden furious action at the sight of his sister clasped in the arms of a brawny man of the working classes, strode out along the platform, his face compressed into lines of fury. His mother was not far behind him, her face like paper, her clear blue-green eyes, so like those of the girl with whom Jamie had just travelled from Manchester, wide with shock.

"Jamie . . . oh, Jamie, if you knew how I'd missed you. All these years and not one letter, you devil. Not one. You promised to write and all I had was news of you from Matty about places . . . but it doesn't matter now. You're home and— "

"Katherine, that's enough. You are making a spectacle of yourself," her brother said icily. "Take your hands off— "

"It's Jamie, you fool," she breathed, her face and voice enchanted. She patted his chest, ready to snuggle up to him again, unconcerned with the delighted stares of Fred Beardsall, the ticket collector, who would have something to tell his old woman tonight, and of Archie Bagshaw, the postman, who was collecting some parcels at the back of the train and would have the scene in every detail all over Crossclough within the hour.

"We know who it is, Katherine" – her mother nodded graciously at Jamie – "and would be obliged if you would be a little more circumspect in your behaviour. You are not a child."

"Oh, Mother . . ."

"Katherine! Go and get your hat before it rolls beneath the train." Her mother's voice had chips of ice in it. The voice of a lady, a lady born to be obeyed as her upbringing and breeding had taught her and there were not a few about who were of the opinion she should have used it more often in the past, particularly on this rebellious girl.

"Mother . . ."

"Katherine, do as I say."

Reluctantly Katherine stood away from Jamie, then turned and hurried up the platform to retrieve her hat which Fred Beardsall had rescued for her and it was then that the mother and her son turned to look again at the girl beside Jamie, as he did himself. What an ethereal creature she was, a snowdrop beside the tall, colourful sunflower who was Katherine Andrews and whether it was because of the journey they had just travelled together or the raw antagonism in Sara Andrews's face, she drew closer to him as though seeking his protection and Chris Andrews's eyes gleamed in sudden speculation.

"You are . . . Chloe Taylor?" Mrs Andrews asked distantly and Jamie noticed that for some reason she gazed slightly to one side of the girl's face as though reluctant to look into it. He was astonished and, if he were truthful, strangely angry, for Mrs Andrews was acting as though the girl was some kind of low person who had accosted them without provocation and must be dispatched with the contempt she deserved.

"Yes, ma'am." The answer was so low it was barely more than a whisper.

"We had your father's letter."

"Yes, ma'am." The girl's head rose, a delicate blossom on a slender stalk, but proud, unbowed, as though to say, frail as she was, she would not be frightened by Sara Andrews's evident hostility. She was frightened, Jamie had seen it in the train and as she stepped down on to the platform, but she would not let this woman know it, her erect carriage said.

Chris Andrews stared at her appreciatively, as bowled over by her delicate beauty as Jamie had been, with nothing to say for himself now that his sister had been removed from the embarrassing spectacle she had made of herself with one of his mother's servants. That was who he was, and he'd best remember it, Chris Andrews's green, flinty-eyed expression had said, and now another expression had come to replace it. Jamie recognised it, for was he not a man and had he not seen it in other men's eyes when they were presented with a pretty and perhaps available young woman.

"Well . . ." To Jamie's amazement it seemed Jack Andrews's ladylike wife had nothing further to say to the girl who must surely be a kinswoman of hers and whose existence Jamie had not been aware of and who, it was very apparent, was an unwelcome guest at Cloudberry End.

Mrs Andrews turned to him. Her eyes warmed and at once she was as he had always known her. Kind, sweet-natured, gracious, affectionate even, for she and his mother had been close friends for years despite the difference in their rank.

"Jamie, it is good to see you. We had no idea . . . your mother never mentioned you were coming home."

"She didn't know, Mrs Andrews. I thought that by the time a letter was posted in Liverpool I would be here before it so I decided to give her a surprise. She is well, I hope."

"Oh, of course, and just as irrepressible. You know how she is."

He smiled. "Indeed. She will never change. And my stepfather?"

"Vigorous as ever. Still driving my carriage as you will see in a moment."

"Mother."

"Yes, dear?" Sara turned to her son who had become restive under the pleasantries his mother and Jamie were exchanging. Her gaze passed over the girl – Chloe Taylor, was that what she had said? – as though she did not exist and again Jamie was mortified for her.

"I had better get Fred to send up the luggage in the station trap," Chris said smoothly. "We shall be hard pressed all to get into the carriage as it is," his insolent tone implying that Jamie Hutchinson's enormous bulk would take up more than his fair share of the seating.

"There is no need, Chris," Jamie ventured politely and at the use of his Christian name Chris Andrews frowned. Though he and his brothers, with a young Jamie Hutchinson, had roamed the moorland together when they were boys it was evident that that boyhood friendship, now that they were grown men, was ended and he did not care for the use of his Christian name without the obligatory "master" before it.

But be damned to him, Jamie thought savagely. He'd call no man master, not now. Jack Andrews he'd address as Mr Andrews as was only courteous with an older man, but if this young puppy thought he'd bow his head humbly to the son of the man who owned Cloudberry End, even if Jamie's mother and stepfather worked for him, then he was sadly mistaken.

"I shall walk up to Cloudberry," he continued coolly, "since I'm sure you and . . . Miss Taylor?" with a warm smile at the silent girl beside him, "will have much to talk about."

"I'll walk with you, Jamie." Katherine took his arm proprietorially, ready to stride off in the direction of the gate, but Jamie felt a strange reluctance to leave the young woman to the cold, dreadful and amazing hostility of Mrs Andrews. She remained still and frozen by his side, awakening a gentle pity in him, a need to protect, to defend. She reminded him of a doe he had once seen cornered by a group of hunters. The beautiful animal had been transfixed, her coat rippling in terror, her eyes sightless, stunned, as though in stillness and silence she might avoid the awful fate which was to be hers. They had shot her just the same.

"No, Katherine, go with your mother and with Miss Taylor," for somehow, though why he should think so since a more careless, unthinking creature than Katherine Andrews did not exist, he had the feeling she might stand as a bulwark between her mother and the girl. Again, why a bulwark should be needed he couldn't imagine, but for all her faults Katherine was warm-hearted, there was no doubt about that, and perhaps with her casual approach to anything which did not directly affect her she might be kind to the girl.

"I don't want to, Jamie. I want to walk with you. There is so much to talk about and I want to know what you think of me now that I'm grown up." She smiled impishly. "What d'you think? Am I— "

"Oh, for God's sake, Katherine, go and get in the bloody carriage," her brother snapped. "You do nothing but talk nonsense and anyway, how in hell's name can you walk up to Cloudberry dressed like that? Look at your shoes."

"Mind your own damned business, Chris." Katherine's face was furious. "If I want to walk with Jamie then I shall. We have so much to say to one another, haven't we, Jamie?" She turned to glow up into Jamie's face, her own telling the world what was in her heart.

"Katherine, take your . . . take Miss Taylor to the carriage while Chris sees to the luggage."

"Mother, please."

It was not often that Sara Andrews could withstand her stubborn daughter. It was not often that she even tried, but she seemed to have about her today a grim air of coldness, of fixed and unbending resolution that would not be denied.

It was so unlike her Jamie could only wonder what had happened to alter her so. It was obviously something to do with this young woman whom she seemed unable to bear to contemplate, but whatever it was put steel in her and her daughter recognised it.

She tried one more time, her mouth set in a tight line of pleading.

"Mother, it will be crowded in the carriage and— "

"Do as you are told, Katherine, and take Miss Taylor with you."

The last Jamie saw of them as he shouldered his sea bag and gathered his packages about him was the bone white face of Chloe Taylor as she stared in what looked to be despair from the carriage window.

4

Chloe Taylor stared sightlessly from the window of the room they had put her in, shivering though it was not cold. Far from it. An enormously extravagant fire roared up the chimney, a fire the likes of which she had never before seen since Mama had not cared for lavishness. In the fireplace behind the brass fender stood a brass coal scuttle, polished to mirror-like gloss, filled to its brim with even more coal, evidence that if she cared to she might build the fire even higher.

She had been here for two hours. A neatly uniformed and obviously excited young housemaid had unpacked her bags, her face crimson with bursting curiosity, her eyes bright with speculation, hanging her gowns, two of them, both black, away in the wardrobe, neatly folding her immaculate, exquisitely made underwear into the top drawer of the chest. Her silver-backed hairbrush and mirror, an unexpectedly extravagant gift on her sixteenth birthday from Mama, and her tortoiseshell comb, now resided in perfect alignment on the dressing-table and her clean nightgown, again fashioned and embroidered with consummate skill by herself and Mama, had been tucked away beneath the frilled pillow on the enormous canopied bed. The maid had fidgeted about the room, straightening the lace runner on the chest of drawers, twitching the curtains into a more pleasing line, giving the fire an unnecessary stir until, unable to find anything further which might need her attention, she had bobbed a curtsey, asking if there was "anything else, miss?"

"No, thank you," Chloe had answered, standing awkwardly by the fire, since she was not used to being waited on, her hand resting on the back of the low, comfortably padded chair which was evidently hers to lounge in if she so desired.

"Rightio, miss," the maid said cheerfully. "I'll get on then."

"Thank you – er . . .?"

"Ivy, miss."

"Thank you, Ivy."

"Lunch is at one, miss, madame said ter tell yer."

"Aah . . ."

"Ring if yer want anythin', miss. Bells by't fireplace," and with another dipping bob and one last wide-eyed, fascinated glance, Ivy left the room, hurrying off back to the kitchen to give a full report to the rest of the eager servants on the looks, the demeanour, the state of the guest's wardrobe and the exquisite colour of her hair which had been revealed when she removed her bonnet. Of course, Freda and Thomas had already seen her, Thomas on the journey from the station and Freda when she opened the front door which was part of her duties as head parlourmaid. It was Freda who had given Ivy instructions on the transfer of the visitor's luggage from the hall to the front corner bedroom on the first floor. One of the best guest bedrooms which surely must indicate the importance of the young lady.

Yes, a fine bedroom, a luxurious bedroom even, Chloe admitted miserably, with two long windows at the front and one at the side in which there was a padded seat, and with a sigh she slowly sank into it. She leaned back against the wooden frame, bending her knees and clasping her arms about them. She lowered her head, resting her forehead on her hands, longing to burst into noisy tears and cry out her pain and grief and heartache, her very real fear and her homesickness for the tall, narrow house in Upper Parliament Street which she had shared with Mama and Papa until Mama's death. She longed to give way, to let go, to shout and bluster as she was sure that tall, red-headed lump of a girl downstairs would do, the one she supposed was her cousin. Let them all be in no doubt that she wanted to be here as little as they wanted her here but she had no choice, as Papa had awkwardly explained to her. The new Mrs Taylor, only a year or two older than Chloe and already pregnant with her first child, had thought it best that a young, unmarried girl like herself should not be exposed to the tribulations and embarrassment of pregnancy and childbirth, she had told Chloe's papa. Indeed, it was not at all "proper" and therefore they both agreed, he and the second Mrs Taylor, that it was best that she go and stay with her relatives for a while.

He had written to Mama's sister, the one Mama had loathed and, she had said, pitied for her disagreeable nature and Chloe was to go and stay with her in some God-forsaken spot in the wilds of the Pennine country, just until the baby was born, Papa had added placatingly.

She had pleaded and begged but it had done no good and so here she was, for where could a girl of her age and social class go but where she was sent, obedient to her father's wishes and making the best of it as her mama had taught her.

But it was worse, far worse than Mama had said it would be. Not that Mama had been up here or seen her sister for over twenty-five years but she had described her to Chloe, painting her in such grasping, self-centred, greedy and Godless colours, Chloe had been hard pressed to believe that such a monster could be related to her own God-fearing Mama. A liar and a cheat who had swindled Mama out of a great deal of money over the sale of a fashion house in Liverpool, though she had revealed none of the sordid details to her innocent daughter. She had run off with some rough man in the building trade, sailing away with him to Canada and them not even married. A woman not fit to lick Mama's boots and Chloe had been appalled and terrified when Papa had told her what was to become of her.

"May I come back home and help to care for the baby when it is born?" she had pleaded, ignoring her stepmama's horror- stricken pretence at a faint since no young, unmarried woman spoke of such things in the presence of a gentleman, even her own papa. "I will take on the duties of nursemaid willingly, Papa, if you would allow it, and would keep out of the way," meaning her stepmama's way, of course. "I like children, you know I do and would not mind at all if you would give your permission and . . ."

"Henry, really! A man in your position allowing your own daughter to play at nursemaid. What would your business acquaintances and friends think if it should get out? No, far better to send her for a while to her relatives where I'm sure she will be kindly treated and, who knows, where eligible young bachelors will be guests. They are well placed, I believe. Mrs Cartwright's husband is connected in some way with the railway and says Jack Andrews is well thought of, apart from his . . . other advantages. So you must put all thoughts of acting as nursemaid quite out of your head, my dear. Your papa has a position to keep up and if it became known that— "

"I wouldn't tell anyone, Papa. I would just stay in the nursery and look after the baby. Oh, please, Papa, you know how Mama felt about her sister. She will not want me, Papa. She will have children of her own, I'm sure, and if she is wicked, as Mama said she was, then . . ."

"Your mama was inclined to . . . to exaggerate somewhat, Chloe," Papa had said distantly.

"Indeed she was—" her stepmama began but Chloe had rounded on her, her white face flooding with outraged colour.

"How do you know what my mama was like? You never met her since she would not have a woman like you in her home. She would be turning in her grave this very minute if she knew you were here, sleeping in her bed, using her things."

"Henry!" the second Mrs Taylor shrieked. "The baby . . ." And Henry Taylor, a chandler in Water Street, who desperately wanted a son, a son who would in time help him in the successful business which, with the injection of his first wife's money after her death and the sale of her own dressmaking establishment, was growing beyond his wildest imaginings.

He half carried his fainting wife from the dining room and the slightly apologetic look he gave his daughter said quite plainly that she could see how he was placed and must surely understand. A man's duty was to his wife, it said, especially if that wife was with child and that child might be a son.

So, here she was, and but for the large gentleman who had helped her from the train, oh, and the smiling housemaid, she had received not one kind word, nor even a friendly glance from a soul this day. Her aunt – she supposed she must admit to her being that – after a cold stare and a brief nod had totally ignored her, treating her like some new servant who was to work in the kitchens. Worse, for most mistresses would find a comforting word or two for a homesick kitchenmaid on her first day of duty. Her cousin, the girl called Katherine, had been in such a taking over her mama's refusal to allow her to walk back with the big man, she had sulked and tapped her foot all the way to Cloudberry End where the man also seemed to live and Chris, as his mama had addressed him, had eyed her with a look on his face Chloe did not care for at all. She'd seen it before on men's faces, of course, even on that of the big man in the train though he'd done his best to hide it. To be polite and careful with her. She was a lady and deserved respect, no matter how pretty she was, the look in his brilliant blue eyes had said, and how could she not be aware that she was pretty? It had been the cross she bore ever since she had moved from childhood to girlhood, causing no end of trouble to her mama who had made her wear her hair dragged back from her face in heavy braids, but it had done no good, for men continued to stare at her in fascinated awe, and in other ways which she did not like to mention.

She turned again to the window, leaning the back of her head against the frame. There were two men working at the far end of the garden. Well, a man and a boy, industriously turning over the soil, their backs bending and straightening in unison, their spades biting into the dark earth at precisely the same moment. A row of plant pots, at least two dozen of them, stood on the path, the plants obviously waiting to be put in the ground and as she watched another man came round from the back of the house pushing a wheelbarrow. On it was a further load of pots, wobbling a bit as he manhandled it, in a short cut, across the grass. Behind him pranced a small dog.

The first man stopped work, leaning on his spade, his face irate, Chloe could see even from the bedroom. His free hand rose and formed a fist, his head nodded angrily and though she could not hear the words he spoke she knew he was giving the newcomer a piece of his mind for crossing the lawn and leaving imprints in its shaved perfection. The man with the wheelbarrow, looking abashed, carefully trundled it on to the footpath, almost carrying it. The dog wagged its tail frantically. Its tongue lolled from its mouth and its ears pricked in anticipation.

Chloe leaned forward for a better look, wondering who it belonged to and as if in answer to her pondering the tall, red-headed girl came skidding full pelt round the opposite corner of the house. Her hair was all over the place. Chloe had never seen anything like it since it seemed to be cut as short as a man's and if Chloe's own mama had been in charge of her the girl would have been in dire peril. It bounced and swirled about her head, glowing like a beacon in the small gleam of fitful sunshine which had decided to peep out, completely unbound by anything at all, even a bit of ribbon. She had discarded her silk gown and now wore what looked like a riding habit in a rich shade of blue. The skirt was long, trained and full and she held it bunched up above her knees and, horror of horrors, showing beneath it were a pair of trousers and glossy riding boots!

"Muffy, come here at once, you devil, or I swear I'll take my whip to you," she was shouting loud enough for Chloe to hear even though the bedroom windows were shut. "Catch him, Billy," and the boy sprang forward eagerly. "Shut him in the stable, will you? I'm off to Woodhead so will you go and saddle Storm for me, Noah?" this to the man with the wheelbarrow. "I can't find Dicken or Jimmy. God alone knows where they get to when they're needed, and if anyone asks you haven't seen me."

The second voice seemed to come from nowhere. "But

I've seen you, Katherine, and I'd be obliged if you'd come indoors at once and change back into your gown. Your mother and Chris are about to sit down to lunch and you are to go upstairs and fetch . . . fetch our guest."

Katherine came to such an abrupt halt she made heel marks in the gardener's obviously prized lawn and a look of resigned horror came over his face. The dog had raced over to her, the boy in unsuccessful pursuit, jumping up at her in ecstasy and leaving muddy paw marks all over her skirt, since he had been rummaging in the soil at the back of the flowerbed where the gardener and his boy were digging. Katherine clapped her hand to her forehead in exasperation. Chloe was not sure whether it was at the dog or the male voice which seemed to come from just beneath her window. She stamped her foot fretfully and Chloe held her breath.

"Oh, Father, really! Do I need to? I did my duty this morning, you must agree and I promised Grandmother I would be over to give her a full description of the girl. I'll have my lunch there so . . ."

"No, you will not, Katherine. You will have your lunch with your family. You know how difficult this is going to be for your mother, and for me, so kindly do as I say."

"Father, please don't make me. Oh, damn that bloody animal."

Chloe gasped in horror, clapping her hand to her mouth.

"Watch your language, my girl," for though it appeared Jack Andrews was at perfect liberty to curse whenever he felt the need for it, a young lady such as his badly brought-up daughter was not.

"If he had been shut up as he was supposed to be I wouldn't have had to chase him all over the bloody garden."

"Dammit, Katherine!"

"But I knew the minute I was up on Storm he'd be after me and I didn't want to take him today." A secretive expression flitted across her face, gone in a moment, but Chloe had seen it even if the man below had not. "Oh, damn and blast . . ."

"Katherine, come inside at once," and Katherine, it seemed, had no choice, vanishing disconsolately from Chloe's view. The two men and the boy huddled together for several minutes, evidently exchanging opinions on the scene they had just witnessed and the dog lay down in a patch of weak sunshine.

Chloe put her feet to the carpet. She was shocked and amazed and she knew her mouth hung open in a most foolish way. She wanted to turn to someone, though of course she had no one to turn to, and ask them if they had ever seen or heard anything like it in their life because she certainly hadn't. The language and bald-faced defiance of the man who must be her cousin's father, and as for that outfit, the indecency of the trousered legs, and the hair, well, she could hardly believe her own eyes. For a young woman to act like that, to look like that and to speak like that, especially to her own father, was scarcely believable and if she hadn't witnessed it she wouldn't have believed it. And in what was supposedly a decent family. They were evidently people who had no respect for one another, she decided, nor even affection and certainly no regard for the niceties of social behaviour. If she had spoken to her papa like that, let alone the cursing, Mama would have locked her in her room on bread and water for a week. She had never heard a man speak as Katherine Andrews had, let alone a woman and the thought of spending even an hour in the company of such uncouth and probably uneducated persons as these, even if they were as enormously wealthy as this room, this house seemed to say they were, filled her with appalled horror. Oh, Mama, you were strict and sometimes harsh, I suppose, but why did you have to die when you did? Why did you have to die at all? It is not even a year yet and barely three months since Papa married that woman who has driven me out, but for all your severity I know you loved me and I miss you.

She stood up, clamping her soft lips together to suppress the wail of misery which wanted to escape. She glanced about the room apathetically, noticing with a part of her mind which, without being consciously aware of it, gloated over its elegance and comfort, the thickness of the rich-piled, buttercup yellow carpet, the lacy white frills about the canopy of the bed, the glowing polish on the satinwood wardrobe, the chest of drawers and the dainty, kidney-shaped dressing-table on which a triple mirror stood. The walls were papered in a pale yellow and silver striped wallpaper. The quilt on the bed, a patchwork quilt, was made up of every shade of lemon, ivory, bold yellow, daffodil and buttercup banded with white and on the low table by the long window an enormous copper bowl was filled with yellow and white roses. Where would they get roses at this time of the year? she wondered, sighing deeply. She smoothed the rich golden yellow velvet of the curtains at the window, marvelling that though the sun did not enter the room, at least at this time of the day, it seemed to be filled with it, deep and glowing. There were pictures on the wall, pastoral scenes done in watercolours, a field rippling with poppies, another of buttercups and daisies with cattle standing knee deep in grasses.

She walked across the room to look at them more closely and was amazed to see that the signature on them was of the famous and talented artist David Bretherton who had been born in Liverpool. If they were original, and they appeared to be, they must be worth a fortune.

On the mantelpiece above the fire was a pretty brass clock set between two pale and pirouetting ballet dancers. She picked one up and smoothed its graceful form with a careful finger. So many lovely things. It was all enchanting and in any other circumstance she would have been enchanted. Though she had not offered the knowledge to Mama she had always been drawn to beauty. She could stand for an hour, and had when she was let, and absorb into herself, through her eyes and the pores of her skin, the glorious, furious, sometimes delicate colours of a sunset. The sky first turning yellow, merging to green as the golden sun vanished and when the sun had gone, dropping gracefully, slowly, below the horizon, the heart-stopping glory of fiery brown, crimson and orange, spreading upwards as the orb of the sun sank to its next day. An arch of rose on rose-pink, lingering as night crept overhead until the pink turned to violet and plum purple.

Enraptured she had watched it happen across the River Mersey, the waters mirroring the sky, until Mama, who liked a brisk evening walk before prayer meeting, pulled at her arm to fetch her from what she called her daughter's "daydreaming".

The moon, mistress of the night, seen from her bedroom window, the earth shine lighting up its surface, the silver stitching about it pulling at her heart in its loveliness. March sunshine filled with the fluttering wings of the first Brimstone butterflies, yellow and blue, blush red and chocolate brown. Bluebells in April, a hazy carpet beneath the close-packed trees of Mill Wood beyond West Derby where Papa took her as a child, and primroses, the first flower of the year. The song of the thrush, the bird looping up in low graceful flight from the garden at the back of the house . . . oh, she could go on and on and on, remembering not only the rich beauty she loved but the unthinking content she had known as a child. She had not, of course, divulged her thoughts to Mama simply because Mama would have thought her "fanciful". She would not have approved, nor understood. Mama had been practical, down to earth, believing in the performing of one's duty and responsibility to others, as the Church taught; in hard work and decency and had certainly not had time in her busy life simply to stand and stare at what she would have called trivialities.

Her own room at home had been a plain, no-nonsense sort of a room with everything in it Mama considered suitable for a young girl. A narrow white bed and a table beside it on which her Bible rested. A wardrobe in which her exquisitely made dresses and mantles hung, the cut and colour of the garments again picked by Mama who knew best, naturally. A square of carpet on the floor and . . . Oh dear Lord above, give me strength, if it is Thy will, but I would exchange the deep-piled comfort and luxury of this room for the plainness and sparseness of my own, and with all my heart if it could only be made possible.

The knock on the door was peremptory and it was flung open without waiting for her to answer. Chloe clenched her jaw even tighter, so tight she feared she would be unable to open it again when the time came, but it was the only way she could keep her composure from shredding away in tatters about her. She had not changed since she had nothing to change into except another black dress but she had unbraided her hair, brushed it vigorously and braided it again, even tighter, if that were possible, coiling it up into an enormous bun at the back of her head. Though she was not aware of it, since she had done it that way because it would have pleased her mama, the style gave her a strange, exotic look, lengthening her blue-green eyes, heightening her already high cheekbones and accentuating the faint hollow beneath them. Her mouth was a rich, ripe coral against the black of her gown which, because of its plainness and absolute lack of colour, emphasised her startling and delicate young beauty. She would have been mortified if she had known.

"Lunch is ready," the girl in the doorway said curtly. "They sent me to fetch you."

Chloe had argued with herself for the past ten minutes, ever since she had known Katherine was to come up for her, warned by the unseen man's voice, telling herself she didn't want any lunch. She didn't want to eat at all, ever again; in fact she was convinced she would just heave it all up again if she did. Or it would stick in her throat and refuse to go down. But it had to be done sometime or they would only come to the conclusion that she was afraid of them and that would never do. She was afraid of them but she'd be damned . . . Oh God, forgive me, I'm already picking up their profane language. But she'd not let them know she was afraid.

"Thank you," was all she said, lifting her chin which was already high, a little higher.

"Are you going down like that?" her cousin asked curiously, just as though Chloe had on some strange and outlandish costume. She herself was in the tawny silk she had worn that morning.

"Like what?" Chloe heard herself say defensively.

"Well, in that black dress."

"I am in mourning for my mama." She tried her best to keep the tears from her voice but it trembled badly.

Amazingly Katherine softened. "Oh, of course, I'm sorry."

Chloe felt a tiny feather of warmth touch her skin and her back relaxed a fraction from its aching stiffness.

"When did she die?" Katherine went on, holding open the door for her to go through. She eyed the scraped-back braids, the high-necked severity of the mourning gown with faint disapproval as though she couldn't understand why anyone would voluntarily trick herself out in such drabness, her expression saying that she certainly wouldn't, no matter who had died.

"Last August."

"Last August!"

They were halfway down the length of the landing along which most of the doors stood open to reveal bedrooms as delightful as the one Chloe had been put in but Katherine's hand on her arm halted her and swung her back to face her.

"D'you mean to say your mother has been dead since last August and yet your father has left it until now to . . ." she almost said "discard" you, ". . . to send you to us?"

"I don't know what you mean."

"Well, he has managed to look after you himself all these months so why has he suddenly decided that you'd be best off with us?"

Chloe had an instant picture of her stepmama's triumphant face as she had waved to her from the window of the house in Upper Parliament Street but she made her own stay calm and expressionless as her cousin blundered on.

"And how did he know we would take you in, anyway? Your mother and mine were not, apparently, on the best of terms."

Chloe could not help it. "And is it any wonder?" she said furiously.

"What is that supposed to mean?" Katherine's chin took

on a truculent angle and Chloe felt a great desire to strike it. Dear Lord, she had only been in this house a couple of hours and already she had been incited to swearing and seized by the desire to hit another human being. Her voice rose to an angry squeak though she did her level best to remain calm.

"How can you ask that after what happened between them? Mama was devastated." Her voice rose even higher in remembered pain and Katherine began to look alarmed.

"Oh, for God's sake, be quiet. You'll have Mother and Father up here in a minute and I'm supposed to be bringing you down to the dining-room. They'll want to know, of course. Why your father sent you here, I mean, so you'd best save your explanations until then. Come on, and do try to look as though you are going down to lunch and not to your own hanging."

Again Chloe clamped her teeth together since it seemed there was no avoiding the confrontation with this girl's family. Best get it over and done with and then she could retire to what she supposed she must call her room and howl herself into oblivion.

Katherine opened the door to the left of the staircase and ushered her into the room. As she had upstairs, Chloe was at once aware of a sense of warmth, of comfort, of polished surfaces, a gleaming and a glittering which was ready to dazzle her until she looked into the bone white face of the woman who was her mother's sister. She did not speak.

The two gentlemen present rose to their feet politely, the older one indicating brusquely that she was to sit on his right with Katherine between her and his wife, holding her chair until she was seated. She had no more than a brief glimpse of a face which would be good-humoured under other circumstances, she was sure, and of deep brown eyes beneath fiercely dipping brows. The younger man, the one called Chris, remained standing until the other man – it must be his father – sat down again.

"I'm Jack Andrews," the older man said shortly, "as you will no doubt have guessed."

Somehow she unclamped her jaw.

"Yes, sir." Her voice was low but steady. There were two women at the back of the room and she was conscious of their curious glances. One of them was the maid who had opened the door to them earlier in the day, the other an older woman, steady, nudging the younger as though to tell her to stop gawping and get on with her job.

"You have met my son and daughter?"

"Yes, sir."

"And my wife?"

"Indeed," though she did not look at her aunt.

"Have you anything you would like to say to us?"

Chloe raised her head to look at him in some astonishment. What on earth had she to say to these strangers who had, as Christians should, taken her in but who were treating her as though she had done them some grievous harm for which they could never forgive her. Even the man, her aunt's husband, seemed to have the greatest difficulty in looking at her, carefully keeping his eyes on his plate, or his wife, or the wallpaper, rather than meet hers.

She cleared her throat and the maidservants who were just about to serve soup, paused uncertainly.

"Only that it is most generous of you to allow me to stay with you, sir." What else could she say beyond the polite response anyone in her position would make? Even those few words stuck in her throat but she supposed, in one way, it was generous of them to give shelter to a complete stranger, for that was what she was.

"You are comfortable?"

She nodded her head. He was doing his duty as a host but she was also aware that he was setting guidelines, letting her know what her position was here in this house. She was not to think of herself as a member of the family. She was a guest, one his wife had obligingly accommodated for as short a time as possible, but no more. Polite they would be with one another, since one was polite to a guest in one's home, but anything warmer, more cordial, more personal was out of the question.

She understood, though she did not know why.

It was the girl, of course, not knowing, nor caring, what the past had held for her parents, who broke away from the icy courtesies which were being exchanged. The maids had served the soup, a deliciously rich soup in which fine slices of leek floated, and they had begun to eat when she broke the silence.

"Do you ride?" she asked, turning to look at Chloe and her dreadful black dress as though assessing what might be needed to smarten her up a bit.

"Ride?" Chloe was clearly startled and Katherine raised her eyebrows.

"Yes, on a horse."

"A horse?"

Katy sighed in exasperation. "You do know what a horse is, surely, even if you have lived in the city. I presume they have them in Liverpool though one wonders how one could possibly get a good gallop in those congested streets."

Her brother spoke for the first time, leaning back indolently in his chair despite his father's frown. "I suppose there are bridle trails and paths in the woods and fields about the city, Katy." Chloe might not have been there. "Johnny Ashwell has some cousins who live in . . . oh, somewhere on the outskirts and I'm sure they have stables. I have a feeling they ride to hounds in Cheshire which, if my geography serves me, is somewhere over that way."

"Well, they would, wouldn't they? The great and glorious Ashwells and what surprises me is that Johnny manages to stay on his animal at all, his seat is so appalling. I saw him the other day going hell for leather up towards Tintwistle Knarr with that imbecile Tim What's-his-name in tow and he was all over the place. He reminded me of nothing so much as a sack of coal, lolling from side to side, his head going ten to the dozen and his mount baulking at every blade of grass."

"Rubbish, he is as good a rider as I am."

Katherine shrugged and rolled her eyes as though to say, "Well, there you are then," then lost interest and the matter was closed, it seemed.

Chris glanced languidly at Chloe and in his eyes was a spark of something which could have been admiration, the look a man allows a woman whom he might just be interested in, a secret look since he knew his father's eye was on him. His eyelids drooped as though he had not had much sleep the night before and he yawned several times behind his hand.

"I hope those yawns are not meant to indicate that you are too exhausted to accompany me this afternoon, lad," Jack Andrews said crisply to his son, pausing in the act of lifting a spoonful of soup to his lips, "because if they are it cuts no ice with me, for I mean you to come along just the same."

"Accompany you, sir?" Chris assumed an injured air and Chloe noticed the two maids exchange glances. Trouble brewing, those glances said and for the first time since she had entered this house she was diverted from her own heartache. This was them as they were when she was not present and she found it intrigued her. For the moment they had forgotten her as their own affairs, the daily and presumably important concerns of the Andrews family took precedence over all else.

"Aye," her uncle continued. "I've a mind to try you out in the paper mill."

"The paper mill! Christ Almighty, Father, surely you cannot mean me to spend my days in that appalling hell-hole? I'd go out of my mind."

"Really! Then how are you to spend your days, lad? It is honest labour," his father began to thunder and at the end of the table Sara Andrews made a small sound in the back of her throat.

"Oh God," she mumbled, staring into her soup and they all turned to look at her, even the maids, and on all their faces, except Chloe's, was an expression of awful dread.

"Sara, sweetheart," her husband began, rising from his seat and Chloe was bemused by the emotion, total and consuming, which lit his face. She didn't know what it was since she had never seen it before. It was tender, gentle, cherishing, all in one, and yet there was a passion in it which was quite embarrassing to watch. It said that he would gladly give his life if it would save his wife a moment's anguish and it was then that she began to have some intimation of what joined Sara and Jack Andrews together. And perhaps an understanding, when it was finally made clear to her, of the past in which her mother had played a part.

She was badly startled by it but at the same time completely fascinated.

"It's all right, darling," her aunt said, the look she bestowed on him identical to the one he had just given her. "No, really, it's just that . . . it's just as though she has come back to remind me."

Lifting her head her aunt looked down the table to where Chloe sat and in her face was such a depth of sadness Chloe felt her own heart squeeze, though she didn't know why.

"It's her, Jack. If I didn't know Alice was dead I would swear it was her."

5

Matty Jenkins smiled at her son or rather at his profile which was outlined, strong and bold and serious, against the flames of the brightly burning kitchen fire. He was sitting in her husband's comfortable chair, his leg bent, his right foot resting on his left knee, reading the newspaper which came across daily from the house when Mr Andrews had finished with it. Not that Thomas was particularly interested in the sort of newspaper his employer read. *The Times* was not really his cup of tea, he had said to her cheerfully, since Thomas was an unfailingly cheerful man, thank the good God, but the paper rolled up into decent firelighters for when the front parlour fire was lit on special occasions, so it wasn't wasted.

Matty was making bread. There was a fine film of flour coating most surfaces of the warm kitchen: the plain deal table where she worked, the stone-flagged floor about the table, her own apron and face and hair, and some had even come to rest, featherlike, in her son's dark curls. Matty was inclined to fling things about a bit when she was enjoying herself and she enjoyed making bread. It gave her a great sense of who she was, and how far she had come from what she had once been, though she didn't dwell on that now. Her Jamie, her illegitimate son Jamie, was living proof of who she had once been, though she didn't dwell on that, neither. Life had been good to her. Life and Sara Andrews whom she'd die for, God's honour, and she gave thanks every day to some faceless, nameless deity, whom she was reluctant to call God, for what she had. This tidy little cottage, for instance, nestling in a dip at the front of Cloudberry End, screened from the house by a well-kept hedge of holly and a dozen or so mature beech trees. For her Thomas who had come with her from Liverpool since she'd not be parted from Sara, even for him, she'd told him, and for the children he'd given her, Dulcie who was a mother herself now and, late in life when they had both thought themselves to be past such things, their Tommy, a scamp of a lad at fourteen but with the warm heart of his mother.

Matty was getting on for fifty and her Thomas fifty-three but they could both still do a hard day's work with the best, though it was seldom they were called upon to do so. Thomas was coachman to Mr Andrews, and to Mrs Andrews whom Matty called Sara. She and Sara had been friends for thirty years nearly and a day never went by when they didn't see one another. They shared their troubles, always had, though thank God there'd not been many of those in recent years at least not until this last one had come along and it was a facer all right.

She glanced again at the dark bulk of her strapping son, watching him frown, wondering what it was in the newspaper that put that expression on his normally even-tempered face. Lord, she couldn't get over how big he was. You forgot in five years the size and shape of even the most beloved son, but then his life at sea had formed him, and, though she could barely remember him after twenty-seven years, his pa had been a big chap an' all.

She gave the dough a last hearty slap then, folding it in a clean cloth, placed it in the hearth to rise.

"Mind yer feet in that there dough when yer gerrup, our Jamie," she said, the nasal lilt of Liverpool still in her voice despite her twenty-five years' exile from the place of her birth.

"Aye, Ma." Jamie continued to read, the toes of his stockinged feet wriggling pleasurably in the warmth from the fire. He had on a pair of corduroy breeches and a rough woollen gansey, the sort sailors wore, and his hair stood up in a mass of tousled curls about his head as though he were in the habit of running his hand through it.

"What yer readin', son? 'Owt interestin'?"

"Mmmm?" Jamie's voice was vague, giving the impression that he had barely heard his mother and if he had he was too engrossed in the newspaper to give her an answer.

Matty was not offended. She rummaged through a basket of washing she had just brought in from the washing line in the garden, lifting out several shirts and flinging them energetically on to a chair. Like a great white sail a flannel sheet was lifted into the air, then allowed to settle across the table. She smoothed it carefully with hands which were worn in the service of others, hands which had once done the most delicate embroidery in Liverpool, though it was many years now since she had taken up a needle and thread to do more than darn the socks of her menfolk, mend a rip in Tommy's shirt, which happened every day for he was a real lad, run up a shirt or a plain gown for herself or put up a hem on an over-long skirt for one of the maidservants at the house.

Bending over her son she withdrew the "sad" iron, "sad" come from the word solid, which the iron was, from the heat of the fire, one of a pair, and with a great deal of spitting and hissing and banging, the first to test the iron's heat, the latter to remove a certain amount of soot which clung to it from the flames, she began vigorously to dash it up and down the first shirt.

"I asked yer what were so interestin' in that there paper, our Jamie? Yer've 'ad yer nose stuck in it this past hour wi'out a word ter say fer yerself. After five years wi'out a sight of yer I'd be glad of a word or two about what yer've bin up to. Yer'll 'ave seen sights yer pa an' me'll never see, or our Tommy fer that matter. Mind you . . ." she brooded pensively, ". . . Tommy's bin that restless lately I'd not be surprised if he didn't tekk off like you did. He's finished school an' Mr Andrews 'as offered ter tekk 'im on in that there paper mill he's just bought but that don't suit our Tommy. Oh no, he ses, I'm not workin' in no mill, though what he do want he can't say. Summat oudoors, likely, but there's nowt round 'ere for a lad, Jamie. Not unless he wants ter get set on in one o't quarries or go fer a farm labourer like them Andrews lads and where's that gonner fetch him up? I said to 'is pa . . ."

Her voice rambled on and her iron hissed and glided in harmony with it. Though his mother had begged him to tell her of what he'd been "up to" in the five years he had been away, her mind had veered back from his travels to the worrying one his boisterous young half-brother was to take in the future.

And could you blame her? Jamie had been out of her life for the best part of thirteen years, ever since Tommy was born, practically, and it was natural that her maternal pride and anxiety should be fixed on her last-born.

He watched her for a minute or two, then smiled, more to himself than at her, his good white teeth a startling slash in his deeply sunbrowned face. He rustled the newspaper and the cat on the hearth-rug at his feet glared up at him irritably, miaowed in a plaintive voice since her place had been partially usurped by the newcomer's feet, curled her tail about her body and did her best to resume her interrupted sleep. Jamie studied his mother, suddenly noticing the dashes of grey in what had been her glossy dark curls. There were wrinkles seaming her lively face, about her mouth and eyes, wrinkles which had not been there when he went away. A shaft of pale May sunlight from the side window caught her as she leaned across him to retrieve the second iron, putting the first in its place to reheat, and it tinted her skin to gold. She was still a handsome woman despite her years but with eyes which were a paler blue than once they had been and her trim figure had thickened at the waist and hips and her bosom was deep and motherly.

"I've told 'im an' told 'im he must settle on summat," she was saying, "but he just laughs an' ses he will soon enough but I'm that feared he might get in with that lot up by Woodhead."

Jamie's indulgent smile died away and he let the newspaper fall to his lap.

"What lot's that then?"

His mother banged her sad iron viciously over her husband's inoffensive shirt, her face falling into a worried frown.

"Them lads o' George an' Will Andrews. Yer know, Jack Andrews's brothers. There's Paddy, he's George's youngest an' at twenty they say he's wilder 'n a caged animal in a zoo. An' the other two're just as bad. Twins, they are, Josh an' Jake an' if Paddy ordered 'em ter jump off Lud's Leap in ter Combes Clough they'd not 'ave ter be told twice. I'm only surprised yer've not come across 'em in yer wanderings, wherever it is yer get to. Anyroad, they're always in trouble, drinkin' an' mekkin' a nuisance o' theirselves with girls hereabouts. Woe betide any lass what finds 'erself on 'er own wi' them three. Oh, no, there's nowt happened yet," seeing the look of consternation on her son's face, "but Ivy Arkwright what's parlourmaid ter Sara, Mrs Andrews, said they didn't half give her some cheek t'other evenin' when she were walking back along t'road from her pa's farm at Thornley Clough. T'weren't even dark. A decent girl on her afternoon off! Well, her pa were all fer goin' over to George's place an' givin' the lot of 'em a good hidin', tekkin' his lads an' all, but Mr Andrews said leave it to him an' he'd sort it out an' I suppose he'd have words with 'em, though what good that'll do I don't know. Anyroad, it's the thought of our Tommy tekkin up wi' 'em what frightens me, our Jamie. He's bin seen wi' the twins, seventeen they are an' far too old fer him ter be goin' about with, an' all of 'em with a shotgun apiece, though where our Tommy got hold of such a thing I couldn't say, and he won't. Shootin' rabbits they were up on Hankeith Hill an' where's it all goin' ter lead to, that's what frightens me. Shotguns an' him only fourteen. His pa's spoken to him but you know how soft he is. Ses the boy's not bad, which is true, an' he doesn't want ter break his spirit."

Matty shook her head and thumped the iron on the table just as though she'd like nothing better than to clout it round the ears of the Andrews lads who were doing their best to lead her Tommy astray. Her face was creased with some dread which her mother's heart did not care to contemplate. Her Tommy was a good lad, sweet-natured but rough and cheerfully rumbustious as lads are. He'd not hurt a lass, or any living thing deliberately but that Paddy Andrews had the charm and devilment of Old Scratch himself and his influence could fling boys like her Tommy and the Andrews twins into trouble before they even knew they were approaching it.

She sighed heavily, still shaking her head as though to clear the cobwebs of alarm from her mind. She looked up and smiled at Jamie, her usual blithe optimism, which had got her through many a rough patch in her life, lifting the corners of her mouth and narrowing her faded blue eyes. Once they had been as brilliant as those of her eldest son, twinkling wickedly at any man with a claim to looks who smiled at her but now, with the disquieting images still lurking at the back of them, they were clouded and flat.

She did her best. "Will yer listen ter me goin' on about what'll probably never 'appen an' you only 'ome a few weeks. We've not seen a lot of yer, lad, an' me an' yer pa were only wonderin' t'other night where yer get to. Saul Gibbon told yer pa he saw yer up on Pikenose Moor, t'other day. Said you was standin' gawpin' at Philcox's farm, that's 'ow he purrit, an' when he spoke yer jumped a foot in th'air. What you up to? Yer've not said a word about what yer mean ter do, son, now that yer've left the sea. Yer *have* left it, haven't yer?" she asked anxiously, since she had a warm feeling that this big lad of hers would be a great comfort to her as she got older. "Yer not goin' back, are yer?"

"No, Mam, I'm not going back. I've finished with the sea and not before time an' all. I'm getting too old to be climbing rigging in a force eight gale."

He stood up slowly and stretched his tall frame – as far as he could in the low-ceilinged room – and his mother admired the long and beautiful length of him. And he *was* beautiful. A strong masculine beauty which had nothing of softness in it, magnificently put together with each part of his body in perfect symmetry with the rest. Long, graceful bones with flat muscles which glided smoothly from the deep curve of his broad chest and shoulders to the concavity of his lean belly which, as he stretched, flattened even further above the belt which held up his breeches. His body, beneath his clothes, was hard and powerful, shaped by the manual adversity of the work he had performed since he was a boy, and he was attractive too, his mother thought proudly. Far from handsome since his face was too rugged for that, but his dark hair curled pleasingly over his well-shaped skull, his mouth was wide and generous, his lips soft and his teeth good.

Aye, a face to please some woman to be sure but it was his eyes which were his most compelling feature, being of an incredible blue, deep and magnetic. A cobalt blue which could change, with his emotions, to the serenity and softness of pale azure; eyes heavily lashed, dark at the roots but tipped with gold. Aye, a good-looking lad, well, man really, was her Jamie and she'd not be surprised to see the lasses come flocking when word got around that he was home. As for being too old to climb rigging in a force eight gale, whatever that was, he was talking through his seaman's woollen hat, so he was. He was in his prime, was her Jamie, and she was right glad he was home to stay.

"Don't you worry about Tommy neither, Mam," he said, as he made his way towards the front door of the cottage, dropping a light kiss on her hair which was still filmed with flour. He had to bend his head to avoid the blackened beams and as she watched him go his mother wondered where her enormous son would fetch up in this working man's world of poky cottages and cramped farmhouses, of low doorways and tiny windows, of minute patches of garden scarcely bigger than a pocket handkerchief, or none at all, which was the fate of frailer men than himself. He needed a great deal of space to accommodate the splendid size of him since he filled any room he entered, overwhelming the more ordinary mortals who shared it with him. A house the size of Cloudberry End, for instance, with its grand proportions, its high ceilings, its vast, meandering acres of garden, not to mention the equally vast acres of woodland and moorland and tumbling cloughs which surrounded it, land owned by the wealthiest man in the district, Mr Jack Andrews.

"Hold on, my lad, don't you tell me not to worry about our Tommy," she said sharply. "A mother can't help worrying about her children no more than she can avoid givin' birth to 'em once they're inside her. D'yer think I never bothered me head over you, not ter mention me heart, when you were away? There wasn't a day went by when I didn't wonder where the devil you were, or even if you were still in the land o't livin." She almost choked on her indignation.

"Well, I'm home now, Mam. Home to stay. I've plans in my head, things I've been thinking on for the past five years and if everything goes as I mean it to, and he shapes himself, there's no reason why our Tommy can't be included in them."

Matty Jenkins's face lit up and she dropped her sad iron to the table with little or no concern for the fate of her husband's shirt which she was just about to tackle. Ignoring the ominous smell of singeing wool, if she even noticed it, she followed on her son's heels to the opened door, her hands plucking at the sleeve of the reefer jacket he had just put on.

"What d'yer mean, our Jamie? What plans? What yer goin' ter do, fer God's sake, an' how does our Tommy fit?"

"Now then, Mam. I'm only right at the very beginning so I can tell you nowt' because the whole bloody scheme depends on someone else and could easily come to nothing. I've someone to see."

"Who, tell me who?"

"I can't. Not until things are more settled. That's if they do settle. Now be patient, Mam, and I promise as soon as I've anything to say you'll be the first one I'll say it to."

"Oh, lad, how can I set meself to . . ."

"You'd better, Mam, or me pa'll have no shirt."

"What?"

"Me pa's shirt. It's burning."

"Oh, my dear Lord, an' it's his best."

Flinging herself nimbly across the kitchen, she picked up the sad iron and placed it in the fire next to its twin then turned back to her son, ready to insist that he tell his mother what he was up to but he'd already gone, in which direction she could not say, for when she got to the door he was nowhere in sight.

"Mr Hutchinson's here, sir." The maidservant bobbed a curtsey. "Ses he's an appointment," which seemed highly unlikely to her, since when did a grand gentleman like Mr Andrews entertain a rough seaman like Matty Jenkins's lad? Not that he wasn't a fine figure of a man and she'd be willing to spend an hour or two in his company, or even more, any day of the week; polite too, with a lovely grin but that still didn't put him on the same footing as Mr Andrews.

"That's right, Ivy. I'm expecting him. Show him in, will you?" the master said, standing up, if you please, just as though Jamie Hutchinson was as good as him.

"Rightio, sir." Ivy was not quite the professional Freda was, inclined to be less "formal", but it was Freda's day off so Ivy had answered the door and right glad she was about it, for it meant she could have a real good look at the enormous young man who strode so confidently into the master's study, holding out his hand to him as though they were equals and him with a pa, well, step-pa, who was Mr Andrews's coachman!

"Will that be all, sir?" she asked, her eyes out on stalks.

"Well, perhaps a drink, Jamie? What can I offer you? I know sailors are said to prefer rum but . . .?"

Jamie smiled engagingly, at least Ivy thought so.

"No, I'd prefer a brandy, sir. Besides which I'm no longer a sailor."

Ivy hung about, hoping to hear what he meant to be.

"Is that so?" the master said. "Well, sit down, lad, sit down, and tell me what you want to see me about." Ivy did her best to make herself invisible, for she would be made up if she could carry the news back to the kitchen. The master moved towards the small table where the silver tray on which several silver-topped diamond-cut crystal decanters stood. He poured out two generous measures and, to Ivy's disappointment, noticed her hovering discreetly by the door, waving her away irritably, the wave indicating that she was no longer needed.

She was tempted to linger outside the study door in the hope of overhearing a word or two but at that moment Miss Katherine clattered down the stairs with a face on her which Ivy and the other servants knew only too well. There had been more rows since Miss Chloe had come to stay at Cloudberry End than could be counted in the days of the month, and the girl in the house no more than a few weeks. Miss Katherine was expected to entertain her cousin, or at least keep her out of madame's way, rumour had it. Go about with her, make a friend of her, it was implied, since they were much of an age but Miss Katherine didn't care for that at all, objecting strenuously, loudly and with no thought for Miss Chloe's feelings who sat beside her each morning at the breakfast table as she did so. Miss Katherine wanted to leap on to her horse's back and go galloping off as she had for the past few years, not wet-nurse some city-bred mouse who had never been on a horse's back in her life, she said rudely.

Miss Chloe had stated coldly that she had absolutely no need of her cousin's company since she could entertain herself and, it being Sunday, she would be obliged if someone would direct her to the nearest church. Anglican, of course. That brought the lot of them to a standstill, particularly Miss Katherine who, as far as Ivy knew, had never been inside a church since the day she was christened.

Now, by the look on her face she was about to make someone's life a misery.

"Who was that, Ivy?" she asked peevishly, turning in the direction of the drawing room where her father had ordered her to sit and sew with her cousin.

"Jamie Hutchinson, Miss Katherine, come ter see yer pa."

If she hadn't seen it herself Ivy wouldn't have believed the transformation that took place in the master's daughter. From a drooping, woebegone, mutinous figure who gave the distinct impression the hangman's noose awaited her, she blazed with a sudden fiery intensity which made Ivy take a startled step backwards in case she herself was burned in the flames. Her head came up and her wilting back straightened to its normal long and graceful curve. Her eyes flooded with a glowing tawny light, a clear transparent brown in which gold flecks danced with joyous anticipation, and before Ivy could stop her, which she wouldn't have tried if she could, Miss Katherine was across the hall and without knocking had flung open the door of her father's study.

"Father," Ivy heard her cry in a voice in which nightingales sang, "why didn't you tell me Jamie was coming?" then the door was banged to behind her and Ivy heard nothing more.

Jamie sprang to his feet as Katherine swept into the room and his first reaction, fond as he was of her, was one of sharp irritation. Damn and blast the girl, why in hell's name couldn't she stay in her place for once? It was not that he was one of those men who believed women were meant for bedding and breeding but this meeting with her father was one of the most important moments in his life. He needed her father's complete attention. He needed time and a degree of calm in which to lay out his plans to the man he fervently hoped would agree with them, his proposition scrutinised and approved, in fact his whole bloody future, and it could hardly be done in the atmosphere of explosive fireworks with which Katherine treated every aspect of her life. He had glanced appreciatively about the room as he had entered it, noting the well-polished beauty of mahogany, the rich-piled luxury of expensive carpets, the fine prints of country scenes on the panelled walls, the smell of leather and good cigars, all speaking not only of great wealth but of good taste. He could not say he aspired to a room such as this for himself but he overwhelmingly wanted the chance to try for it. He couldn't honestly say he wanted to be as rich as Jack Andrews but he wanted to be as successful and if this girl who was flaunting herself so gloriously for his inspection ruined it he would never forgive her.

Jack Andrews sighed. He had no idea why Matty Jenkins's lad should have asked to speak to him, though he suspected that money might be involved. That's what most men wanted from him these days, knowing him to have an abundance of it. Schemes for this or that, wild ideas which needed an injection of ready cash, his, and which they were sure he would be only too eager to provide once they had presented their daft plans to him. Crackpot inventions, most of them, ill-thought-out businesses which would go under in six months or less, but which their innovator was convinced with a hundred guineas, again Jack's, would turn them into millionaires. He was also none too pleased at Katherine's very obvious delight in Jamie Hutchinson's presence in his study, wondering as he took another sip of his fine brandy how she had learned he was here. Not from Sara who was the only one to know of this meeting since both he and his wife were already a trifle alarmed at their daughter's lunatic attachment to the man who was their coachman's stepson. Five years ago at the age of eleven it had not unduly concerned them when she had clung passionately to his twenty-year-old coat tails, weeping and wailing when she was detached from them, but she was sixteen now and must be made to see that her position, and Jamie's, were very far apart. She was a young lady, her mother's daughter and would, in the fullness of time, marry some suitable young gentleman of her own sort. He himself had a working-class background but he didn't want to see this headstrong lass of his consigned to a labourer's cottage, living on a labourer's wage which must provide for her and the children she would undoubtedly produce on an annual basis. She would be a gentleman's wife, living the life her own mother lived, the life for which Sara had raised her. This . . . this attachment she seemed to have developed for Matty Jenkins's lad, her illegitimate lad, must be firmly nipped in the bud.

He reached out to a box on his desk and, offering it politely to Jamie, who refused just as politely, took a cigar from it and lit it, blowing fragrant smoke to the ceiling.

"I didn't tell you, Katherine," he said wearily, "because it does not concern you."

She glided, there was no other word for it, in a way which would have pleased her erstwhile governess, graceful as a lady should be, until she stood directly in front of Jamie, her flushed face smiling radiantly up into his. Her father might not have spoken – or even been there.

"I've tried to get over, Jamie, really I have," she said softly, positive that he had been as frustrated as she was at her failure to call, "but you know we have my cousin Chloe with us and it has made it very difficult but I promise— "

"Really, Katherine, it is of no consequence."

"Oh, but it is. I am being made to . . . to be with her every minute of the day. I don't know why since she does not want me but my mother insists."

"Katherine, I would be greatly obliged if you would go and join your cousin in the drawing room. Jamie and I have something to talk over and— "

"Really!" She whirled from her ardent contemplation of Jamie's embarrassed face to her father, then back to Jamie again who, like Ivy a few minutes ago, had the distinct urge to step back from her, from the overwhelming impact of her appeal which could threaten and, at the same time, bewitch any man. Her face became even more animated. Her eyes widened in excitement and she put her hand on his arm, waiting, he could see, to be enlightened.

"Well?" she demanded.

"It is a private matter, Katherine," her father said brusquely. "Jamie . . ."

"I wouldn't tell anyone, Jamie." She was enchanted to be part of anything which included him. "You can trust me, you know you can," she cried joyfully, longing for him to share whatever it was with her, her young, self-absorbed soul yearning towards him in a way her father did not like. There was a strange fervour in her eyes, a moistness to her parted lips, an unconsciously sensual lift to her full breasts which arched in the direction of Jamie Hutchinson.

Jack Andrews's face darkened and his eyes narrowed dangerously, but the man towards whom she was leaning was not responding to Katherine's wilful charm. In fact his face was grim and in it his eyes were a cold ice blue. His blunt-angled jaw was set in a purposeful way and aimed straight at Jack's daughter and, astonishingly, she faltered, even dropping her over-familiar hand from his arm.

"I'm sorry, Jamie," she said demurely, amazing her father with her sudden restraint. "I didn't mean to be a nuisance, really I didn't. I'll go now and leave you and Father to your business and perhaps later, when you're ready, if I may, I'll come down to Matty's and you can tell me about it, that's if you want to." She smiled repentantly.

"Oh . . . of course," Jamie faltered, as flabbergasted as Jack Andrews by the abrupt about-face of this girl who had never, to his knowledge, been humble, decorous, or sorry about anything in her life. She was a young princess, or so she believed, who could do as she liked with her father's subjects, taking what she wanted when she wanted it and kicking up such a hell of a fuss until she got it no one, except now and again this father of hers, had tried to curb her. She said the first thing that came into her head with little or no regard for anyone's feelings but now, with a quiet smile at her father and a last innocent look at himself, she moved gracefully across the room and went out, closing the door noiselessly behind her. The gleam in her eyes was hidden from them both.

"Well," her father gasped, "that's the first time I've ever seen her back down from a confrontation without a fight. What in hell got into her, d'you think?" raising amazed eyebrows, asking Jamie's opinion since he knew Katherine as well as any of them. "She's been a hellion since her cousin arrived and that's God's truth, fighting like a navviewoman, and I've met a few, against the constraint her mother is . . ."

He stopped speaking abruptly, clamping his teeth about his cigar, for though this lad's mother was almost one of the family it did not do to be gossiping about what was really none of his business. Matty would know all about it, of course, but still, it was not the kind of conversation which two men involved themselves in.

He "humphed-humphed" a time or two, clearing his throat awkwardly before leaning back in his chair as though to indicate that they might continue. He studied the man who stood before him, taking note of his strong, decisive face, his fiercely dipping eyebrows, the resolution in his firmly held mouth, his clear, direct gaze which did not falter from his own. Jack Andrews had dealt all his working life with men, navviemen who were the hardest, most intractable men in the world. He knew men. He could read a man's character from so many things. The easy way he stood before him, or otherwise. What he did with his hands, or his feet as Jack looked him over. His eyes, of course, which were the clearest indication of a man's temper and what he saw in Jamie Hutchinson's he found he liked. He had noticed him, at a distance, naturally, about Cloudberry End from time to time. As a young boy larking with his own sons, and, at Sara's request, sending him, again with his own sons, to the grammar school in Crossclough. The lad had had a good education, particularly for one whose mother and stepfather aspired to be no more than servants, but at fourteen he'd given it all up and gone away to sea, foolishly in Jack's opinion, who could have used him in his own business, or at least found him something more fitted to his learning and with more future in it. He hadn't even tried for promotion in his chosen employment, or if he had he hadn't got it. A man with his brains and education would have had more than a fair chance of gaining his master's ticket, but Jamie had remained no more than a common seaman, a deck-hand on a sailing ship for the past eleven or twelve years. Now he was home and for good, it seemed, and what did he want from Jack Andrews?

"Sit down, lad. Will you have another brandy?" he asked genially, testing him right from the start.

Jack lowered himself into the handsome leather chair on the other side of the desk.

"No, thank you, sir. I'm not much of a drinker though I've had my share in the past few years. Sailors are not known for their temperance, as you can imagine. Besides, I need a clear head for what I want to discuss with you." He grinned engagingly and Jack found himself returning it. Jamie had passed the first test, it seemed.

"Oh aye, and what might that be?" Jack asked. He drew deeply on his cigar, one hand in his pocket as he leaned back nonchalantly in his chair, at ease with himself, with his state in life and not particularly concerned or so he would have him believe, with the proposition – that's what it would be – that this enormous young man was about to put to him. Sara had begged him this morning for Matty's sake, she said, to give Matty's son whatever he might need in the way of cash for whatever he might have in mind, and Jack supposed he would, in the end, if only to please Sara, but he'd be damned if he'd just hand it over without a bloody murmur.

Jamie Hutchinson took a deep breath.

"Valley Bottom Farm, sir. It's on your land and I want to rent it from you. I've saved every penny I could, even invested some of it in . . . well, when I was home last you spoke of shares you had. D'you remember?"

By God, he did. He and the lad had met up on the path to Tintwistle Knarr and had walked back together. He had been surprised by Jamie's interest in the market, pleasantly surprised and quite willing to talk about it.

"Well, sir, I took your advice."

Advice! He didn't know he'd been giving any!

"It's taken me five years but I've enough to set myself up as a farmer."

"Have you now?"

"Yes, sir. I don't want anything from you but to rent the farm and some land."

"Do you now?"

"Yes, a small dairy herd, perhaps, sheep up on the high ground, some crops, whatever will grow up here. I'm no farmer, sir, but by God, I can learn. I've been studying farm journals for years."

"As long as that?"

"Yes, sir. I made up my mind when I was last home and if hope and optimism and bloody hard work are the ingredients needed to be successful then I'll be the most successful farmer in the valley and when I am I propose to buy your farm from you and if you won't sell it then I shall look elsewhere."

"By God, lad, I believe you would." Jack began to laugh and Jamie was astounded by his merriment and by the expression on his good-humoured face which Jamie failed to realise was recognition. Recognition by Jack Andrews of himself thirty years ago.

"Then . . .?" Jamie asked carefully

"Let's have a chat, shall we, lad, about your financial position. Always remember, should I agree to your . . . er . . . offer, that the financial position of any man, combined with his bloody and absolute determination to get what he wants from life, is the key to either success, or failure. Now then . . ."

6

Jack Andrews had bought and made extensive improvements to Waterway Paper Mill primarily as an investment and as an interest to fill his days after he retired from railroad building, but with his usual enthusiasm he had become so involved in its day-to-day running it had turned into what was essentially a new career for him and well worth the five thousand pounds he had spent to regenerate it.

There had been a paper mill on the site for one hundred and fifty years or more, driven by water power, of which there was a plentiful supply tumbling down a dozen cloughs into the valley. Paper-making by hand, sheet by laborious sheet, producing only a few hundredweight a week, each sheet as it came out of the vat laid by the "coucher", alternated with a sheet of woollen felt, into a pile. The owner, who had died penniless, unable to compete with the new mechanism for which he could not find the cash, had simply let the small business and the buildings which housed it fall into a state of tumbledown disrepair.

Jack soon put that right.

Of the one hundred and ten paper mills established in England after 1861, thirty-four had a short life: twenty-five less than five years and no more than one-third were still in business after ten years. There was a great increase in the demand for paper, of all sorts, due to the growth in industry, in trade, in the reading of newspapers and books, and with the enlarging of the supply of materials, again of all sorts, how could a paper manufacturer fail? was Jack's astonished question and he proceeded to show them, those who failed, where they went wrong.

He began by chucking out the old vat method of paper-making in which for generations the water-driven mill had produced the hand-made sheets of quality paper. He was a man who had done things on a grand scale all his working life, being involved in the sheer immensity of the Grand Trunk Railway in Canada and the Victoria Tubular Bridge which carried it across the St Lawrence River at Montreal.

Before that, and closer to home, he had shared the heroic savagery, the bloody determination and punishing labour which went into the building of the three-mile-long Woodhead Tunnel under the Pennine range. No one had kept an account of how many men died there, blasting through the millstone of those ferocious hills, though not a few of them were buried in unmarked graves in the graveyard at Woodhead Chapel, no more than a mile or so from Jack's home.

"I'm not fooling around with machines which were out of date before I was born," he told his family, none of whom, at the time, were particularly concerned. "I've ordered a couple of Fourdriniers – paper-making machines, darling – which, with the beating machines, should employ getting on for ninety people, something that will be welcomed by those in the district who are desperate for work."

"Beating machines, darling?" his wife asked vaguely, doing her best to show some interest.

"Aye, that's where it all starts, in the beater."

"But what is it?" She smiled encouragingly and Jack needed no second asking.

"It's a big oval tub with a revolving horizontal roll set with knives," doing his best to make his explanation as simple as possible. "Something like a paddle wheel. You put in your china clay, your sulphate of ammonia and other chemicals and mix it all together with the pulp."

"What pulp is that, my love?"

Jack was never less than unfailingly patient with his beautiful and much loved wife even though he was well aware that she was asking these questions to please him.

"It is the pulp made from the esparto grass that has been treated in the digester. That's the first process. The next is on the Fourdrinier, called that after the chap who designed it. Well, sweetheart" – smiling at her tolerantly, seeing that she was doing her best to understand, which was more than could be said of his children, Chris and Katy – "it's a bit complicated but when it's all ticking over to my satisfaction perhaps I'll take you round and let you see how it works for yourself."

"Thank you, darling, that would be nice," returning his smile for they both knew she would never set foot in any place Jack considered to be dangerous, or even the slightest bit uncomfortable for his well-bred wife to endure.

Jack had not the same compunction about his youngest son. When his factory was running smoothly in the efficient way he liked and since his son still showed no sign of buckling down to anything beyond enjoying himself – at Jack's expense – he had let it be known that they were both to be at the gates of the paper mill, the Waterway Paper Mill, as the grand, newly painted sign proclaimed it to be, by seven thirty each morning.

"If the hands know you're on time, lad, then they will be," referring to the punctuality of his journeymen paper-makers, the men who worked on the digesters, the beaters, the women who sorted the esparto grass which came from Tunisia; those who worked in the drying and pressing rooms, the cutting rooms and the men who tended to and fed his two steam engines with the endless tons of coal on which the whole thing depended. And naturally, an eye must be firmly kept on his manager and his foremen since it was on their honesty and efficiency his profit depended.

"Get yourself down here," he would roar at the foot of the wide staircase at Cloudberry End, "for we've a business to run. Aye, I'm sorry you've had no breakfast but that's your fault, not mine, for I'm sure Freda called you at the same time she called me. So you can take that look off your face and make an effort not to look so pingling, lad. I heard you come in last night but it makes no difference to me if your head's rolling about on your shoulders like a bloody cannonball. You've still a day's work to do and the carriage is at the door. I take it you'd like to continue to receive that generous allowance I give you? Aye, I thought so."

Chris would follow his father, scowling fiercely against the light which hurt his eyes and the thundering movement of his lean body which hurt his head, hastily shrugging his way into his jacket, ramming his curly-brimmed bowler on to his auburn curls which seemed to ache as well.

For almost four months now he and his father had made this journey, sharing the carriage, crunching down the smoothly raked gravel driveway to the ornate, wrought-iron gates of Cloudberry End, turning left towards Crossclough and the factory which stood on the edge of Torside Reservoir.

The drive along the reservoir was a pleasant one, at least his father thought so, and said so almost every morning. When they entered the gates, promptly at seven thirty, or sometimes before since Jack liked to keep his workmen "on their toes", they were greeted by bobbing heads, the touching of a respectful finger to a peaked cap, even a dipping bob here and there from a grateful woman since Jack Andrews was known as a fair employer and, though he did not do so, could boast he knew the name of every man and woman in his employ. It was something he had learned in his years on the railway.

But, on this particular day neither father nor son received more than a surly glance from beneath the fiercely scowling eyebrows of a broad-backed labourer who was shouldering an enormous sack of china clay from a waggon. There were several other men working alongside him and it was noticeable that, in so far as the job they were doing would allow, they were giving him a wide berth. The yard, even at this time of the morning, was as busy as an ants' nest. There were other waggons loading and unloading, all pulled by the enduring patience and indomitable strength of handsome Clydesdale horses. Their harnesses were jingling as they tossed their heads up and down; their broad backs and flanks glistened with spit and polish, for they were much loved and fawned over by the men who drove them. Their gigantic hooves were garlanded with a smoky cream fringe of hair and their tails, of the same colour, swished constantly against the attack of troublesome flies. In their cream-coloured manes were tied a multitude of bright ribbons.

The men grunted as the heavy sacks were placed on their shoulders, sagging slightly as they took the load, all except the tall and powerful man who accepted his as though it were a sack of feathers. He kept his gaze on the two men who were alighting from the carriage, his head, on which sprang a mass of dark brown curls, held high. The angle at which it was carried might even have been described as disdainful, though his rough, working man's garb of trousers tied below the knee with twine, his stout, unpolished boots and faded, collarless shirt were exactly the same as every other man's in the yard.

Waterway Paper Mill was built around three sides of a large mill yard. There were two storeys, the upper storey housing the offices and other administrative workrooms where once the waste cotton material, from which paper had previously been made, had been stored.

On the far side of the yard a waggon loaded with esparto grass had just drawn up to the wide open doors of the sorting shed where the new material would be separated ready to be directed to the various treatment sheds. There the esparto grass, or alfa, would be cleaned and bleached with solvents, its uniform length of fibres and its free-draining qualities making it particularly suitable to be converted into the pulp which in turn would be manufactured through several processes into close-textured, resilient, porous and clear paper.

Up until a decade ago most of the pulp from which paper was fabricated had been made from the waste materials, cotton and linen rags, of the mills which abounded throughout Lancashire and which gave the county its lead in the production of paper. There was a variety of the necessary chemical products immediately available. There was a constant supply of industrial labour, for Lancashire had a long-standing tradition of skilled work in its mills, but the most important factors were the proximity of coalfields, an abundance of soft, pure water and the availability of transport, in the early days by canal, then by rail, to take its finished products to market.

Though Crossclough was, strictly speaking, in Cheshire, placed as it was on the narrow peninsula of land which reached out eastwards through Lancashire and Derbyshire and into Yorkshire, it had the same favourable factors which operated in the paper-making industry in Lancashire. Esparto grass was easily and swiftly transported from the port of Liverpool forty miles away by the fast trains which hurtled almost on the hour every day of the week through Crossclough, the finished product taking the same swift journey back again, mainly to Manchester which was by far the largest market for Jack Andrews's product. Esparto grass imports had risen from fifty-one thousand tons in 1863 to almost one hundred and fifty thousand tons annually in 1876 but the possibility of the large-scale use of the timber resources of the world was opening up with the invention of a chemical process for producing good quality cellulose from wood, and already Jack was talking of importing wood pulp. You had to keep up with the times, he told his family when they met at mealtime, frowning in the direction of his son who, as usual, looked glassy-eyed with boredom, since he heard it a dozen times a day at the mill.

It was going to be a hot day. It was mid-August and even at this early hour the men were sweating with the strength of their exertions, their muscled backs and shoulders, their brawny forearms rippling in the mist-hazed sunshine. Jack Andrews employed over ninety people in his mill. He had installed two steam engines to drive eight beating machines and two paper machines and it was on these that the skilled men worked while the women sorted and prepared the esparto grass. The men in the yard were unskilled labourers, rough and ready men, somewhat like the navviemen he had once directed, using their muscles not just in the carting of bales of grass and rolls of finished paper wherever they were told, but on one another in the fist fights which broke out on pay day. Some of them, those who were family men, not only loaded and unloaded the waggons, but drove them to and fro between Crossclough railway station and the paper mill. They were decent men with wives and children to support and because of it could be trusted to convey their loads to the waiting railway trains without succumbing to the temptation of the inns which lay along the way. Sometimes, when a delivery was urgently needed and was within driving distance they could be trusted to convey it directly to the buyer by what was now considered the somewhat old-fashioned method of horse-power. They looked after their animals as though they were their own, trustworthy reliable men, which could not be said of Paddy Andrews.

"Good morning," Jack called out to them, nodding civilly to the man who was, after all, his nephew. It was two months since Jack's older brother George had approached him somewhat sheepishly, not liking to ask a favour, but asking it just the same, for he was of the opinion that if his lad could just get himself set up in some decent, permanent work it would be the making of him. With Jack to see he kept at it, perhaps he might give over this shilly shallying from job to job, this liking he had for fighting in the boxing ring and make something of himself. George and Will and Harry, who were also Jack's brothers, were labourers on other men's farms and had lost most of their sons and even a couple of daughters to that promised land across the seas known as the New World, since there was little to keep them in the Longdendale Valley. The brothers were sadly aware, though they did not admit as much to their children's mothers, that they would never see their offspring again. America, where it was said the streets were paved with gold and if, when the seekers after a new life found it was not true, then an enterprising chap could buy himself a mule and a pick and go and dig it out of the ground for himself. George had only this one lad left, he said disconsolately to Jack, and if he were ever to have a grandchild or two at his knee then his only hope was Paddy. So, if Jack could find him summat in that there mill of his – and if Paddy could be persuaded to it – George would be eternally grateful. There was only him and Paddy living in the muck and muddle of the crumbling and untidy cottage since his Ethel had died a year or two back. If Paddy could be kept occupied happen he wouldn't be as wild and daft as he was. Fights and the like, drinking, a bit of poaching, not only game but other men's wives but a bit of steady work might settle him, didn't Jack think so?

"I'll try him out, George." Jack always felt slightly uneasy in the presence of his poorly educated, poorly placed brothers and for that reason was often inclined to allow them to persuade him to something he did not always care for. "Just in the yard at first but if he shapes . . . well, I can't promise anything. It's up to him. Send him down tomorrow."

Paddy had given no trouble, indeed he worked hard, was punctual and if not exactly civil at least he was not blatantly defiant with the foreman. He had a tendency to let thirty seconds or so go by when given an order, a curious smile on his lips which could be unnerving, or so the foreman, who knew his reputation, said. You were never sure whether he was going to obey, he told the manager.

"And does he?"

"Oh aye, eventually, but it's a bloody long thirty seconds while yer wait ter see what he'll do."

The other men seemed inclined to keep their distance from him, which was again a bit awkward, for they had their jobs to do as he did, grinning nervously when Paddy addressed some remark to them, and Jack could see why. Paddy was a big lad, there was no doubt of it and his talents with his fists were legendary.

Men moved purposefully or languidly, according to their

nature, about the yard. They seemed to have the inconsequence of mechanical figures to Chris Andrews, set in motion by the order of his father to perform inconsequential tasks and he was constantly amazed that these men could accept their lot so tamely. Chained to the two huge steam engines which in turn bound them to the beating machines and the paper-making machines which moved like great undulating slugs across the length of the machine shed. The pulp flowed out through a strainer into what was known as a head box. From there it spread out on the endless copper screens which lay across the machines, the screens so finely woven the fibres in the pulp remained on them while the moisture was drained off.

The screen moved on and on, travelling remorselessly forward, but with a sly, side-to-side motion which settled the fibres and knitted them together until they reached the suction roller where any excess water was finally extracted. The pressed fibres then ran on in a continuous sheet of paper almost one hundred inches wide, ready for the next mechanical process.

Chris loathed it. His flesh crawled every time he entered any of the sheds. For one thing he felt as though the ammonia and other chemicals with which the esparto was incorporated was coating his skin and not only on the outside but within him as well. It seemed to slide down his throat the moment he took a deep breath, making his eyes sting, catching at his lungs until he thought he might choke. His stomach which, the night before, had been saturated with an enormous amount of brandy, and nothing since, for his father's voice at the foot of the stairs did not allow him time for breakfast, rolled over uneasily and he was forced to clamp his mouth tightly shut, only opening it to deliver a shouted message from his father to the manager, to the man in charge of one of the sheds, to a brawny labourer on the matter of his careless handling of a roll of paper. That's what he was, a messenger boy and nothing else and he was painfully aware that every man in the factory knew it. He had to shout because of the noise which was quite deafening, the clatter and crash of the machinery, the rhythmic bang of the head box as it took on another load of pulp, the hiss and swish of the live pulp as it snaked along the copper screen. They watched him, the men in the yard and the sheds, nudging one another as he went by, smirking, since they knew he was only employed because he was the owner's son, a young man pretending to be about something important but what he actually did at the factory not one of them could really say. He was a man trapped between his own belief that as the son of a wealthy father he had no need to work, and his father's belief that, as a man of the working classes, it was dishonest not to be gainfully and decently employed.

"Reckons 'iself too fine a gentleman ter dirty 'is 'ands in trade," they whispered behind his back, since he made no attempt to hide his distaste for factory life and indeed for all those involved in it. He was fit only to do what gentlemen did, which was to shoot grouse in season up on his father's grouse moor beyond Arnfield, drink brandy and claret until he fell insensible into his bed, play cards and other more dangerous games with the sons of the gentry. The men his father employed were forced to toil for twelve hours a day, six days a week, a total of seventy-two hours for a wage of just twenty-five shillings and threepence, and their womenfolk who laboured just as strenuously were rewarded with ten shillings less than that. They lived in tiny cottages in and around Crossclough, mostly four-roomed, two up and two down, each one crammed with the children which came with tenacious regularity every year, paying rents which varied from three shillings and sixpence to five shillings and sixpence each week. There was no such thing as running water and only the most basic pretence of sanitation. Cooking was done in the front room and the weekly washing in the one behind it and on wet days the family wash, and sometimes others people's wash if a woman took in washing to make ends meet, hung flapping damply about the cottage for days. Their homes were cheaply furnished and their families were cheaply fed and the sight of the master's son all tricked out in his silk waistcoats and expensively tailored suits taking a job which might have gone to a more deserving and needy man caused a great deal of resentment. Strangely, though Jack Andrews was just as immaculately tailored as his son the men had no such thoughts about him since he did as hard a day's work as they did and had done since he was a lad.

And none knew this better than Chris Andrews as he dragged himself, or at least that's how it appeared to his reluctant body, across the yard in the direction of the beating shed where he was to tell Mr Harrop, the factory manager, that Mr Andrews, senior, of course, would be glad of a word with him at his earliest convenience.

At his earliest bloody convenience, Chris repeated through gritted teeth. He felt like some half-grown schoolboy entrusted with a message from the headmaster to a lesser teacher. It was a wonder his father didn't make him write it down so that he wouldn't forget it, or better yet, write it himself, telling his son to be a good boy and deliver it as quickly as he could.

A dog was snapping and snarling over something in the corner of the yard, his fur bristling, his ears laid back as his vicious jaw closed about a rough brown object which squealed in terror and pain. The dog threw back his head and the squealing stopped immediately but, not quite satisfied that his victim was properly subdued, the beast shook it savagely.

It was the ugliest dog Chris had ever seen. His muzzle, from which the dead rat swung, was short, wide, his lower jaw protruding beyond his upper. His eyes had such a look of vicious malevolence in them Chris came to an abrupt halt. The dog studied him intently, not making a sound, his whole body tensely still just as though, should Chris consider taking his prize from him he had better be prepared to lose a hand, or perhaps his life.

There came a short, sharp whistle from the direction of the waggon which was still being unloaded of its cargo of china clay. Was it the same waggon, or a second one? Chris wondered mindlessly, since time had no meaning in this place. A minute ticked on endlessly for an hour, an hour dragged like a day and at the end of each day he felt as though he had been incarcerated for a week in the Waterway Paper Mill.

The dog pricked his ears and with a speed and fluidity astonishing in one of his clumsy-looking bulk, swerved away, racing across the yard on his short legs as though he were a greyhound fresh from the trap. He skidded to a halt at the feet of the man who had whistled, lowered his rear end to a sitting position on the cobbles, every inch of him quivering in ecstasy-ridden adoration, his tiny eyes fixed slavishly on the man's face as he offered him the dead rat.

"Good lad, there's a good lad," the man said, in what could only be described as doting fondness, placing his big hand on the animal's broad head, rubbing it and his slavering muzzle with obvious signs of devotion. He took the rat from the dog's mouth whilst he watched him anxiously as though in some doubt that his offering might not suit and when the man threw it back to him with a "Good lad", falling on it joyously before waddling off into a corner to enjoy his kill.

The man was Paddy Andrews.

Those about him who had all stopped work to watch did not smile or joke with him on the skill of his dog as a ratter. They did not indulge in light banter, nor nudge one another in amusement at his unbelievable and what, in another, would have been called a fatuous display of affection. They did not move nor speak, not to him or each other until, with a growl at the two men who stood on the waggon placing the sacks of china clay on the labourers' shoulders, Paddy indicated that he was ready for another. They obliged quickly and the men resumed work.

Chris didn't know why he did it. The dog had not menaced a soul in the yard except for the rat and was now lying placidly in a square of sunshine tearing it to bloody pieces. The incident had held up the work for no longer than two minutes and yet something about the man, about the dog and the former's perfect belief that the animal had as much right to be there as the horses, as the men themselves, set his teeth and his nerves, which were stretched to breaking point anyway, on edge and before he had given himself time to consider the consequences he was across the yard tapping on Paddy's shoulder.

"Just a minute," he said to him as he was about to enter the shed. "I'd like a word with you."

Paddy turned and from his bit of space by the wall the dog lifted a suspicious head, ready to lumber to its feet should an order be given. Paddy didn't speak, just waited for his cousin to do so, one brawny arm lifted to balance his burden, the other flexing in readiness for a move he might not care for, which could be anything he considered to be insulting, every man in the yard knew that. An affront to Paddy Andrews which could take the form of a sidelong glance, a lift of the eyebrows, an innocent frown, even a smile which just did not suit him.

"It seems to me that dog of yours is somewhat dangerous," Chris went on, narrowing his green eyes in an unconsciously menacing manner. "He should not be hanging about the yard where there are women and possibly their children. He looks vicious to me and though he has undoubted talents as a ratter I think it would be wise to keep him at home in the future. Besides which, if every man we employ brought his dog to work we would be inundated with them. See to it, if you please."

The fact that he was talking to his own cousin did not seem to occur to him and if it did it made no difference. They had never been friends, even as youngsters, though they were of the same age, for the difference in their upbringing, their education, their standing in the community – since Paddy's family had none – was quite unbridgeable.

Paddy's few years at school had not made him familiar with words such as "inundated" though he knew exactly what his cousin meant.

"We employ," he returned contemptuously. "Who dost tha' mean by we? I don't work fer thee, lad, not a pipsqueak what can't do nowt but run messages so tha'd best scamper back ter tha' pa afore tha' ends up in all sorts o' trouble tha' might not like."

Chris Andrews was not a coward but nor had he the size and strength of his cousin who was known to go in for the art, if you could call it that, of bare knuckle prize fighting for the entertainment of the gentry, who liked to see one working man batter another senseless over twenty or thirty bloody rounds. Indeed Chris had been present when Paddy had done so and had won money on him. Paddy was famous for it, as his dog was famous for its prowess in mauling and mangling other animals in the illegal dog fights which took place after dark in secret places on the moor.

"You'd best watch your mouth if you want to keep your job," Chris answered hotly, ready, despite the three or four stones in weight and six inches in height his cousin could give him, to bristle up to him. He himself was lean, fine-boned, a whippet challenging a bulldog and Paddy's face creased in a satisfied smile. He dropped the heavy bag of china clay, which hit the ground with a noise like a clap of thunder and, bending his knees and back, lifted his fists and began to weave a graceful circle about his employer's son.

The men in the yard, open-mouthed in amazement, for surely not even Paddy would take on Jack Andrews's lad, Jack Andrews who was a man of power and influence in these parts, closed their mouths and, gesturing to others who had not heard the exchange, scurried to get a good spot in the crowd which quickly gathered about the two young men.

It might have become dangerous. There was no doubt in the minds of the men who watched that Paddy Andrews could batter their employer's son with one hand tied behind his back and it was evident that Paddy thought so too, and relished the idea. He grinned, the grin itself like a slap in the face to the lighter man. Paddy jabbed at him playfully, making no move as yet to mark him with a fist the size of a horse's hoof, his grin deepening as Chris whipped back hastily.

"What was it tha' wanted ter say, lad?" Paddy asked pleasantly. "Summat about my dog, were it? Come on, speak up . . ."

"What the bloody hell's going on here?" a voice thundered, before Paddy had managed to land even one serious blow on the dancing, shifting, light-footed grace of his cousin's person. Chris, who had done some boxing at school, had at least learned how to avoid a blow if not to land one, though how long that state of affairs would have lasted was uncertain since Paddy was just as sure-footed and just as determined to knock him senseless.

"Clear a way there and you men, get back to your jobs, that's if you want to have one by the end of the day. Andrews, pick up that bag and take it to wherever it's meant to be, now, yes now, I said and look lively and as for you . . ." turning to his red-faced son, ". . . you'd best follow me into the office. I've a word or two to say about— "

"I don't think so, sir," Chris Andrews retaliated, his face draining of its inflamed colour, of his fury, his bloodlust, his frustration and his disenchantment with the life he was being forced to lead.

"Don't you answer me back, you young limb," his father bellowed. "Get up to my office . . ."

"Not while that man works in this mill," his son said quietly then, to his father's astonishment and that of the watching men, including Paddy Andrews, he calmly turned on his heel and strode from the yard, his red hair gleaming in the bright sunshine, his head high, his back tall and straight.

They did not see him that evening at dinner and his bed had not been slept in, Ivy said fearfully the next morning to Mrs Tiplady who reported it to her mistress, but after all he was a man of twenty, nearly twenty-one years and though his father despaired of him, short of tying the lad to his coat tails, what could he do about it? The slightest thing seemed to unsettle the lad. Oh aye, they'd all heard of the scuffle down at Waterway and the sacking of Paddy Andrews because of it, but what had become of the master's son? Probably in some tavern, drinking off his ill humour or senseless in some floozie's bed. He'd come home when he ran out of money, no doubt.

He did, unrepentant. Cocky, Freda was inclined to think, she told Mrs Tiplady after she had served the family their evening meal, not sorry for what he'd done, for fighting and drinking and staying out all night and his pa spoke sharply to him, Freda reported, though not sharply enough in her opinion, for he worried his ma no end and his pa told him so.

"Well, Father," he had said flippantly, "it's heartening to know that someone cares about my welfare but then a child's mother is bound to be concerned about her child, wouldn't you say, even if that child is worthless."

7

He was standing on the cobbled track which divided the farm from its outbuildings when she saw him. His hands were pushed deep into the pockets of his corduroy breeches. He wore no jacket and his shirt sleeves were rolled up for it was a mild day and his smoothly muscled forearms were as brown as a gypsy's. He was utterly relaxed, his manner one of dreaming contemplation since he thought himself to be unobserved, like a man whose mind has gone drifting off somewhere pleasing, leaving his physical self behind.

To the right of the track was the farmhouse, surrounded by a broken-down drystone wall and crowded up against it, its foliage casting a shadow over him and the track, was a somewhat stunted horse chestnut tree in still gloriously red flower, which was surprising since the fierce winds which raged over these stark hills and through the valley bottom did not allow for a profusion of growth.

She almost turned back. It was several months since she had last seen him on the Manchester to Sheffield train and in that time she had barely given him a thought as she wrestled with her own unhappiness and the tribulation of how she could escape it. She still harboured in her sorely tried heart, foolishly she knew, the hope that she might find some employment which would suit her and her talent for dressmaking, taught her by Mama, and perhaps some little place of her own she might make into a home. She didn't know where. She had, of course, given up completely the idea that she might live again with Papa and his new wife. Indeed she had had no word from Papa since she left Liverpool, though she had written regularly every week since she had arrived at Cloudberry End. She was lonely, she admitted it and it was perhaps this which made her hesitate, which made her study the man on the path for a moment or two longer, unseen.

She felt she knew him, for his name and what he was up to were for ever on her cousin's lips. Jamie this and Jamie that was her sole topic of conversation and there had been many arguments between her and her father, since Mr Andrews did not care to have Jamie Hutchinson's activities discussed at every meal, he thundered, and if Katherine did not stop dwelling on it morning, noon and bloody night he would begin to regret he had ever let the man have the damned farm in the first place. Katherine had been threatened with the most horrible punishments if she didn't let Jamie alone, since apparently she had been seen at Valley Bottom, her mare tied to the wall of the farm, on several occasions and her poor mother's nerves were in tatters just as her daughter's reputation would be if she did not learn to be more circumspect. She seemed determined to be included in every detail of Jamie Hutchinson's new career as a farmer and from her conversation it seemed the man could not make a decision or take a step without her supervision, from the purchasing of his small dairy herd, the seeds for his crops, the farm machinery he had bought second-hand at a farm sale, even a puppy given him by some chap or other Katherine had known and which was to make Jamie a splendid sheepdog. Katherine was his right-hand man, his mentor, his inspiration, to hear her speak, which Chloe was sure was not true, not from what she had seen of him and his quiet air of resolution which he had displayed on the journey from Manchester.

She looked at him now, the man who, or so she would have everyone believe, belonged exclusively to Katherine Andrews. He was very still, at ease, Chloe thought and in the most curious way something in his demeanour touched a chord in her. Something which spoke of tranquillity, of a man of peace and perfect content, of which she herself was in short supply these days and it was this which drew her towards him up the track and even gave her the courage to speak to him cautiously

"So this is it?" she said, quietly enough not to disturb him, to shatter his deep reverie but loud enough to announce what she hoped was her unthreatening, uncritical presence.

He turned sharply, still caught fast in his brooding contemplation of the land sloping upwards from the farm in a patchwork of browns and greens, fields divided by grey, stone walls, most of them urgently in need of repair. The wind, coming straight from the moor above them brought the fragrance of heather and bracken and the coarse, damp smell of hare's-tail cotton grass.

He seemed to feel no surprise at seeing her there. He smiled at her and again she felt that faint pull of something pleasurable inside her, something which drew her on until they stood almost shoulder to shoulder on the track looking up at the rough moorland together.

"Aye, this is it," he said simply, almost dreamily, his eyes following the track which led away gradually before disappearing towards Round Hill and Spond Moor. The drystone wall beside it meandered like a bit of abandoned grey ribbon, threatening to collapse in many places, its stones scattered beside the track where no one, for many years, had bothered to pick them up.

"When are you to begin?" she asked him, following his gaze up to the ridged outline of the hill at the back of the farm. Though it was high summer and the sky was a cloudless blue, it was grim nevertheless and she shivered inside her light summer cloak, wondering at the folly and bravery of those who lived up here wresting a livelihood of sorts from its poor ground.

"I've begun," he answered, turning back to her, smiling, still in perfect harmony with the elements about him and with her, it seemed, though they had met only once before. "I'm living in the farmhouse already."

Now that he had pointed it out to her she could see a thread of grey smoke whipping from the one chimneypot sagging at the apex of the roof. She turned from her bemused perusal of Valley Bottom Farmhouse, this man's farmhouse now from all accounts, and smiled back at him.

"So you have."

There seemed to be no more he wished to say and they remained in what appeared to her to be a rather pleasant and companionable silence. She leaned her back against the crumbling stone wall and so did he, his arms folded now across his broad chest. She could hear the sound of running water, a sound which was becoming very familiar to her, and from the shelter of the tussocky grass where it had built its nest a skylark rose on the air, going up and up until it was no more than a tiny dot in the blue arch of the sky. They both watched it in that silence which did not seem to be strange to them and when he spoke it was softly as though the great peace on the hill must not be shattered.

"You've found a place for yourself then, at Cloudberry, I mean?" His voice was hesitant with no intention to pry.

"Not really, though I find I have taken to country life."

"Does that surprise you?"

"Oh yes. I was born and brought up in Liverpool, you see. I am used to bustle and noise and the absence of both up here alarmed me at first."

"And now?"

"I have grown used to it. I walk a lot and then there is my sewing. It's something I enjoy."

"So I see." He smiled down at her, indicating the pale dove grey gown she wore.

She smiled back at him, relaxed and astonished that she was. "I decided to discard my mourning black. My aunt and uncle are surprisingly generous with their money and my allowance, as my uncle calls it, is quite enormous."

Silence fell again, and again it was an easy one, then, "Would you like to take a cup of tea with me?" he asked her, his eyes clear and steady as he smiled down at her, untroubled by her beauty, by her unexpected arrival, by the strangeness of a tough-fibred farmer like himself – he hoped he was that – inviting this elfin-like creature to take tea with him. It seemed natural somehow, with none of the complexities of Male and Female in it, merely two people who might be friends taking another small step towards that easy relationship.

To her own surprise, since she was often shy with strangers, she found herself agreeing.

"Yes, I would, thank you."

"The kettle will be on the boil. It always is so it shouldn't take long," he told her as he led her through the ramshackle gate which would one day keep his livestock out of his bit of garden. "Mind the cobbles. They need relaying but I'm afraid the job is a long way down my list of what needs doing. Yes, I can tell you know what I mean," as she smiled widely at him in what he realised was sympathetic humour. "My cattle are to be delivered tomorrow."

"So I believe."

"Pardon?" He looked bewildered.

"Mr Hutchinson, I do assure you there is no part of your life, nor your plans for it which I do not know. My cousin is most enthusiastic."

"Oh God," he groaned, "that girl will be the death of me, really she will. She means well but she cannot believe I can manage this new life of mine without her at my elbow."

"I know, so she implies." Chloe dimpled in the most delightful and amazing way and he realised she was teasing him. He grinned at her ruefully, wondering how to explain the relationship between himself and the wayward Katherine Andrews but she did not seem to care about it, merely saying, "Do go on, Mr Hutchinson. You were talking about your livestock?"

"Yes, so I was. Well, my sheep, what I could afford, are up on Spond Moor and I must hire a man to mend the walls before the foolish creatures all vanish into another farmer's flock. There are crops to sow but my brother is to give me a hand."

"So we heard," laughing again. "You are going to be busy," she continued in her gracious, ladylike way, though her laughter was warm and friendly. "I only wish I could help," she added, "since I would be glad of something to do, something useful. Of course, I could make curtains . . . or the bedlinen, pillow cases, things like that," she went on breathlessly as the idea grew in her mind. "I must be honest with you, Mr Hutchinson, I'd be hopeless at cobble laying, or wall building and as for sheep and cows I should be terrified if I came face to face with either one." She began to laugh unrestrainedly and so did he. "But a bit of sewing, I could manage that." Her face brightened even more, just as though a lamp had been lit behind it, the very thought of doing something specific, even for this man who was really a stranger, filling her with pleasure.

He was astounded. "That's a most generous offer but I couldn't possibly ask you to do it, Miss . . .?" He could not recall her surname and he raised his eyebrows enquiringly. He knew he sounded pompous but he was so bowled over by her offer he couldn't think of anything else to say.

"Why not? It's one thing I'm good at and my name is Taylor, but I would like it if . . . if you . . . my name is Chloe." She knew it was forward of her and her mama would have had a fit since a well-bred lady did not invite a gentleman to call her by her given name on almost first acquaintance. Except for the occasional conversations she had with Katherine and the somewhat furtive exchanges Chris Andrews tried to draw her into when they found themselves alone together, no one had called her by her Christian name in three months. Her aunt and uncle demanded nothing of her and gave nothing to her beyond a distant politeness. They met only at mealtimes, and after a while, as the weeks passed, it seemed they had grown used to her quiet presence at the table, barely noticing her, as they would barely notice a chair or a salt-cellar or a fork. They had long given up attempting to force Katherine into taking Chloe about with her, for which she at least was truly thankful and so, for the most part, Chloe was free to do as she pleased. This walk was one of her favourites. The track led from the woodland at the side of her uncle's property, across an easily traversed hillside meadow and on up to Valley Bottom Farm, which, though it didn't actually rest in the valley, did so in comparison to the high peaks of Black Hill and Bleaklow. The track went nowhere else, petering out beyond the farm and up until today she had met no one in her solitary meandering.

"I know," Jamie said, a small smile playing round his mouth.

"Pardon?"

"I know your name is Chloe."

She began to laugh. "Katherine?"

"Katherine."

There was a puppy just inside the kitchen door, his body wriggling in ecstasy as Mr Hutchinson held it open for her, yapping and nipping at her boots, and then at her hesitantly outstretched hand as she knelt down to him. His huge paws reared up against her, planting themselves on her shoulders. She scratched his ears in some trepidation and he turned his head to attack her hands with a rough, over-exuberant, scratchy tongue.

"Careful, he'll have you over if you don't watch him. He's supposed to be a sheepdog, or will be when I've finished with him," his owner said cheerfully. "Get down, Captain. I call him Captain after the many masters I've sailed under. Now mind your manners, lad," but it was too late and as Chloe landed on her backside, her pale grey cotton skirts up about her knees, revealing not only her white stockings, her many white frilled petticoats but her white, lace-trimmed drawers, the puppy leaped into her lap and turned his attentions to her face.

"Oh my," she squealed, her breath gone, her gold-shot russet hair tumbling about her laughing face, her cloak coming undone and slipping from her shoulders, her long, white slender neck arching in a lovely line as she attempted to avoid the puppy's avid tongue. "Oh my, Mr Hutchinson, I'm afraid it's too late for manners. Will you please rescue me from this rough scamp before he eats me alive."

Jamie Hutchinson turned from his host's duties at the glowing coals of the fire where the kettle had rested, the expression on his face one of good-humoured exasperation but it slipped away as his eyes came to rest on the girl who sprawled in his doorway. Her severely dragged-back hair was gone in an eruption of glorious, tangled curls about her shoulders and down her back to where it swept the old stone flags of the kitchen. Her legs, slender but shapely, were revealed to the knees and as the puppy redoubled his efforts to get at her flesh, any bit of flesh would do, her skirt rose even higher until it was about her waist. Her heels scrabbled frantically on the flagged floor as she tried to escape but her efforts only excited the puppy further in what he evidently considered to be a game she was devising for his enjoyment. She was giggling helplessly, her cool young dignity completely gone, her composure, which no one at Cloudberry had ever broken through, or if they had she had not allowed them to see it, flung to the winds in her joy in the puppy.

Jamie was spellbound. He had the kettle in one hand, the teapot in the other, just standing there, he realised later, with his mouth foolishly open, his heart violently thumping and the sudden thrusting ache in his loins hurting him quite intolerably. She was the most enchanting thing he had ever seen, her eyes sparkling like turquoise through the curtain of her hair, her mouth wide as she laughed, her small tongue pink and quivering between her perfect white teeth. Perfect! That's what she was, he told himself as he fell mindlessly and irrevocably under her spell. But what the bloody hell was he doing, gawping at her like some ignorant farm lad who had never before seen a pair of drawers except on his ma's washing line.

Oh God!

"Please . . . Mr Hutchinson . . . rescue me . . ." she was pleading between squeaks of laughter.

"Right," he said, continuing to stare at those slender

white calves and the expanse of white frilly drawers above them.

"Mr Hutchinson . . . I beg of you . . ." and as a note of something he did not quite recognise as awareness sharpened her voice he hastily placed the kettle and the teapot on the table, realising with that part of his brain which still functioned logically that the soot on the kettle's base would leave a mark on the chenille cloth his mam had given him for his kitchen table.

"Captain," he managed to bellow, but the dog, not yet recognising his name, nor the authority in his master's voice, continued to lavish his young devotion on Chloe and it was not until Jamie had picked him up by the scruff of his neck and flung him outside the door, where he howled plaintively, that peace was restored, at least inside.

When Jamie turned back to her Chloe had arranged her skirt to a more decorous length, though she still sprawled somewhat awkwardly on the floor. He held out his hand to her and she took it, aware of the sharp tension in it, in the hard palm and the strong brown fingers, for though she did not know what it was that had happened between them she knew something had.

He pulled her to her feet, then, unable to bear the lovely closeness of her, the dishevelment of her spectacular hair, her fragrance, her softness, her brilliance which he wanted more than he had ever wanted anything in his life before, even this farm, he stamped back to the fireplace, giving the strange impression that she had seriously offended him in his determination not to let her see the effect she had had on him. He rattled about with spoons and tea-caddies, with cups and saucers and milk jugs, giving her time to recapture the profusion of her hair and himself his badly strained peace of mind.

"I think I'd better get back," she said hesitantly behind him and he whirled to face her, his face stern and paler than usual.

"No, please don't go. Stay and have your tea," and he at least was well aware that he was saying something else. Stay, yes. Don't go, yes, but nothing to do with cups of tea.

She was bewildered. "Mr Hutchinson . . ." She was about to trot out the platitudes her mama had taught her which were meant to rebuff, politely, of course, any gentleman who was becoming a nuisance but the words just seemed to die in her throat in a way which had never happened before. Even before life was breathed into them they withered away and she found herself moving, trancelike, towards him.

"Mr Hutchinson . . ." Her voice was husky with something she did not recognise as her awakening sexuality.

"Jamie, please," he heard himself murmur, studying her mouth, waiting for her to say his name for the first time.

"Jamie . . ." It thrilled him. He watched her helplessly as she drifted even closer to him and he knew she was hypnotised by something he was directing at her and he was acutely aware that it must be he who put a stop to it. Christ Almighty, what in hell was happening to him? he asked himself, knowing what it was even as he denied it. He'd known many women since he'd become a man but in ten years no one had ever touched his heart. He had thought her lovely, enchanting even, on the train and had been surprised by the enormous urge he had felt to protect her, which he had put down to her defenceless fragility. Her face at the carriage window as the Andrews drove away had awakened a strong feeling of pity in him but he had not once considered her as a woman on that train journey. A young, frightened girl she had been and that was what his maleness had responded to.

But now he wanted her. Sweet Jesus, how he wanted her but she'd not thank him if he made advances to her here on the old rag rug his mam had given him and on which countless dogs and kittens and children had rolled in play. She was too fine for that, too . . . special. Yes, that was the word and though it surprised him, for he had always been a man to take an opportunity when it presented itself to him, he was reluctant to do so now.

"Sit down, Chloe," he managed to say, "and let me pour you a cup of tea to hearten you on your journey." He knew he sounded bloody ridiculous. It was one of those trite remarks a hostess might make to a guest but it was the best he could think of at that precise moment.

She did as she was told, her manner still dream-like, her eyes a soft, clouded, greeny blue, her lashes drooping, her lips still moistly parted, a flush of apricot in each cheek. Jesus, but she was beautiful, with some physical thing her mama had not taught her, nor even thought to warn her about, but by Christ, he'd not take advantage of it, nor of her ignorance, her innocence, no matter how she damn well looked at him.

"I'm to rent this farm from Jack Andrews, did I tell you?" he heard himself babble, glad of anything to dissipate the languorous warmth which still had a hold of them. "I saved enough and invested money . . . Mr Andrews helped me."

"Really." Her voice was low and still thready but he could see reality touch her gently.

"Yes. I intend buying it one day when I've the money. Here's your tea . . . sugar? And perhaps some milk? It's fresh . . . well, as I was saying . . ." His own voice was almost his own again. "I can't buy yet or I would have nothing left for beasts and machinery, you see."

"Of course." She sipped her tea obediently though it was

strong, not what she was accustomed to drinking, and the mug was thick and sturdy, again not what she was used to, never taking her eyes from his face, mesmerised, it seemed, by the sound of his voice which was murmuring of everyday things, but which appeared to electrify her.

"You'll have heard of the Agricultural Holdings Bill which was passed in March?"

"No, I don't believe so." The personification of exquisite politeness.

"It gives tenants rights which they didn't have before."

"Really."

"Yes," taking a sip of his own tea, wishing it had a shot of whisky in it to steady his overstretched nerves.

"If a tenant makes an improvement to a farm, like this one, say, then he is entitled to compensation from the owner. And of course I shall be improving it."

"What will you do?" It was with great relief Jamie could see she was taking a genuine interest now, coming out of her trance, out of the bewildering web he and she had blundered into.

They both turned to look round the comfortless room. The farmhouse was in poor repair, since it had been unlived in for many years. He and his mother had done what they could, scrubbing the floors, the windows, even the walls but there were none of the homely appointments to be found in Matty's cottage. A solid table left by the previous owner since it could not be got through the doorway, a couple of rush-seated, spindle-backed chairs made from cherrywood, and a lopsided dresser on which several pieces of serviceable pottery stood. No more than a plate or two and half a dozen knives, forks and spoons. The enormous hearth, characteristic of farmhouses and cottages of the previous century, sported a huge, crackling log fire, the kettle and what appeared to be an all-purpose iron pot. There was nothing else. Nothing that was not strictly practical, not even a jar of flowers which after all could be gathered for nothing. The walls had suspicious patches of what looked like damp and the woodwork about the windows was crumbling with age and neglect.

"Well . . ." Jamie sighed somewhat helplessly, seeing it for the first time as it would appear to a woman such as her, but knowing there was nothing to be done about it. "The drystone walling for a start."

"And the cobbles up to the farmhouse door." She smiled, a natural smile which he returned.

"Yes, and then visitors will not fall and damage themselves, and of course," he went on hastily since it seemed she knew exactly who one of those visitors would be, "there is the farmhouse itself. It is barely fit for the mice to live in let alone humans."

"Mice!" She shuddered and looked about her apprehensively and he wondered, fast in the throes of helpless fascination, why it was women were so afraid of mice, at the same time enchanted with her because she was.

"Oh, they'll be long gone soon," he soothed her. "There's a fine litter of kittens in the stable at Cloudberry, all looking for good homes so I'll fetch a couple up here and they'll soon be rid of them."

"What about Captain? Won't they fight? I thought cats and dogs were mortal enemies. Not that I know much about it since I'm familiar with neither." She leaned forward confidentially, putting her elbows on the table, cupping her chin in her hands, and he wondered at the sad echo of – was it loss? – in her voice. What had she known in her young life? What was she doing here? Even his mother seemed reluctant to talk about her and why had her father, who surely could not help but love this beautiful young woman, sent her here to a house where she was very evidently not welcome?

"How old are you, Chloe?" he heard himself ask abruptly.

She did not seem surprised or offended by his question which was not one a gentleman asked a lady.

"I'm eighteen, nineteen in September."

"I shall be twenty-six in December."

"I see," she breathed and though she was not exactly certain what she meant by that it seemed to satisfy him.

"I think you had better get home now, don't you?" he asked softly.

"Where is that, Jamie?" It was said with no appeal for sympathy.

His insides wrenched at the sadness in her voice but he resisted the temptation to take her hand and bring it to his lips. God Almighty, he had got up from his narrow truckle bed this morning, his first night spent in this new home of his, his first day of his new life ahead of him and like a thunderbolt, striking at him with ferocity and yet at the same time exquisite tenderness, this girl had walked into his farmyard, into his farmhouse, into his heart even, and settled herself in it, whether she knew it or not, with the serenity of a cat curling itself before a good fire on its own hearth. His thoughts were wild and foolish for how could he believe that this would be her hearth one day, an easily broken creature like Chloe Taylor who should by rights be adorning some rich man's home where she would have need to do no more than take a stitch or two of fine embroidery each day. Jamie Hutchinson should be looking about him for a brave-hearted, strong-shouldered, wide-hipped young woman – like Katy Andrews, his bemused mind whispered, who would scrub and scour, plant seeds and plough furrows and give him a dozen healthy children while she did so.

Of course he should, but could he? Now?

"I'll walk you to the edge of the wood," he told her, already expecting her to do what he thought best for her.

"Can we take Captain? Poor puppy shut outside and it wasn't his fault. I shouldn't have knelt down beside him."

"He knew exactly what he was doing, the young devil. And he must learn to live outside, Chloe. He's not a pet but a working dog."

She looked quite horrified. "Outside! By himself? How could you? He's only a baby even though he is so big. Oh, Jamie, I couldn't bear to have him fretting in one of those awful outbuildings on the other side of the track. Surely he could be allowed to sleep on this mat before the fire? It must be damp and cold out there, particularly in the winter and I'm sure it will do him no good. Oh, please, Mr Hutchinson . . . Jamie, let him come inside now and I'm sure he will behave for you when he is properly trained. I could make him a blanket of his own."

He was helpless before the appeal in her voice, in her body which surged towards his in desperate defence of the dog. He was left without resources as the natural barricades which a man puts up about himself in order to get through life without mishap shattered and came crashing down about him. Jesus Christ, how could he possibly deny her whatever she asked of him when her little flower face, which had paled with the strength of her outrage over the dog, swam inches below his own. She was up on her tiptoes, her nose on a level with his chin and he had only to reach out and pull her to him, press her face into the curve beneath his chin, fold his arms across her back and simply hold her. Assure her that he would do anything she wanted, with the bloody dog, with this farm, himself, his life. Oh, Jesus God, if he could . . . if he could . . .

He held up his hands as though in submission, palms towards her and with a great effort he managed to smile.

"I give in, I give in, really I do. The animal shall sleep in my bed if that's what you think's best for him and shall eat the best steak the butcher in Crossclough can supply."

Her face broke into a smile of huge delight.

"Oh, Jamie, do you mean it? You don't, do you, not about the meat, but you will let him sleep in the house?"

He sighed, defeated. "Very well, but next time you come bring that blanket, for I'll not have him upstairs."

"Oh, I will, I promise, I promise."

She collapsed into the chair, her face rosy again, her laughter bubbling up, high and lovely to hear and the girl who was just about to tie her mare to the iron ring at the gate lifted her head in shocked surprise. Her fingers became still for a moment and then clumsy as she did her best to loop the reins through the ring and the mare, sensing her mistress's flaring unease, backed off, eyes rolling, ears pricking.

"Stand still, you fool, for God's sake, and not a sound," she hissed, her face turning in bewilderment towards the farmhouse, but it was too late as the puppy, who had flopped disconsolately in a bit of sunshine by the doorstep, sprang to his feet and galloped frantically towards her. He began to bark, knowing already that this was his domain and that inside the house were his people whom he must guard, but at the same time, since he was still very young, he could not resist greeting with great affection this new human he vaguely recognised.

"Oh, God alive," Katherine Andrews moaned as several pounds of ecstatic dog flesh leaped up against the skirt of her blue riding habit. Her mare reared and whinnied in alarm and from a rotting pile of wood in which she had cornered what she was positive was an enemy, her small terrier flew to defend her. The puppy, who had meant no harm, began to howl as Muffy showed him her teeth in a savage snarl though she was half his size, backing off in great haste towards the safety of the door. When it opened he thundered inside and cowered behind Chloe's skirts.

When Jamie, who had opened the door, saw who his visitor was, his heart sank like a stone to his boots but he did his best to smile.

"Katy, what a commotion. I thought a pack of wolves was attacking us. I'm afraid my brave hound has not yet learned any manners and I'm sorry if he has damaged your gown. He was the same with Chloe, jumping up and almost taking her off her feet. In fact he did take her off her feet, didn't he, Chloe?"

Katherine's eyes narrowed suspiciously. The sight of her cousin lurking in Jamie's kitchen was not one she had expected and she did not like it. This was her territory. It belonged to her, with Jamie, for had they not brought it to its present state which was one of being ready to begin. To plant and . . . and all the other things Jamie meant to do which, as yet, she herself was not too clear about. Sheep and cows and hens and . . . and things. For weeks she had been coming up here and standing, hands on hips, feet apart, as a man might stand, gazing with proprietorial pride over the land which Jamie was to farm. As Jamie did. Side by side they had discussed what Jamie and his brother were to do. Sometimes Tommy would come with them which was a bit of a nuisance but as he was to work for Jamie it couldn't be helped. The joy of being alone with Jamie was indescribable. She had never been happier. She and Jamie were going to do this together, though neither of them had said so in so many words. There was no need. It was understood. She loved him and when he had a moment to turn round and see her, really see her, he would know he loved her. She only had to be there when he did.

So what was her cousin Chloe doing in his kitchen, smiling, almost purring, Katherine would have said, like the cat who has just had the last saucer of cream?

She felt the confusion press around her heart. She didn't really know what to do, how to feel or even how to behave at this precise moment, which was unlike her since she had always said and done the first thing that came into her head but something, some instinct, some female sense begged her to be careful, to watch her mouth, to guard her tongue, even to hide the expression in her eyes since, her senses told her, she was in great danger.

"Really," was all she said, clamping her lips firmly about her teeth.

"It seems I am to be honoured with visitors today which is just as well for I shall be up to my eyes in work as soon as the herd arrive. Tomorrow, they said, and I am to collect the plough at the end of the week. Tommy is coming up later to give me a hand so I shall have no time for entertaining. Chloe and I have just had . . . there's tea in the pot, Katherine, if you fancy a cup. Come in . . . do come in."

He knew he was saying more than was needed and so did Katherine and she felt the first stirring, not just of alarm but of real fear. Why should Jamie, a man, not a callow youth, be in such a taking, such a state of jabbering foolishness, like a husband who has just been found in awkward circumstances with his wife's maid?

She walked towards them, aware that Chloe, whether on purpose or not, had moved to stand beside Jamie in the doorway. Her face was composed, pale, and her eyes were clear and untroubled. She looked as she had always looked, unapproachable, detached from those about her, her dove grey gown falling, unwrinkled, in soft folds to her feet, not a button awry, not a hem out of place. Yes, just as she always did except for several tendrils of red-gold hair which fell about her ears, drifting to her neck and to her placid white forehead as Katherine had never seen it do before.

Their eyes met and held and though Chloe Taylor, until this moment, had been only vaguely aware of the empathy which had blossomed, the warmth which had been kindled today between herself and Jamie Hutchinson, perhaps of no more than friendship since she had no experience of men, nor of need, she did recognise the challenge in her cousin's eyes for were they not both women? Jamie was an extraordinary man. They had met only twice but each time he had given her something, something unrecognised but which had made her feel . . . what? Safe, comforted, at ease and she had liked it. And him! Something unusual had happened between them today. As yet she had had no time to study it, to mull over its contents, to examine it in depth, to visualise what she would do with it when she knew what it might be. She would go back to Cloudberry and her room there, sit in the window seat overlooking the garden and call up every moment, bring each one forth and listen to what Jamie had said to her and how he had said it. Remember the expressions on his face and what had been softly inherent in his voice.

And she knew something else she would do as well. She would come again to Valley Bottom Farm to visit him, as she sensed he wanted her to and that brooding look in Katherine's eyes, which she had been allowed to see, would not stop her!

8

Chris Andrews watched his cousin come towards him in that straightbacked and yet supple way she had of walking, placing each foot on the rough path with sure grace, one before the other as a cat does. Even though she was making her way uphill it did not hinder her. Her head was up. She wore no bonnet and despite the dullness of the day there appeared to be a gleam, a gloss about her hair, as though the sun touched it. It was held at the crown of her head with a froth of peacock blue satin ribbons, a small unconscious rebellion, he thought, surprised, against the pale grey sombreness of her half mourning. She was a young girl who should have been in pretty colours, defying convention with a touch of frivolity though there was none to see it and none to care if they did. Her hair hung in an enormously thick, curling cable, giving the impression it longed to be free, strands of it falling across her breasts, the rest hanging down her back from the confining ribbon to just below her waist. The damp in the air had wound her hair into tight ringlets at her forehead and neck and put spangles of mist in it, like tiny diamonds which, again, though there was no sun to reflect in them, sparkled like dew on early morning roses.

He saw all this from beneath the overhang of the enormous rock which formed part of a tumbled group lying at the side of the clough. The water accelerated past him, hurtling white drifts dividing on either side of grey rocks which, blackened by the moisture, resembled enormous lumps of coal, shiny and polished to ebony. It thundered down to each level in a skirt of misted gauze edged with lace, floundering and hissing, leaping from rock to rock so that there was nothing but the sound of its frantic race to reach the reservoir in the valley. When he stepped out on to the path up which Chloe climbed she recoiled savagely, almost overbalancing into the demented stream.

"Whoops," he said, laughing, reaching out to take her fine-boned arm in his strong, horseman's hand, steadying her but at the same time drawing her closer to him. "Careful, or we'll both be in the clough, though I must say I have often wondered how long it would take to get to the bottom by water instead of the more conventional way. Not long, I shouldn't wonder, though in what state one would arrive . . . well . . ."

He grinned engagingly into her startled face which was very close to his own, leaning even closer in a way which she recognised, for it was not the first time he had accosted her this way. His smile had in it the impudence of a young gentleman who knows he is flirting with a female who is not a lady, at least in his opinion, and she felt her anger erupt.

With a violence which astonished him – she could see it in his transparent green eyes – she snatched her arm away from his over-friendly hand and, brushing past him, continued up the path without speaking, her face taut and furious.

He had lain in wait for her on many occasions since she had been sent to Cloudberry End and though she would not let him see it, since she despised him for his weak character, his belief that no woman could resist him and what she saw – or what her mama would have seen – as a most immoral determination to avoid doing a hand's turn if he could help it, she was beginning to be somewhat nervous of him. Well, perhaps not exactly nervous of him since that implied she could not control him, had no power to stop the silly games he played with her, but she did wish he would accept she had no interest in what he called "being friendly".

There was the time in the wood when she had gone to sit in a patch of sunlight to read a book she had taken from her uncle's library. *Far from the Madding Crowd* by Thomas Hardy, it was, published only a year or two back, and she had been deeply immersed in the passionate exchanges between Bathsheba and Captain Troy when a shadow had fallen over her, blotting out the sunshine, blotting out her pleasant hour of forgetfulness from her own dispiriting life. He had laughed and chattered and done his best to draw her into his own, what she saw as facetious nonsense, talking about how pretty she was and how lonely she must be and if ever she needed a friend she had only to turn to him. She would sooner befriend Katherine's little dog.

Then there had been the incident in the back parlour where he had done more than try to be her "friend". A little kiss, he had said, which naturally she wouldn't miss and would certainly enjoy sharing with Chris Andrews. His face had been so serious when he had drawn her into the room she had been completely fooled and had allowed herself to be enticed from the narrow passage but when his true purpose had been revealed it was all she could do not to strike him.

He had stepped into her path in Crossclough, bowing and doffing his hat, asking her where she was going and did she mind if he accompanied her and perhaps, afterwards, they might . . .

She had not allowed him to finish but had swept up her skirt and continued on her way to the haberdasher's where she meant to purchase velvet ribbons to match a new gown she was planning for the winter.

There had been other times when he had been more determined and she had almost had to struggle with him to avoid the delights of what he called "being friendly" and so she had learned to watch for him, note where he was going and with whom and when he was gone to slip away across Cloudberry End wood like some stealthy intruder. When she knew he was at the paper mill she could relax but even then, sent on some errand or other by his father, he would sometimes pop up in the most unexpected places, his grey cropping the vegetation behind some handy huddle of rocks, his grin engaging, pretending to be apologetic for alarming her but leaving her in no doubt that he was not at all sorry, not really.

She climbed steadily away from him, moving through the undergrowth which, nourished by the spray from the fall of water, grew in great abundance. Ferns fringed the water, beautiful in their display of misted droplets which slid from frond to frond and then to the ground, turning last year's leaf mould into a quagmire. There was a path of sorts, with rocky outcrops and from every bit of ground where sustenance might be had grew saplings of rowan and sycamore in their full summer glory. Chloe had, on Katy's advice, bought herself from the generous allowance her uncle gave her some sturdy leather boots which gripped her about the ankle, supporting their tendency to turn on the uneven ground and their serrated soles gripped the wet stones and were impervious to the boggy ground. She had been out walking almost every day since she had come to Cloudberry End and had become strong, able to stride out for hours. Chris, in the well-polished boots he wore to the office at Waterway Paper Mill, had a job to keep up.

"Chloe, wait, don't run off like that," he gasped, his predilection for good brandy and good cigars, hours at the gaming table and other, more punishing pastimes, leaving him out of breath. "I'm not used to this, cousin," he heaved. "I'm not a great one for the outdoors unless I'm on horseback. Please, have mercy," laughing, "take pity on me and let's have a breather. Why don't we stop and admire the view? Can you honestly tell me that it's not worth looking at, even on a day like this?"

They had reached about halfway up the Black Hill from where the watercourse flowed. The gritstone cliffs which formed the clough were about twenty feet high on either side at this level, the water which flowed through it gentler now, just a mild froth and dither, with miles of boggy moorland beyond where the bog-cotton grew and curlews piped a tune. Just heather and broom and rough stone, a rabbit or two flirting their scuts and high, high above, a hawk lay on the air with nothing more than an occasional flicker of its wings to keep it there.

The moorland stretched on and on to the murky horizons, vast wastes of hazed purple and golden explosions of gorse, the tawny brown of bracken, all divided by the narrow paths where sheep trod.

Chloe emerged from the tangle of vegetation, sparser now, striding out across the springy turf, skirting tumbled projections of half-buried rocks from behind which sheep got clumsily to their feet and leaped away in alarm.

"Chloe, dammit, won't you stand still for a bloody minute? Anyone would think you were afraid of me."

It was perhaps this which stopped her. The idea that he might think he frightened her; even if he did she had no intention of letting him see it. He was a boy, a silly boy playing silly games, dangerous games, for should she tell his father it might be awkward for him. The Andrews family might regard her as an unwanted visitor who must be put up with until the time came for her to leave, but she was a relative, a defenceless young woman and she was sure Jack Andrews would be mortified if he knew what his son was up to.

She turned, looking back to where he struggled in what she recognised as his "city" shoes to get a foothold on the rocky, tussocky ground. His face was aflame with his exertions of the last ten minutes but when he saw she had stopped, so did he, his hand dramatically to his heart, grinning in that imbecile way which he thought so irresistible. He was a handsome young man, she could not deny it, and neither would he if she told him so. There was no doubt he would have girlish hearts atwitter up and down the valley and there was talk that eighteen-year-old Miss Diana Ashwell of Ashwell Hall, where Chris was on good terms with her brother Johnny and where Aunt Sara called at least once a week, was very taken with him. It would be considered a good match. His money and her breeding but it seemed Chris Andrews had other things on his mind at the moment and if his relentless pursuit of herself over the last weeks was anything to go by, Diana might have a long wait for her trip up the aisle with Chloe's cousin. Not that she suspected his intentions towards herself were anything but dishonourable. The narrowed gleam in his eye distinctly told her so.

"What do you want?" she asked sharply, hoping to put him off with her icy rudeness.

Though it was midsummer the air had no warmth. Indeed it might even be said to be what her uncle called "hearty", giving one the inclination to walk briskly, not stand about admiring the view, spectacular as it was. She pulled her warm cloak more closely about her, clasping her arms across her breasts beneath its folds so that she looked like a dark finger of flinty stone, only her hair bright and lively as a flame in a grate.

"I can't say I want anything, cousin."

"Then why do you keep following me around?" she asked accusingly. "Every time I go out I can guarantee I shall meet you somewhere along the way. I swear I don't know how you do it since I am sure your papa does not allow you to spend a lot of time away from the mill."

He shrugged, a shadow darkening his discontented face. "True. My father would chain me to the damn paper machine if he could but even he knows better than to do that. He sends me to collect parcels from the station and to deliver notes. They are tasks with little or no responsibility, for which he believes, by the way, I am not yet ready, but I am perfectly happy to perform them. They get me away from clanking machines, spinning wheels, pulleys and rollers, pipes and straps and wires and the everlasting "stuff" which pours from one end of the bloody place to the other. And it gives my father a reason to justify the allowance he makes me, to pretend I'm working, d'you see. But whatever am I thinking of? I came up here to get away from it, not to talk to you about it. I'm sure you and I can find more pleasing subjects to discuss without a great deal of trouble."

For a moment, as he spoke of the paper mill he had regained that strained, strung-up look he wore to the mill every day, a little pale, a transparency in his eyes which spoke of his aversion to manufacturing and his own seemingly inescapable burden of being involved in it. But now he changed, his face deepening into a curving smile, his eyes narrowing in that way which had become so familiar to her. An acquisitive face, she called it, since he did not try to hide the very obvious fact that he would like something from her.

He strolled indolently up the last bit of slope towards her then, with a courtly gesture, he swept his arm across his chest inviting her to rest on a lichen-covered rock beside the path.

"Do sit down, Chloe and if *you* are not out of breath, then at least allow me to catch mine."

"Catch your breath by all means but I shall get on. No doubt I shall see you at dinner."

Her contemptuous rejection of him and his attempt to be "friendly" hardened his face and, taking her by surprise and before she had time to turn away or even free her arms to defend herself, he sprang forward and caught her to him, all pretence at being "civilised" cast on the wind which blew across the tops. Their faces were so close she could see the tiny golden brown flecks in the depths of his green eyes and the long droop of the copper-coloured lashes which surrounded them. His skin was flushed, so much so she could feel the heat of it against her hastily averted cheek and when his lips laid themselves on the line of her straining jaw she was not surprised to find them on fire.

"Let me go . . . let me go, Chris."

"Now don't be silly, sweetheart," he gasped. "You know I won't hurt you."

"Take your hands off me, you fool." She jerked herself away from him, no more than an inch or two, but her wriggling body seemed to fan the flames of his male excitement.

"You don't mean that, my love. You have been telling me for weeks with those cast-down eyes of yours that you would not be averse to . . ."

"Don't be so bloody ridiculous," she gasped, suddenly realising why it was her uncle and Katy seemed to find such satisfaction in swearing. "Really, if I were to tell your papa . . ."

"Tell my papa!" His voice was clipped, his own jaw stiff as he did his best to reach her mouth with his. "It would be your word against mine, sweet Chloe, and who do you think will be believed? The son of the house or the unwanted cousin whose character and morals are known to no one. We met you only three months ago so how are my parents to know what kind of girl you are or what you got up to before you came to Crossclough? Come now, don't struggle, my pet. You know you want this as much as I do."

Dear God, where did men get their bloated sense of their own desirability to women, any woman, and how could this fool seriously believe that her frantic struggles were a sign of her own willingness? she agonised, as she did her best, if she could not escape his mouth, at least to sink her teeth into his lower lip. It seemed to please him. He began to laugh.

"Spirited as well, eeh? Well, that's all to the better. I've been wanting to do this to you ever since you stepped down from that train. Eyes on you like a startled deer and a mouth as luscious as a ripe peach . . ."

"Oh, for heaven's sake, get away from me, you idiot." Strangely, now that he had caught her she was no longer afraid. It was all so silly, even his words seeming to come from some cheap melodrama. "Let me go and I promise I'll say no more about it. I know this is the sort of thing young gentlemen get up to but . . ."

"I see, so you *do* know more than that innocent face and those great wide eyes imply you do."

"No, of course not . . . please, Chris."

"Give me a kiss then. I promise you'll enjoy it. I'll let you go at once if you'll allow me just one kiss. I know Mother and Father treat you as though you didn't exist and Katy is too concerned with involving herself with Jamie Hutchinson to befriend you but I'm more than willing to make up for their— "

"I have no wish to be your friend, can't you see that?" She snorted derisively, doing her best to get her arms out of her enveloping cloak, to bring her knee up into what she believed was the most vulnerable part of a man's body. Even if she didn't hurt him, which she wanted to do most savagely now, at least it might force him away from her, but he bore her back relentlessly until she felt the damp and rigid hardness of stone behind her. Her head swung frantically from side to side as she did her best to avoid his burning mouth, her face screwed up with deep revulsion, when, suddenly, so suddenly she almost fell over, he let her go, stepping back from her, straightening his jacket, smoothing down the alarming bulge in his breeches, then pushing both hands through the dishevelment of his auburn hair.

"I'll force no woman," he spat out. "I've no need, for Chris Andrews can take his bloody pick."

"Then why pick me?" she panted, doing her best to draw a deep breath into her lungs, putting up shaking hands to her own hair from which the ribbon had come loose, lying in a vivid splash across one grey-clad shoulder.

"Oh come on, stop playing the innocent with me. I've seen the way you look . . ."

"*At you!*" Her voice was incredulous and not only that, but scathing.

There had been, though neither of these two young people knew it, way back in the dark generations of the Andrews family, a labouring man by the name of Bartholomew Andrews whose temper was so short and vicious those who lived and worked in his vicinity walked about him on tiptoes lest they disturb the uncertain equilibrium of his nature. A word, a look, even the lift of an eyebrow, it was said, could set him off and his first wife, who had died young and rather mysteriously, might have told a tale or two had she lived. Black Bart's temper was a legend up in the wild dales of Yorkshire where the family then lived and every now and again, as the generations came and went, it flared up, sometimes in a female but more often than not in a male descendant of Black Bart Andrews.

Though it had not yet manifested itself in Jack and Sara Andrews's youngest boy, who had never as yet been seriously crossed, it lay dormant in Christopher Andrews.

At Chloe's cutting words it exploded into life, surprising not only her but him, and before she could lift her hands to defend herself or even steady her back against the rock, the palm of his lean hard hand lashed her across the cheek, rocking her head and neck with such force she thought she heard a bone click somewhere and an agonising pain rippled through her body. She felt her senses begin to slip away, not just with the torment of her ricked neck but by the sheer horror of being struck by another human being. Never in her life had anyone offered violence to her and the shock of it flung her giddily into reeling blackness which threatened to bring her to her knees.

At once Chris Andrews was filled with remorse. Unlike his rough ancestor, Chris had a veneer of the civilised, cultured upbringing a woman such as his well-bred mother thought fit for her sons and though the violent flash of uncontrollable rage had been real enough, the sight of his cousin fainting against the rock where his blow had knocked her brought him instantly back to the realisation of who he was, of who she was, of what he had done. He was amazed at himself, stunned as to where that explosive white light of passion had come from, even wondering if it had actually happened it was so incredible.

But his cousin's cheek, which had the fiery red imprint of his hand upon it, her rapidly puffing eye and a small bleeding cut by her mouth where his signet ring had caught it were enough confirmation, if he needed it.

"Dear sweet Jesus . . . Oh, Christ, Chloe, I'm sorry. Hell's teeth, I'm sorry . . . there, let me . . . won't you sit down? I honestly don't know where that came from, really I don't."

His demeanour was anguished, bewildered, his own dreadful action so completely out of his own range of what he believed himself to be, which was a gentleman, of course, he could only stammer like a child. He would never forgive himself, his manner said and if she would just allow it he would, if necessary, carry her home on his own back, or at least to where his grey was tethered.

The pain, and the man who had inflicted it were too much for Chloe and she began to shake in great rippling tremors, putting up her hands in horror to him when he would have helped her.

"Don't . . . please," she mumbled. Her mouth was numbed and inclined to be unmanageable so that she could not speak properly. Her head lolled on her neck as though something had snapped and she could see the rocks and trees, the clouds and other, quite unrecognisable objects, flying round and round, going past her blurred eyes in the most dizzying way. Her stomach heaved and she had the greatest difficulty in keeping within it the last meal she had eaten which, for the life of her, she couldn't recall. Was it breakfast or lunch? And her face was beginning to burn with a pain which was unbearable.

"No . . . of course not," Chris was stuttering. "I'm sorry . . . so sorry but . . . will you ever forgive me?"

"No."

"Jesus, I deserved that."

"Go away." Her eye was already so swollen she could barely see out of it and Chris knew and was appalled, since he had knowledge of such things at school, that she would have a livid bruise about it by this evening. God in heaven, what would she tell them at home? He had meant her no harm, none at all. She had intrigued him from the first day she had come to stay in his home since, not only was she exceedingly pretty but she was unknown, a mystery, a challenge which he would enjoy conquering, and though he had been told she was his cousin, his young unmarried cousin and therefore untouchable, he had not quite believed it. She was very like his mother, of course, and would not have been accepted if his parents had the slightest doubts as to her ancestry, but his male curiosity and desire only knew that she was a young, beautiful woman whose body his lusted after. He would not, naturally, he told himself, have gone further than a kiss or two, had she been willing, for the consequences of such actions would have been disastrous for them both, particularly him! A bit of harmless fun, that was all, a kiss that no one would know about and now, through his own amazing loss of control, he had put a mark on her that could not be missed, or explained. If only she hadn't fought him. If only she hadn't been so bloody scornful, sneering, none of this would have happened. Oh God, women were the bloody limit.

"I can't . . . well . . . just leave you here, Chloe," he said helplessly, moving from anxious foot to anxious foot and on his face, though he was not aware of it, was a growing look of exasperation that said he wished to God he had never clapped eyes on her.

"Please leave me alone," she mumbled, hiding her face in the fall of her hair.

"But . . ."

"You have injured my . . . my face, not my legs. I can walk back."

"Well, if you're sure . . ." relieved, it seemed, to be rid of her. "Only Father will be . . . you know how he is and then there's Zack."

"Zack?"

"My grey."

"Of course."

"Then I'll go." He hesitated, his handsome young face creased with concern, not for her now, she realised, but for himself. "Er . . . what will you say . . ." He cleared his throat and pulled at his cravat. "I mean, how will you explain . . ."

"Don't worry, I won't tell them what happened. As you said a few minutes ago, a girl who leads on a gentleman deserves all she gets."

"Chloe . . ."

"Oh, for goodness sake, go." Her tone was bitter. "But I have this to say. If you touch me again I shall go, not to your father but to the local constabulary. I shall make such an outcry no man will trust you about his daughter ever again. Even if, like you, they wonder about me, they will say there is no smoke without fire."

"Chloe, I promise, honest to God . . ."

"Don't bring God into this, please. I'm beginning to wonder if He has the slightest concern for . . ." Her voice from beneath her curtain of hair broke and she turned away.

When, several moments later, she turned back, he was gone.

The sky was beginning to lose its light, changing slowly to that deep shade of damson which heralds a summer thunderstorm when Jamie found her. He had been up to Browden Meadow where his small flock of sheep were grazing, checking on the state of the pasture and the nourishment his Lonks might get out of it. It was poor and there were flocks from several small farms like his own to share it but Lonks were hardy beasts and those he had found with his own brand on them seemed to be thriving. There was a storm brewing, a vivid lightning storm which would have the moorland creatures, including the sheep, cowering under any cover they could find and he meant to do the same when he got home. His young dog, Captain, who slunk uneasily at his heels, was already turning his head this way and that and pricking his ears, his coat beginning to ripple in alarm.

He could not at first put a name to the dark huddle of something which crouched at the base of the rock beside the path. Captain was not inclined, as he normally would be, to bound madly forward and investigate, his fear of the coming storm keeping him fastened as though by a rope to Jamie's ankle.

Jamie hesitated, his heavily booted feet sending several small pieces of stone clinking into a narrow crevice and at the sound the huddle moved. The head . . . yes, it was a head, lifted and reared back and a small gasp escaped from the whiteness of what Jamie now recognised as a woman's face. And not just any face, but the face of the woman who had been in Jamie's mind and thoughts for weeks now, in the very heart of him, like the thrilling notes of a songbird, or the perfection of that songbird in flight across the evening sky. An exquisite flower which cannot be forgotten, a bright star in the firmament, an image of all the dreaming thoughts men have when they contemplate the woman they will love.

Chloe! Chloe!

Throwing off his perplexity on what the hell she was doing up here alone and more to the point why she was crumpled up like some child's discarded toy at the base of the rock, he leaped down the path towards her. She had seen him come to a halt higher up the path and even in the deepening gloom he could not fail to notice the way she drew herself into her cloak as though she would dearly love to slip quietly under the rock and hide away from him, as though she were afraid of him, as though his presence was something she did not care for.

"Chloe . . .?" His voice was uncertain though he knew without doubt it was she, hoarse with his fear since it was very evident she was deeply distressed.

He slithered wildly on loose stones and wet grass, scrambling to her side, sinking to his knees and bending his head to peer into her face. His heart was pounding with something he recognised as fear and his voice was rough with it as he spoke.

"What is it? What's happened? Have you fallen? Where are you hurt? Here, let me lift you a little," reaching out with strong, yearning arms but not as yet touching her, since he did not know where she was injured. Her hair hung in a tangled mass of curls about her head, falling across her face, over her shoulders and down her back, darkened by the damp, and through it her clouded blue-green eyes peered up at him.

Well, one did. The other seemed to be half shut, sunk in folds of swollen flesh, shadowed by something he could not as yet recognise. As he put out a hand to her she shrank away from him and he was left in no doubt that his touch, perhaps even his presence was unwelcome to her. That indeed she was frightened of it.

"Chloe, it's me, Jamie. Don't be afraid. Won't you tell me what's happened to you, my dove?" Neither of them noticed his use of the endearment. "You have obviously hurt yourself . . . well, your face," for as he looked even closer there was no question Chloe Taylor had a spanker of a black eye and a livid weal down one side of her dazed face. Neither injury was consistent with a fall. More like a fist . . . a clenched fist, or perhaps . . .

She was in a state of shock. He had seen it before when a man had an accident at sea. A sort of a daze, stunned, not senseless but in such a deep well of distress all thought and feeling and speech are impossible. He didn't know what or who had done this to her and in any case that could wait until later. What she needed was warmth and comfort, a compress, perhaps some sort of lotion, though he didn't know what, for her face. Cherishing was what Chloe Taylor needed and he, who loved her, was the one to give it to her.

Murmuring gently, the soft, incomprehensible sounds with which a mother would soothe a hurt child, he persuaded her to allow his arms about her, to be lifted from the damp, cold ground, to be wrapped against his chest in his own warm jacket, to be held tenderly, her face hidden in the curve of his shoulder. She was light, insubstantial, as tiny and breakable as a bird, as the dove he had likened her to in her plain, pale grey gown which was revealed as her cloak fell open.

"Come, my little dove, let me take you home," he whispered, his mouth against her damp hair, and strangely, they both knew he did not mean Cloudberry End.

9

No one missed her until the next morning which, later, Chloe though wryly, was an indication of her importance in the household of Cloudberry End.

Chris Andrews was relieved when he entered the dining room that same evening to find that his cousin Chloe had not put in an appearance. He knew it was only a matter of time before Chloe's face, which he was sure was a sorry sight by now, was noticed and remarked on, but he had been worried all day on how she would explain it to his family. A fall, perhaps, or that old adage that she had walked into something, but her non-appearance was a relief. Though she was treated with cool politeness, no more, by his mother and father, somewhat in the manner of hosts who are too well bred to question an unwelcome guest on when she might be expected to leave, and with casual indifference by Katy who saw no benefit to her in her city-bred cousin, surely her absence would be noticed and something said. They could hardly start dinner, at which she was usually present, without a well-mannered murmur of curiosity on where she could be and, sure enough, his father raised his eyebrows at her empty chair.

"Aah, if you're looking for Chloe, sir," Chris said smoothly, "when last I saw her she spoke of feeling unwell."

"Did she now? Well, she might have sent a message to inform your mother she wouldn't be down."

Jack Andrews glowered at the place where his niece's quiet presence normally hovered, for that is how she appeared to him who was used to his own daughter's noisy and colourful occupancy of the space about her. "Surely it is only good manners to let your hostess know you will not be dining, I should have thought. I don't know, the ways of the young never cease to amaze me, and if I were to treat my mother that way— "

"Never mind, dearest," his wife interrupted him gently, taking up her spoon in readiness for the fragrant bowl of soup Freda had just placed before her, her smiling expression saying quite clearly that, as she was not here, that cuckoo which had invaded their nest, why did they not enjoy her absence while they could. Not that the girl was any trouble and to tell the truth Sara had become quite used to having her about the place. If she had not been so uncannily like Alice, indeed it was just like having her dead sister sitting at her table, she might have made more effort to be civil to Alice's daughter. She was not an unkind woman and often felt guilty that she could not find it in her heart to be warmer towards her niece but each time she did so what had happened would come back and haunt her. Those years when . . . well, she was not going to dig up the past, nor bring Alice's ghost into the present but, being a woman who in her young days had known what it was like to be desired by more than one man she had not failed to recognise what was in her son's eyes when he looked at his new-found cousin, which wouldn't do at all! In fact she fully intended writing to her brother-in-law at the earliest opportunity demanding that he remove his daughter as soon as possible. They had given her a home for almost four months now and surely that was long enough for him to have resolved whatever difficulties he might be having with his new young wife?

"Shall I send Ivy to see how she is, mum?" Freda asked her mistress when the family were all served and tucking into Mrs Tiplady's splendid soup.

"No, I don't think so, Freda. If she is unwell then a good night's sleep will do her good."

"Very well, mum." Freda exchanged a glance with Ivy, for none of them ceased to be amazed at the cold-hearted way Miss Chloe was treated. A nice little thing, she was, with a kind word or a smile if she met you on the stairs and no trouble at all, not like the headstrong daughter of their master and mistress. Right sorry they were for her at times but then it was nowt to do with them, was it?

Jamie Hutchinson's small farmhouse had undergone a quite startling transformation in the four weeks since he had moved into it. He had returned to Crossclough on the first day of May and now it was the last day of August and thanks to his mother and the girl who was curled up like a terrified child in the chair before the glowing embers of the fire, the interior was as snug and comfortable as any you could find and a perfectly acceptable home to bring any bride to, which, he had acknowledged subconsciously, was what he had been working towards. Once his flock were out on the grazing moor and his small dairy herd contentedly browsing belly deep in the fenced pasture he and Tommy had prepared; once his fields in which he was to plant his first attempt at crops were ploughed, again with young Tommy's assistance and the plough horse he now owned, he and his brother had turned their attention to the actual farmhouse. The cows had to be milked daily, of course, a task he and Tommy shared, and when that was done they had set about repairing the drystone walls, the loose stones on the cobbled path, the gates and the roof and the rattling window panes, while inside his mother had a lovely time arranging his few bits of furniture to her own satisfaction.

The girl, as his mother called her somewhat suspiciously, since Chloe was not the sort of female Matty Jenkins could see as a farmer's wife, had brought up red plush curtains for the windows, both kitchen and bedroom. She had made them herself, after a great deal of measuring, from some stuff she had found in the attic, she said simply, the ethics of removing what was not hers to remove of no concern to her, it appeared. They were warm and bright and sturdy enough to keep out the most searching of the winds which blew up on the bleak winter moorland, with brass curtain rings which ran on a brass pole.

She had sewn plain pillow cases and sheets since, she explained regretfully, she had not had time for the exquisite embroidery with which she would normally decorate such things. Jamie needed bedlinen at once, and blankets, and then there was the quite incredibly lovely bed quilt she had "thrown together", again racing against the clock, and if Mrs Jenkins would give her permission she would go upstairs at once and make up the enormous brass bed she knew Mrs Andrews had sent up earlier in the week. Hadn't they all been driven to distraction by Katy's constant reminder to her mother that it was needed up at Valley Bottom Farm? The folding truckle bed would do for Tommy when he stayed over, as Chloe knew he sometimes did. Oh dear, her hand to her mouth, she did hope Mrs Jenkins did not think she was interfering, really . . . please forgive her, but it was so lovely to have something useful to do at last.

The kitchen glowed as the fire Jamie had replenished roared up the chimney and Captain hutched himself a bit closer to it, his eyes rolling in ecstasy. The hooked rug he lay on had been a gift from Madge Andrews, brought up by Katy who had no talent for such things, worked in rich colours of red and yellow and orange which made a bright splash against the grey, well-scrubbed stone floor. The ovens on either side of the fire winked and twinkled in the reflected glory of the flames, blackleaded by Matty to a gleaming ebony and kept that way by Jamie who had a sailor's passion for cleanliness and neatness. Along the mantel above the fire stood a row of copper pans of varying sizes. Beside them were candlestick holders, a couple of enormous seashells Jamie had brought back from some exotic beach, a tea caddy and a bunch of hardy wild flowers which had survived on the high peak and which Jamie had picked and arranged, for some reason known only to himself, in a glass jar.

There was a highly polished dresser, a settle at right angles to the fire, its back to the door to avoid the draught, and an elaborately carved child's chair with the initials TH and the date 1788 set in its back.

The chair in which Chloe had been placed was a rocker, a man's chair, big and deep, lined with bright cushions at its back and seat. There was a clock tick-tocking against the whitewashed wall, its face colourful with paintings of the moon, the sun and a sprinkling of stars and in the centre of the room was a plain deal table covered with a red chenille cloth. In its exact centre was a bowl filled with red polished apples. Hanging on hooks from the beams, so low that Jamie had to bend his tall frame to avoid them, were several iron pots, left, like the child's chair, by the previous owners.

It was delightfully warm in the kitchen, tranquil, quiet, and when Jamie turned to look at her as he lifted the kettle from the fire to make the tea, Chloe had fallen asleep. Her head was to one side resting on the back of the chair and her hair, which had rippled concealingly about her, had fallen back to reveal her pale, defenceless face. Pale, yes, pale as bleached bone, except where the bruise lay, the livid outline of a hand, the small cut which had bled and dribbled to dry down her face, the deep, purple plum of the socket about the eye and the eye itself which though closed in sleep was deeply embedded in her swollen flesh. All he could see was the pathetic coppery brown tips of her lashes protruding slightly from the slit of the injury.

Someone had hit her!

He felt it begin to rise in him then, the slow, deep, moving tremors of a rage so terrible he wanted to sweep to the floor all the homely things he and his mother had arranged so carefully in this, his first home. To smash and savage everything, anything he could lay his hands on since it was the only way to let it out of him. To do something, even if it destroyed his own place, to release the explosion of hatred, of venomous, perilous, terrifying rage – it terrified *him* – which needed, since it could not reach the man who had done this to her, to destroy what lay readily to hand. His hands clenched into fists, so tight he could feel his fingernails cut into his palms. He wanted to crash them against the walls, the table, to howl dementedly at the hurt which had been done her. His mouth twisted back on his teeth in a snarl like that of an enraged leopard and he felt his blood run hot and fast in a need to kill . . . to maim . . . to hurt . . . really hurt . . . but then to kill the man who had lifted his hand to this fragile girl, to the delicacy, the sweet vulnerability of this young woman whom Jamie Hutchinson loved and lived to die for. He would die for her if he could find the bastard who had struck her, die for her and bloody swing for him, whoever he was and if it was the last thing he did he would find him.

He knelt at her knee for over an hour, pushing aside the reluctant dog in order to be closer to her, slowly, slowly beating down the hating rage inside him, bringing it under control so that he might be as she needed him to be when she awoke. Chloe had her feet tucked up under the skirt of her gown and he was able to lean gently on the arms of the chair, his face no more than six inches from hers as he studied her. The hot rage had gone, leaving what was worse, a cold thirst for revenge but at that moment, until she awoke, he was content to kneel on the hard stone and drown himself in the beauty of his sleeping love. To protect her sleep which was nature's way of curing, and which Chloe had entrusted with him, to defend her innocent belief that no harm could come to her while she was in his care. In all the times she had been up to Valley Bottom Farm, no more than half a dozen, he supposed, if that, there had been no reawakening of the strange feelings which had linked them on that first occasion. She had been friendly, glad to be of help, eager to be doing what she was so good at, sewing something to make his home more comfortable, even making, as she had promised, a cosy blanket bed for the dog. She had drunk his tea, chatted shyly with his mother, had a word or two to say to Tommy who had been struck unusually dumb by her exquisitely tinted loveliness, and listened attentively while he himself told her of his plans for the future. She never spoke of the Andrews family, who, he heard from his mother, treated her shabbily, though was it any wonder after the suffering Chloe's own mother had caused Jack and Sara Andrews? She would not say what form that took since it was not her tale to tell, she said, but it must have been devastating to make Sara so bitter against her sister's daughter.

She began to stir, making small mewing sounds in the back of her throat, stretching a little, then catching her breath as she moved her neck too hastily. Her eyes opened, at least one did, and as he eased back a little so as not to alarm her by his closeness, smiling his slightly lopsided, good-humoured smile, she opened her mouth on a wide yawn.

"Ouch." She winced, lifting a hand to her cheek, looking into his face as though there was nothing untoward in waking in Jamie Hutchinson's kitchen with Jamie Hutchinson at her feet.

He grimaced in sympathy. "It would be daft to ask does it hurt, wouldn't it?"

"Yes, it would, and yes it hurts but I imagine it looks worse than it feels." She did her best to smile and his heart lurched.

"That's good," he managed to answer.

"You think so? I must admit to a great reluctance to look in a mirror."

"Wise, I think, at least for a day or two. In the meanwhile no one need see you if you don't want it. Only me, and I'm quite . . . I don't count seeing that— " He stopped abruptly. He felt the hot blood rush to his face in embarrassment. Him, a grown man blushing and awkward and yet her eyes . . . oh bloody hell . . . her one good eye was clear and steady, as though she had already acknowledged and accepted the strangeness of their situation.

"What are you trying to say, Jamie?" She had become very still, holding her breath almost, for there was no doubt that this moment, this moment of pain and awkwardness and bewilderment at what was taking place, was very important. She was no longer alarmed for she had no fear of this enormous man who gave her shelter when she needed refuge from the storms and tempests of the Andrews family. Who gave her his company when her heart was weary with loneliness. Who gave her laughter when she was despondent. She had found tranquillity in this small farmhouse, a certain peace and content, a place of serenity away from the alarums and excursions of Cloudberry End. She had come to like Mrs Jenkins, despite knowing Jamie's mother was suspicious of her and her motives in coming here, and young Tommy, so full of boyish, boisterous good humour, made her feel as though she were no older than him. Though she had come up to the farm no more than half a dozen times in the last few weeks – timing it when she knew Katy was at her grandmother's – she was strangely at ease here.

"What am I trying to say?" he repeated, his voice low and sweet and deep as only a lover's voice can be. "I think it might be that I love you, Chloe Taylor. That I have loved you from that moment at Crossclough Station when I saw your face at the window of the carriage taking you to Cloudberry End. I love you, my dove, and I want you to feel the same way about me, if you could. That is what I am trying to say."

He bent his head as though afraid her answer might be too much for him and his wide shoulders trembled briefly, then he looked up at her. He lifted a hand and almost dreamily ran a tender finger down the curve of her chin. "I love you, Chloe, and I want nothing more than to serve you but if you could . . . feel just a little of what I feel for you I would be eternally grateful." He smiled. "My life is yours, sweet Chloe. I am yours. Yes, that is what I'm trying to say and though I am sorry about your face, the slight . . . rearrangement does not offend me. There, will that do for now?"

"Oh, Jamie . . . Jamie . . ." She smiled back at him a smile of lilting sweetness, though it turned into a moue of pain which had her gasping. "I don't know what to say to you."

"I love you, Jamie, would do admirably." He grinned but there was a depth of seriousness in his eyes.

She hesitated. There was no one she trusted or liked or admired or respected more than this big, quiet, dependable man but did she love him? She knew nothing of love in its romantic form. Her mother and father had not shown love, to each other, or to her, and what she would have described as the excess of passion her aunt and uncle shared seemed too extreme, too frantic to be quite real. She was aware that Katy Andrews was devoted to Jamie, indeed she probably loved him in her young and ardent way. Chloe would like to be in love with him, for what would be more glorious than to leave Cloudberry End and its unwelcoming occupants for good and have a home, a home of her own? To depend on no one, not her Aunt Sara and Uncle Jack, not her papa and stepmama, and put herself in the strong, protective, loving hands of this man in whose face, as she hesitated, was dying the hope of his love.

It took no longer than thirty seconds to decide the course of her future but, just to make sure, to make sure she could not go back she must begin it at once.

She leaned forward with perfect trust and placed one small hand on the flat plane of his brown cheek.

"I do love you, Jamie," she said, meaning it, though not in the way he wanted her to mean it and as she said it she swore he would never know the difference.

She watched his blue eyes come brilliantly alive and the wide mouth open and stretch in a smile of triumph. The colour surged again beneath his skin so great was his emotion and he seemed incapable of speech. Turning his mouth into the palm of her hand he kissed it reverently and she knew with a certainty she wondered about, since she was no more than an innocent girl, that this man idolised her, idealised her and it was going to be difficult arranging matters without distressing or offending him. Marriage he would need. Marriage he would have, and naturally so would she, but marriages took time to arrange and she wanted no time in which to think, to have people think for her, to be argued at, screamed at – by Katy, there was no doubt of that – to be the subject of gossip which might, or might not, rage about Cloudberry End. In fact, she never wanted to see Cloudberry End again.

Lifting her gently to her feet Jamie stood her on the colourful mat and her cloak which had been wrapped about her fell to the ground. Holding her by both arms above the elbow he bent his head and placed his mouth on hers in her first kiss, then, with the tenderness of a mother, moved his lips to her ravaged cheek and eye, gently, so lightly she could barely feel it.

"Jesus God, if you knew how much I love you," he breathed. She could feel his heart pound beneath her cheek as he pressed her tenderly into his arms and his body quivered with his effort to hold himself back from her. In his eyes she was an innocent, inexperienced girl who, one day, or night, she supposed, he would gently, slowly teach the ways of physical love. The act which would unite them, the technicalities of which she was only vaguely aware, but that would not do. It must be now, tonight, not as was usually the case the seduction of an ignorant girl, though she was that, but of this man who loved her with the devotion and respect a man shows to the woman he truly loves. How to begin? How? What must she do to get him to . . . to make love to her?

Afterwards she was to realise that two healthy, normal young bodies have no need of thought, or planning, or indeed of anything but where they can lay themselves down together in the act of love. Male and female, a certain interest and attraction, desire she supposed it was called and before her untried body and mind could jib at it, perhaps become awkward with shyness, she was in his arms, her toes barely touching the ground, her arms twined about his neck in a way that amazed her. His mouth was firm and warm, sweet and soft at the same time, parting her lips, his tongue hesitating enquiringly as it caressed the soft, moist inner flesh of her opening mouth. He moved his head from side to side, and so did she, she found, his lips taking hers, first the top then the bottom, then letting them travel along her jawline and down her throat to the breathlessly leaping pulse at its base.

She found it . . . not unpleasing! Her body had a sudden need to stretch and her back to arch and she seemed inclined to purr as a cat will as it lies in the warmth from a fire, she didn't know why. Greatly daring she began to nuzzle with her mouth beneath his chin, just where a wisp of silky hair protruded from the neck of his open shirt. His hand moved to her throat, holding her as his mouth rose again to hers and it was then that she became aware of the changes in his body. Hers was nailed against his and as, instinctively, she pressed it even closer, he began to breathe hoarsely and for a moment she felt fear. This was how Chris Andrews had been when . . . when . . . but this was not Chris Andrews, this was Jamie who must become, if not in name then in deed, her husband tonight.

She could sense him drawing away as though he were making a great effort to control himself, the fierceness of his need giving him what seemed to be a great deal of pain.

"Chloe," he almost snarled, kissing her, hurting her with it, he knew, savouring the satin smoothness of the skin at her throat with his open mouth. Her body was enclosed by the length of his, the trembling of his limbs mingling with hers.

He stood away for a brief second, his eyes glazed and

helpless then swayed back again, his hands going to the buttons of her bodice, tearing them apart, pulling the soft cotton fabric away to reveal the creamy white smoothness of her shoulders.

"Oh God, Chloe, stop me," he whispered hoarsely. "I shouldn't be doing this . . . stop me . . . please . . . stop me."

But it was too late for anything which might be called restraint. Her breasts broke free of their covering, her small, almond-tinted nipples hard, like the ripe berries in the hedgerows in the valley and his mouth went to them eagerly, taking each one in turn between his lips, his tongue circling them, licking them with delight before allowing his hands their turn. They were big and brown, Jamie Hutchinson's hands, hard with the calloused palms of a seaman, or a farmer, but they were gentle with love and so were his eyes as he picked her up and carried her towards the stairs.

The one bedroom was in the sort of half gloom which heralds the coming of a thunderstorm but the bed and its plain, exquisitely sewn linen gleamed whitely beneath the two slopes of the roof. Its brass head and foot were bright with polish and Matty's elbow grease. Folded at its foot was the glowing bed quilt just as though in preparation for the lovers. There was a plain dresser and a wardrobe. Nothing of value but it was clean and immaculately tidy, everything stowed away as Jamie had been used to below decks.

She hung her head shyly when he began to undress her, hiding herself in her silken curtain of hair, uncertain, waiting hesitantly for him to tell her what to do and yet willing, not holding back or recoiling when his hands and mouth began softly but surely to explore her trembling body. She held his head to her naked breast, her own hands in his thick hair and then moving to smooth the long rippling muscles of his back since she meant to do this thing well, to give him no cause for complaint, to please him. She was not offended by him, by his weight and size and dark masculinity nor by his growing and strange male excitement. Her body found his not unwelcome and when, at last, his pierced and entered hers, though it was painful she did not cry out.

Later, when he was calm and she almost asleep in what she found to be his comforting arms, he turned her so that her back was pressed close to his chest. He cupped her breasts with marvelling hands and sighed, his breath moving in her tumbled hair.

"So, my dove," he murmured wryly, "this is to be our wedding night, is it?" pretending resignation but glorying in his mastery of her.

"So it seems, Jamie. Do you mind?"

"I'll not have to for it's done. You'll sleep in my bed tonight and every night of your life, my darling. You belong to me now and God help any man who tries to take you from me for I'll kill him."

They slept through the thunderstorm in one another's arms. He would find out who had beaten her tomorrow.

It was Ivy who discovered her bed had not been slept in and for an hour there was chaos since no one could imagine where she might have got to.

"It's not as if she's any friends, Mrs Tiplady," Ivy said plaintively, her heart going out to the poor young lady who had done her best to fit into this family, indeed to find some niche in their lives which she could call her own. "'Appen she's gone back to 'er pa in Liverpool," for of course by now all the servants were aware of the circumstances of their mistress's young niece.

"Happen she has, Ivy, but that doesn't mean we shouldn't look for her here. Anyway, no doubt Mr Andrews has sent a telegram to Miss Chloe's pa by now so we'll soon know. Eeh, this is a bad do and no mistake. See, you, Tommy Jenkins . . ." turning on the coachman's lad who for some reason was hanging about the kitchen doorway. "You'd best be occupied looking for Miss Chloe instead of dithering on my doorstep. Go and find Angus and he'll tell you what to do. Him and Billy are to go up to Tintwistle Knarr since Saul Gibbon says he's seen her up there a time or two. Now then, Lottie, fetch me that saddle of lamb from the larder and you'd best start on the veg, Mabel. What? Who?"

She turned irritably to where Mabel, who was her kitchen maid, pointed her finger at Tommy Jenkins who still remained glued to the doorstep.

"I thought I told you to report to Angus, my lad, and I'd be obliged . . . what? A note. Who for? The master? Well, why didn't you say so? Come in, come in and mind them feet on my clean floor."

All about the kitchen work came to a complete standstill as eager young women, excited as those who have nothing in their lives but drab routine often are, crowded about young Tommy Jenkins, eyeing the piece of folded paper he held in his hand. But it was not just the paper which captured their attention but Tommy's air of positively bursting with something which threatened, if it was not let out soon, to explode.

"I'm ter put it in master's hands an' no one else's, Mrs Tiplady," he said politely, his own importance almost too much for his boyish composure, which was none too steady at the best of times. "That's what I were told ter do an' if Jamie were ter hear that— "

He stopped speaking abruptly and the maids exchanged

bewildered glances for what had Jamie Hutchinson to do with all this? They were not awfully sure what they meant by all this, nor why this young lad's older brother . . . well, half-brother, should be involved but it was all very intriguing. Happen he'd found her wandering on the moor, poor little mite, and taken her in, but the note would reveal the truth and they could hardly wait to see what it might be. They nudged one another, whispering and lifting enquiring eyebrows, but even in the midst of this crisis Mrs Tiplady was not about to allow any slacking in the strict regime of her kitchen. Mrs Tiplady was not only cook here, but housekeeper and Mrs Andrews trusted her to keep these twittering housemaids and kitchenmaids employed as they should be and not wasting their time and Mr Andrews's good money in idleness.

She clapped her hands and at once, like a flock of starlings disturbed from a tree, they darted away to their respective tasks, leaving Tommy in the sole charge of Mrs Tiplady.

"Give me the note, lad," she said kindly. "I'll see the master gets it." But Tommy, just as though he expected her to snatch it from his hand, put it behind his back, his brother's words still echoing in his astonished head. He had taken it in, of course he had, for their Jamie's hard grip on his shoulders, which had made him wince, had forced him to, despite the incredible sight of Miss Chloe who was curled up wrapped in nothing but a quilt, from what Tommy could see, in his brother's fireside chair. And as for her face, well, if Jamie had done that to her he wanted a good thrashing and no doubt Mr Andrews would see to it when the time came. Not that Tommy could imagine his big, good-natured brother bashing a woman in the face, nor anybody's face for that matter, since he was the gentlest, most even-tempered man Tommy had ever known. Go out of his way to mend the broken wing of a bird, he would, or fetch home a lamb in need of shelter, but somebody had landed her one, which was another puzzle in the quite mystifying events which were taking place at Valley Bottom Farm.

"Nay, Mrs Tiplady, I can't," he protested. "I'm ter give it ter't master an' no one else." Tommy set his jaw at its most truculent angle, ready, it seemed to her, to dart away if she so much as put a hand out to him.

She tutted irritably. "Very well then. I'll take you through myself but make sure them boots are clean. Mrs Andrews is very particular about her carpets and Dilly doesn't want to have to brush them again, do you, Dilly?"

Dilly shook her head dumbly, her eyes popping, her mouth agape.

They were all in the breakfast room, Mrs Andrews and her daughter eating a late breakfast as was their custom, Mr Andrews stalking round and round the table in what looked to Mrs Tiplady to be a state of considerable annoyance, though there was an anxious frown dipping his eyebrows. Master Chris, who lounged against the window frame gazing out over the rolling lawns and crowded flowerbeds, had returned from the mill with his father when his mother's rather frantic note regarding her niece's disappearance had been delivered there by Dicken, mounted on Master Richard's chestnut bay. Mrs Tiplady couldn't quite see why he was needed since he had made no effort to offer his services in the search for his cousin, but then any excuse was better than none to the master's son to get out of doing any work.

"Yes, Mrs Tiplady?" the master enquired, pausing for a moment in his pacing, eyeing Tommy Jenkins and his hobnailed boots to which wisps of what looked like cow-dung still clung with some amazement.

"The lad has a note, sir, which he won't part with, only to you." She pushed Tommy forward unceremoniously, still somewhat incensed by his refusal to trust her in the delivery of the message.

"A note! Who from?"

"Nay, sir, he wouldn't let me see it, but happen . . ." She left the sentence unfinished, for all their thoughts were centred on the missing girl and what else could it be about despite what seemed to be some involvement on the part of Jamie Hutchinson?

You could have heard a feather drop, Mrs Tiplady thought, so quiet did they all go and from his favourite position before the small fire, Katy Andrews's dog, who had no business being there in Mrs Tiplady's opinion, raised an enquiring head.

He read it through twice, the master, without a word, without lifting his head, without looking at his wife, absorbed, or was it stunned, Mrs Tiplady was to wonder, by its contents.

"Jack?" Mrs Andrews quavered, her face as white as the napkin she held to her lips.

"Father, is it from Chloe?" his daughter asked, her young voice trembling with what seemed a genuine concern to Mrs Tiplady, while by the window young Master Chris said nothing at all.

"Jack?" Mrs Andrew repeated. "Please, Jack . . ."

Mr Andrews sighed heavily, his hand holding the crumpled sheet of paper falling to his side.

"Aye . . . oh aye, lass . . . she's safe enough."

"Oh, thank God, Jack."

"Hang on . . . hang on."

"What is it, Jack?"

"Well, I don't reckon tha'll like it over much when I tell thi'," reverting to the broad vowels of his youth in his distress.

"It seems she's spent the night wi' Jamie Hutchinson. She's . . . she's his . . . his wife, he ses. Bloody hell, tha' knows what that means, don't tha', my lass? They mean to make it legal as soon as— "

Katherine Andrews stood up violently, so violently her chair flew backwards halfway across the room, and throwing back her head began to howl like a badly wounded animal.

10

It was a bad, bad time and how they managed to get through it was a wonder to them all, Mrs Tiplady was often to say sadly to Freda, the head parlourmaid. Well, she had to talk to someone, hadn't she, and Freda was a decent, sensible woman of more than thirty years, fifteen of them spent in the service of the Andrews family.

They'd known nothing like it before, even in this household where the children had been allowed a freedom no member of their generation and class was accustomed to. Miss Katy had been a law unto herself since she was a little thing, going where she pleased and when checked bellowing her outrage from the cellars to the rooftops. The boys not quite so bad, particularly the two older ones, though Master Chris caused almost as many ructions as Miss Katy, even if it was Mr Andrews who made the most noise about them.

But they had been . . . well, it sounded daft and she was sure Freda would understand, they had been wholesome disagreements with no badness in them. Hot and hasty but soon over. Tantrums really, the kind children have, if it was not out of place to call Mr Andrews childish. They all wanted their own way, every member of the family, that was the trouble, and with the exception of Mrs Andrews, fought one another to get it. It seemed Miss Katy had had plans for herself and that big lad of Matty Jenkins, from the way she carried on. In front of Tommy Jenkins, too, but they had turned to ashes on her tongue and she would never recover from it, she shrieked in her first dementia.

Mrs Tiplady, frozen for several long, appalled seconds, as they all were, by Miss Katy's heart-rending cries, by her absolute determination to hurt herself badly as she threw herself from wall to wall, had hurried Tommy from the room so fast the pair of them had almost fallen headlong over the damned dog which whined at the door to get out. To safety and sanity, she supposed, and who could blame the poor beast? Young Tommy was as white as the driven snow and she herself was shaking badly, but Mrs Tiplady had been in service for a good many years and had survived many crises and she was not about to allow this one to interrupt the smoothly running machinery of her kitchen.

The maidservants, having heard the commotion from the breakfast room, were milling about the room as she had fully expected them to be, except Freda who had more sense, and they turned as one as she hurried Tommy towards the kitchen door.

"Go home to your mother, lad, and say nothing. D'you understand? Not to anyone. Now I'm trusting you, Tommy Jenkins, to act like a man. They'll know soon enough, your ma and pa but it's up to the family to say when. Can I . . .?"

"I'll say nowt, Mrs Tiplady, 'onest ter God," but she could see the excitement in his eyes and the flush of anticipation in his face and, since he was only a boy of fourteen she was not awfully sure he would keep his promise. After all, it concerned his family just as much as the Andrews.

She sighed deeply. "Right then, off you go, and as for you lot," turning to her handmaidens as Tommy ran off across the back yard, "who gave you permission to stand about with your mouths hanging open? Mabel, have you done them veg? And what happened to the saddle of lamb I told you to fetch from the larder half an hour ago, Lottie Earnshaw?"

"But Mrs Tiplady, them screams . . . is someone 'urt? Miss Chloe?"

"Whether they are or whether they're not is none of your business, Ivy. As I told Tommy, when the master sees fit to let you in on his private affairs, then you'll know and until then you've a job to do so I suggest you go and do it. I'll say this," relenting a fraction for they had all been worried sick about Miss Chloe, "the mistress's niece is safe and sound. Now then, Dilly, I reckon you'll have to go over this floor again, don't you? That lad's boots look as if they've traipsed through a farmyard and he's left a trail from here to the breakfast room so you'd best get your bucket out again. Freda, you come with me and Janet, make a fresh pot of tea and bring it to my room and then you can make a start on— "

It was not vouchsafed to Janet what she was to make a start on, for cutting off Mrs Tiplady in mid-sentence, the door, which led from the hallway to the kitchen and which she herself had just come through, was flung open with such violence Dilly dropped the bucket she had picked up. They all turned, Mrs Tiplady included, their faces filled with dread, the expression on them sharing the identical thought: What now?

When they saw the apparition in the doorway, every last one of them, even Mrs Tiplady, fell back from it in horrified silence.

Katherine Andrews's eyes recognised them for they were part of her everyday life and had been, some of them, since she was a child but they meant nothing to her now. She didn't acknowledge them just as she didn't acknowledge the table and chairs, the pots and pans or any part of the familiar room. She had been in and out of it since she had learned to walk, sitting on Mrs Tiplady's footstool before the fire, eating Mrs Tiplady's delicious biscuits, quite at home there since, as was her way, Katy Andrews could see no reason why she should not go where she wished to go.

Now she was to make her way to where she didn't wish to go at all but where she must. She had no coherent thought in her head, nothing that made sense or was reasonable, just a deep, primeval instinct which drove her on to what her breaking heart must know for itself. Her brain was numbed, empty really, and her body suspended in some merciful oblivion which, she knew quite definitely, would not last long. But while it did she was driven to this journey she must take.

She was dressed in her simple day dress, a separate skirt and bodice of jaconet, a fine cotton material in a colour somewhere between pale blue and green, with a sash of the same colour. The skirt had what was known as an apron front but as she was not yet seventeen her mother had forbidden her, and her dressmaker, the overskirt and bustle which were the fashion. Her shoes were high-heeled, dyed to match her gown, shaped like slippers with long uppers.

A very elegant and lovely young woman but somehow it was all tossed about, dishevelled, creased, even torn in places, the sash hanging loose, several buttons come undone. Her hair, though it was short by the day's standards, was hanging about her face in some curious way and from beneath it her eyes stared, blank and unfocused, the lovely, rich golden amber to which they were all accustomed turned to the colour of the brown mud which edged the reservoir when the water was low.

She stood for a moment or two in the doorway and from behind her her father's voice called out to her but she appeared not to hear him as she blundered across the kitchen towards the back door, banging her hip savagely against the solid table in its centre as she went.

"Miss . . . Miss Katy," Mrs Tiplady quavered, while all about her the maidservants stood rigidly in the position of whatever it was they had been doing before Miss Katherine crashed into their domain. Dilly held her scrubbing brush in a hand gone cold and numb and Lottie clutched the saddle of lamb to her bosom as though it were the only sane thing in a world gone mad, while in the chimney corner where she had been about to reach for the kettle for Mrs Tiplady's tea, Janet began to weep silently since she could not bear to witness the pain which was written on Miss Katy's face, she blubbered later.

Katherine moved through them with the speed and force of a charging bull, opening the yard door and flinging it back on its hinges against the wall. Through it they watched as she rushed headlong across the yard where she disappeared through the arch which led to the stables.

Jimmy was grooming Master Richard's horse, a bay mare called Jenny which he had just exercised in the big paddock at the back of the stables. When he had finished he would do the same for Hal who was Master David's chestnut. Neither animal was ridden as much as Jimmy would have liked but Mr Andrews wouldn't dream of getting rid of them, he had told the groom. When his sons came home they would need a decent mount and so the pair of them, groomed and glossy with good health and loving care, if a bit overweight, were quartered in the stables and paddock, eating their pampered heads off.

Dicken was mucking out, sweeping the malodorous contents of the loose boxes into the yard, and sitting on a bench against the stable wall, a pipe in his mouth and a tangle of harness in his hands, was the third groom, a wiry, bandy-legged little man called Noah. Jamie Hutchinson's father was nowhere to be seen.

They all three turned to stare at Katherine in much the same way the maids had, mouths open, eyes wide, for though they were used to Miss Katy's tendency to pop up, however inconvenient, at any old time of the day, demanding her mare, Storm, be saddled, she wasn't dressed for riding today. In fact she looked bloody queer, Dicken was to remark later to Janet, with whom he was "walking out" and it was perhaps the strangeness of her attire and manner, her complete oblivion to any of them, just as though the yard were empty, that allowed her to stride into the stable, release the sorrel from where she tossed her head in her stall and lead her out into the yard without a word from any of them. If it had not been for Noah's pipe which fell from his slack lips into his lap, scattering hot ashes on his "vitals" they might have been frozen to paralysis for the next hour, Dicken told Janet, they were all so bloody mazed, though of course Mr Andrews would have fetched them out of it soon enough!

There was a mounting block in the yard. She led the sorrel to it then, bunching her full skirts about her waist, unconscious of the men who stared in wonder at her frilly drawers, leaped astride the mare's back, thrust her hands deep in her mane, dug her dainty heels into her side and flew out of the yard like a bird on the wing just as her father staggered into it.

"Katherine . . ." he bellowed, his face like paper, his brown eyes flat and muddy, so great was his fear for his girl. "Katy. Oh, dear God, that bloody woman's come back from't grave to haunt us."

The bewildered men had not the slightest notion who he was talking about, continuing to stare, first at the open gate out on to the drive through which Miss Katy had disappeared, then at the frantic man who was her father.

"Jimmy, get up on that animal and follow her . . . bring her back. Be quick, man, for Christ's sake. No, don't bother with a bloody saddle, you fool. If my lass can ride bareback then so can thee. Hurry, man . . . hurry. You, Dicken, saddle me a horse an' one for thissen an' we'll follow."

She went by the most direct route through her father's wood and out on to the pasture beyond. There was a gate leading to a field in which cattle stood and which she usually stopped to open and close behind her, since her father objected to Jamie's small dairy herd, which for the past month had grazed there, wandering willy nilly on to his property. It was all his property, of course, including Valley Bottom Farm but it was leased to Jamie who was now her father's tenant.

Ignoring the gate, for she had not the time to be concerned with it, she set the sorrel at the stone wall which ran round the field, clinging with her strong hands and legs to the little mare's back. The animal took it bravely though her eyes rolled frantically as her hooves dislodged one of the top cam stones. The cattle scattered, flowing towards the edge of the field, ungainly in their alarm and Archie Bagshaw, the postman, who was riding placidly along the valley road, twisted about in his saddle so vigorously to see what all the commotion was about he damn near fell off his horse. He was on his second delivery of the day and with two more to go he couldn't afford an accident, could he?

It was a soft, late summer day. The thunderstorm of the night before had washed the skies and tossed away the clouds, leaving the sun to shine where it would, gentle and warm and benign. On any other day Katy would have idled along, drinking in the wine-like air, dreaming her dreams, admiring the wild spread of flowers in the long meadow grasses, and the heady lilt of the songs the skylarks poured out. It was not often the high peaks were favoured with such benevolence. The sound of water from above was a soft background to the loveliness of it all but Katherine Andrews neither saw nor heard any of it.

Jamie had not left Chloe's side since the moment he had carried her through the door the day before, like a bride, he had whispered to her later in the warm, comforting depths of what was now to be considered their marriage bed. She had awoken, dreadfully alarmed for the space of ten seconds, with his arms still about her, the weight of him tipping the bed so that her body had no choice but to lie directly against his. He was awake in the growing half light which the cock in the yard was declaring to be time to get up and when she opened her eyes his serious face was straining towards her.

"Have you any idea how much I love you?" was the first thing he said to her.

"I . . . think so," she murmured hesitantly.

"Are . . . are you still of the same mind, lass, because if you're not you are bound by . . ."

"What do you mean?"

"I mean that if you have . . . are having second thoughts I'll not hold you to . . . to anything. I'm glad what happened to us happened but I'm afraid I might have stampeded you into it."

She must have made some sound of distress for at once he turned her to him and, lifting himself on one elbow, looked down into her face.

"What have I said?" He smoothed her hair back from her brow, marvelling on how beautiful she was, even with half her face swollen and bruised.

"I'm . . . I wasn't . . . stampeded, Jamie. I wanted to." She ducked her head shyly and he was enchanted. "I was happy at what happened but if you . . ."

"Dear sweet Christ, no," he almost shouted, and at once she relaxed and smiled, for only she knew what had really taken place. She regretted nothing and her smile said so and when, gently, tentatively, as though she were some breakable thing which should he damage it would be beyond repair, he kissed her moist, rosy lips and cupped her breasts with big, tender hands, she responded willingly, wanting nothing more than to please this man who loved her.

They made love again, easier this time since she knew what to expect, her heart flowing with gratitude towards him, for she sensed he was holding back what could be a stronger passion than she could cope with just yet. He shuddered and gasped at the end of it and she held him more confidently, glad that he seemed to get what she supposed men wanted from a woman. Her body accommodated his quite readily and painlessly despite the enormous difference in their weight and size, and when, later, he brought them tea on a dainty tray, his strong and beautiful male body completely naked, she allowed her eyes to study him for a matter of thirty seconds and, finding nothing in his masculinity to repel or frighten her, was glad when he slid back into bed beside her and, holding her close to him as though he could not bear to have her even an inch from his side, began to talk to her of his life at sea. He made her laugh and he made her gasp in wonder at some of the things he had done and seen and when, suddenly, he clapped his hand to his head and said, "Oh, my God, the bloody cows," she was sorry when he leaped out of bed and into his clothes.

"Get up when you're ready, lass," he said, leaning over to kiss her. When she did, wrapping herself daringly in the quilt she herself had made, and ventured down the narrow, crooked stairs, Tommy had been there, his face thunderstruck. A note was to be delivered to Cloudberry

End and put into Mr Andrews's hand, Jamie had told him as Chloe curled herself in the big chair, and no one else's, and now, here was the result of it in the form of Katherine Andrews herself.

They heard her coming, her mare's hooves striking sparks off the newly restored cobbles on the track and though they had expected something they had not specifically imagined it would be Katy herself.

Jamie opened the door, placing himself in the frame of it, filling it, his body ready to protect Chloe from what promised to be a degree of violence. He was alarmed by Katy's appearance, which seemed to convey an ordeal through which she had gone and which she could barely manage. Her face was the colour of the ash in a dead fire and her eyes, for that moment, were blank and lifeless, just as though the flame of Katy Andrews which had burned so brilliantly, so jubilantly, so joyfully, had been snuffed out. Her gown was torn and she wore only one shoe which, like the hem of her skirt and her bare, stockinged foot, was filthy with cow muck, for Jamie's farmyard was not in the immaculate condition of her father's stable yard. The cows had been brought up and milked, then turned loose again and their excreta was thick and stinking in the churned-up ground. He should have cleared it himself, Jamie had time to think, but the truth was he was so enchanted with his new love he could not find the strength of mind to tear himself away from her.

Katy's hair was wild and tangled and from beneath it her eyes peered like an animal's from its den. When he glanced over her shoulder he was not surprised to see she had ridden bareback.

"Katy . . . ?" he said, keeping his hand on the latch, beginning to be afraid now, not just for Chloe who, he imagined, could possibly receive another black eye to match the one she already had if Katy reached her, but for this silent, empty young girl who stared at him so senselessly, on whose face was an expression of such crazed and terrible pain he was appalled. There would be more than black eyes exchanged this day, he told himself, for this was no temper tantrum thrown by a young girl who had been crossed in love, calf love, he had always thought it, but some deep and agonising emotion which might destroy the girl who suffered it, and anyone in her path who she thought had caused it. An explosive nature such as Katy's which she had never learned to control was a dangerous thing to encounter and he must keep it from inflicting damage to the woman he loved.

But Chloe Taylor, despite her fragile appearance, the wisp of swansdown look which implied she might blow away on any stray breeze, was deceptively strong and was no coward. All her life she had been protected from the outside world by her well-bred, devout, church-going mother, but the last year had taught her that it didn't matter whether you believed in God or not, followed the teachings of the Church, read and lived by your Bible, the blows came just the same and there was only one way to deal with them when they knocked you to your knees. Get up and get on! Face them and if you couldn't do that, then bend a little which prevented you from breaking. Courage, she had learned, came hard and though she had done wrong last night, and this morning, a wrong her mama would condemn her for, it had not felt wrong. Jamie had done what he had done to her in love and she had responded in the same way and if her cousin Katy had come to castigate her, Chloe could manage a bit of castigating herself.

When she opened the door wide and peered round the

large frame of Jamie she was astounded by the sight of the swaying, what seemed the almost insensible figure of her cousin on the path. She would barely have recognised her had it not been for the colour of her tangled hair and the blown horse who stood, head hanging, beyond the mended gate. It was Storm all right, and it was Katy all right, but . . . Oh, dear merciful heaven, what had happened to her? How had she come to be in this pitiable condition, this state of near collapse, of suffering so great it was not to be borne? She was in pain so deep it was ready to destroy her, ready to drain her life's blood away, her eyes moving slowly, like that of a wounded and downed beast, from one tormentor to the other.

Herself and Jamie! Sweet Jesus!

"Jamie, bring her in," she murmured without hesitation, doing her best to dodge under his arm to get to the girl from whom, she realised fully now, Chloe had taken the only man Katy had ever wanted. Jamie Hutchinson. It was too late now, of course, for ignorant as she was she was fully aware that she could already carry Jamie's child in her womb. They could not go back, none of them, even had she and Jamie wanted to, despite what he had said this morning, but her compassion for her cousin, who had treated Chloe with nothing warmer than casual indifference, was immense. She must be brought inside, put in a cosy chair by the chimney corner, given tea, or perhaps brandy if Jamie had any, comforted, if such a thing could be managed, until her father came to get her. She could hardly be left to weave about in such a mindless fashion. So deep in shock her mind was gone.

But Jamie knew Katy Andrews better than did Chloe and when, with a shriek which lifted a flock of starlings from the trees at the back of the house and sent her mare skidding and flying back down the track, she launched herself at her cousin he was ready for her. She had nothing but her bare fists, her feet, her teeth, her fingernails to tear him to pieces with, then do the same to Chloe if she could reach her, but her despair gave her a strength which was not far short of his own.

"You bitch . . . you filthy whore . . . he was mine . . . mine . . . all my life, since I was a child I've loved him and . . . yes . . . left alone . . . waiting . . . he would have loved me. He would have seen me . . . Oh, God, I should have done what you did, taken my clothes off for him . . . anything . . . but I didn't know . . . you see, I thought you were nothing . . . I was blind . . . God damn you to hell, you bitch . . . your mother did something . . . to mine for which she never forgave her . . . and now . . . now you've done the same to me. Let me get at her . . . Jamie . . . please . . . I'll kill you both, I swear I'll kill you both . . . she's taken you from me, Jamie . . . Oh, Jesus, Jesus, what am I to do with the rest of my life? . . . let me go, dammit, let me go . . . let me hurt her, Jamie . . . I beg you . . . don't do this . . ." and all the while she shrieked and howled her pain and loss and devastation she struggled in the straining arms of the man she loved, not to claim his kisses as she had yearned to do, but to tear out his eyes, rake his cheeks with her nails, damage him, particularly his manhood, for if she couldn't have it then Chloe Taylor certainly wouldn't.

She drew blood as her teeth sank into the fleshy part of his hand between his thumb and forefinger and his left cheek had four bleeding tracks down it where she had run her nails. When she was free she would start on Chloe, her maddened eyes told her.

Chloe, appalled, her one good eye enormous and glittering in her bruised face, backed away from the scene of horror which was being played out on the doorstep. The young dog who had come to the door in welcome at the sound of the visitor was cowering on the blanket bed Chloe had made him and with a moan of anguish she sank down beside him, putting her head down to his.

"It will be all right, Captain, it really will," she kept repeating as though it was his fear she was calming and still, from beyond the door which Jamie had managed to close when she stepped back from it, the sounds of the struggle, the shrieks of demented rage and pain and desolation continued. She could hear Jamie's voice as he did his best to calm her cousin, soft, tender, even, for he was aware that it was because of him Katy was suffering. He had done nothing, ever, to encourage her belief that one day he would come to love her, as a man loves his woman, but all the same he felt guilty. She was a child, sixteen, a child who had suffered no pain, no unhappiness in her carefree life, not even the normal restrictions put on a girl of her class. She had got what she wanted, always, from the world she lived in and she had expected to get him and now, when she found she couldn't, she was ready to inflict any injury she could on those who had prevented it.

He couldn't calm her. Without physically hurting her he couldn't restrain her, so he did what he had to, which he had done before with recalcitrant, drunken seamen and when she fell, senseless as a stone, he caught her to him, ready to weep for her.

"Open the door, Chloe." His voice from outside was as cold as ice, just as though this was all her fault but Chloe rose to her feet and did as she was told.

"A blanket, if you please," he added and she ran to do his bidding as he laid the insensible figure of Katy Andrews on the settle, placing the quilt which was the first thing to come to hand across her cousin. There was a livid red mark on her chin, just to the right and below her jawline.

"You . . . you hit her?" She put her hand to her own bruised face and the eye which, this morning, would not open.

"I had to." His voice was stony.

"But surely there was no need?"

"There was every need. She would have injured you if I hadn't stopped her."

"Dear God, Jamie, was there not some other way to prevent her?"

"None. She was not herself." His voice was clipped and flat and Chloe was distraught, wondering where the loveliness, the sweetness, the promise of last night and this morning had gone. It could not be destroyed. Not so soon. It had been . . . lovely. He had been . . . she had liked his arms about her, his blue eyes shining into hers with the brilliance of his love. She had been ready to . . . what? Well, whatever it was she had been content with it, longing to see where it might lead. Was it now destroyed? Had her cousin killed it, as she had threatened to kill her?

"Jamie?" Her voice was soft and despairing and when he turned to her, his worry and distress plain on his strong face, she began to cry soundlessly.

At once everyone, including the unconscious girl on the settle, fled from his mind and he was across the kitchen in a stride, pulling her half-dressed figure into his arms. He cradled her against his chest, his cheek resting on her hair, his hands smoothing and stroking her bare shoulders, her back, her face.

"Don't, my dove, don't cry. I can't bear to see you cry. It breaks my heart . . . hush now . . . I love you and this doesn't change anything, you must know that. I was aware that she had . . . tender feelings for me but I thought, hoped, she would grow out of it."

"Oh, Jamie . . . poor Katy . . . poor little girl."

"I know, but you are my love, my heart, my very soul. Do you not know I would die for you? Your flower face is engraved in my mind so that if I were to go blind I would always see it." He was close to tears himself. "I love you . . . kiss me."

The girl on the settle opened her eyes and they were clear now, despite the blow to the chin she had suffered. It was as though Jamie's fist had jolted the mist of despair and fury from her head, leaving it steady and able to organise her thoughts for the first time since her father had read out the note from Jamie. She knew she would hurt savagely again, not physically of course, but in every other way and she must get away from here before it began, away from the man and woman who murmured in one another's arms on the other side of the room, away from this farm and from the family which was hers at Cloudberry End. She didn't know for how long. She didn't even know where she would go, but she must leave. She must leave at once. She didn't want to hurt anyone now. That was over and done with and the next step must be taken towards whatever was to happen to her.

Katherine Andrews, a child no longer, rose quietly and, with only the dog to watch her go, slipped from the kitchen. When she reached the gate she hesitated, bewildered that her sorrel was not there. She whistled softly, beginning to walk back down the track and with a whicker of greeting Storm appeared, nuzzling at her mistress's shoulder, recognising that the mad possession had gone.

Using the wall beside the track as a mounting block, Katherine climbed up on to the mare's back and, turning her round, steered her up the track towards Little Crowden Intake and the long climb towards the Black Hill.

11

Everything went in threes, they all knew that, Mrs Tiplady murmured to Freda, who had become her confidante, and as if the situation wasn't bad enough, what with Miss Chloe and her goings-on and then Miss Katy vanishing off the face of the earth, Mr Andrews's brother George had to go and have an apoplectic stroke right at the bar of the Old Swan, which was enough to put any man off his ale and no mistake, and all on the same day. Dead before he hit the sawdust on the floor, they said, and could the master, who was already out of his mind with worry over his girl, ever be the same again?

Three days now since Miss Katy was last seen at Valley Bottom Farm, or so Jamie Hutchinson reported, though how he dare show his face at Cloudberry End after what he and that hussy had got up to was beyond understanding. The mistress prostrate, shut up in her room with only the master and Matty Jenkins allowed to go near her, but then she and Matty had a lot in common, what with Matty's lad living in sin with that mim-faced niece of Mrs Andrews, who'd taken them all in, and the mistress's lass vanished as though the ground had swallowed her up.

Which, of course, was what they were all afraid of. Everyone in the district was aware of the vast areas of wet, boggy land which lay on the high wastes above the valley. The underlying stone cupped the water like a bowl and the peat held it, sponge-like, so that even in the driest summer there were still many places where the moor was a quaking morass, pitching and tilting and sucking the unwary into its depthless clutches. Whole waggons had been known to vanish without a trace so the ground would have no trouble absorbing a mere horse and rider, would it? The groom, Jimmy, muttered to Dicken, not in Mr Andrews's hearing, of course, that if Miss Katy's appearance that morning was anything to go by, the last thing she would have on her mind was where her mare might tread. Out of her bloody mind over something, though they were not privy to what it was. The events in the house were relayed to them third or fourth hand but it must have something to do with the other one, her cousin, who had gone missing the day before, apparently. What was up with them, he asked Dicken to tell him, as they set off on Hal and Zack to search the faint, stony tracks which criss-crossed Tintwistle Knarr. Couldn't the master keep his womenfolk in better order than this? If they were his girls they'd feel his belt on their bums, choose how. Not sit down for a bloody week, they wouldn't. Causing all this hullaballoo when he had work to see to in the stables, not to mention all the men whom Mr Andrews had mustered to search for his girl and must leave their jobs unattended.

And how would anyone know if she and the horse she rode had been sucked into a bog? the maids whispered to one another in the kitchen, their eyes wide and frightened at the very idea of it, the sheer horror of it. Without trace, without a footprint or hoofprint, with no one but the larks high above to hear her cries or see her . . . her . . . struggles. Dear Lord, it didn't bear thinking about, did it? Janet moaned and perhaps another cup of tea would be in order.

Every man in the district was drawn into the search,

those who knew Butterley Moss, Sliddens Moss, Tooley Shaw Moss, all barren, shaking wastes which lay about the steep, sloping land up to the Black Hill. To the south on the far side of the reservoirs, Birchen Bank Moss and Featherbed Moss, for who knew which direction she had taken? Last seen at Valley Bottom Farm, they were told, but she could have crossed the railway track in her demented state, the one Jimmy and Dicken described to the searchers in shocked whispers.

They were forced to stop as darkness fell, for no man could search in the dark, Saul Gibbon said patiently to Mr Andrews who was nearly off his head. Saul was a shepherd and he knew what he was talking about, for he was as familiar with these hills and moors as he was with his own snug kitchen. If anyone could find Katy Andrews, he could, and so, with the sergeant from the local constabulary, who after all had the authority, Saul was more or less in charge, sending men where he thought they should go, quartering the valley and the hills which rose out of it with almost military precision. It was no good thrashing about in the dark or there would be more than Jack Andrews's lass missing, and as soon as it was light they would begin again. Farmers and their sons, labourers, those who worked the quarries, any man who could be spared, and Saul would set his own two sheepdogs on the trail, those which searched for sheep when the deep winter snows fell. It was lucky it was mild out, and dry, he added comfortingly to the distraught father, and the lass would take no harm.

Chloe saw next to nothing of Jamie for three days, nor indeed of anyone. She had been left with the problem not only of how one made oneself a meal of any sort on the open fire, but on how to light the thing if it should go out, which it did. She knew how to boil an egg and make a pot of tea since she had done it for Mama when she fell ill, but not on an open fire. And then there was the question of a change of clothing, especially her underclothing. She had nothing but the clothes she had worn on the day Chris Andrews had accosted her and she had no money to buy the materials to make others even if she could get into Crossclough. Jack Andrews had been more than generous with the allowance he had given her – she suspected more to ease his own conscience than for any other reason – but naturally she had not carried money about with her when she went for a walk. Now, when she was really in need she had nothing to ease it.

Not that that mattered when compared with the terrifying strain of her missing cousin. Jamie was like a man possessed, just as though he were to blame for Katy's disappearance. Jack Andrews, when he had followed close on the heels of his groom up to Valley Bottom Farm – for where else could Katy have gone? – had made it plain that this tragedy could only be laid at Jamie's door. Of course he was not himself and when he was, being a fair man, would realise that it wasn't so. If every man or woman who was rejected by the object of their own desire acted as Katy had done the world would be in a constant state of upheaval, her uncle would know that, Chloe told herself, but he wasn't thinking straight and, she supposed, the sight of herself lurking at Jamie's back half an hour after Katy's disappearance had not helped his normally reasonable mind.

"I'll bloody kill you for this, Jamie Hutchinson," he thundered in his demented fury. "If she's not found soon you're off this farm by the weekend, you and that trollop with you," before digging his heels into his mount's side and heading off back to Cloudberry End, the awkward groom behind him.

So Chloe could only remain in the farmhouse, her only

company the dog, and wait forlornly for the moment, usually just after dark, when Jamie came stumbling home to fling himself in the chair and fall asleep. She knew she was no good to him. She could do nothing to ease his sense of guilt, to comfort his aching, weary body, not even cook him a warm meal to sustain him.

"It's all right, lass," he would mumble, his haggard face doing its best to smile reassuringly. "A bit of bread and cheese will do."

On that first day when she had been left so frighteningly alone she had moved slowly about the farmhouse, going from room to room, opening cupboards and drawers, the dog at her heels, familiarising herself, or trying to, with what was to be her home from now on. She had lived a comfortable life for eighteen years in the tall house in Liverpool, with a parlourmaid to answer the door, a cook and a skivvy in the kitchen and during the last four months in absolute luxury at Cloudberry End. She had never been in a kitchen except to convey an order from her mama to the cook, until the last weeks of Mama's life when she had learned how to boil an egg and make a pot of tea, but the rudiments of cooking, of cleaning, of how one went about the everyday tasks of washing and ironing one's own garments were a dark mystery to her. There was no running water in the kitchen and Jamie explained to her that every drop must be brought from the pump in the yard. These were the buckets to be used, he had explained, his eyes so dark and forbidding, she felt herself shrivel inside, wanting to weep for the loss of the loving warmth which he had shown her before Katy's disappearance. He was no longer the ardent, gentle lover who had taken her to his bed and then, after loving her, for she recognised that was what he had done, loved her, held her in strong, protective arms while she slept. He was no longer the smiling, good-humoured giant who had treated her as though she were a fragile stem of cut crystal who should not be allowed so much as to lift her own teacup to her lips and, in the soft depth of the bed they had shared for the first time only a night or two ago, he turned his back on her and slept the sleep of the exhausted, only to fling himself out of the farmhouse with hardly a word the minute it was daylight.

How Katy would have relished it, Chloe thought bitterly, her disappearance having separated the man she loved from the woman she loathed as effectively as death itself.

She found an old but clean white shirt presumably belonging to Jamie at the back of a drawer, one which had a frilled, tucked front, wondering in astonishment when he had ever worn it. She hoped it was not something he treasured as she cut into it with a pair of sharp shears she found in the kitchen drawer, not sure of their purpose but at least they suited hers. From the worn material and with a needle and some thread – black – she discovered in a small box on the mantelshelf she fashioned herself some rather skimpy undergarments, but at least it meant she could wash her own, though the ironing of them was beyond her. It had taken all her strength to pump the water into the bucket and carry it, half a bucketful at a time, into the house and then to ponder on the means to heat it. There were pans on the shelf and the fire, which Jamie had patiently relit with instructions not to let it go out, pointing to the plentiful supply of wood which was stacked in the yard, was crackling cheerfully in the barred grate. But in the end she had washed them as best she could in cold water, then draped them before the fire to dry.

The bread, which was all but gone, was as hard as rock, and the cheese box empty and she was wondering despairingly what she might give Jamie for a meal on this, the third and what was to be the last day of searching, when she heard the sound of horse's hooves on the track. For a second her heart leaped gladly for surely it was Katy come back from the . . . well, from the dead, but when she flung open the door it was not her cousin who stood there but Jamie's mother.

They looked at one another, the two women, for what seemed an eternity to Chloe, the expression on Mrs Jenkins's face quite inscrutable and yet in her eyes there was surely no mistaking the utter contempt and dislike. Chloe felt it slither inside her and wrap sinuously around her fast-beating heart. Mrs Jenkins was walking, leading a placid old horse which lowered its head and began to crop the rough grass just beyond the gate. On its back was strapped the faded, much worn carpetbag which had once belonged to Chloe's mama.

Chloe, with what seemed so much to do in this new life of hers, the bringing in of water and logs, the constant replenishing of the fire, the washing and sewing and even the sweeping out of the kitchen which she thought she should do, had not had the time to fasten up her hair in its customary neat chignon. It hung in a wild tangle of curls – since she had no brush and Jamie seemed uncertain of where one could be found – tied up with a bit of twine she had found with the needle and thread. Her dove grey gown was stained around the hem with the muck from the yard and though she had sluiced her hands and face at the pump and even stripped and washed her body in a bucket of cold water, there was about her the kind of dishevelment usually seen in those who care not a jot for their appearance. Her stout walking boots were weighted down with mud and muck and the scrap of towel she had tied about her waist in an effort to protect her one dress was torn and dirty.

Jamie's mother continued to study her, her blue eyes, so like his, running down the length of her, then up again to Chloe's face, her lip curled in what appeared to be almost a snarl.

Matty Jenkins had nothing against this girl as such and perhaps, if she'd proved strong enough to be the farmer's wife Jamie needed, could have taken to her. She was well bred, though that didn't matter, and good-hearted, they all agreed at the house. She'd kept her head up and her graceful back straight despite Sara's aversion to her, and Matty admired that, but Jesus God, she'd overturned the life of the Andrews family like a child with a stick stirring an ant-hill. She had created havoc and destruction, not just because of who she was, which Sara had found so hard to cope with, but because of what she had done to Katy and to Jamie. Jamie must be bewitched, his mother agonised, as she stared in growing horror at the slut in her son's doorway. And she'd no shame neither, standing with her tatterdemalion head up and her shoulders squared, just as though she were some elegantly gowned hostess welcoming a guest on the doorstep of her mansion.

"Mrs Jenkins," she enquired politely, "won't you come in and . . ." She was about to say "take tea" but she had used the last of the tea leaves an hour ago, having mastered the kettle and the trivet which held it, as she meant to master all the other strange gadgets in her new home. When Jamie was himself, of course, and could show her.

"I don't think so, lass. I'm doin' Sara, Mrs Andrews, a favour fetchin' yer things. She wants shut of 'em, yer see. Aye, I could've sent one o't lads but they're all out searchin' fer Miss Katy, poor lass, an' if she's not found tha'll not 'ave an easy life in these parts an' neither'll my lad."

Chloe's face spasmed in horror as the words struck her

but she found her voice bravely though it was broken with her strong emotion.

"Why? Dear God . . . why? Why do you blame me and Jamie for all this? Even Mr Andrews has threatened Jamie with eviction but it is not his fault, nor mine that— "

Matty cut her short, her face contorted with rage. "So, yer've summat else to answer for, 'ave yer? For if my boy loses this farm an' everythin' he's purrin' to it he'll not forgive thi'. Miss Katy'd not've run off but fer thee an' what tha' tempted my lad ter do. Traipsin' up here an' doin' yer best ter get yer claws in 'im."

"No, no, it wasn't like that. Jamie has never loved Katy, not in that way. He was entirely honourable in his dealings with her but she refused to accept it. She wanted him for herself, you see and when she heard that we . . . that Jamie and I . . ."

Chloe stepped out from beneath the shadow of the porch, throwing out her hands in desperate appeal and for the first time Matty saw her face. She gasped and put her hand to her mouth.

"Dear sweet God in heaven, tell me my son didn't . . ."

Chloe tutted impatiently. "No, of course not. Surely you know Jamie better than that."

"I thought I did, lass." Matty's shoulders slumped. "But if it were'nt 'im, then who?"

Chloe hesitated. Should she tell Jamie's mother who had beaten her across the face in his frustrated temper? But if she did would it not cause more trouble for the Andrews family? So far only she and Chris Andrews knew who had given her the bruised and blackened eye, the swollen, red-wealed face but if Mrs Jenkins was told and it got out, Jamie would without a doubt go down to Cloudberry End and wreak havoc on . . . Well, he would have done a few nights ago, she told herself bleakly, but now . . . now, who knew what his reaction would be? From his attitude towards her since Katy had slipped out of the kitchen and vanished, probably that she had got what she deserved.

"It was . . . a man up on the . . . on the moor," she mumbled, hanging her head as though in shame, then looking up again sharply. "He wanted something I was not prepared to give him so . . . he struck me. Jamie found me and brought me here. Neither of us planned it, Mrs Jenkins, please believe me, but . . . well . . . Jamie has asked me to marry him and I have said I will. I cannot return to Cloudberry End, not now. Even if Katy had not run away, I could not return to the house where . . ."

Matty knew then who it was who had savaged Chloe Taylor's face, for had they not all noticed the way he waylaid this lovely girl, in the garden, according to Angus and Billy, and on the back staircase where Ivy had found them. He was the weak son of a strong father and though Matty did not like to believe that he would strike a defenceless girl, who else would have done it? Some rough fellow intent on rape? Hardly, for a refusal to allow it would have been ignored and Chloe would have got more than a smack in the face.

Matty sagged against the patient horse and pushed a hand through her windblown hair, her own head bending as though in pain. She believed her, that was the trouble. She believed every word this girl said, which made it hard to go on despising her. Sara was lying in a semi-drugged state in her bedroom at Cloudberry End, moaning for her girl to be returned to her, and if not her, then her husband on whom she leaned so heavily. Sometimes, when Matty looked back to the days when she and Sara had lived and worked in Liverpool, she could scarcely credit that this was the strong, resolute young woman Sara Andrews had then been. She had suffered sorrow and loss and the dreadful mischief her own sister had caused in her life but she had been unbowed by it. It was not until she married Jack, who insisted on treating her like a hot-house flower which would wither in the cold winds of everyday life, that she had become . . . weakened. He, with his strength on which he insisted she leaned, had weakened her imperceptibly day by day until she could barely function without him beside her, no more than an arm's length away. It had saddened Matty. It was not that Sara was melancholy. Far from it. When all was well she was as merry as a child but it had to be within sight and sound of Jack Andrews, which was probably the reason he had retired from the business of building railways so as to be always near her.

"Tha's ter marry my Jamie?" she said at last, raising her head, surprised by the compassion she saw in Chloe's eyes, just as though the girl could sense Matty's pain. She didn't take after her mother, at any rate, which was something, for Alice Hamilton had been a cold-hearted bitch if ever there was one.

"Yes, I believe so."

"Don't tha' know?"

"Well . . . since Katy left he has been distraught. Like Mr Andrews, he blamed himself, you see."

"Nay, she were always hangin' about him when he were home. Puppy love, it were."

"Oh no!" Chloe looked shocked. "It was not that, Mrs Jenkins. She truly loves him."

"Loved him, lass."

"You can't mean . . . she's dead?" Chloe slumped against the door frame and the dog huddled up to her skirt, bewildered by the tides of emotion which flooded in and out of what he had begun to think of as his territory.

"Nay, she's not bin found. There's a hue an' cry out for 'er in every town within forty miles an' she'd hardly be missed, lookin' like she did, that's if she got that far. Them bogs up there . . ."

Matty shook her head dumbly and tears began to slide down her cheeks. She had not wept nor broken, as Sara had, for the three whole days of Katy's disappearance but now, in the presence of this quiet, dishevelled but dignified young woman, she felt it begin to break inside her and flow towards the surface of her skin.

"Oh, God, lass, where is she?" she wailed, then was amazed to find herself in the slender, but surprisingly strong arms of the girl she had been prepared to repudiate, even if she was Jamie's choice. She was led inside and placed gently in front of the lively fire, her hands chafed by the girl who knelt at her feet while she wept and wept and then, as women do, felt better for it.

"Put kettle on, lass," she said at last, sniffing her last sniffle, blowing her nose vigorously on the scrap of clean linen in her sleeve.

Chloe sighed disconsolately. "Mrs Jenkins, I would most willingly but . . . well, you see, there's no tea. I am so sorry. I feel quite mortified, but Jamie is . . . is so worried . . ."

"D'yer mean ter say he's gone off an' left yer, a gently reared girl ter fend for thissen? Is there nowt?"

"Well, milk by the churnful, for the cows have to be seen to," Chloe said brightly, just as though the routine of the farm was well known to her. "Tommy has been up."

"Aye, he would. A good lad is my Tommy."

"But he didn't stay to tell me where things were."

"What about potatoes in't barn? An' them carrots an' onions?"

"Carrots and onions?" Chloe said faintly.

"Aye, an' there was a rabbit in the ice house."

"Ice house?"

"Jesus God, girl, what 'ave tha' bin livin' on?"

"Cheese, and bread . . . and milk, of course."

"An' Jamie an' all?"

"He said he wasn't hungry, Mrs Jenkins and I didn't want to add to his . . . his burdens. He was so tired he slept like a log."

"Aye, well . . ." Matty wasn't sure she wanted to become acquainted with her son's sleeping arrangements but it was very plain that this lass needed a bit of help and who else was to give it to her but the woman who was to be her mother-in-law?

She began to feel more cheerful than she had for days. "Now then, let's get ourselves started. Tha's no tea, tha' say?"

"No." Chloe was devastatingly sorry.

"Well, we'll see about that. Put some water in't kettle."

"Oh, I can do that, Mrs Jenkins."

"Good, then go an' fetch some eggs an'— "

"Eggs?" Chloe looked bewildered.

"Don't tell me tha's not collected th'eggs?"

"From where?"

"Eeh lass, tha's a lot ter learn about bein' a farmer's wife."

"I know." Chloe's answer was humble, but Matty patted her hand comfortingly.

"Don't tha' fret. Now then, why don't tha' tekk that there basket an' go outside. Search about the yard an' round the places where tha've seen the 'ens scratch and look ter see if tha' can find any eggs. I'll be surprised if tha' don't. Mind you, I don't suppose Jamie thought ter tell thi' ter feed 'em, did he? No, I thought not," as Chloe shook her head in bewilderment.

"Now, I'll fetch in tha' bag. There's your 'air brush, which tha'll be glad of," eyeing the tangled mass which fell about Chloe's face and shoulders, "all tha' things, not much, lass, but enough ter tide thi' over till tha're wed. Oh, an' I found a little bag in't drawer with some money in it so tha'll be able ter mekk thissen a decent dress, fer I'll have no one in this valley say our Jamie wed a . . ."

She had been about to say "trollop" and she could see the awareness of it in Chloe's eyes and she was sorry. This girl was not the trollop they all called her. It was that lad down at Cloudberry End who had sent her running for cover with his greedy hands and lustful eyes. It was not the first time he'd gone after some girl, though usually it was a pretty maidservant or a dairymaid he'd taken a fancy to. Got a girl into trouble up Penistone way a year or two back and cost his pa a pretty penny to hush it up, the story went, and all this trouble could, in a way, be laid at his door. If he'd not done his best to seduce this lass would she have been as willing to wed Jamie who, though a decent, hardworking, attractive man, was not in the same class as she was and was illegitimate into the bargain? And happen, if there'd been no one else to take his fancy, who knows, Jamie might have settled with Katy who usually got her way. He'd have been in clover then, her Jamie, with the Andrews' endless supply of cash ready to flow into his pocket, and his infant farm. There were some bad seeds in the Andrews family, like that Paddy and now, it seemed, Chris Andrews was going the same nasty way. His brothers were as even-tempered and worthwhile as their father and young Davy was at this moment somewhere up on Ramsden Edge where Ramsden Clough plunged, cliff-like, into the turbulence of the rock-strewn water, searching frantically for his sister. Called home from the university in Edinburgh he had been, and there was young Master Richie, who was expected home in the next few weeks since the railway he was helping to build was all but finished, and how would he be affected by his sister's disappearance? Chris was galloping about here and there and every bloody where, they said, strangely excited by the drama, and glad, of course, Matty was convinced, of anything that got him out of the mill.

The horse beyond the gate was quite prepared, it seemed, to browse on the sparse, almost colourless grass which grew there and when the sun came out the dog wandered into the bit of warmth beneath the kitchen window, happy with the feeling of calm which now flowed about his domain. Matty produced scrubbing brushes, polish and dusters from where they were kept in a tiny, hidden cupboard under the stairs and which Chloe had not even known was there.

"We'll give t'place a good bottomin', lass, then tha'll know how to go about it by thissen, then I'll show thi' where Jamie stores 'is veg an' the like an' how the ice house works. Made it 'isself, did Jamie. Oh aye, he's a clever lad is yon an' tha'll want fer nowt he can give thi'."

Having decided that she might as well accept this lass who could, for all Matty knew, already be carrying Jamie's bairn, she was bent on teaching her, in no more than a couple of hours, how to look after Matty's son in the way he deserved, and she demanded. She'd keep an eye on her, of course. Come up every day or so to make sure she was going on in the right way of things and, if there was a bairn, the lass'd need all the help Matty could give her. She was willing, give her that, setting to with the scrubbing brush as though her life depended on it and, when the place was as immaculate as Matty liked to see it, listening and watching intently as she was shown how to make a rabbit stew.

"It needs a bit of celery in it ter give it best flavour which we 'aven't got but these'll do fer now. No, don't fiddle wi' it, lass, give it a good chop across its legs," for Chloe had paled slightly, not only over the skinning and cleaning of the rabbit but the chopping of it into decent-sized pieces.

"Plenty o' carrots an' onions, that's right, an' a dash o' salt an' in the oven it goes."

She was quite flabbergasted to find that Chloe had no idea that those were ovens on either side of the fire, but then, could you blame the lass, for when had she ever had the need to know such things? She promised she'd come up tomorrow, and show her how to bake bread . . . aye, that was flour in that crock, patient as patient, and then was ashamed when she realised that for the best part of two hours she hadn't given poor Katy Andrews a blessed thought and what was worse, for she loved her like a sister, Sara Andrews would be awake now and fretting for her.

It was completely dark when Jamie Hutchinson staggered up the path towards the farmhouse door which stood half open. He had tramped thirty miles since daybreak and his mind was blank and empty of all thought but the need to lay himself down somewhere and sleep until the cock crowed. He knew she would be there, where she had been for the past three nights but somehow he couldn't seem to find the strength to care. He loved her, he knew that, deep in his bones and heart he loved her but just at this moment he had no time for her. She would be there when all this was over, he knew that, too, for she was not the kind of girl . . . woman . . . to run away, or have a paddy if she was neglected but just for now he wanted nothing but oblivion.

She was standing over a pot which she had just brought from the oven, a spoon in her hand, a delighted smile on her face. She turned as he entered. The room was lovely with firelight and candlelight and the aroma of cooking mixed with what smelled like lavender. It was clean and sparkling across every surface, even the snow white tablecloth which she had rooted out from somewhere. She was in her black gown but the top half a dozen buttons were undone to reveal the sweet cleft between her creamy breasts and their top curve almost to her nipples. She wore a snowy cloth about her waist to protect her gown and her hair had been brushed and brushed to a gleaming tawny gloss. It tumbled carelessly down her back in a curtain of living flame, caught casually with a knot of ribbons at the crown. She was flushed and bright-eyed and looked quite, quite enchanting.

"Rabbit stew," she said, smiling shyly in his direction before turning to put the dish back in the oven. "The potatoes will be ready in ten minutes if you want to have a wash."

"Bugger the wash and bugger the rabbit stew," he said.

"Your mama was here," she ventured breathlessly as he pulled her into his arms.

"Was she now?" His lips folded about hers in a way that drew the most delightful feeling to the pit of her belly. His arms held her tight against him so that even through her petticoats she could feel his need of her, knowing exactly what it was now, despite her lack of experience. He bent her back and his lips travelled down the column of her throat to her breasts and when his fingers pulled her bodice apart she made no objection.

They ate the rabbit stew later, much later, she on his knee, their naked bodies wrapped in the quilt while the dog dozed contentedly before the fire.

They were not to go out again since they had searched every square inch where she might be, quite fruitlessly, he told her quietly, holding her, guarding her, loving her while she wept for her cousin.

12

Katherine Andrews awoke from her deep and troubled sleep and for a moment or two could not recall what was troubling her, or even where she was. She felt calm. She had felt calm ever since she had slipped out of Jamie's house, climbed on to Storm's back and ridden away towards the summit of the Black Hill. As calm and frozen as an iceberg which floats imperturbably on an Arctic sea and which Jamie had once described to her. The sea is cold and the air is cold and so nothing melts it, just as nothing would ever melt Katy Andrews's heart again. She had the most curious feeling that she was not really present in her own body which had had things done to it in these last few days which she had never dreamed of. She existed in the tearless agony which had come upon her when she had seen Jamie and Chloe in one another's arms in Jamie's kitchen. Yes, agony, excruciating and yet at the same time numbing, and nothing, nothing of what was happening now touched her. She knew she must live for ever with these days, these hours, these minutes which ticked by so slowly, and yet flew backwards like birds tumbled in a windblown sky. They would be a part of her life, burned in her brain, sunk deep in her heart with the painful remains of her love for Jamie and whatever she did, whatever became of her, whatever else was forgotten as she grew old, this would be as clear in her memory as though it had just happened. Time would never dim or heal her pain. There was nothing she could do, nothing, except gather her strength to go back. She could not stay here, not in this cottage where no woman had dwelled for years and where the man who remained was content to live in the confusion her death had left.

She was naked under the sleazy sheet, the bedlinen which a week ago would have made her shudder. Now, if she noticed it, which appeared unlikely, it made no ripple on the flat, smooth surface of her clouded mind.

She turned her head towards a window festooned with cobwebs, the small panes of glass smeared and dull. There was a jumble of objects on the windowsill, a pint pot from which he drank his ale, a sturdy boot with a sock hanging from it, a hammer, a picture of a dog and a cat in a basket, a relic from the days when Emily Andrews was alive, a small, rose-painted jug and a half-eaten sandwich on a plate. He had been munching on it as he came up the stairs last night, she remembered, but his eyes had become hot and narrowed when he saw she was awake and the bread and cheese had been unceremoniously put aside as he made himself as naked as she was.

She had not been out of this bed for . . . how long was it? . . . she didn't know, nor did she care at this precise moment. She was quiet, empty, without, for the moment, any need to make a decision. She needed this quietness, this emptiness, totally apart from those who, she supposed, loved her at Cloudberry End and who would, by now, imagine she was dead but it didn't seem to matter.

It was the dog who had found her. Strangely, she had not gone far, which was perhaps the reason none of the others had looked for her there, imagining that she would have galloped for miles before stopping. Just on the edge of Pikenose Moor which lay up beyond the back of her grandmother's cottage there was a circle of rocks, a curious outcropping of grey-pitted stones, some teetering on top of others to form an overhang. It made a shelter of sorts, a stockade in which she and Storm could hide. The beaten-down, springy peat created a soft bed on which to lie and for a long time, while Storm cropped the grass, in total silence and stillness, just as though she were dead, she lay and stared up unblinkingly into the clear sky. Grouse rose now and then, unafraid of her quiet presence, and invisible skylarks sang their hearts out as if to say though hers might be broken theirs certainly weren't.

He only found her by accident and had the dog not caught the scent of the mare and gone to investigate he would have tramped by on his way back from Crossclough to his cottage higher up the hill. He wasn't even looking for her, since he didn't know she was missing, he told her later, for when he picked her up in his strong arms and, leading her sorrel, carried her to his cottage, she was senseless and in a state which she would not have understood had he tried to explain. The mare was tied to a broken, hanging gate, then Paddy Andrews turned his attention to his cousin.

Carelessly he laid her on the littered table on which were the remains of not only his breakfast but his and his pa's supper last night. He had spent the morning seeing to the arrangements for the disposal of his pa's body, and had then gone rabbiting, and what the hell Katy Andrews was doing lolling about like a rag doll with half its stuffing missing was a bloody mystery, but as soon as he'd had a bite to eat he'd take her back to that mansion she lived in and perhaps his uncle, who, after all, was pa's brother, might be persuaded to chip in for the funeral.

She turned her head to look at him as he was shovelling

a cold bacon sandwich into his mouth, and then sat up, making nothing of finding herself lying on the frowsy table, and Paddy was slightly unnerved by the fixed, unfocused depths of her transparent, golden eyes. Had she heard, he asked her, since he was a chap who liked a bit of a tongue wag while he ate, that his pa had died last night? He was not unduly concerned about it, though there was the question of this cottage which belonged to Jed Miller of High Shine Farm and was meant only for those Jed employed. George Andrews had laboured for most of his fifty-odd years for Jed Miller and Jed Miller's pa. Paddy had been born in this cottage and his ma had died here, a year or two back, did Katy know that? wondering what the bloody hell was wrong with her since she was obviously not what he would have called "right", not the Katy Andrews he knew and had fought with at his gran's cottage a month or two back. She'd not have allowed him to lay a finger on her then, let alone pick her up in his arms and cuddle her to his chest as he carried her to his house.

"D'yer want summat? A cup o' tea, 'appen?"

"That would be nice," she answered, her polite voice hoarse as though from misuse.

"Right, I'll put kettle on."

"Thank you."

"I were goin' ter clear up but then I got word me pa was dead . . . well, you know 'ow it is." He shrugged his broad shoulders and smiled deprecatingly, his face not wearing its normal arrogant grin, nor his chin its usual truculent angle. He turned back to the kettle, the teapot, the tea caddy, the domesticity of his tasks seeming to soften him, though neither he nor the girl was aware of any change in him, or indeed why he should be changed at all. He had to rinse a couple of mugs out, for there was not a pot clean in the house and the milk was off but, Paddy decided, glancing at Katy, she'd not have noticed if he'd given her the contents of the chamberpot to drink.

What was up with her? he asked himself wonderingly for the umpteenth time, as he threw one long leg over the bench and sat down beside her. She was still perched on the table, her feet on the bench which he straddled. He pushed aside several plates, and the cat who had licked them clean, propping one elbow in the space he had cleared, studying the state of his visitor's dress and the windswept tumble of her hair. He knew she often roamed the moorland which surrounded her home, he'd seen her himself, even nodded to her as she passed him by when he had been tramping off with his dog to a fight in which either he, or the dog, was to take part. Dressed up to the nines she had been then, in her blue riding habit and polished boots. She'd returned his greeting in that haughty way she had, just as though Paddy Andrews was nowt a pound to her, a cowpat in which even her little mare would not be allowed to tread, but she'd lost it now, that hoity-toity "I'm better than you" look with which he was so familiar. Dragged about, she appeared to be, and for the first time he noticed she had only one shoe.

She sipped her tea in total silence, her great golden eyes staring somewhere over his shoulder to the greasy window, or sliding to the open door which led out into the cobbled yard. There were chickens strutting and pecking, several of them sidling into the kitchen and coming to roost on the top of the dresser but the constant sound of their cackling did not appear to trouble her. The dog lay on the step watching without interest, his little eyes half closed though he was alert to any danger which might threaten him or his master.

Paddy didn't know what to say and she didn't seem to care, or even notice the lack of conversation. When she had finished the tea she just sat there, incongruously, on the edge of the table, her feet together on the bench, waiting, it seemed to him, for someone to tell her what to do next. Had she had a fall from her horse, he wondered, perhaps a blow to the head which had stunned her? How could he tell without asking her and when he did she turned to stare at him as though he were talking a foreign language.

"Is summat up, Katy?" he asked her, bewildered by his own concern for her, for when had any of Jack Andrews's family ever given him the time of day, let alone their goodwill? But she was so unlike her usual self, almost like a bairn . . . well, no, not with a figure like hers, bits of which were showing through her torn, stained dress, but despite his curiosity and a strong need to know what had been done to her to get her in this state, he'd best get her home to her pa before a hue and cry was sparked off. It was already beginning to dim into the dusky, end of summer evening which fell at this time of the year and the track down to Woodhead was steep and tricky.

She had not answered his question, nor even turned to look at him when he spoke.

"Well," he said at last, his eyes moving across her face. He rubbed the stubble on his chin and gave her a sort of half smile as though to encourage her, to let her see he meant her no harm. That despite his reputation with women he had never yet damaged one, nor forced one against her will. He liked a joke. He liked to tease and frighten them a little, those he sometimes came across walking a quiet lane alone but Paddy Andrews had no need to force a lass. No need at all. There was a certain dairymaid on a farm near Woodhead who regularly and willingly dropped her drawers and spread her legs for him, so he didn't go short and he'd never paid for it in his life, never.

He sighed in some irritation, pushing a none too clean hand through the rough thatch of his short, curly hair. He wished to God the damned dog had not found her, and wondered why, when he did, he hadn't taken her straight down to her folks instead of fetching her all the way up here. Why had he even bothered to pick her up, for she'd no doubt have got up on her horse and gone home herself when she was ready? She was nowt to do with him. He'd enough to see to with his pa dying like that and the question of cash, or his lack of it. He'd been working as a labourer in the local quarry ever since Chris Andrews had got him the push from the paper mill, soft prick, and one day he'd get even with him, choose how, but in the meanwhile, with fights a bit few and far between, he was short of ready cash. Surely, if he took Katy home his uncle'd be so bloody relieved he'd not refuse his help with the laying to rest of his own brother? It was a worrying time, for this cottage would not be his for long, neither, for it would be given to the next labourer Jed Miller employed. Paddy thought he might sling his hook and find something for himself elsewhere. Perhaps America, if he could get together the fare, where their Lester and Walter and Arthur had gone years ago. He was strong, afraid of nothing and no one and the thought of carving out a new life for himself in the wilderness which he'd heard of out there appealed to the adventurer in him. He couldn't settle to anything here, and now seemed as good a time as any to leave.

He stood up. "Right then, we'd best get tha' home ter tha' pa, hadn't we?" he said, his voice almost soft, him, Paddy Andrews who had never in his life had the grace to see any woman home but then he was short of a bob or two and Uncle Jack would be very grateful to have his lass home safe and sound.

He was seriously alarmed, as was his dog which leaped to his feet when Katy began to rant and rave like a woman gone off her head.

"No . . . no . . . I won't go," she screamed, rocking backwards and forwards on the table, tearing at her own hair and face. Her mouth was wide and so were her eyes, as though she stared at some horror which was not vouchsafed to him. She swung about as though searching for some means to escape it, he thought, whatever it was, and as much to protect her from her own savagery as anything else, he sprang towards her and pulled her to him.

"Christ, Katy . . ." He was appalled, for the first time in his life totally at a loss as to how to handle a woman. He shoved the bench back and stood before her while her fists beat against him, but by now her cries were muffled in the open neck of his shirt though her words were still audible.

"I can't . . . I can't go home . . . not yet . . . oh please, don't make me . . . let me stay here."

"Bloody 'ell, lass, tha' can't stay 'ere."

"Why not? Why should you care? You've no time for us so why should it worry you what happens to me or my family?" Her voice was rough and gasping. Her arms went round his back and her hands clung to the thick fabric of his shirt as though she were resolutely determined not to be prised loose from him.

It was true. He'd despised them all, particularly that high, mucky-muck wife of his uncle's who, like her daughter, had looked at him as though he were no more than his own dog when they passed him in the lane. This girl's brothers with their grand horses and expensive boots and whose expressions of disdain, whose eagerness not to be associated with him were as plain as the nose on his face. Jack Andrews had made a lot of money and for reasons best known to himself had come back here to lord it over his own brothers, over his nieces and nephews and it had been a festering sore beneath the skin of Paddy Andrews ever since he had been old enough to understand. Stuck-up buggers, the lot of them and his greatest wish was that one of them would pick a fight with him so that he could knock the living daylights out of him. He'd almost had that bloody little sod, Chris Andrews, a month or two back but old Jack, who at least had guts, had come out and chased his son off in a funk.

Katy shook so much the table on which she was still perched trembled and all the crockery jumped and dithered. The dog growled warningly, not sure what at but ready to show his willingness to fight it, whatever it might be, and Paddy, in a state totally unlike his usual cocksure, defiant self, held her steady against him, his handsome face creased with an expression no one who knew him would have recognised.

"I won't go, Paddy." At least she knew who he was. "If you turn me out I'll simply run away again and they'll never find me."

"What were tha' runnin' away from?"

"Never mind that. Just let me stay with you."

"Lass, don't be daft . . ." but he was beginning to weaken since, from some deep, primeval part of him, some fundamental source which is buried in all men, it began to occur to him that here was a perfect way to assuage his desire for revenge on Jack Andrews and his family who had always been, in their eyes, so far above the rest of them. They'd done nothing to him, or his, he knew that, it was simply that their sneering attitude, which said that Paddy Andrews was not fit to lick their very boots, needed to be shown that he could do far more than that. And here, to hand, was the girl who would help him to it.

"Please, Paddy, let me . . . let me stay until . . ."

Until I feel better, she wanted to say, which was ridiculous for when would that ever be, but just a few days. No, she did not care that they would be out of their minds, her mother and her father. They shouldn't have tried to prevent her from . . . keep her from . . . from Jamie. Aah, God . . . God, she could not stand it. She must surely die from the wounds which had been inflicted on her . . . but a few days on her own . . . it would give her time to begin the building of the shell inside beyond which no one could reach, beyond which no one could touch, hear her cries of grief, see her suffering. They would be looking for her, even Jamie, she knew that, but let them hurt a little, or even a lot, for whatever it was they were suffering it would not be a fraction of her own.

She became aware of the change in the man who was standing between her legs. He had begun to breathe heavily and his hands had moved to her ankles. He removed her shoe and began to smooth the arch of her feet, then, his face closing in on hers but not yet touching it, his hands moved slowly up her legs beneath her petticoats. They reached her knees, stroking behind them, pushing her legs further apart, slipping beneath the ribbons at the bottom of her drawers, finding their way to the soft flesh between her thighs. With one enquiring finger he pushed his way through the thick mat of her pubic hair and moved very slowly into the warm, moist crevice at the junction of her thighs, stroking gently, experimentally, as though waiting to see if she had any objection. When she made none, he smiled.

"Good lass. Now, I'll just go an' 'ide the mare in the outhouse," he murmured, his warm, heavy-lidded eyes running over her. "Don't move."

"No, I won't," she said obediently.

He returned quickly, moving to stand in the position he had left a moment ago. He put a hand to her cheek, cupping it without force, then letting it slide to her chin. She looked up at him, not afraid, for what would Katy Andrews ever fear again, her eyes deep and fathomless, great golden pools in which there was no life. She blinked as his mouth came down on hers. He was still holding her chin with one hand and as she sat in blank acceptance his other hand went to the back of her head beneath her hair as though to prevent her escaping.

She felt nothing, no surprise, no offence, even at his first intimacy, no warmth, no fear or distaste. She merely let him kiss her. Let his eager hands begin again their exploration of her body. What did it matter? If this was what he wanted and was the price for a few days of respite for Katy Andrews, could it concern her who, having offered her body to one man who had refused, must give it to another. Why not Paddy? One man was as good as another if his name was not Jamie Hutchinson and it was nothing to her. She was numb, cold, so perhaps Paddy's big warm body would help to bring her back to some sense of who she was. Not yet, of course, since she didn't want to be troubled with who she was. Not yet, but soon, when she was ready to leave. What did it matter?

He lifted her skirt and removed her drawers, bending her legs apart so that he could "have a good look at her" he said hoarsely. He seemed to find a great deal to interest him in that warm, secret part of her body which no one had ever seen, she supposed since she was a babe in arms. He parted it and even put his mouth to it, groaning in the most peculiar way while she sat obediently and stared out of the window at the moors where once she had been so happy.

He told her to remove her clothes then, one by one and slowly, and she complied obligingly, sitting on the littered table, her back straight, her breasts full and jutting. He was like a boy with a new toy, one which is his alone to play with, gloating, his hands and mouth roaming over her and into her before removing his own garments and coming to stand again between her legs. The rod which stood out from him was quite enormous but he tucked it up flat against his stomach between them, not yet ready, he gasped, to do what the stallion at Johnny Ashwell's place did to the mare. What did it matter?

He stood back from her for a moment, trembling as though he were ill, groaning deeply in his strong chest. He lifted her from the table, turning her about, bending her over it so that her breasts were flattened in a plate which had once held a joint of bacon. His hands were everywhere, smoothing the curve of her buttocks, lingering in the crease between, probing the centre of her. What did it matter?

"Jesus God, but tha're beautiful, Katy Andrews," he grunted huskily, "and tha're bloody mine. Tha're mine, dost tha' hear me? That bloody pa o' thine and the prick who's tha' brother . . . By God, if they could see thi' now, wi' me, Paddy Andrews who's scum of the earth ter them. But I'll tell thi' this, my lass, tha'll not forget what I'll do ter thi' in the next few days an' no man'll suit yer after that. Only me, I promise thi'. Now, I'm tekken thi' ter bed an' yer ter stay there, d'yer hear me? Wherever I go I'd like ter think of yer there, waitin' on me. On me, Paddy Andrews, waitin' in my bed whenever I want thi'. God Almighty, it'll 'ave ter be now cos I can't wait ter get yer up them stairs."

Sweeping the table clear with one mighty crash which made the dog leap towards the yard with a howl, and scattered the hens into a flapping frenzy, he laid her on it, her long and lovely back squashed against the litter of George and Paddy's last meal, opened wide her legs, put her heels on the edge of the table and tore through her virginity until her thighs were red with her own blood.

She did not cry out. What did it matter?

That had been several days ago, she supposed vaguely. How could she tell in this dream world, this nightmare world in which nothing existed but Paddy Andrews's powerful body and what it did several times a day to hers. He couldn't get enough of it, he said. He'd always had a fancy for one of them there slave girls he'd heard tell of, he said, and if she got out of his bed, even when he was forced to leave the cottage for an hour or two, he'd beat her until she was black and blue.

He fed her on something or other, mostly eggs and milk and cheese, introduced her to a chamberpot which she supposed he emptied. She slept like the dead in his arms at night, for which she was eternally grateful and when he wasn't making love to her, if what he did could be called that, or studying her in the poses he put her in, or instructing her in what she was to do to him, she dozed in the bed, the minutes and hours and days running in to one another in one long, timeless blur.

"How long has it been, Paddy?" she asked him that night. He had been to his pa's funeral, he had told her, which her pa and her brothers had attended but he did not divulge to her the quite dreadful appearance of all three. It was just a week since Katy Andrews had ridden off, never to be seen again, it seemed, and hope had long since gone that she might have survived, though there were still a few men paid by Jack Andrews who were to keep on tramping the hills and moors for some trace of his lost daughter.

They were all in black at Cloudberry End, it was reported

and Sara Andrews had gone into such a decline it was only the constant presence of her husband prevented her from slipping completely away; but her eldest son was to be home in a day or two so that should perhaps take her mind off her loss, they were saying.

They'd not found her. They had been all about Paddy's own cottage only yesterday, wanting to poke into his outhouse and chicken house but he'd told them to bugger off, threatening them with murder if they didn't, doing his best not to smile at the thought of the girl they sought, naked and waiting in his bed only a few yards from where they argued.

She was sitting up in the bed, the sheets about her waist, her glorious breasts, on which there were several bites and bruises, flaunting, golden, rose-tipped in the candlelight. He had roasted a chicken which he had stolen from Jed Miller's chicken run on the way back from the funeral at Woodhead Chapel. He had chickens of his own, of course, but why use up your own provisions when you can "borrow" from someone else, he laughed. She had a drumstick in her hand and she bit into it with evident relish. Her white teeth sank into the flesh as they had at times sunk into his own and he felt the urgent, explosive desire for her flood the pit of his belly. Sweet Christ, but she was superb, his Katy, for she belonged to him now, the most superb woman he had ever had in his bed, or ever would, come to think of it. She was all he had ever wanted in a woman and now, she was his. He knew that, even if she didn't and though he wasn't sure how he would manage it, he intended that she would remain his until one of them died.

Tearing off his clothes, he threw back the tangled, greasy sheets, his eyes hot with passion on her long, stretching body but in them was also a strange expression which might have been tenderness, a soft look of something she did not see and he was not aware was there.

"Aah, lass . . . my lass," he whispered. His hands reached to smooth and fondle her, his fingers and mouth insistent, his tongue, his breath touching every full curve and exploring every cleft of her, fierce and possessive, and within her she felt something unfurl itself, like a bud in spring ready to burst into flower.

"Katy . . . Katy, tha're the most beautiful thing I've ever known," he murmured, out of his mind with some emotion he did not recognise, his body moving over hers. She arched her back, surprising them both, for though she had never resisted him her part in their coupling had always been passive. No matter what he did to her, sometimes rough and animal-like, she had made no demur, allowing him the most extreme and even painful familiarities.

Her hips rose eagerly to his and when he entered her he felt her muscles grip him fiercely, spasming about his thrusting manhood, gripping him in what seemed to be a reluctance against his withdrawal.

"No," she moaned, "no . . . I'm not . . . not ready . . ." then with an explosion which they both felt, the bud opened. It flowed and rippled and shimmered inside her, moving from the centre of her where she and Paddy were joined, to every tingling nerve and pulse in her body.

She cried out then in her first climax, clinging to him as though should she let go she might be flung into infinity for ever.

He smiled afterwards, holding her in his arms, well pleased with himself, for he knew what had happened to her and it would help to bind her to him more closely. A woman will follow anywhere a man who loves her well. Who gives her body what it needs. She was of the earth, as he was; the last few days had proved that, not like those high-nosed, gently reared ladies who, so he had heard, found their man's attentions distasteful and to be put up with only when they could not avoid it.

"Tha're truly mine now, lass," he murmured into her hair and for some reason she was sorry.

When he awoke she was gone.

Jimmy and Dicken and Noah froze into paralysed, slack-jawed silence, all three turning a sickly grey-white as she rode slowly into the yard and, throwing her leg over the mare's neck, slid to the ground. She wore only one shoe. Apart from that and the muck which coated her, she looked just the same, just as she had done when she high-tailed it out of here a week ago like a wild thing on its way to hell, except that she was quiet now, thinner in the face, her eyes cool where they had flashed with madness.

"Dear God . . . Dear God, Miss Katy," Jimmy stammered, the comb with which he was currying Master Davy's chestnut falling with a clatter to the cobbles. The horse shied, startled, and Jimmy was dragged a foot or so as he tried to calm it. Noah, who was an old man and who had been the first to put this lass up on a horse when she was no more than a tiddler, began to sniffle, bringing out a big white square of linen from his pocket into which he trumpeted, and Dicken could do nothing but stand and stare before a grin as wide as the stable door split his young face. A bugger she had always been but he was right glad to see her back just the same.

"Mrs Tiplady . . . Mrs Tiplady," he bellowed as he ran towards the back door of the kitchen, sent by Jimmy to warn them, for the mistress was very frail and a shock like this . . . well, who knew what a gently bred lady like herself might do?

"What, for heaven's sake?" Mrs Tiplady did a bit of bellowing herself as Dicken flung open the door, for she'd have none of the stable yard muck in her kitchen.

"'Tis 'er, Mrs Tiplady . . . 'tis herself tell the master. Look," turning to sweep his arm in a theatrical manner, somewhat like a magician producing a rabbit from a hat, towards the gate where Jimmy and Noah were slowly escorting Miss Katy, one on either side of her, longing to hold her up, to carry her if needs be, in her triumphal, heartfelt homecoming. She walked steadily enough without their help, not smiling nor showing much of anything in her face, though her eyes were glad to see them, they said.

The state of her was appalling, Mrs Tiplady had time to notice before the maids began to scream their joy, throwing their aprons over their heads and, from the corner of the chimney, a small brown bundle of rough fur flung herself rapturously against Miss Katy's skirt, leaping up in great bounds until Miss Katy caught her in her arms and held her, wriggling and licking her dirty face ecstatically. The blasted animal had never been out of the kitchen except on matters of duty since Miss Katy left, hanging about, first at one door, then the other as though, when Miss Katy returned she would be at the right one to greet her. Fretted she had, poor little thing, gone to skin and bone and now would you look at her. At least she brought a smile to Miss Katy's haggard face.

"Miss Katy," she breathed, sitting down hastily in her chair before the fire. "Lord save us and may we be truly thankful for His blessings. Oh child . . . child . . . Quick, Freda, run for the master."

"Oh, miss, we thought you was dead."

"We've bin asearchin' and asearchin' for yer." This from Dilly who gave the tearful impression she herself had been out with the men.

"See, sit thi' down, lass and . . ."

". . . a week an' we'd give up 'ope, 'adn't we, Ivy?"

"Where've tha' bin, child?"

And in the doorway the three grooms hung, elbowing one another aside for a better look, their weatherbeaten faces split into grins of huge delight.

"I must go through, Mrs Tiplady. My mother and father will . . ."

"Eeh, o' course, lass, get thi' gone. They're in't drawin' room."

Mrs Tiplady was so overcome with emotion she broke out into the thick, long-drawn-out vowels of her northern heritage, that which she had managed to eradicate from her speech for years now.

They all wept over her, her father, her mother, even her two brothers, though she herself shed not a tear. Dry-eyed, she stood first in one embrace and then another, saying nothing except, yes, she would like a bath and a change of clothing, and no, she was not harmed and they had no need to worry over her.

"Worry over you, lass. Worry over you! We thought you were dead . . . in the bog . . ." Weary tears slid down her father's face, her strong, unbowed father who, as far as she knew, had never wept in his life.

"Darling . . . darling, we thought we had lost you," her mother cried, her frail body shaking in her daughter's arms which were so much stronger than hers.

"God, you're a bloody nuisance, Katy Andrews, but bloody hell, it's good to have you home," Chris whispered, his keen male eye wondering what it was that had changed his spoilt brat of a sister into this quiet-eyed but strangely exotic young woman. He recognised it, that look of maturity, that look of . . . Jesus, what was it? He had seen it on many women's faces, young as he was, but it made no sense in connection with his sixteen-year-old sister.

"Where have you been? Christ, we've been out of our minds," Davy said, hugging her swiftly and thanking God, she was well aware, that he could now get back to his studies.

She wouldn't tell them. Her father thundered, her mother wept quite frantically, her brothers threatened, since they were well aware that she had been sheltered somewhere. She could not have survived out in the open, dressed as she was, with nothing to eat but bilberries so where and with whom had she been?

She wouldn't tell them.

It was no concern of theirs.

13

Chloe Eleanor Taylor and James Paul Hutchinson were married in a quiet ceremony at Woodhead Chapel on Chloe's nineteenth birthday, the only persons present beyond the parson and his wife, Jamie's mother, his stepfather, his half-brother Tommy and his half-sister Dulcie, who would not have missed the occasion for the world, she told her mother.

The Andrews family, even if they had been invited which they were not, would have declined, since Katy's disappearance for a whole week was still far too fresh in their minds. Of course Jack Andrews had not made good his promise to evict Matty's son from the farm he rented, but there was still that feeling that none of what had happened would have happened but for him and Sara Andrews's flighty niece.

The quiet service, the unhurried and peaceful tranquillity of the old church which had stood since it was founded in 1487 as a "Chapel of Ease" for outlying parishioners, the absence of prurient spectators gave their wedding day a dignified joy which pleased both the bride and groom. They had told no one of the date they were to be married except Jamie's small family, and as they came out from the plain, foursquare little chapel the autumn sunshine laid its golden rays about them in what seemed a blessing, a delightful omen which augured well for the days and years ahead.

Chloe wore a gown of rich cream muslin over silk. A collar of frothy ruffles stood up at the back of her neck under the fall of her loosely fastened gold and copper curls. The neckline was square cut just above the tops of her creamy white breasts. The bodice fitted her like a second skin, the ruffled sleeves ending just above her elbows and the skirt was a full waterfall of gathered flounces, each one edged with cream satin and scattered with cream rosebuds, gathered up at the back in a small bustle. She wore a "Dolly Varden" hat tipped slightly over her forehead, the front of the brim turned down, the back turned up. It was decorated with cream satin ribbons and roses to match her gown. She held a single cream rosebud in her hand, begged by Thomas, who had been told of the colours she was to wear, from Angus the gardener.

Her delicate beauty – thank the dear Lord her face was healed – was startling, not quite of this world, her mother-in-law decided. Totally unsuited for a farmer's wife with her dashing hat, her lovely dress which she had made herself, the pale cream of her kid boots which peeped from beneath her skirt. Jamie had had to carry her across the yard to the gig Thomas had borrowed from the Andrews' stable, so as not to spoil the hem of her dress and her dainty boots, but could you help but be struck dumb with awed admiration for her? Matty couldn't. She'd grown fond of her during the past month, for no matter what Chloe was asked to do, no matter how hard the task, by God she had a go at it and every surface of the little farmhouse shone like the newly burnished copper pans which winked on the mantelshelf. You couldn't help but take to her. A little bit of a thing doing her best to hump great buckets of water from the pump in the yard, the skirt of her black dress which she wore to work in tucked up in her waistband. Her hair tied up in a bright froth of coloured ribbons, her boots caked with cow muck, she'd even had a go at milking the cows, squealing with delight when she had squirted her first milky stream into the bucket.

Jamie worshipped her. His eyes were a narrowed, vivid blue, blazing with a love for his wife you'd have to be blind to miss. A bit embarrassing really, his mother was tempted to think, for it was very evident what he had planned for her when he'd got rid of his guests. And it was not as though he was the usual bridegroom who, having been held at straining point for months, years sometimes, was at last to get his hands on what he'd ached for. That big bed of theirs, which Matty had helped to change only this morning before the gig had brought them down here, had been most thoroughly used ever since Chloe had been brought to Valley Bottom Farm, for it seemed they cared nought for Crossclough's opinion on the sinfulness of their situation.

Of course, Katy Andrews had diverted a lot of the talk away from Matty's son and his intended bride, and they *were* to be married, Matty made sure everyone knew, those in the kitchen included, for she'd have no talk in front of her about loose morals and such like. It had been hard not to disclose the date of the wedding, which would have made her feel better, but Jamie and Chloe had been adamant that they wanted no curious spectators.

Now her joy was unbounded as she watched her son and her new daughter-in-law move in what might have been described as a "languorous" fashion – had she known the word, which she didn't – down the short, steep path to the chapel gate. They held hands and looked fondly into one another's eyes and Matty took her Thomas's arm, turning to smile at Tommy who looked most uncomfortable and not at all himself in his new black suit. A big lad was Tommy, like Jamie, and she hoped to God he didn't grow any bigger, for the suit had cost a pretty penny and would be hard to replace. He was like Jamie in looks, was Tommy, both of them taking after her, she thought complacently, dark-haired and blue-eyed and with any luck, though she was narrow-hipped and as insubstantial as the daisies growing in the grass between the graves, James's Chloe might put a blue-eyed baby in Matty's arms by this time next year, or even sooner!

They hadn't a lot to say but they were all smiling broadly except for Tommy who couldn't wait to get his bloody collar off. Thomas was smart in his one good suit, Matty quietly elegant in a blue silk gown she had made herself, for Matty had been a seamstress in her younger days, and a good one, like Sara Andrews. Her blue hat, decorated with a racy-looking stuffed bird, was stylish and she was proud of her family, of her new daughter-in-law who was "respectable" now and of her eldest son who, for the first time in his twenty-five years, wore a dark grey suit with a light grey waistcoat and could be mistaken for gentry any day of the week.

"Right, lad," she said cheerfully to her husband. "Let's be off ter cut t'wedding cake, an' give over kissin' tha' wife, Jamie Hutchinson. Tha'll have plenty o' time fer that later," glorying in the fact that she could make a joke of it now since Jamie and Chloe were decently wed.

The girl who crouched behind the stone wall at the side of the chapel waited until the gig was out of sight then straightened up stiffly, just as though she were as old as her own grandmother. Her face was bleak. Her eyes were brown and dull like the soil on a newly dug grave in the cemetery about the chapel, staring at nothing in particular, empty of any expression. Her wide, full-lipped mouth, the colour of the red berries in the hedge, was compressed into a thin white line but she made no sound as she made her way slowly up to the back of the chapel where her mare, her reins fastened to a cam stone at the top of the drystone wall, cropped peacefully.

By the simple expedient of keeping her eye, not on Jamie or the girl he was to marry, but Matty; on Thomas and his comings and goings and the sudden use of the gig this morning, she had ascertained when the wedding ceremony was to be. She was the only one who knew.

Katy Andrews wore breeches of doeskin, well cut, in a shade of creamy beige, made for her by her mother's dressmaker who had at first refused flatly to be associated with such a disgraceful, indecent item of clothing.

"Very well, I shall take my custom elsewhere," Miss Andrews said coldly, picking up her reticule and turning towards the shop door. "There are other dressmakers besides yourself, Miss Mason," which was true and, seeing a great deal of business leaving her establishment, for Mrs Andrews, who no longer made her own clothes, was a wealthy client, Miss Mason hesitated.

"Can you not make such a garment?" Miss Andrews wanted to know. She was alone. She had come in her father's carriage, driven by her father's coachman. She was beautifully dressed in a gown of white muslin, her sash a lavender blue to match the ribbons on her small hat. Just as a girl of her age should be.

"Naturally I can, Miss Andrews, for have I not made the breeches you wear with your riding habit? I can make any garment I set my mind to but I'm sure your mama . . ."

"My mother is not well, Miss Mason, otherwise she would be here beside me."

"I'm sorry to hear that, my dear, but really, would it not be . . .?"

"Can you do this, Miss Mason?" Katy Andrews continued doggedly. "And will you do it?"

Miss Andrews was perfectly polite, calm and more dignified than Miss Mason had ever seen her, but there was a certain look about her, in her brooding eyes, in her unruffled belief that she would get what she wanted which made Miss Mason uneasy.

Resigned, Miss Mason gave in. She had heard, as who had not in Crossclough, of the worrying state of Mrs Andrews's health and if Miss Andrews were to be allowed to wear such a garment, as it seemed she was, who was Miss Mason to argue? She measured her customer, not only for one pair of breeches but two, several jackets of various materials and colours, an enveloping waterproof cloak lined with a sturdy woollen material which Miss Andrews explained must be full enough to be spread back over her mare's rump, and half a dozen pairs of riding gloves.

Miss Mason watched from her window as her client walked calmly across the road to Mr Wilson's, the hatter, where, she heard later, she ordered a man's tall riding hat, and from there to Mr Potter who made riding boots for gentlemen.

Miss Mason shook her head. What was the world coming to, she asked her young apprentice to tell her, but the girl had no answer.

Katy sprang lightly on to Storm's back, unhindered by the full length of the riding habit she had once worn. They made no attempt to force her now, her mother and her father; to stop her going where she pleased since she went anyway. Her father might have made more fuss, created the dreadful arguments which upset her mother so, but the very fact that they did kept him tight-lipped and grey-faced with the growing realisation that his daughter, his Katy, was gone for ever. Ever since she had returned from the dead, so to speak, she had, without fuss, or any of the shenanigans she had once got up to, gone wherever she pleased and there was a rumour rippling about the valley which made her smile, since it said she had been seen with a man up on the high moorland of the Dark Peak.

It was hard going up through the stand of trees which lay at the back of Woodhead Chapel, oak and birch and rowan, acorns lying thickly on the spongy ground, last year's growth of leaves forming a carpet which deadened the sound of her mare's hooves. The downy birch trees, which were the only species to survive in the cold uplands of the north, their leaves turning a bright yellow and ready to fall, showed their gleaming trunks, a pale white in the soft shafts of sunshine and russet bracken crowded about their roots. Rowan, its handsome trunk covered with smooth, slate grey bark, its foliage providing a glorious display of bright, shiny fruits ranging in colour from orange to vivid scarlet. It would be short-lived, this splendour, for already the woodland birds were stripping the trees bare.

She came out from beneath the trees on to the tussocky moorland, allowing Storm her head, galloping flat out, her hair, which she no longer bothered to cut or fasten back and which had grown quickly, streaming out in a molten copper flag behind her. The wind plastered her silk shirt to her full, round breasts and it was very evident that she wore nothing under it. Her face, despite the force and drive of her gallop, was white and strained, her eyes glazed, anguished.

The sky was shining and translucent, like silvered mother-of-pearl with barely a hint of blue in it but she did not see the beauty around her, nor above her. Her expression was haunted and she gave the appearance of being in a kind of dreadful limbo in which nothing was real or relevant. She was sunk in her own agonising, dry-eyed grief, washed up alone on some deserted shore where her inner self had nothing to do with her body which continued to function as those about her expected her to function. The armour of numbness, which had formed about her in Jamie Hutchinson's kitchen and which had shielded her to a degree, had begun to develop chinks in it which would soon become great gaps and eventually fall away altogether and Katy knew she would be raw and vulnerable. Her face felt cold, clamped tight with the pain which devoured her, a pain so deep it seemed to come from somewhere inside her she had not known existed.

Despair, that worst of all emotions, tore at her, for at last she truly knew she had lost him. He was married, husband to Chloe, lost to her for ever and somehow she must find a way to go, something to fill her days, and nights, a purpose in life which would exhaust her so that she might sleep.

Jamie. His name slashed across her heart like a saw-edged blade and she doubled up in agony, her face pressed to Storm's wind-tossed mane. The piercing sorrow hollowed out a space inside her that only Jamie could fill and at last, with her hair falling to mingle with the mare's mane, she wept. Not a cascade of tormented weeping but silent tears which slipped from beneath her closed eyelids and fell in slow desolation to Storm's neck.

The wind whined over the moors but she dawdled about the tops for several hours, stopping now and then to alight and lean against her mare's strong back and stare down across the rolling uplands of the valley far below. The hills went on and on into the distance, rising up in dark-shaded, gold-shaded, blue-shaded grandeur. There were deep grey cloughs littered with stones and, winding like a thread of silver ribbon, Great Crowden Brook which emptied just by her grandmother's cottage into Woodhead Reservoir.

She rode again, stopped to rest again, her back against a sun-warmed rock as big and as square as the stable block at Cloudberry End and all about her great chunks of stone rambled down the slope, cracked and broken as though a giant hammer had shattered them and a giant hand flung them away.

She was just inside the encircling woodland which surrounded her father's property when he sprang out at her from behind the broad, gnarled trunk of a vast oak tree. His arms went round her waist, dragging her from the saddle but her feet were still in the stirrups and for a moment, as her legs twisted agonisingly, they were both carried along by the terrified mare.

"You bloody fool," she snarled in his ear. "You'll injure her," but already her teeth were beginning to nip at his flesh and her tongue to lap about his chin like a kitten at a bowl of cream.

He brought them to a halt just before the wood ended and the smooth lawns and ornamental gardens of Cloudberry End began. The mare tried to escape him, rolling her eyes, ready to snap at his hand for she was afraid of him, as most animals were, but he hauled her back deeper into the wood and tied her to a sapling.

Paddy Andrews turned to Katy, his eyes burning pits of brown coal in his strong, sunburned face. He had not shaved for days nor had he bathed and the smell of his male sweat was acrid in the leaf-scented, fern-scented fragrance beneath the trees, the familar scent of him already uncoiling that sensitive bud deep in her belly which she had come to know so well in the past weeks.

He swayed towards her and she began to smile, for by God this was what she needed to block out the sight of her cousin Chloe in her wedding dress and the look in Jamie's eyes as he brought his bride out of the chapel on his arm.

They came together with an impact which jarred the breath from their lungs, tearing at one another, their mouths opened wide as they bit and snapped and sucked and licked, their snarling breath growing hoarse with desire. Frantically they threw off their clothing though her bloody breeches were not as easy to remove as her skirt and drawers had been, he growled at her.

They smiled as they circled one another like two prize fighters, both totally naked, both strangely beautiful in their fierce lust. They had shared many hours together since the days he had turned her into a woman, up on the moorland, lying on the springing turf among the rocks, their bodies turning to lustrous shades of burned honey and polished amber in the hot sunshine which had bathed the Dark Peak throughout the month of September. He had loved her until she purred like a cat, hurt her until she screamed for mercy, then loved her again until she slept in his arms. On waking, bruised and sore, he would take her again and it was as he had said it would be. She could not get enough of him, nor he of her. He put his mark on her, though she would have denied it, as though he branded her with a hot iron and the clamour they made silenced the small moorland animals and flushed out the larks which rose crazily into the sun. He caressed her body until, her hips and buttocks rolling boisterously, she laid herself along his hard body and impaled herself on his jutting manhood. When it was done, not satisfied, she explored him from the curling, tumbled hair on his head to the soles of his none-too-clean feet with her fingers and her mouth until he groaned in agony, her breasts, golden and tipped with rose, big and full and exuberant, poised above his face until her nipples slid into his mouth and this time it was his turn to dominate her, flipping her over on to her back, the full weight of his muscular body pressing hers down into the soft grass. He took her every day and longed for her every night, careless who knew it, for she was his.

They were quiet at last. It was the first time they had lain together so close to her home and it was in his heart to wish that her father or her poor sap of a brother would come across them, sprawled naked together on the sorrel-carpeted woodland of Cloudberry End. They'd have to accept him then. Accept him as a husband for Katy Andrews, for what man would want damaged goods when it came out she'd been had by Paddy Andrews? He'd like that. It'd suit him down to the ground to have not only Katy Andrews in his bed but Jack Andrews's cash in his pocket. A decent job at the paper mill, not too exacting, for he fancied the life of a bloody gentleman and by Jesus, he'd put that little pipsqueak's nose out of joint, see if he didn't.

He had hoped, in the last few weeks, that she'd tell him she was pregnant, for with what joy would he have greeted such news. He had to smile when he thought about it, for in the five years or so since he had taken his first woman he'd done his best to avoid the very situation he now hoped for. It was what all men dreaded, the accusation that they were the father of what was in a woman's womb, but by Christ he wished he could claim that predicament with Katy Andrews.

"I'll have to go." Her eyes were a deep, glowing golden brown surrounded by the faint smudges he recognised were the result of her utter satiation. Her face was flushed and there was still a patina of sweat between her breasts and on the inside of her thighs. He began to lick it with a greedy tongue but she pushed him away and he knew it was all over. She had had what she wanted from him and the familiar feeling of frustrated fury ran through his veins. He did his best to be patient. He had never been patient in his life but then he had never loved a woman in his life and if he was to have this one, who had become his life, then he must show restraint. At the moment she was mad for him, as he had told her she would be on that first night, but she still did not consider him as anything but a lover. A plaything, an interlude to relieve her boredom and fulfil her newly awakened needs in much the same way men looked on a mistress. Until he had her in the palm of his hand, eating out of the palm of his hand, pregnant, then he must not try to rope her or she would simply turn her back on him.

It was hard but he managed a grin, a grin of great wickedness and she began to smile as she pulled her breeches over her hips. She wore nothing beneath them. She sort of wriggled and twisted and slithered into them, her breasts bouncing, her waist and belly sinuous and fluid and for a moment he was diverted. Hurriedly he reached for his own trousers, holding them in front of him before she noticed his renewed interest.

"What?" she asked him. "What mischief have you got planned? You're up to something I can tell, so you'd better spit it out."

"I'm fightin' ternight."

She stopped fiddling with the buttons of her breeches and her eyes widened. He was fascinated to see that, for some reason, her nipples had hardened, standing out from the dark circles which surrounded them. She was excited, he suddenly realised and at once his hands reached out to hold them. She did not stop him.

"Fighting?" she murmured, her breath beginning to quicken again.

"Aye, would tha' like ter come an' see me fight, Katy Andrews?"

"Yes . . . oh yes," making no resistance when he began to pull her breeches down about her thighs.

She slammed through the back door and, about the kitchen as it always did, everything came to a halt, just as it had done in the stable yard where the men's eyes didn't know where to look. Dilly's hands froze in the water in which she was peeling carrots and her eyes swivelled wildly in her head. Her mouth dropped open and she almost fell off the box which elevated her to the right height for the scullery sink. They'd seen her before, naturally, in this "get-up" but it took some getting used to. No wonder her poor ma was not in good health.

Ivy carefully replaced the fine bone china milk jug on the tray which she had been about to take through to Mrs Andrews, afraid she might drop it in her spellbound contemplation of Miss Katy's rolling behind and Janet, who was diligently following Mrs Tiplady's instructions on the making of light, fruity scones, dropped the baking spoon on to the clean floor where Muffy leaped upon it in great glee.

It had been noticed and remarked upon that Miss Katy no longer took her little dog with her on her daily outings to only God alone knew where. They didn't know why, for the animal had gone everywhere with her at one time. Another mystery to add to the one which none of them could solve and all, probably, to do with the week she had spent, again they didn't know where, when she had gone missing.

"No, naughty girl," Katy told the dog, scooping her up into her arms and kissing her. She handed the spoon to Janet with an apologetic shrug, then, "I think I might have something to eat, Mrs Tiplady. I'm famished." She threw herself down in the chair Mrs Tiplady had just vacated, the dog in her lap and waited with absolute certainty that she would be fed.

"Will you not go through to the drawing room, Miss Katy?" Mrs Tiplady wheedled. "The mistress is about to take afternoon tea and I could bring some extra . . ."

"No thanks, here will do, Tippy," calling the cook by the name she and her brothers had used as children. "I can't be bothered to change and Mother will only go on about my breeches."

And could you wonder, Mrs Tiplady's expression suggested as Miss Katy placed her right ankle across her left knee, as her brothers did, and waited.

"Those scones smell good, Janet. I love them hot," she went on. "Lots of butter, please and a cup of tea. I've no idea what's made me so hungry," and neither had they and they had never seen her look so well. She was flushed and shining, like a rosy apple, her skin right down to the opening of her shirt a soft, honey brown, as were her bare forearms, her neck and where else they shuddered to think for not a bit of white flesh could be seen anywhere. The Lord alone knew where she went all day long, what she got up to and with whom, for nobody reported seeing her in Crossclough or Woodhead so what were they to make of that? Her eyes were sort of unfocused, deep and somehow dreaming, her lashes lifting and drooping slowly, her long body lying boneless and graceful in the depths of the chair. The dog draped herself across her stomach while her mistress ate half a dozen scones, watching each mouthful unblinkingly, rewarded now and again with a morsel which went straight down without touching her teeth.

Katy stood up and placed the little mongrel on her cushion by the fire, dusted down her indecent breeches beneath which they could all see, as plain as plain, the crack in her behind and in . . . in another unmentionable place, smiled her thanks and strode out of the kitchen.

"Well, I don't know what ter say, really I don't," sighed Freda. "She were a handful before, we all know that but since she come back from . . . wherever it were she got to that week, she's like some . . . well, I dunno . . . Her poor ma and pa must be outa their minds with worry. She's lost that wildness, wouldn't you say, Mrs Tiplady, but what's come ter take its place, tell me that? A madam she might have been, and was, but she was always warm with it, you know what I mean? Now she's so damned cool, composed like, it's frightening. Ride roughshod over everyone, she will, to have what she wants, whatever that might be, an' I for one wonder where it will all end, honest to God."

Chris Andrews yelled with the rest of the howling mob as the bare fist of the smaller fighter glided off his opponent's cheek and whistled past his ear. They fell against one another, the blood which slicked both their bodies glueing them together for a moment before one pushed the other off and danced away on light feet. He was graceful, the big one, lean and dangerously cool-headed, his powerful shoulders shining with sweat in the torchlight.

The contenders were not restricted by the 1867 Marquis of Queensberry rules here, fighting bare-knuckled, throwing, gouging, tripping, hair-pulling and scratching being the order of the day. There were no weight divisions, though the two who fought each other tonight were evenly matched, one being slightly taller than the other. There were no timed rounds, for they lasted as long as it took one man to knock down the other which was followed by a thirty-second rest period when both challengers were then required to "come up to scratch". This was a line drawn in the centre of the rough ring and the loser of the fight was the man who was unable to crawl or stagger to the "scratch" line. A test of endurance then, with no real skills required. This fight had already lasted two hours.

The purse was for twenty guineas and the bets were flying, tempers rising, other scraps threatening to break out as men extolled or belittled the skills of the men in the ring. There was an enormous crowd, working men mingling with the gentry who were diverted by the sight of one labouring man beating the living daylights out of another. They yelled hoarsely, then guffawed mindlessly as one almost slipped in the blood. There was an avid hush, a dreadful silence followed by an explosion of maniacal noise as one of the fighters went down.

"Get up, man, get up."

"Yer bloody nancy, it were nowt burra tap."

"'Ang on theer, lad."

"Come up to scratch, for God's sake, I've a guinea . . ."

"What's up wi' yer?"

"Gerrup . . . gerrup an' kill 'im."

The crowd howled and swayed, mindless in its bloodlust, wanting murder, or at least mutilation and Chris Andrews, who was already deep in debt and would be deeper still if his "man" did not win, clapped his hands to his head in a ferment of excitement.

It ended suddenly when the taller man drove one of his hard fists into the centre of his opponent's face, smashing what was left of his nose to bloody pulp and with the other almost lifted him from his feet with an upper cut to the jaw. He went down with a thud which seemed to make the ground judder.

"Come up to scratch . . . come up to scratch," the time-keeper roared after the required thirty seconds had gone by, but the man was coming nowhere, not even round, and the arm of the winner was lifted high above his head as the crowd howled its approval, or not, depending on where the wagers had been laid.

They were spellbound, the hundred or so men who surrounded the ring, falling silent at the spectacle of the tall, blood-streaked winner striding from the ring and taking in his arms a tall, slender, cloaked, top-hatted young gentleman who, to their astonishment, kissed him again and again on his bloody mouth, so vigorously his hat fell off, his cloak fell open and he was revealed to be, not a young man but a young woman!

And not any young woman, either, but Jack Andrews's lass, who had vanished a month or two back and then returned in the most mysterious fashion. Now she was hanging about Paddy Andrews's neck, Paddy Andrews who was her own cousin, and in a way which could only be called disgusting. Not only disgusting but surely criminal for her even to be here. Impropriety apart, she was in real danger amongst such rough company, though the way she and Paddy were carrying on it was obvious what was between them and there was not one man ready to insult her, not with the winner of the fight to protect her.

But Chris Andrews had no such compunction. With a roar which could be heard a mile away in these silent hills and in this silent company, he launched himself across the slippery ring, his arms going round Paddy's waist, his face twisted, contorted into a rage and disgust so powerful he actually pulled the bigger, more powerful man from his feet. Katy Andrews staggered, losing her balance but was saved by the hand of an excited onlooker who leered at her brazen, what seemed to him almost naked body beneath her cloak as though he would dearly love to lay more than his hand on her.

"Chris," she was shrieking, shaking herself free. "Get off him. Paddy, for God's sake, it's Chris, damn you. Chris . . . Oh, dear sweet Christ, he'll kill him," for Paddy, not recognising his attacker in the flickering light of the torch and who would not have cared if he had, was raining blows on her lightweight brother's face and head, doing him damage from which he might never recover.

Paddy still had the killing force in him and did not understand or care for the troublesome fly which buzzed about him.

"Paddy, stop it . . . stop it," the fly shrieked and when he at last recognised her and who it was he was murdering, he stepped back in disdain from the bleeding, crumpled heap at his feet. He wouldn't soil his hands, nor his reputation on a bit of shite like Chris Andrews, his expression said.

"Leave 'im," he snarled as Katy would have gone to him.

"He's my brother."

"An' what am I?" His eyes were menacing, not allowing her to see his fear. She must choose between them, his slitted eyes told her, here before this assembly who were watching, hypnotised and soundless, but this was Katy Andrews who feared no man and was beholden to no man. Katy Andrews whose warm, loving heart had been broken then effectively hardened until it ached for no one.

Still, she did not ignore him.

"I'll come back, Paddy, but I must see he gets home. Johnny, is that you? Is his horse here? Oh Tim, thank God . . . get him into the saddle and make sure he gets home, will you? Thanks."

She turned when her brother was draped across his saddle and led away and with a shameless, graceful stride which silenced even those who whispered at the back of the crowd, moved across to Paddy Andrews and kissed him again on his torn mouth.

He grinned triumphantly, turning to the men who watched, his arm possessively about her waist, his grin confirming that, yes, this woman was his and if there was any other man who wished to dispute it then now was the time to do it.

They shuffled their feet and lowered their eyes, not in shame for themselves but for Katy Andrews who was breaking her family's heart.

14

The full and shameful horror of it rocked not only the house of Cloudberry End but the small town of Crossclough and the length and breadth of the Longdendale Valley as well. They talked of nothing else and it was then that Madge Andrews, who had scarcely had a day's illness in her life, suddenly seemed to falter, to look frail, to look her age, saying she did not feel up to fettling and would have a day or two in bed. Her son's lass, Dorcas, a sensible young woman, plain to be sure but trustworthy, was sent over to stay with her until she was up to her old fettling ways but Madge was beyond that now. Paddy was her grandson. A young devil, if ever there was one, and Katy, her granddaughter, the joy of her heart and she just could not reconcile the two, nor the talk about them.

Katy Andrews, during the week she had spent in Paddy's cottage, her mind numbed with grief and despair, had given no thought to those who loved her, who searched desperately for her, since their feelings had not mattered. In a curious way she had been half ready to believe that her father and mother were to blame, for if they had encouraged Jamie to think of their daughter as, perhaps, a prospective bride, had him up to the house to dine, allowed him to become a welcome guest and not treated him as merely the son of a servant, could not the result have been vastly different? After all, her father was of humble stock and so could he not have been less rigid in his refusal to accept Katy's obvious feelings, for she had never kept them hidden, for Jamie Hutchinson? Calf love, puppy love, those were the words which had been bandied about, no one ready to believe that her young love was given whole-heartedly, irrevocably to Jamie.

So, let them suffer, let them weep, let them spend sleepless nights and heartbreaking days; the only person whom she regretted hurting during that week was her grandmother who had never, in all the years Katy had been galloping over to Woodhead, reproached, or criticised her arbitrary defiance of the rules of society. Nor had she treated her granddaughter as other than a human being who must decide her own course through life. As Madge Andrews had. Even if it proved to be the wrong course, then that was all right as long as one had the guts and resolution to recognise it and get back on the appropriate track, then no harm was done. Katy had respect and love for her grandmother and it filled her with guilty shame in the weeks following her homecoming to see the way her grandmother, worn out by that dreadful week, was fading. Of course she was very old, well past the time when women could expect to live, but Katy could not forget how spry her grandmother had been only a few days before Chloe Taylor ran away to Valley Bottom Farm.

"What were tha' thinkin' of, my lass?" she asked Katy sorrowfully when her granddaughter rode over to visit her a few days after the fight. Chris was still lying in his bed, no bones broken, no more than two black eyes, a bloody nose and a livid bruise below his breastbone, but the damage to his self-esteem, to his pride and sense of who he was in this community, not only in the valley but in the eyes of Johnny Ashwell and Tim Warren, was vast, brooding and hidden, ready, though no one knew of it, to do murder to

Paddy Andrews when the time was ripe. His mother had risen from her own couch where she was fast becoming a semi-invalid, exclaiming in horror, clinging to her husband but refusing to leave her son's bedside until the doctor had assured her that he was in no mortal danger.

Later that night, when she had drifted home on the back of her mare, Paddy's kisses still hot on her mouth, the bruises he had given her chafing her thighs, Katy had not been astonished when her mother had turned on her.

"This is your fault," she had hissed, ready to clench her own fist and drive it into the face of this girl child of hers, but Katy had merely shrugged, her own eyes untroubled, for whatever had caused her brother to be as he was could not be laid at her door.

"Why, lass?" her grandmother repeated, putting out her hand to her, beckoning her to sit beside her on the bed where she lay. "Dost tha' enjoy hurting them as loves thi'? And what did tha' think to achieve by going to watch a prize fight?"

Katy, in deference to her grandmother, wore her blue riding habit, though naturally Madge Andrews had been told of her granddaughter's indecent outfit which she ostentatiously sported up hill and down dale and even in the centre of Crossclough where the sight of her lounging on her mare's back in a man's silk shirt and riding jacket, doeskin breeches and a dashing top hat had brought the traffic to a standstill.

"Nothing, Grandmother. I just wanted to see how men spent their time. To find out what pleasure they get from such a spectacle."

"An' did tha'?"

"No, not really. But I did find out something and that is that I need the choice to see such things, if I wish to. I may not go again but I shall decide one way or the other. I have been persuaded, all my life, to follow other people's inclinations and not my own. I have not, as you know, been easily persuaded." She grinned. "Now I have decided to consider no one's preferences, only my own. The other night my . . . my cousin was to fight and when he invited me to watch him I accepted."

"No matter who tha' hurt?"

Her grandmother's eyes were misted with what looked like tears and in a fit of remorse Katy lifted her blue-veined, liver-spotted hand to her face, brushing the back of it with her lips.

"I'm sorry, I know it hurts you but sometimes . . . I hurt so much myself I seem unable to feel for others, even you, Grandmother. I love you."

"I know that, lamb, an' I know what ails thi' but tha' must get on wi' tha' life an' not try to destroy others."

"I don't, Grandmother. I'm not trying to destroy others but I feel the need to live as I want to live. Is that wrong?"

"An' how's that then, Katy Andrews? Tha' can't go through life treatin' other folk as though they meant nowt. Tha's chosen a hard road to walk, lass, if tha're to be at odds wi' everyone tha' meets on it."

She put her gnarled old hand against Katy's cheek and in her face was a mixture of sadness and yet a pride in this headstrong granddaughter of hers.

"Paddy Andrews, though he's me grandson an' I'm fond of 'im fer all his wild ways, will bring tha' nowt but trouble, Katy. Don't play wi' fire, lamb, fer that's what tha're doin'. He's a man not a boy an' won't be put down an' picked up again when tha've a fancy for . . . for whatever it is he is ter thi'."

Though Katy still obstinately refused to reveal where she had spent the week of her disappearance, the farrago at the prize fight surely pointed to only one conclusion and that was Paddy Andrews's place, and what had gone on there?

Madge Andrews asked herself despairingly. And had the same thought occurred to Jack, this girl's stricken father who, short of tying her to the bedpost to keep her at home, since the law was on his side, had no control whatsoever over her movements?

"Grandmother!" Katy was ready to be appalled.

"I'm old an' me time's nearly up but I'm not blind, lass, nor soft in th'ead. I've heard the rumours, aye, even lyin' here in this bed for Annie Lennox an' Jinty Pickles are only too glad ter tell me tha's bin seen wi' him up on Tintwistle Knarr. Saul Gibbon tells his Agnes who passes it on ter Percy Clarke's missus whose maid tells Jinty when she goes up theer to do't laundry. Leave well alone, lass. Paddy's not the sort ter tekk up wi' any lass unless theer's summat in it for 'im, one way or t'other. Theer's nowt round 'ere fer a lad such as 'im an' I'd not be surprised ter see 'im tekk 'imself off across the world ter join his brothers, that is unless he found summat here more to 'is likin'. And tha' pa's got a bob or two in his pocket."

"I'm not sure I know what you mean, Grandmother."

Madge Andrews's face was filled with compassion and understanding. She should be worried about this girl of Jack's and she would if she had the strength for it but somehow these days she found her mind turned more and more to Chris, her Chris who had died so long ago but who had lived on in her heart ever since. She'd not mind seeing him again and as soon as the good Lord liked. And then there was George, her eldest, dead only a few weeks ago which did not seem right, for surely a mother should go before her child. She'd not attended his funeral, letting the men of the family see to the putting away of one of their own, but sorrow had burdened her and helped to bring her to this bed of hers.

Aye, she could understand her granddaughter's misery, her sense of loss for she'd known it herself. Katy was young, seventeen next month and though it sounded heartless, she'd get over this pain she felt over Jamie Hutchinson. You got over everything in the end. You had to, or go under.

"I'm tired now, my lass," she murmured, her interest in and concern for the events of this world slipping gradually away from her as she edged towards the next. "Off yer go an' mind what I say. Listen to tha' pa an' ma for they only want what's best for thi', as we all do."

It was the last time Katy saw her grandmother alive. Her heart had simply stopped beating as she slept, the doctor informed them, but it made no difference to Katy Andrews, for she knew beyond question that she had killed Madge Andrews as surely as if she had held a pillow over her face and she knew also that she would never forgive herself for it as long as she lived. She sat on the edge of her chair in her mother's drawing room, her hands in her lap, her face carved from grey granite, her eyes wide and tearless in shock as her father discussed the funeral arrangements with her mother as casually, it appeared to her, as though his mother were no more than a slight acquaintance. It would be a splendid affair, of course, and so it was, for, contrary to Katy's belief, Jack Andrews had been very fond of his mother. But she had been ready to go. It was the natural order of things for the generation ahead to "pass on" and Jack accepted it and what he had to do.

There was a vast crowd all but swamping the small cemetery at Woodhead Chapel and standing in silent rows beyond the wall and down to the road which meandered alongside the reservoirs. Katy had been unable to contemplate the funeral, saying she was off to the tops to do her own mourning, but her father, speaking quietly and in a voice which brooked no argument, of his mother, and his mother's love for Katy herself, her hurt at not having her granddaughter to stand at her graveside in a last respectful farewell, persuaded her, and she stood on that cold autumn day, staring out over the heads of her cousins, one of them Paddy Andrews. She did not look at the coffin, just as she had not looked at her grandmother's dead face as it reposed in it, not caring how beautiful she looked, not believing them when they told her she was only sleeping. She was dead, the only person she had ever truly loved besides Jamie, which was quite a different sort of love. She felt irritated by the tears about her, for what did they know of true desolation? She and her mother wore black silk gowns beaded with jet, hats with black, silk bows and feathers and knee-length mourning veils. She did not see, or care what the rest of the family had on, the shuffling rows of them, men and women. There was a black-draped hearse and several carriages, black horses and a blackness about her which did its best to drag her into the grave with Grandmother. How blissful that would be.

It was then she saw them standing on the far side of the drystone wall which surrounded the cemetery, their heads bowed, his arm solicitously about her as though she were as fragile as a newly flowered snowdrop. She was in black, the black she had worn on the day she had climbed down from the Manchester to Sheffield train, pressed and sponged for the occasion. She lifted her clouded, blue-green eyes from her sombre contemplation of the freshly dug earth about the grave and her glance was nailed to Katy's, neither of them able to look away. They were trapped, as the parson droned on of everlasting life and women wept as women do, in a timeless moment of what could only be called remembrance. But remembrance of what, since neither of them could recall memories, shared memories that were pleasing to them both. It was then, as blue eyes searched brown, that they realised it was not what had been but what might have been that they shared. What, in time, might have grown between them if a man had not forced them apart.

Chloe had not known Madge Andrews and could not honestly mourn her as Katy did but her warm gaze said that she understood Katy's desolation, for had she not lost her own mama not so long ago? It was all there, the sympathy, the sadness that she could not give to Katy what she needed. She seemed inclined to smile a little, no more than the compassionate lifting of the corners of her soft mouth. They had never been friends, as they might have been and now, with Jamie Hutchinson standing irrevocably between them, they never would. But for that moment Katy allowed the gentle giving of something which might be of value, perhaps comfort, from her cousin, a willingness, if Katy could bring herself to . . . what? What could there ever be for Katy Andrews and Chloe Hutchinson now?

Nothing but bitterness and knife-edged pain, Katy's eyes told her, hardening to brown pebbles in the absolute stillness of her white face. Then the moment, the strange moment was over almost before it was acknowledged and it was Chloe who looked away first. She turned her face into Jamie's shoulder and at once he bent his head tenderly, murmuring something to her. They had come as a mark of respect to the family who had been closely involved with Jamie and Jamie's mother for nearly thirty years and for no other reason. Certainly not to be stared at, though there were those who were staring since not many had actually seen a couple who had lived in sin.

Now, as the coffin was lowered into the ground, as Sara Andrews, pale and frail as a drift of lily of the valley, swayed in her husband's strong arms, Chloe and Jamie moved away, Jamie's arm still comfortingly about his wife's shoulders.

Across the gaping hole in which their grandmother was laid to rest, Chris Andrews stared grimly at his cousin Paddy, his livid face quite without expression. There were still deep plum circles about his eyes, turning mauve and yellow at the edges and he was seen to take his brother Davy's arm as he moved slowly away towards the carriage.

Richard Andrews, recently arrived from some God-forsaken place none of those hereabouts had ever heard of, put his arm about his sister's stiff shoulders, attempting to lead her away, and those who watched were diverted to see her shake it off, indicating that she would join the others in a minute.

There were only herself and Paddy then and those who had gone would have been astonished to see the expression on his somewhat battered face and hear the soft words he spoke.

"Are thi' managin', Coppertop?" A name he had given her at his cottage when she had flamed into life for him. His usually rough voice was warm, soft-toned.

"Not really," she sighed, showing only to him the true depth of her sorrow.

"Can I . . .?"

"No . . . no, Paddy. It will get better. I loved her."

"Aye, I know that, lass. Listen, I'll not come round ter't house wi' rest."

"It would be . . . for the best."

"I'll see thi' soon, Coppertop?" The longing in his voice was very evident and she smiled a little. The men were shuffling about them, their spades ready to fill in the grave but Paddy moved round to stand beside her.

"Katy?" he insisted.

"Yes . . . soon, Paddy, I promise," and for a second or two the gravediggers were confounded to see Jack Andrews's lass lower her head to Paddy Andrews's broad shoulder.

They trudged or rode back to Cloudberry End where Mrs Tiplady had prepared some sort of repast. How would these plain working folk, Jack Andrews's brothers and sisters-in-law, his nephews and nieces and their offspring, fit in there? But they were Madge Andrews's family when all was said and done and must be sustained. Madge had left a will, at Jack's insistence, since he meant to have no haggling over her bits and pieces, he told her. There was her china tea-service, her mother's chiffonier standing in the parlour, some trifling pieces of jewellery, but best to say who got what, he said firmly, and now they were to find out.

They ambled about the house in their Sunday clothes, Will and his wife, Anna, Harry and his wife, Jane, their children and grandchildren, those who had not died or emigrated. Dozens of them, it seemed to Freda and Lottie and Ivy who were seriously offended to find the women gawping about the first floor of the house, peering open-mouthed into bedrooms, one even trying out Mrs Andrews's pretty summer parasol of cream lace and silk which she had discovered on a chair in the master and mistress's own room.

Will Andrews's two youngest, Josh and Jake, had frightened Dilly to death when they loafed into the kitchen demanding a "proper" drink of ale and not this sweet stuff which tasted like bloody medicine, referring to Mr Andrews's best sherry. Their big, dark, powerful bodies had seemed to fill the kitchen with some dreadful male menace, since it seemed they were ready for a bit of "fun" with the younger housemaids. Mrs Tiplady soon put them in their place, of course, sending them off with a flea in their ear, the pair of them, and she didn't care if they were related to the master. The housekeeper was heard to remark that it could have been worse. Their cousin Paddy Andrews might have accompanied them.

None of them was quite sure why they had been assembled in Sara Andrews's elegant drawing room. They jostled one another, the young ones inclined to giggle and stare at this uncle of theirs and his frozen-faced, gimlet-eyed sons, his stiff-necked daughter whose curling lip said she despised them all, and his wisp of a wife whom none of them had cared for, and most, truth to tell, had never met. A will! What would old Grandma Andrews want with a will, the men muttered amongst themselves, twisting their Sunday bowlers in work-roughened fingers while their womenfolk looked about them wondering what half the objects in the room were meant to be.

"This is a short, simple will," the solicitor from Crossclough began, deciding from the first to use short and simple words in order to be understood. "Bequeath" would be beyond most of them so, to save time he went right at it.

"Mrs Andrews has left everything she owned to her granddaughter . . ."

There was a stir. Which granddaughter?

". . . from whom, she says, she received more affection than she could ever repay."

What in hell's name did *that* mean? they asked one another, turning to stare about them.

"There is only the property in Woodhead . . ."

Property? In Woodhead?

". . . a cottage, but it, and everything in it is . . ." Should he say *bequeathed*? No, best not, ". . . given to my granddaughter Katherine Andrews."

He could see that even Jack Andrews was pole-axed. It was he who had insisted on his mother making a will but he had no idea what its contents might be and if he had known that Madge Andrews had actually owned her sturdy little cottage he might have discussed with her the disposal of it and would certainly have done his best to dissuade her from putting it in his daughter's careless hands.

Ever since he had begun to make money in what he called "a fair way of things", he had arranged for a generous weekly sum to be sent to his mother and, he supposed, over the years, more than twenty of them, she had been able to put some by. And why not, since there was quite a lot of it, at least by her standards, his twisted, feverish thoughts whispered and she had spent it on nothing for herself. He had been aware, but had said nothing, that she often put her hand in her purse to help out one of her family but the rest, it seemed, had gone towards the purchase of her little cottage on the shores of the Woodhead Reservoir. The cottage which she had just passed on to her wilful, headstrong, uncontrollable granddaughter, giving her a bolt-hole to which she might escape whenever the fancy took her. Which would be frequently.

"Jack . . ." his wife faltered, reaching out for him though the expression on her face was bewildered.

"Christ!" Chris Andrews pronounced, turning to look at his two brothers who, being away from home so much, were not aware of the implications, while the silence continued as those not quite as quick-witted as their educated cousins did their best to grapple with what they had just heard.

"D'yer mean ter say the . . . that it belonged to th'old woman?"

"I allus thought it were rented."

"Wheer'd she get brass?"

And then, when the explosion settled slightly another began.

"She's give it to . . . to 'is lass?"

"Talk about much gets bloody more."

"That'd 've medd a right nice little 'ome fer our Patty," who was to be married at Christmas, as they all knew.

"T'aint fair."

"What's she ever done that we didn't, tell me that?"

"Bloody nowt that I can see."

"I allus liked them cups an' saucers."

"Aye, an' I 'ad me eye on them copper pans."

" 'Tis wicked . . . wicked."

In her straightbacked chair Katy stared at the solicitor, her eyes ready to shed tears at last, bright and hot, though her face was perfectly still and as blank as an empty page. There was no expression there. Not gratitude, not remorse that she should benefit from her grandmother's death where others, perhaps more deserving, hadn't. Not relief, nor speculation of what she might get from such relief. She simply sat, a study in black and white, even her glowing hair completely hidden beneath the black hat and ruched black veiling which swathed the brim.

They had stopped muttering when they finally left. By then they were in a full-throated roar of resentment, swearing they'd not let it lie even though the solicitor told them firmly again and again that Mrs Andrews had been in full control of all her faculties when she made the will and there was nothing to be done about it. It could not be overturned, though they were not awfully sure what he meant by that, harbouring the thought that somehow they were being diddled. She had been their mother and grandmother and so surely, just as much as Katy Andrews, who was no better than she should be, they must be entitled to something, even if it was only a copper pan or two, Harry's wife Jane said aggrievedly.

Katy sat where they had left her, the solicitor's card in her hand for, he said, he would be obliged if she would call, at her convenience, of course, at his offices in Crossclough since there were some legal papers to be signed. He had tried to settle the appointment with Jack Andrews, who, as her father and legal guardian was surely the one to deal with, but she had coolly told him, with a polite smile of apology at her father, that she was quite capable of settling her own affairs. The days had gone when a woman's inheritance went at once to her nearest living male relative, her cool smile reminded him, and she would be down the following day to see it all neatly tied up. She was just seventeen years old.

They had all gone their separate ways, her mother and father to the room they shared where, presumably, they would console one another with the thought there was simply nothing more to be done with her. Her father, doing his best not to upset her mother, had done everything in his power to persuade Katy to put it all in his hands. He would sell it and put the proceeds into something which would bring her in a small income. She had no need of it, he begged her to admit, since it was not the sort of home she would ever live in when she married. Or she could rent it if she didn't want to part with it, he pleaded, while her mother wrung her hands and her two older brothers looked bewildered, wishing to God they could get away to their own worlds, she could see.

While her father argued, Chris sat and stared into the fire, his face brooding and unreadable, his eyes hooded, a brandy in his hand, a cigar between his lips and it was a measure of his father's distress that he noticed neither. He said nothing. He didn't look at her and it seemed to her it was then, at that moment, that the frail but up to now determined thread which had tied her to her mother and brothers, to her father and to his ruling of her, frayed and snapped, leaving her suspended in a light bubble of time, which, when it burst, would drop her into a completely new and undeniably shiny world which might be to her liking. She had never been tied to the conventional mores of her mother's world, and her father, though he had done his best to tame her when he was at home, had been too engrossed with her mother to concern himself unduly with his growing daughter who had, after all, a nanny, then a governess to take charge of her.

So what, her calculating mind asked, was she to do with this gift her beloved grandmother had put in her hands? Was she to waste it as her father wished, or was she to use it to her own advantage, as Grandmother, in giving it to her, seemed to be telling her to do?

She lifted her head, turning it as though to listen for something which sounded on the edge of somewhere far off, then let out her breath on a long, exhausted sigh. She had seen put in the ground today the only person who had truly loved her and how was she to replace that? She sensed that there was a depth to Paddy Andrews's feelings for her which had not been truly revealed but he meant very little to her except as someone to warm her cold body against. His flesh set hers alight, while in the midst of the consuming flames her cold heart beat, perhaps faster but certainly not warmer. Her heart! Dear sweet God, her heart, that bothersome organ which nothing and nobody could cure of the dreadful injury inflicted on it by Chloe and Jamie Hutchinson.

Pain knifed her as her closed eyes saw them as they had been today. Jamie's tender care of the slim, flower-like woman who shared his bed, who had stolen his heart and love, who lived his life with him, the life which should have been Katy Andrews's.

She could go away, she supposed. Pack a bag and take the train to . . . to somewhere and make a life for herself, but she was trained for nothing and certainly not for earning a wage on which to live and anyway, that would be running away and Katy Andrews had never been known to back off from a challenge in her life.

Her mind shifted in subtle shades of warmth and light and then to the cold greyness of despair. For the life of her she hadn't the faintest notion of what she wanted to do. What looked exciting to her, thought-provoking, a gamble, a risk in this safe world which her mother and father had built around themselves and which included her? What was there? What could there be? And all she could see was Paddy Andrews's wicked grin, his narrow-eyed desire, his strong demanding body which was as familar to her now as her own. At least when she was with him she felt alive, recklessly alive, which was what she needed to soothe the wounds a girl of just seventeen should not have been asked to suffer. Why did she feel as she did? Why was all her life, her love, her heart and mind and soul focused on one man, a man who was husband to another woman? Five short months since Chloe had come to Crossclough, stepping – ominously, why hadn't she seen it? – from the same carriage as Jamie and in that time had successfully taken the meaning of life from Katy Andrews.

Her eyes narrowed then. She leaned forward in her chair, focusing on the chuckling flames in the fire, yellow, orange, gold, a touch of blue here and there as the coals hissed.

Meaning, that was what life must have. A purpose, and surely the cottage her grandmother had given her must have some purpose otherwise her death would have been for nothing. Love had gone, not only with Jamie but with Grandmother, but perhaps in Grandmother's own house Katy might find what she sought. God knows what it was but even if it were only a space in time to be alone, a space to think and plan and hope, then she must take advantage of it.

Slowly she rose from her chair, left the empty firelit drawing room and went upstairs to pack.

15

The five men were no more than shadows, the outline of them revealed only as slightly darker than the black night itself.

It was Christmas Eve and the inn on the far side of the moorland road near Saltersbrook was raucous with men's voices, men who were merry with ale, with mulled wine and spiced rum and Christmas spirit, men who had just been paid and, with a week's wages in their pockets, were eager to pour it down their throats as fast as the innkeeper and his barmaid could refill their glasses. Through the small leaded windows, the low, smoke-blackened, age-blackened bar-room could be seen to be jammed with working men and not a few of the gentry who had a fancy to drink in what they considered to be the "quaintness" of a working-man's bar. There was the sound of drunken singing, appropriately, "The Holly and the Ivy", and each time the door opened a beam of golden light spilled out in a long rectangle across the track.

It was bitterly cold, the ground beneath the waiting men's feet crunchy with frost. A dark night with no moon as yet, though there was a wind getting up which would shift the clouds to reveal it soon enough. The weight of the darkness pressed down on them and they shifted uneasily, but what they had come to do needed doing, they all knew that, distasteful as it was. Distasteful, yes, but at the same time each one felt that small, completely male frisson of excited anticipation which comes to soldiers as they wait to go into battle.

The door to the inn began to open and close with more frequency, letting out the merrymakers, most of them in amiable groups, their arms about one another's shoulders, their feet inclined to stumble. There were shouts, appropriate to the season, shouts of farewell, shouts of derision as one of the group lost his footing, and of warm friendship, that of men who had the drink in them.

"Is this him?" one of the five waiting men whispered, his voice rising in excitement.

"Be quiet, you bloody fool," the soft answer came and for another half-hour they shivered in the biting wind which searched among their warm clothing.

Moonlight suddenly flooded the land, carving areas of grey shadow in the dips and hollows about them and the silver-white glitter of the hoar frost created a mysterious beauty which the waiting men were too preoccupied and nervous to notice. They bobbed down hastily, looking about them as though expecting shouts of discovery, then, just as suddenly, the moon disappeared behind a cloud again, leaving them in the welcome pitchy darkness.

The inn door opened once more and one man came out, a tall, broad-shouldered man who called back something to those still inside, his laughter carrying across the cold air to the men who crouched in the dark.

"It's him," one of them whispered. "Let's hope to Christ he hasn't got his bloody dog with him." There was a tense pause then, when it was apparent the man was alone, a collective sigh of relief. "He'll have to come this way to get to his place," the man continued, "or to Woodhead." There was a bitter note in his voice. "Wait until he's got past us and don't move until I tell you."

"What if he . . .?"

"Be quiet and wait until I give you the signal."

The man who had come out of the inn crossed the track and, unbuttoning his trousers, casually urinated in a long arc on to a clump of gorse, the steam from its warmth clearly seen in the light from the inn's window. He was about to take the rough path which led off the track where the inn at Saltersbrook stood when he paused as though some deeply buried, primeval instinct in him sensed danger. He stood, as silent and indistinct as one of the trees which were grouped in a small acre of woodland to his left, his head turning this way and that, like an animal which scents the air, but he had drunk a great deal of ale that night and his normally keen awareness of all that went on about him, wherever he was, had been lost in his glass.

Grunting as though at his own foolishness, he moved on up the path which led from Saltersbrook, across Longside Edge and on to the village of Woodhead which was his destination.

They let him go half a mile. He was blundering and cursing as the moon slid in and out behind scudding, silver-edged clouds. He sang "The Holly and the Ivy" with great gusto and the night creatures cowered down as he went by, creeping out as the sound died away only to scuttle back to safety as another group of intruders disturbed them.

The clouds had fled away, leaving a blue-white radiance, when the man they followed finally sensed them at his back, whirling in crouched alarm, wary in that moment but relaxing contemptuously when he saw who it was. He picked out the face of the man who was his enemy and began to laugh, despite the four shadowy figures who were grouped about him. Five against one, his mocking gaze said, not at all alarmed and it was obvious he felt he still had the advantage in view of who the five were.

"Well, well, well, if it's not the Andrews boys, an' who's these two mannikens wi' thi', lads?"

Paddy Andrews's laughter became more merry and he slapped his thigh in huge delight but Chris Andrews did not share his humour, it seemed. His voice was cold, cutting, belying the white-hot, dangerous anger which burned inside him.

"Yes, the Andrews boys, Paddy. My brothers Richard and David who are home for Christmas as you see." His voice was as smooth as silk but heavy with menace. Paddy appeared not to care. "And allow me to introduce my friends, Johnny Ashwell and Tim Warren, who are of the same opinion as myself and my brothers since they have sisters too."

"Aah, so that's it, is it? Tha've come ter tell me tha' don't like the idea of a common chap like me makin' free wi' a lady like Katy. Is that it?" He laughed derisively. "Well, Mr Andrews, sir, your sister needs no persuadin', believe me. Drops her drawers, or should I say 'er breeches, whenever I 'ave a fancy fer it, which is most days, let me tell thi'. That cottage o' Gran's 'as come in right 'andy an' when me an' Katy's ready fer it 'er an' me'll be married an' settle down in it."

"You bastard, you filthy rotten bastard," Richard Andrews screamed and before his cooler-headed younger brother, who knew exactly what Paddy Andrews was capable of, could warn him he leaped at his cousin and swung at his face with the cudgel he carried.

Paddy Andrews's reputation was as a hard and vicious fighter who would use any means at his disposal to injure his opponent. A champion he was, for three of them had seen him fight and had even won a few guineas on him. But only in numbers could he be bested, Chris

Andrews had emphasised and his older brother, in his rage, had forgotten. Only if they moved in on Paddy as one man could they hope to defeat him. They were all aware that they could not tackle a man who fought in a bare-knuckle boxing ring, not unless they had something to knock him down with and even though Richie had such a weapon Chris distinctly heard his brother's arm snap as Paddy caught him and threw his lighter frame towards the other four.

"Stay together, dammit," he yelled, brandishing his own club. "Move in together. At his back, Davy . . . Johnny, over to his right . . . here, Tim, beside me. Together, damn you, together."

Stepping over the prostrate form of his groaning brother who was doing his best to get out of the way, Chris Andrews, whose mean temper and boiling rage, whose frenzied need for revenge, not only on his sister's account but his own, made him strong, moved in and the rest followed, and though he put up a long and deadly fight, damaging each one of the young gentlemen in some way, they steadily beat him down, striking in unison, using their boots as well as their weapons when he was on the ground, five dark, intent, mindless figures, since Richie found he could still utilise his feet, mangling and mauling Paddy Andrews until he was compelled to curl himself up in an attempt to protect the most vital parts of himself.

There came from the brow of the small rise behind them the sound of someone singing. A Christmas carol, probably one of the last revellers from the inn making his cheerful way home, since there were a few men from the direction of Woodhead who liked to drink at the Feathered Cock in Saltersbrook where the ale was cheap and the barmaid saucy

"Someone's coming," Johnny Ashwell hissed, launching a final kick at the foetus-like form on the ground.

"Dammit, dammit . . ." Chris Andrews's voice was almost a moan, a thwarting of his violence which was not yet spent.

"Help Richie."

"For Christ's sake, come on, Chris."

"I hadn't finished."

"An' neither 'ave I," the man on the ground mumbled.

Shambling and stumbling with Richie Andrews between them, the five young men made their way on the moonlit path while their victim fell into a merciful state of insensibility.

Katy Andrews, surprised that she had not seen Paddy since early the night before, had ridden over to Cloudberry End. It was Christmas morning, which meant nothing to her since she would spend it as she spent every morning. A ride up to the peat moor to drink in the peace and grandeur of the undulating hills and valleys and cloughs about her. A good gallop across Arnfield Moor, leaping Arnfield clough and then back down through Spring Intake and eastwards beyond Spond Moor and Crowden Brook to the cottage at Woodhead. She meant to have a word with Annie Lennox about the state of Grandmother's cottage since she had moved into it. Annie was a decent woman, of course, and probably would refuse to have anything to do with her and the cottage her grandmother had once kept in such an immaculate condition but Annie was recently widowed with three children to feed and clothe and perhaps the inducement of a few shillings a week might overcome her aversion. Katy felt her grandmother's reproving presence there whenever she herself noticed the muddle in which she lived, for she knew Madge Andrews would not have approved. The place had not been cleaned properly nor the bed in which Katy herself uncaringly slept changed for weeks and, if only for her own sake, after all she was used to better, she must see that it was cleaned up a bit.

She didn't really know why she had felt the compulsion to ride over to Cloudberry End just because it was Christmas Day. Perhaps because her father and mother had, at last, begun to treat her as an adult and not some silly girl who could not be trusted to cross the lane on her own. It had taken a great deal of tight-lipped resolution on her part. Indeed, on that first day when her father had driven over to Woodhead accompanied by Jimmy and Dicken with the express intention of bringing her home by force, she had been ready to defend herself, and her intentions, with anything which came to hand.

"Fetch her to the carriage," he had thundered, ordering the grooms to lay hands on her, but when they hesitated, looking apprehensively from their master to their master's narrow-eyed, spitting daughter, it had been Mr Andrews who had slowly bowed his head in despairing compliance. His shoulders had slumped. He had ordered them out of the cottage, telling them to go home and only that dog of hers and the four walls of the cottage had heard what was said between them. She had defeated him and he had driven home to tell his wife so. If they wanted to keep her they must let her go and that meant allowing her a weekly sum to feed and clothe herself. She was their child and they could not see her starve or go about in rags.

She was shunned wherever she went, not only by those who were her parents' friends and acquaintances, but by men and women from the lower classes who treated her with the insolence she deserved. She became invisible to the tradespeople of Crossclough, Miss Mason the dressmaker and others averting their faces and pinching their lips, for if they should be seen to serve her who was a harlot then they would be bound to lose customers who were not. She flaunted her looseness, for it was widely known that Paddy Andrews often spent the night at that cottage her grandmother had left her. She was cut dead by everyone who knew her but somehow it didn't seem to matter. When it was ready, the shape her future was to take would come to her and in the meanwhile she had Paddy to make her laugh, to set her flesh on fire, to exasperate and irritate her and it was enough for now.

She was surprised when her three brothers came into the breakfast room, where she was tucking into one of Mrs Tiplady's excellent breakfasts. They were inclined to strut, she thought, their faces, or at least those of Davy and Chris, somewhat knocked about and Richie with his arm in a sling which he held to his side as though in some pain.

"Are you sure this splint and sling is enough, Davy?" he was asking his brother. "Should the arm not be strapped up more firmly and do you think you could make up some more of that stuff you gave me last night? It eased the pain considerably and it hurts like the very devil now."

"It's as good as old Dr Highcroft could do, lad. Probably a lot better since his methods will no doubt be completely out of date by now. No, don't fiddle with it, it's perfectly all right as it is. You will be somewhat handicapped for a week or two but a fine, healthy specimen like yourself should soon heal. I'll get down to the chemist after breakfast and knock him up. See what he's got in stock. I don't carry vast stores of medicine about with me, you know."

They were all three grinning in what seemed to be high good humour and a vast degree of self-approval and Katy sighed in resignation. They had evidently been involved in some boyish prank, the kind of brawl to which young men seemed prone, but she'd be damned if she would ask them to tell her about it as it appeared they would like to do. Chris, glancing in her direction, smirked and whispered something in Richie's ear which made him laugh out loud, then wince as whatever it was he had done to his arm pained him.

She stood up abruptly. She was well aware that her brothers would have liked to cut her dead like the rest of the community and were quite appalled at their parents' willingness to have her at Cloudberry End. It made their own position, with people like the Ashwells and the Warrens, extremely delicate and it took all their tact and charm and exquisite manners, their crushed and sorrowful oppression of spirit which would obviously strike a man whose sister was no better than she should be, to remain on good terms with the circle in which they had always been welcome.

Katy was as unwilling to be involved in the usual family Christmas Day as her brothers were to have her here. The giving and receiving of gifts, the drinking of sherry in the drawing room, the enormous Christmas dinner, and meant to leave as soon as she had greeted her parents. For some reason, perhaps a residue of feeling which she did not care to call compassion for her mother, she had resisted the temptation to put on her breeches and instead wore her riding habit of blue boxcloth. Her hair was long enough now to sweep up and tie in a tumbled knot of ribbons at the crown of her head and the curls bobbed merrily as she moved towards the door.

"Well, I'm off," she declared. "Tell Mother and Father I'll see them later, perhaps for dinner. I've . . . well, I've left a gift or two under the tree so . . ."

"And may one ask where you're off *to*, little sister?" Chris drawled, his cat's eyes narrowing in a way which puzzled her, for everyone knew where she went to these days and nobody tried to stop her. Not now.

He was helping his brother to bacon and eggs and kidneys while Freda and Ivy stood awkwardly to one side, sensing something unpleasant was about to take place and unwilling to be caught in the midst of it.

"No, you may not," Katy answered coolly, sweeping the wide hem of her skirt to one side as she manoeuvred her way towards the door, "and quite honestly I wonder why you ask me. I no longer live in this house and am not bound by its rules. What I do is my own concern and I'd be obliged if you would keep out of it."

"I wouldn't dream of interfering with anything *you* might do, my pet." Her brother sat down, exchanging smiles with Richie and Davy who had arranged themselves on either side of the table, setting to with gusto as though whatever it was they had been up to had given them an appetite. Davy leaned over and helped his older brother to cut up his food and their smiles became deeper, almost, Katy was inclined to think, if they had been females, turning to giggles.

She hesitated at the door. The you, the emphasis on the word, suddenly caught her attention. Not *you*, Chris had said, as though . . . as though . . .

"Are you trying to say something, Chris, or is this just you being your usual fatuous self? I've no time for games and you should know that by now."

"Oh we do, little sister, but then neither have we, have we, brothers? We are very serious when we have a mind to be, is that not so, lads?"

Davy shrugged and speared a morsel of bacon, a small smile still playing about his mouth. Richie nodded at Freda who sprang forward to refill his coffee cup and, in the tense atmosphere, for there was no doubt it was tense, Ivy looked calculatingly towards the door as though measuring the distance and how long it would take her to cover it.

Katy took a step back into the room and despite her own determination not to, said in a cool voice, "What have you done?"

"Done?" Chris took a bite out of a piece of toast. "Done about what?"

"Don't play the fool with me, Chris Andrews. The three of you have been up to something. A fight of some sort, I'd say, by the bruises you carry."

Her brother raised his reddish brown eyebrows, still smirking, and Richie and Davy exchanged further meaningful glances.

"Yes, you might say that, my dear," he drawled, "though I think a beating would be a more apt word, would it not, brothers? A well-deserved beating. Sometimes a man needs teaching a lesson when he interferes with something which is not his to interfere with. When he gets above himself and so must be shown the error of his ways."

Katy took another step in the direction of the breakfast table, her eyes slitted, her fine eyebrows dipping, her mouth thinned to a narrow line of annoyance with this exasperating brother of hers. She was seventeen and for the past ten years or more her two older brothers had been first at school, then at university and in Richard's case abroad and she was close to neither of them. And it was at neither of them that she flung her concentrated gaze.

"Who are you talking about, Chris Andrews?" she snarled, though of course it was becoming clearer with every moment and every exchanged smile who he was talking about. "What have you done to . . .?"

"To Paddy Andrews, is that the name which comes to mind? Why, only what he deserves, little sister," and Chris's gleaming eyes told her he would like nothing better than to do the same to her. She had shamed them, made a laughing stock of them with her blatant and persistent preference for the coarse, uncouth labourer who was their cousin and though Chris Andrews was just as wild, just as rebellious, just as disobedient, he had always stuck to the codes of the society in which he had been brought up; besides which, he was male and she was not. She had been seen as far afield as Tintwistle, Mottram, Holmfirth and Penistone, following the prize fights in which Paddy took part; at the illegal cock fights and dog fights which took place at the back of isolated inns on the moors and was known to smoke cigars and drink a glass of claret, or brandy. She did, in fact, what young gentlemen did, what her own brother did and her own brother was incensed by it. Paddy Andrews was his cousin. His father and Paddy Andrews's father were brothers and in some way Katy's behaviour had been, if not accepted, then overlooked when she lived at home.

But she no longer lived at home. She treated her mother and father with politeness, only turning into a spitting, clawing she-cat when her father tried to remonstrate with her which he did less and less.

In short, she was beyond anyone's control but perhaps with Paddy Andrews out of the picture, which he undoubtedly would be after the thrashing they had given him last night, then she might, for lack of a companion if nothing else, be forced to return to her parents' home where she belonged. The chances of getting her decently married were long gone but they might be able to unearth some member of the lesser gentry who would be willing to take her on with the right amount of inducement. Hard cash, of course.

"You bastard," she spat at him, then turned to glare savagely at Richie and Davy. "You bastards, all of you. D'you mean to tell me the three of you took on Paddy?"

Suddenly she smiled and the colour which had fled from her face flooded back beneath her skin.

"D'you honestly expect me to believe that you three gave Paddy a beating?" And as it had on Paddy's face the night before, an expression of sneering mockery lit hers. "I don't believe you. He could whip the three of you with one hand. In fact it seems he did for Richie's arm, which I presume is broken, and those cuts and bruises you are all three wearing . . ."

"Not three of us, my pet." Chris interrupted.

"Not . . .?"

"Oh, we are well aware of Paddy Andrews's prowess with his fists and not being fools, and not needing to fight him but merely to thrash him, as one would a disobedient dog, we took along— "

"You bastard," she shrieked again. "You cowardly bastards. How many of you? Jesus, you're quite unspeakable, all of you. Where is he? If you've hurt him . . ."

"Hurt him! He'll be lucky to walk again . . ."

But his sister waited to hear no more. Whirling frantically, her skirt tipped to reveal her tight breeches, she tore open the door and, leaving it standing wide open, made for the back kitchen and the stables.

The two parlourmaids listened to her feet pound up the hallway, their eyes wide and appalled, both of them wondering what on earth was to happen to this family, and therefore them, if this tearing one another to pieces was not stopped. First Master Chris and his father, then Miss Katy and her father, and now Master Chris and Miss Katy.

"Should we not try to stop her, Chris?" Richie asked anxiously, nursing the arm which was broken and which his brother, who was almost a doctor, had set for him. "Or perhaps fetch Father, surely."

"Listen, Richie, my lad. You've been away a long time so you don't really know the state of affairs in this family. But let me say this, there is nothing you, nor Father, nor anyone . . . well, perhaps there is one man but he is . . . not available, could retrieve our sister from the path she is on so let her go and look for our cousin, which she will do if only to defy us. When she sees the state of him she'll be back within the hour, for our sister is not known for her mercy, or compassion."

He was wrong. They brought Paddy Andrews to Katy's cottage, for where else could they take him, his cousins Jake and Josh Andrews, sent for by the man who had found him on the moor. When Katy flung herself up the stairs and into her bedroom they were standing beside her bed, awkwardly sorry since they had never seen Paddy Andrews take a beating. In all his years as a prize fighter he had managed to avoid having his body broken or even his face seriously marked but now it lay on the none-too-clean pillow, hideous with torn skin, one cheek gashed to the bone, both eyes blackened and almost closed, and his nose peculiarly askew. He was a big, solid, well-nourished man, strong in body and mind, refusing ever to lie down, but now his flesh all over his fine body was black with bruises, scraped raw and clotted with dried blood.

"Tha' . . . can . . . clear . . . off now, lads, thanks," he gasped to his cousins who were glad to go, his tongue in the hole where a back tooth had been torn out, his breath rasping in a way which obviously hurt him. "Me . . . nurse is . . . 'ere ter . . . 'old me . . . 'and. Tha' 'ave . . . come ter . . . 'old me . . . 'and, . . . 'aven't thi', Coppertop?"

He did his best to give her his usual wicked grin which she knew quite certainly was causing him a great deal of pain and effort. Between the blood-caked slits of his lids his eyes were asking her something. The muscles in his throat were taut with unspoken words and his hard, fighting jaw was inclined to tremble, she thought.

"Do you need your hand holding, Paddy Andrews?" she asked him, her own voice wobbling a bit.

"Just . . . fer a day . . . or two, I reckon. But tha'd . . . best ride . . . fer't doctor, lass, fer I've . . . an idea . . . me leg might . . . be broke."

With great difficulty he pushed aside the bedclothes which the twins had piled on him, since that was what one did with an invalid. They had removed his trousers and though Katy was not aware of it, while they did so, and on numerous other occasions on the long drag home, he had mercifully lost consciousness.

When Katy saw his leg she felt inclined to do the same. Pushing through the oozing skin of his shin was a shaft of white, jagged bone.

"God above, Paddy," she gasped, fighting off nausea as she backed away, her shaking hand to her mouth, then she turned, threw herself down the stairs and on to her mare's back, clattering off as though "owd scrat" was after her, Jinty Pickles remarked.

It was several hours later, the doctor gone, the light going, when Paddy mumbled from the laudanum-induced sleep the doctor had put him in in order to set his leg.

"I'm . . . a bit bashed . . . about, lass, as tha' . . . can . . . see. It were tha' brothers . . . what did . . . it. I'll not let . . . it pass, Coppertop, tha' knows that. When . . . I'm on . . . me feet . . . again, an' it'll . . . not be long . . . I promise thi' . . . I'll teach 'em . . . a bloody . . . lesson they'll not . . . forget."

The effort of talking had opened the deep gash at the corner of his mouth and the blood ran freely on to the grimy pillow. It was this, this added stain which seemed to draw her attention to the state, not only of the pillowcase, the rest of the bedlinen, the room itself, but the whole disreputable cottage, and it stiffened her resolve to put it all back to what it had been before her grandmother's death. Besides, she would need help to nurse Paddy.

She smiled and knelt down beside the bed. "Well, we'll talk about that, later. They had no right to do this to you but I suppose they thought they were defending my honour but it's too late for that, isn't it, Paddy-me-lad? Far too late."

She bent forward and placed her strangely tremulous mouth on his, soft as a butterfly but still he winced. "You're not ready to have me climb into bed with you, then?" She grinned impishly.

"Sweet Jesus, girl . . . don't . . . make . . . me laugh."

"Who's laughing?" and she winked broadly. "Righto, then, I'll just go and . . ."

"Tha'll . . . not . . . leave . . . me?" he asked her anxiously, his expression telling her he was furious that he, of all strong, fighting men, should be brought to this and she knew it would be difficult. Begging for help from a woman, for a woman's comfort, but most of all from her over whom he had always held dominance.

"No, I'll not leave you but it's time I stopped living like a pig in shit, Paddy Andrews. You must surely remember what this place was like when Grandmother was alive?"

"Aye." His eyes wandered as best they could round the room. There were garments strewn about the floor, his own, bloodstained and torn, hers just tossed anywhere they fell. There were riding boots and a plate on which the last meal they had shared reposed, a half-drunk glass of wine. On almost every surface there was some littered object, even a trap with which he snared rabbits and which he had dropped carelessly as he flung off his clothes to get into her bed with her. Paddy had not worked for months now, ever since the week of Katy's disappearance in September. Not even at the casual work which had allowed him to wander the moorland to trap rabbits, to shoot whatever came into his gun sights to supplement his table. He still went out on most days from the cottage belonging to Jed Miller from where, as yet, they had not managed to evict him, trapping and shooting, and a week barely went by when he did not win a decent purse in the boxing ring. A fighter, a hunter was Paddy, skilful and cunning, a man who called no other man master but who, though he had not yet fully admitted it to himself, had bowed his head and his knee to this girl who knelt at the bedside.

"What . . . tha' gonna do . . . then? I can't . . . see thi' . . . in a . . . pinny, my lass," he mumbled through his broken mouth.

"No, neither can I but I can pay someone to put one on and give this place a thorough clean."

"Eeh, Coppertop . . . must tha? I've a . . . mind . . . fer a bit . . . o' . . . peace," closing his eyes fully and turning his head away from her.

"You shall have it, Paddy, never fear."

Annie Lennox took a bit of persuading. Well, Katy Andrews was considered a loose woman by decent folk like her and Jinty, and that ox of a man who frequented Madge Andrews's trim little cottage was no better than he should be, neither. But how could she refuse the money Madge's granddaughter slapped briskly on Annie's well-scrubbed table top, not with her Frank gone and three young 'uns to rear. She did a bit of scrubbing at the Queen's Head in Crossclough and for the parson's wife and anyone else who would employ her and the offer of regular work, and only next door, was surely something she couldn't afford to turn down.

"I'll not come in when the pair o' tha's theer," she said doggedly.

"I'm sure a time convenient to yourself can be arranged, Annie."

"Mrs Lennox ter thi'."

Katy felt a spurt of irritation rise in her, quickly suppressed, for how could Annie Lennox's opinion, or anyone else's for that matter, concern her? Beggars can't be choosers, she told herself and she really couldn't quite see herself tackling the clutter which had accumulated in Grandmother's cottage since last October. Besides which, Paddy would need some looking after until his leg healed. Bedpans and such and the invalid food the doctor had advised and which she herself hadn't the faintest notion how to contrive.

"Very well, Mrs Lennox," she answered crisply, "but I would like you to make a start right now."

"Nay, I saw 'im bein' brought 'ome a while back. Drunk as a lord, 'e were an' I'm goin' nowhere . . ."

"Then the arrangement is cancelled, I'm afraid. Either you start now or I shall find someone else to . . . to help me."

It was perhaps those last few words that did it, for beneath her grim exterior Annie Lennox had a kind heart. She didn't bow her head, though, not to this baggage, but she nodded it stiffly in compliance.

And so it was Annie Lennox, having committed herself punctiliously, as was her way, to the job in hand, which was the scrubbing and deep scouring of Madge Andrews's cottage, as she still thought of it, who told Katy she'd best send for the doctor again.

"Why? The leg is set and surely that's all that's needed. Paddy is a strong man and will soon heal."

"I don't like look of it."

Katy's voice was sharp. "What do you mean, you don't like the look of it?"

"Just what I said. I've not seen it fer a few days an' . . ." since Katy had taken over the dressing of the wound.

"What, for God's sake?"

"'Ave thi' not noticed smell?"

"Well, yes, but . . ."

"An't colour's not right."

"The colour? What's the colour got to do with it? Really, Mrs Lennox, don't you think you are . . ."

"Never mind that, lady. You get Jinty Pickles's lad ter run fer't doctor an' tell 'im ter be quick about it before it's too late."

But it was already too late, the doctor said, none too pleased to be brought back to the foul-mouthed brute who seemed intent on doing them all a serious injury if they so much as came near him with a knife.

"It's no good cursing me, my good man. The flesh is already dead due to the lack of a healthy blood supply to the affected part and if something is not done soon you will— "

"Don't talk so bloody daft. It don't even 'urt."

"That is why. Because it is already dead."

Seeing where the doctor was leading, Paddy began to scream.

"No . . . Oh no . . . yer not cuttin' my bloody leg off . . . oh no . . . I'll not 'ave it . . . no . . . no . . . please, Coppertop, don't let 'im cut me leg off, please . . . please." His voice took on the high-pitched hysteria of a man in mortal terror, his mouth a cavern of horror in his bleached and sweating face.

"Oh, dear God in heaven," Katy moaned, "please, Doctor, can you not . . .?"

"There is nothing else to be done, young lady, nothing."

It was like a nightmare. The stink of it in Madge Andrews's once sweet-smelling cottage made them all gag, though the doctor and his nurse, and Annie herself, were accustomed to the nastiness which illness brings. Annie's own Frank, who had died in the grip of some fever, had suffered a violent emptying of his bowels which Annie had patiently dealt with but this was even more punishing to the nerves and stomach.

But worse, far worse than the abomination of the stench of his flesh was the sight of Paddy's body tissue which had degenerated in two weeks from the well-muscled firmness of a young and healthy man to the blackened, oozing, wet mass which had simply rotted away below the knee and was visibly spreading upwards.

It took five of them, one the hastily summoned and reluctant Barty Pickles, to hold down the writhing, screaming, demoniacally strong figure of Paddy Andrews while Doctor Highcross administered the merciful chloroform.

"Well above the knee, I think, Nurse," the doctor stated matter-of-factly when Paddy was at last still, "if we are to part it from the healthy flesh. And perhaps it might be as well if you were to leave the room now, Miss Andrews," he told Katy, turning from the kitchen table where, with the help of Barty Pickles, they had laid out the unconscious man. "Now I am aware that it is not a pretty sight," referring to the repulsiveness of Paddy's leg which seemed to have in it every colour from the deepest purple and black of the dead flesh to the green and yellow of the pus which exuded from it, "but it will soon be put right." It was as though he had suddenly become aware that though this girl no longer lived in the bosom of her family, indeed had been cast from it by her behaviour with this man, she was still the daughter of one of the most influential men in the neighbourhood. He himself would not be here if that had not been so, since he did not give his services to any Tom, Dick or Harry who had an accident.

The last thing Katy saw was the lethal-looking surgeon's saw which the doctor took from his bag before she fell into the compassionate arms of Annie Lennox.

It was two weeks later that Katy Andrews's brother Chris was found at the bottom of Deep End Clough. Drunk as usual and fallen off his horse, the rumour was and had it not been for Saul Gibbon, who was up that way searching for some of Farmer Clarke's flock which had wandered up beyond the snowline, and who had heard his weakening cries, he would certainly have perished. The clough was deep, filled with jagged rocks, almost impossible to climb out of, especially in the dark, but the puzzle was, what on earth was he doing riding up there at that time of night? Crossclough asked, shaking its collective head. And if he had fallen why was he not injured? Apart from the effects of a night spent out in the icy depths of January and which, as he was young and healthy were no more than a chill and a "wheezy" chest, he had suffered no injuries.

A lucky lad was Chris Andrews who, strangely, had nothing to say on the matter.

16

The following July Chloe Hutchinson had reason to believe that she was pregnant but she told no one, not even her husband who she knew waited and watched her every month for the sign that they were to have a child. It was nine months since they married and really, she often smiled to herself as she did her best to make her butter "come", something which was often beyond her for it required strength, it was not for want of trying on Jamie's part.

Not that she was an unwilling partner, far from it. She had known no man's body before Jamie's but despite her previous ignorance she was aware that Jamie was a considerate lover. How did she know? she often wondered, lying in his arms, her breath beginning to slow and her heartbeat to calm, her body slumbrous and stretching after the touch of his hands and mouth and the enchantment they brought to her.

He seemed to delight in studying her naked body for hours on end, turning her this way and that, placing the candle a little closer in order to alter the shading of gold and honey and tawny rose which played over her skin in the candle's flame, arranging her hair to please some need in himself, the very manner in which he did it, even before his touch began to delight her, putting a taper to the excitement which was lit in the pit of her belly. Every night this happened, and sometimes when his waking body turned to hers in the early morning.

Once they had been in their bed on a sunny, wintry Sunday afternoon when her mother- and father-in-law had taken it into their heads to walk up from Cloudberry End. The silent laughter had been quite hysterical as she and Jamie had fumbled their way back into their discarded clothing, Matty shouting up the stairs – since they had neglected to lock the door – demanding to know what they were up to. Flushed they had been, and dishevelled, Jamie's shirt on inside out and his hair, which her hands had been clutching as he explored with his tongue the exquisite tenderness between her thighs, standing up like that of a porcupine.

She had caught the blue twinkle in Matty's eye and though Thomas had been so embarrassed he had stamped off with the excuse he wanted to check on Jamie's plough horse, she and Matty had shared a conspiratorial smile which they had not allowed Jamie to see.

She was happy. She was well aware of her own shortcomings as far as being a farmer's wife was concerned. There were some jobs about the farm which were beyond her strength which was where Adah-May came in and glad of her, Chloe was. A big, strong girl of fourteen whose mother had despaired of ever getting her in work, for Adah-May was simple and could do nothing without constant supervision. Sweet-natured and hardworking with a smile on her that lit the darkest day, she was a willing workhorse which no amount of work could tire. Show her, tell her, stand over her for five minutes to make sure she'd got the hang of it and whatever it was she'd go on doing it until she was told to stop. She'd scrub the colour off the kitchen flags if left alone but couldn't be trusted, even when watched, to handle the pretty, bone-china tea-service which had been a wedding present from Mr and Mrs Jack Andrews.

And put her to the butter churn, watching her, of course, as she dashed the long plunger up and down, and she would go on long after the thump which said the butter had come.

Jamie had promised to look out for one of the new "end over end" churns without paddles which would make the job simpler and easier for Chloe, but in the meanwhile Adah-May went at the old one as though it were a mortal enemy she was determined to best.

Chloe was very proud of her dairy and of the butter and cheese Jamie took to market each week, along with "her" eggs. The dairy was sited next to the farmhouse on the cool, north side, though as Jamie said, there was seldom a warm side up here on the edge of the moorland. There were two rooms to the dairy, one for butter-making and one for the making and storing of cheeses. Jamie made sure there was a good water supply from the pump. There was a boiler, a stone floor with a slight slope to allow for drainage, and walls lined with plenty of stone shelves. Adah-May kept it spotlessly clean, pails and crocks scrupulously scrubbed out along with the floor, the shelves and indeed every blessed thing Adah-May could lay her hands on. She idolised Mrs Hutchinson, who was everything Adah-May was not and if Mrs Hutchinson needed carrying about the farm on Adah-May's back then Adah-May would get down on her knees and gladly do it. She went home to her ma every night, her round, dough-like face as lugubrious as a hound-dog's and presented herself each morning, sometimes before she was required, as Jamie made love to Chloe in their deep, warm bed, her face lit up with a smile of pure heaven.

They lived a solitary life at Valley Bottom Farm with only Adah-May and Tommy, who helped Jamie in the fields with his small dairy herd, in the planting of his crops and up on the intake where his sheep were grazing, but when the two of them went home it had become a matter of deep pleasure to Chloe to share the warm, firelit, candlelit evenings with the man she considered to be not only her husband, her lover, but her true friend. She could still not bring herself to say that she loved him, she only knew that when he was away from the farmhouse she felt a small prick of loneliness, of unease as though the drawbridge had been left down, allowing in perhaps a presence she would not care for. His weatherwise, earthbound calm was a joy to her and she lowered herself into it each night as into a warm and easeful bath. He was a constant source of comfort, of quiet protection against a world which, though it had held no particular terrors for her, had held no particular joys either. When she heard his step in the yard or his cheerful whistle to Captain as he came down the track at the end of the day, her head lifted thankfully and she could not help nor deny her inclination to run out into the dusk to embrace him which she knew pleased him inordinately. He loved her. He said so at least twice a day and she sensed his own happiness with her, in what she gave him.

She had not failed nor disappointed him, she knew that, but did she love him as a woman loves her man? she asked herself. In that unique way which exists between a woman and the man who is all the world to her. In that blissful committed state shared by two people who cannot live apart and the answer was she didn't know.

She was a farmer's wife now and though she sewed in the evening by the fire it was no longer the intricately embroidered pretty things her fingers were accustomed to but warm winter shirts for her husband, skirts and blouses for herself in practical colours of chestnut brown, burgundy and charcoal grey, but all well fitting and beautifully made, simple but at the same time elegant since her mama's training and her own sense of good taste were deeply ingrained in her. She made pretty underwear of sturdy white cotton, smothered in lace and frills, for she knew her husband liked it, the fabric all bought from the accumulated allowance her uncle had made her. She replenished Jamie's slender stock of bedlinen and soon it would be tiny garments by the score.

When spring came they spent long Sunday afternoons together, climbing the tortuous, stony paths and the winding tracks between walls of heather in the direction of Bare Moss at the back of the farm. They found a sheltered spot in a grassy hollow, tall rocks at their back and admired in companionable silence the splendid panorama of the valley set out below, threaded with the shining expanses of the reservoirs. Jamie would stretch out beside her, his hand holding hers, telling her the names of the grasses and wild flowers, of the trees below and the birds above, many of which he could identify by their song.

"However did you come to know such clever things, Jamie? You were away at sea so long."

"I was a boy round here, my little dove, and grew up knowing country ways from the grooms and stable lads at Cloudberry End, the shepherds on the hills and all those who came from these parts. It was this which encouraged me to think I might make a farmer." He smiled from under the shade of his hand, his eyes soft and dreaming.

"You're an amazing man, Jamie."

"A lucky man, my dove."

When Jamie went into Crossclough she accompanied him on occasions, bringing back farming manuals from the second-hand bookshop which they both studied in the evenings, for was she not a farmer's wife and would it not be beneficial to Jamie to share his work with a woman who knew what he was talking about? She could milk a cow, care for the hens, the sow and her piglets, and even, when Jamie got up in the night to attend a sick cow or deliver a calf, get up to help him – aided by the good advice in the manual – and had managed to quell the churning of her stomach at the sight of the blood and detritus of birth.

Matty came over to see her perhaps once a week, a fount of sensible, practical advice, glad to be of help to the slight but stubbornly determined girl her son had married and it was these visits more than anything which helped Chloe to decide to keep her suspicions about her own condition to herself for the moment. She knew that once Matty was told that she was to be a grandmother nothing short of an earthquake, a tidal wave or a blizzard would stop her from making her way up to Valley Bottom Farm as many times in the week as there were days.

And there had been a few of those in the winter. Blizzards! Jamie had been tied to the farmhouse for two whole days just after Christmas, going no further than the manure-scented, steaming barn where his beasts were quartered, to the hen house and the pig sty, Captain floundering comically at his heels. The world had become a magical place – at least to the eye – when the storm was over, its coming announced by bottom-heavy, fat clouds bouncing over the hills. A world of vast white spaces in which only the hazed shapes of snow-laden trees were visible and the solitary white-topped greyness of a farmhouse down in the valley. Chloe had stoked the fires and drawn the warm woollen curtains she had made for every window and they had not wasted the hours they had been shut in together.

It was in April that she conceived. One of the days on which she and Jamie had climbed up the track as far as Crowden Meadow. There had been no sign of life beyond a skylark high above and a few cropping sheep and when he had drawn her to him in love, cradling her, caressing her until she moaned her delight, he had eased himself into her and planted the seed which grew in her now. She had conceived. That was the word for it, the proper word which she knew her mother would have shuddered over, just as she would have shuddered over the very idea of making love, not just in broad daylight, but out of doors. But as a farm wife Chloe had no time for shuddering or being ladylike. She knew exactly what lay ahead of her when her time came, for the farm manual on breeding described it to her in detail and she supposed it was pretty much the same for humans as it was for animals. Lambing time had come and gone by then and she had helped her husband with several weak lambs, feeding them by hand and nursing them in the warmth of her own hearth.

She was content.

She saw nothing of Katy Andrews but her mother-in-law brought her the news from Cloudberry End, none of it good.

"They say he sits in that special chair what she had made fer 'im, the one wi' wheels, though he never turns 'em, an' does nowt but shout at her as if it were all her fault. She has ter keep out of 'is way, Annie Lennox told me t'other day in Crossclough, when the black mood's on 'im or he'd knock her teeth down her throat. Them cousins of his, Jake an' Josh, fetched him downstairs an' he sleeps in a bed in the parlour, Annie said. God only knows how Katy'd manage if it weren't fer Annie." Matty shook her head sadly. "That girl waits on 'im hand an' foot. Lord, will yer listen ter me, poor bugger only has one foot ter wait on. Mind you, I reckon it's a good job he can't gerrup them stairs or the poor lass's life would be a hundred times worse than it is."

The mental picture of the one-legged hulk it was said

Paddy Andrews had become doing to Katy what Jamie did so lovingly, so joyfully to Chloe was too much for her and she turned away in distress, the slight nausea which had troubled her recently turning her stomach over.

"Dear heavens, Matty," she whispered, "what is to become of her?"

"Nay, lass, she made her bed an' now she must lie in it." Matty's face was grim.

"But don't you think . . . circumstances . . . have helped to shape what has happened to her?"

"Aye, happen, but you should see her. You'd think she were Queen of England the way she carries herself. There's just summat about her . . ." Matty's eyes became unfocused as they dwelled on what it was about Katy Andrews that was so fascinating. "She's . . . matured. No, that's not the right word . . . she's become a woman, gloriously beautiful. Eeh, will yer listen at me?" Matty sighed. "But it's her poor mother I'm sorry for," she continued dolefully. "She's not strong, what with all them miscarriages. Oh aye, in between Master Richie an' Master Davy an' them with only eighteen months between them. One she had then. Only a couple o' months gone, she were, but she'd a bad do. Then after Master Davy she'd another two before Master Chris come along and then if she didn't have another after him. Four in all an' her like a bit o' swansdown with no substance on her to speak of. That's why Jack, Mr Andrews, is so clucky wi' her. Fusses like a mother hen, he does but then, after what happened years ago is it any wonder? It seemed for a while, afterwards like, he just couldn't bear her out of his sight. An' then them years she spent in Canada did her no good. Great cold place it were, not fit fer humans, I shouldn't wonder. Well, I'll say no more but when she come back I was shocked at the change in her, I can tell thi'."

"What *did* happen, Matty?" Chloe tried to keep her voice light as though to reveal her true interest might bring her mother-in-law back from the past just when it seemed the mystery about Sara and Alice Hamilton might be about to be revealed.

"She were only fifteen when they met, Sara, I mean. Jack were a navvy buildin' the railroad near where the Hamiltons lived and . . . well, they fell fer each other like a ton o' bricks. But Sara's pa were a doctor, her ma related to a lord or summat, an' Jack were nowt burra rough workman. Miss Hoity-Toity didn't like it one bit from what Sara told me— "

"Miss Hoity-Toity?" Chloe was enthralled. That day she had made her first successful batch of fruit scones in the hard-to-manage ovens beside the fire and she had been so pleased with them she couldn't wait for Matty to try one with the cup of tea she was sipping, but the scones stood neglected as did her newly churned butter while Matty wandered back into the past and Chloe encouraged her. Adah-May was warbling on about, ". . . going to Scarborough Fair . . ." in the dairy and in the cosy kitchen Alice Hamilton's daughter leaned forward expectantly towards her mother-in-law. At last she was going to find out what it was that made her mother's sister, her Aunt Sara, unable to bear the sight of her. In all the months Chloe had lived at Cloudberry End she had received no more than a cool "Good morning" or "Good evening", her aunt's eyes unable to find the courage even to meet Chloe's gaze. Since then, apart from the tea-service which Thomas had delivered with not even a note to accompany it, there had been no word from the Andrews family.

"That were what they called 'er. Miss Hoity-Toity. We all did 'cos that's what she damn well was." Matty's face became flushed with the memory of some offence she still obviously felt and she folded her arms grimly over her matronly bosom.

"Who?"

"Alice bloody Hamilton, that's who . . ." Then, suddenly appalled as she realised what she was saying to this girl of whom Matty had grown enormously fond, and about her own mother, too, she clapped her hand to her mouth.

"Eeh, lass, will yer listen ter me babblin' on about summat what's got nowt ter do wi' me. An' about yer ma an' all. No matter what she did, she were yer ma an' yer must 'ave bin fond of her."

"What *did* she do, Matty?" Chloe clutched at her mother-in-law's arm, her eyes quite frantic in her face from which all colour had fled. First of all there had been the revelation of Sara Andrews's frequent miscarriages, which, to a woman who was possibly three months pregnant was not exactly the kind of conversation which should be embarked upon. Of course, Matty didn't know about Chloe's condition and would be stricken with remorse if she did but it was Matty's evident loathing, her bitter contempt, even after all these years, of Chloe's mama, which demoralised her.

"Please tell me, Matty," she pleaded desperately. "I know I am hated by all of them at Cloudberry but none of it can be blamed on me. I had nothing to do with Aunt Sara and Mama and what happened between them. Uncle Jack and Aunt Sara . . . well, you know how they are and now there's Katy. I feel to blame about that. She has run wild and now look at the consequences. If I hadn't married Jamie, well, who knows, perhaps he and Katy might . . . but that was forced on me by Chris. Oh God, Matty, I don't mean I was forced into marriage with Jamie," for Matty's face was becoming more and more horror-stricken. "It was Chris's . . . attentions . . . he hit me, Matty. That's where I got that . . . that . . . last year. Jamie found me and brought me home . . . Oh, dear Lord . . ."

She began to weep, all her pent-up emotions, which she had not really been aware she was clenching inside her, those that she had pushed to the furthest corner of her mind, flooded in a torrent from her wide, distressed mouth.

"I haven't told Jamie though he's asked and asked . . . Matty, he'd kill him . . . you know how he is about me."

"Aye, chuck, aye, now give over greetin'." Matty had her in her arms, pulling her along the settle on which they were both sitting until Chloe's face was buried in Matty's capacious, comforting bosom, patting her back and shoulder consolingly, sniffing a bit herself, for she was the sort of warm-hearted, emotional woman who would always weep in sympathy for another's tears.

"Promise me, Matty," Chloe begged her frantically. "I want no more trouble which can be laid at my door."

"Nay, lass, none of it can be laid at thy door." Though Matty was Liverpool born and bred she had lived in this land which was somewhere between Lancashire and Yorkshire for so long, it showed in her speech. Now and again she lapsed into the "thee"s and "thou"s and other dialect of her neighbours. "I had me suspicions about Master Chris fer he's allus bin a birrov a lad. For ever sniffin' round every maidservant with a claim ter looks but I'd not've believed he could hit a lass."

"I wouldn't allow him to . . ."

"So he hit yer?"

"Yes."

"A bad bugger he is an' he deserves a good thrashin' but I don't want our Jamie givin' it 'im. I'm frightened he'd not stop there."

Matty hugged Chloe closer to her, hesitating before she spoke again.

"Did yer know there's rumour goin' round it were Chris what did fer Paddy Andrews?"

Chloe lifted her head in amazement. "Chris couldn't do that, Matty. He's half Paddy's weight and size. Paddy would kill him."

"Aye, I know that but with his brothers and them pals of 'is from't gentry he could manage it. Chris an' Davy were a bit knocked about at Christmas an' Richie had a broken arm which he said he got fallin' off his 'orse."

"Oh Matty, Matty, ever since I came to Cloudberry End there's been trouble."

"An' none of it your fault, so yer not ter dwell on it, d'yer hear?"

There was no more said on the subject of Sara and Alice. Chloe calmed herself enough to butter a scone for her mother-in-law which Matty thought was a "fair treat" and later, when she had gone and Chloe lay drowsing on her husband's lap before their fire she told him she was to have his child.

It was another week before Matty heard the news, whispered with great delight in her ear by her son, who had called to bring her some eggs, but within the hour it was all over Cloudberry End.

Katy had taken to galloping up to the top of the rough hill at the back of Jamie's farm, though it was becoming increasingly difficult as the months passed, dismounting from Storm's back and standing, sometimes for more than an hour, amongst a huddle of tall concealing stones. Wrapped about in her capacious cloak she would watch as Chloe moved about the yard from the farmhouse to the hen run or the barn, or, if the day was fine, merely standing and gazing about her in evident pleasure. That was what stabbed Katy to the heart,

Chloe's pleasure, her great content, her settling like a cat which has finally found a place by a welcoming hearth, the hearth which should have been Katy Andrews's, and the contrast with her own devastated life was horrific. She didn't know why she rode up here for it did no good. It was as though the clean, sweet, undisturbed direction of Chloe's life with Jamie might somehow deaden the hideous distortion of her own with Paddy. As though, if she came within a certain radius of its goodness it might warm the frozen stillness in herself, though the thought often amazed her, for it was Chloe's fault, wasn't it, that this had happened at all.

Her face expressionless, her eyes dead, she remounted Storm and made her way back to Cloudberry End where the mare was still stabled since there was nowhere to house her at the cottage in Woodhead. She would walk back from there as she always did. But today, with the peace and goodness of Valley Bottom Farm still laid about her she found she could not face it, not yet. Paddy, and possibly the twins, would be there, swilling down the whisky they bought him with the money, her money, he gave them and she needed an hour or so to regain her strength for the never-ending war which was waged in Grandmother's cottage. She would go and sit in the kitchen of her old home and drink a cup of Mrs Tiplady's hot chocolate, eat a mouth-watering biscuit, just as she had done as a child. She would be a child again if only for a short time.

"What's all the excitement about, Tippy?" Katy smiled up at the housekeeper as, seated by the fire and still wrapped in her figure-disguising cloak, she accepted the cup of chocolate and the plate of biscuits which were pressed into her hand.

The housekeeper beamed. It was not that the coming event would in any way affect her, or indeed any member of the Andrews household, but Matty Jenkins had been so enraptured, so overwhelmed with joy, flinging open the kitchen door to announce the news as though it were world-shattering, her delight had infected them all, even Mrs Tiplady. Well, Matty would be excited. Her Dulcie already had little ones but they all knew Jamie Hutchinson held a special place in his mother's heart, him being her first, perhaps, and this coming child would bring her a special joy. Matty had grabbed the squealing Dilly and whirled her about the kitchen table, the scullery maid ready to have hysterics about it and it was all Mrs Tiplady could do to disentangle her from Matty's ecstatic embrace and restore order.

"Now sit down, Matty, and calm yourself," she had told her. "See, Janet, pour Matty a cup of tea and I'll have one myself. Now then, when's it to be?"

Matty had gone but the happiness such events bring had remained in the warm, bread-scented kitchen and before she had time to consider the advisability of revealing to Miss Katy the fact that Miss Chloe was with child, since they were all aware of Miss Katy's feelings for Miss Chloe's husband, it was out of Mrs Tiplady's mouth with a smile of pure delight. For a moment she had forgotten the connection Matty Jenkins's grandchild would have with this family. Babies were a delight, Mrs Tiplady believed, though she'd had none herself and Matty was so overjoyed, so proud you'd have thought it was all her doing.

"It's Matty, Miss Katy. Mrs Jenkins. She's just heard she's to be a grandmother and she's that tickled she's got us all in a . . ."

Mrs Tiplady had been about to use the word turmoil but that didn't say much for her own control of her staff, did it, besides which Miss Katy was looking at her as though she had said something offensively rude.

"I mean . . . well, I know it's not her first but with it being . . . well . . ." Mrs Tiplady's voice ran down to a whispered entreaty for forgiveness as she realised what she was saying.

"Indeed," was all Miss Katy said, but she stood up so violently Lottie, who had been about to pass her another plate of biscuits was almost knocked from her feet.

"I beg yer pardon, Miss Katy," she babbled, though it was not her fault that the biscuits were all over the floor and the plate smashed to smithereens.

They all stood in paralysed silence, the servants, each one waiting for another to speak, or move, or for Miss Katy herself to explode which she seemed in imminent danger of doing.

"Miss Katy, won't you sit down and let Lottie get you another plate of biscuits?" Mrs Tiplady begged nervously. They didn't see her all that much but when they did they were all like that with her. Nervous, for she was as unpredictable as one of the storms which blew up over Black Hill and just as dangerous, and could you blame the poor child though what had happened had been brought on by her own wilfulness. Even so, Mrs Tiplady wouldn't wish on her worst enemy the life Miss Katy lived with that . . . that brute up at her grandmother's cottage.

Katy Andrews didn't answer. From the secret part of herself to where she withdrew when she could stand no more, she peered out at them, quiet as death, pale as marble, and Freda and Mrs Tiplady exchanged glances, for they were of the private opinion that their master's daughter was not far from the edge of . . . well, they hated to call it "madness", but surely, "out of her mind" might describe the state into which she seemed about to topple and it frightened them all to death.

As though to confirm Mrs Tiplady's thoughts Miss Katy began to laugh. Her hand made some gesture which might have been denial of the news just disclosed or simply a matter of steadying herself against something which threatened to consume her, then, still laughing merrily, she turned on her heel and left the kitchen. They heard her footsteps clatter across the cobbled yard and when Janet ventured to peep through the open door she could be seen striding towards the drive which led to the gates, and from there to Woodhead and what awaited her there.

17

It was a day of warm summer sunshine. Jamie and Tommy had gone up to the high intake to check on the almost full-grown lambs, ready to select which to keep and which to send to market and Chloe knew, as she slipped her light cloak over her shoulders, that they would not be back for hours. She sat down to pull on her sturdy boots since she had a fair walk ahead of her, then, after one last glance round the peaceful, sweet-smelling tranquillity of her kitchen, she stepped out into the yard.

"I'm off, Adah-May," she called, turning in the direction of the dairy where a tuneless rendition of "O God our Help in Ages Past" was being performed. It was Monday and yesterday Adah-May would have gone to church with her family which explained the hymn, the words and music which would have been the last Adah-May had heard and so retained in her memory. A bucket clattered against the rim of the old stone sink and there was the sound of one of the wide, shallow slipware bowls in which the milk cooled being placed on a shelf. Adah-May was to scrub the dairy from floor to ceiling which included the shelves and the sink. She was to remove the gauze which was placed over the windows to keep out the flies and when she got back "the missis" was to help her to put up fresh. All Adah-May had to do for the moment was scrub, since it was the only job she could be trusted to do on her own and having no idea how long she would be, Chloe had given her the most time-consuming task she could think of. When she was finished she was to go home, Chloe had impressed on her, though she could see Adah-May was bewildered. She didn't actually ask her mistress where she was going, or why Adah-May was to go home so early, for her thought processes could not cope with more than one order at a time.

Her alarm at the idea of being here without Mrs Hutchinson to run to should something go wrong showed clearly in the biting of her lip and the screwing up of her homely face, but when Chloe popped her head round the dairy door Adah-May turned to beam at her and Chloe knew she had forgotten all that she had been told no more than fifteen minutes ago.

She sighed. "Good girl, just keep on in the dairy and then . . . well . . ." Perhaps she would be home before Adah-May had finished the scrubbing and if she wasn't then the girl would just have to manage as best she could. She would come to no harm, surely, in the farmyard where there was nothing more dangerous than the strutting, pecking hens.

"Goodbye, Adah-May," she murmured, working on the assumption that if she were quiet and calm and matter-of-fact Adah-May would be the same and accept her leavetaking without noticing that she had actually gone.

"'Bye, missis," Adah-May answered shyly, returning at once to her deep scouring, for was that not what the missis had told her to do?

There was still a hint of mist on the tops, breaking up into floating wisps and wavering curtains as larks rose to greet the sun. Heather flowed away like a purple sea, lapping in wavelets against the outcropping of grey spotted rocks, golden with lichen. The cotton grass rippled in the gentle breeze and Chloe sighed in contented pleasure as she stepped out on the path. She had come to love what she had once called "this God-forsaken spot". The great empty spaces in which the serenity of it all wrapped about her, with no sound but the chuckling of the water, the lyrical song of the birds, perhaps the faint barking of a distant dog. Blue shadows filled the valley below, moving steadily to climb the opposite hill in unison with the clouds.

Growing in shy clumps in the rough grass and sprouting from fissures in the rocks were the white, mauve-tinged delicacy of eyebright and the yellow and purple of mountain pansy. To her right and just below her, where the track led up, was an acre or two of woodland: sessile oak, birch and mountain rowan which were native to this part of the high peakland.

She sighed again in pure happiness. It was just over a year since she had left Liverpool, sent with scant regard for her own wishes to her mama's sister, an aunt Chloe had never met, nor indeed scarcely knew the existence of. Forwarded like a parcel to get her out of the sight of her new stepmama who was to have her papa's child and now, fourteen months later, she was to have a child of her own.

Had her papa another daughter now, or perhaps a son to carry on his name? Why had he not written, at least once, to tell his first child of the birth of her new brother or sister, or even to enquire of her if she was managing in the strange and unfamiliar life to which he had abandoned her? But the triumphantly smiling face of her stepmama came between her and her thoughts and her question was answered.

She stopped for a moment on the track which led to the road, basking in the warm sun of midsummer, chasing the thoughts away since she did not wish to cloud her new happiness with bleak memories of the past. She was happy with Jamie. Happy and loved as she had never, she realised it now, been loved before. Even her mother-in-law showed her a deep affection, inclined to hug her and give her a smacking kiss on the cheek to show her approval, and though Chloe had not been accustomed to it with Mama and Papa, she did not find it unwelcome. Her world was small, isolated but she was happy in it. She was not to be afraid of the coming birth, Matty had told her stoutly for she would be there and Chloe was given the distinct impression that if Matty could manage it she would labour alongside Chloe.

The faint, morning breeze moved in her hair which she wore loose, since it seemed Jamie liked it that way and it was always her pleasure to please him. Only when she was busy at her household chores, or working about the farm did she tie up her hair in a three-cornered kerchief. The moor above her was loud with birdsong, lulling her to a state which was almost like sleep-walking but she knew she could not afford to dawdle. Not only might she lose her nerve, so bravely scraped together over the last few days, but she had a long walk there and back and if Jamie were to come home and find her not there he would be frantic.

There was a short cut from the farm in a direct line across Great Crowden Brook, through Springfield Wood and on behind Woodhead Chapel. From there it would take her across ploughed and planted farmland and meadowland, over the steep-sided Enter Clough which was tricky and then on to the road which led to her destination.

The trouble was she was not really familiar with the route although she had been on it with Jamie, and if she lost her way, or her footing, she could be in real trouble. Jamie had taught her a very real respect for these parts which could be treacherous, even on a sunny day. She placed a protective hand on her still flat belly – though Jamie swore it was fuller – and turned towards the safety of the muddy road. It might take her longer but at least she was on a well-used thoroughfare.

The sun was bright on the water which lapped peacefully on her right. Torside Reservoir, as placid and unruffled as a duck pond, the blue of the sky, the mottled brown and green and gold of the land and the brilliance of emerald-leaved trees reflected in its mirror-like surface. It stunned her heart into silence with its beauty, the silence and stillness which only the land in its glory can command. There was nothing to intrude in the peace as she passed Woodhead Chapel, her face smiling in remembrance of the joy of her wedding day and all the joyful days which had followed.

There was a cottage at the foot of Enter Clough, its garden vivid with the blue of Michaelmas daises, the spikes of yellow hollyhock and the scarlet of dahlias. The hedges which bordered the road flamed with ripening berries and beyond them the corn was turning a rich gold. Cattle dozed in the shade of the trees and the small golden domes of beehives hummed with thronging bees in the frantic activity of making honey. Had it not been for the hazard ahead Chloe would have enjoyed every lovely mile.

The track turned off about halfway along Woodhead Reservoir, moving upwards steeply then turning to the right, and as she clambered up it, her heart pounding in her breast, there they were, perched like a row of birds on a washing line. The half a dozen or so cottages which made up the hamlet of Woodhead.

Her mouth became instantly dry and she would have given a great deal for a long drink of the cold, clear water Jamie drew from the pump in the yard. Oh, Lord . . . Oh, Lord . . . it was not just what she was about to attempt that frightened her, though that was bad enough, but what Jamie would say, and do, when he found out. Of course it would be done by then and too late for anything but the inevitable recriminations but if he should be aware that she was hazarding not only herself but their unborn child in this foolhardy venture, his rage would be unimaginable.

The end cottage which was her goal was quite, quite enchanting. There were roses scrambling up its walls in their full summer glory and even sprawling over the well-kept tiled roof. In comparison with the other cottages, some of which were in a sad state of repair, it was freshly painted. The windows winked cheerfully in the sunshine, the step was freshly scrubbed and even the bright daisies and lobelia in the window boxes stood up proudly to attention.

Hesitantly she approached the front door, clutching her cloak about her as though for protection. She could feel pulses she had not known she possessed beating frantically in various parts of her body. Her last thought as she lifted her hand to the bright, freshly buffed brass door-knocker, which was in the shape of a lion's head with a ring in its mouth, was that this surely could not be good for a woman in her third month of pregnancy?

She had lifted the ring in the lion's mouth and was about to let it fall when, from the other side of the door, there came a roar which nearly stopped her heart beating. She felt it falter, then race in an even more rapid tattoo and despite her courageous determination to do this thing she took half a dozen steps backwards. There was a window open upstairs which allowed the sound, the bellowing, free escape. A dog howled ferociously from somewhere in the cottage, a great angry tidal wave which washed out and over her and beyond to join the waters below, a sound so terrifying she had turned to run, to scurry home to the peace and security of where Jamie was, when a woman screamed.

The scream was even more terrifying than the roar and the howling dog and it seemed to Chloe that every living thing within hearing distance had curled up and put its hands over its ears to shut out the horror of it. A high scream of pain and yet even worse was the whimpering which followed, a whimpering which said that the woman who was doing it was in a state of total terror.

Dear sweet God above, what shall I do? Chloe distinctly heard someone say out loud, unaware that it was herself. She was conscious that she was shuffling about indecisively, moving from foot to foot and she could hear someone moaning in the back of her throat and realised that it was her own throat and her own voice which was making the sound.

"Don't, Paddy . . . I'm warning you . . . don't," she heard the woman say in a high, pain-filled voice and she knew as she had known from the first that the woman was her cousin and that something dreadful was happening to her on the other side of the beautifully painted door.

She didn't give herself time to think, since she knew if she did she would pick up the skirt of her second-best gown and run like a hare down the track for the safety of her home. Paddy Andrews might be murdering Katy Andrews in the cottage which had once belonged to her grandmother but it was nothing to do with Chloe Hutchinson, was it? Chloe Hutchinson was to have a child and she must protect it, her female, breeding body was screaming, but the screams from inside the cottage were just as insistent for they were female too.

Flinging herself at the door, ready to shout and bang and create as much noise as she could in the hope of distracting the man from what he was doing to Katy, Chloe found it opened before her onslaught and she was flung into the room almost at the feet of the seated man and the woman who knelt in front of him.

He had her by the arm, which he had twisted up behind her back at what seemed to be an impossible angle, her hand almost hidden under the tangle of her own hair. Her head was thrown back and her mouth was wide and straining in a rictus of agony. Tears poured from her eyes and as Chloe scrambled to her feet and began to back away, the man in the wheelchair grabbed Katy's hair with his other hand and forced her into an even more awkward position, one that had her almost on her back but with her legs twisted under her.

"You whore . . . you filthy whore," he was spitting, the saliva from his mouth spraying her face. "I'll bloody kill thi', I swear it. I'll 'ang fer thi' gladly since there's nowt much else ter be done wi' me, an' when I find out who it is tha've bin with . . ."

"Paddy . . . Jesus, Paddy . . . would I be likely to go out and lie with another man like this? Let me go, you bastard, or I warn you I shall abandon you to fend for yourself. Take your bloody hands off me."

"I've not done wi' thi', bitch, not yet. It's not often I get me 'ands on thi' now but I reckon . . ."

It was at that moment that Paddy suddenly became aware that they were no longer alone. The sunlight from the open door fell in a golden stream across the kitchen, touching the hem of Katy's dishevelled gown which was somewhere up about her thighs and Chloe remembered wondering when it was that her cousin had discarded the breeches which she had flaunted about the valley for so long. She wore no stockings or shoes and the skin of her shapely legs was white, smooth as porcelain but mottled with unsightly bruises, some of them deep and fresh, others fading to green and yellow.

Paddy Andrews, an expression of surprise taking the place of uncontainable rage on his red and sweating face, stared over the sprawled body of the woman he was abusing, and so great was his amazement to find the dainty wife of Jamie Hutchinson in what he had come to consider as *his* cottage, since he now lived here with Katy, he allowed his grip to slacken and at once Katy scrambled awkwardly away. Not far but far enough to be out of his reach. She remained on the floor, her skirts still bunched up about her, hugging the arm Paddy had nearly torn from her shoulder, rocking slowly in pain as she nursed it to her. Her hair hung about her face like a curtain, hiding all but her bitten mouth, but from the tangled mass of red-gold curls her tawny eyes, narrowed and venomous, glared at Paddy.

"You do that again, Paddy Andrews, and it won't be you who'll swing but me." Her voice was low, husky. It was as though her throat hurt her and Chloe had time to notice that the bruises on her legs and thighs were repeated on her neck. "I'll kill you, I promise. I'm sure I could persuade my brother who is now a qualified doctor and who hates your guts to give me some potion which would do for you. Slip it in your whisky, I would, and no one the wiser and, what's more, no one to care, not even those two idiots who— "

"Now then, Coppertop, that's enough of that. Can thi' not see we 'ave a visitor an' that's no way ter talk afore a visitor. Good day ter thi', Mrs Hutchinson, an' what can we do fer thi' on this fine, bright an' lovely mornin'?

He grinned and for a moment, from inside the ruined, sweat-streaked face, the bloated flesh, the bloodshot eyes and twisted, bitter features of the man in the chair, the old handsome, winsome charm of Paddy Andrews shone through. Chloe could remember him clearly, striding athletically down the track from his father's old cottage, jumping lightly across rocks and crevices, his powerful, muscular body quite magnificent in its flagrant masculinity. Tall, strong, invincible, winking devilishly at her as she gathered bilberries for a pie.

"Good mornin' to yer, Mrs Hutchinson," he had cried out then, for it was just after she and Jamie had married, bowing and doffing his cap with a sweeping gesture, his dark curls alive and springing about his head. "A lovely mornin', is it not?" he had gone on, before disappearing jauntily in the direction of Woodhead and, presumably, this cottage.

Chloe simply stood there, her slight figure outlined by the shaft of sunlight, slender enough as to be almost transparent, her body as fragile and breakable as the lark which soared in the sky and yet prepared, or so it appeared to the grinning Paddy Andrews, to defend to the death her cousin who hated the very air Chloe Hutchinson breathed.

"Look 'oo's come ter visit us, Coppertop. It's Mrs Jamie Hutchinson as I live an' breathe. Tha'd best gerrout that fine tea-service Grandma left us, fer I'm sure a cuppa tea'd be most welcome, wouldn't it, Mrs Hutchinson?"

She turned her head then, Katy Andrews. Her face, still hidden in the curtain of her hair, showed no surprise, for Katy Andrews had learned in the last, bitter seven months to hide all emotion, all thought, all feeling, to keep to herself what once had exploded from her in a great fiery conflagration, since then she had seen no need to suppress it.

Slowly she hauled herself to her feet, hampered, Chloe thought, by her injured arm, clinging to the corner of the highly polished dresser but as the hem of her gown fell down about her bare feet, the reason for her discarding of her breeches became clear. Chloe felt the blood drain from her face and almost succumbed to her own need to fall down if she could not, and as soon as possible, find something of her own to hold on to.

Katy Andrews was in what looked to be the last month of pregnancy. Not that Chloe knew much about pregnancy. She was in her third month and barely showed. Her stepmama had been in her sixth month when Chloe last saw her and had appeared quite enormous but not nearly so enormous as Katy, whose belly jutted out from her straight and slender frame as though it could not possibly be a part of it. It was like some monstrous appendage which had attached itself to her, dragging her forward, altering the way she stood, forcing her back to a concavity which made her look deformed.

She stood as straight as she could though, her head held high, her jaw thrust forward. She pushed her hair back from her face with both hands, fastening it with a scrap of ribbon she retrieved awkwardly from the floor before she spoke.

"Get out of my house."

That was all, just those five words, but in them was a venom which plainly revealed all her loathing, all her revulsion, all her bitter, pent-up enmity for her cousin who had caused, knowingly or not, the nightmare world in which Katy now lived. Her face was cut like a cameo as she turned icily away, clear, unblurred by her pregnancy, white as marble, and as cold, but she had not bargained for Chloe's frail but resolute courage which had brought her here. Chloe had not known of Katy's condition. She had come, persuaded by the conversation she and Matty had had a few days ago, to see if . . . well, to find out if perhaps . . . perhaps . . . If Katy would allow it, she might give her cousin . . . dear God, it was so hard to put into words since she wasn't even sure what she meant herself, what she meant to offer, but what it boiled down to was . . . was a helping hand! A sympathetic . . . no, oh no, that was the last thing her hot-headed, stiff-necked, brave-hearted cousin would want, sympathy, so really it was anything that Katy might have a need for which Chloe could give.

She spoke for the first time since she had erupted into the pleasant kitchen – and it was pleasant, as clean and fragrant as her own – but it was not to Katy she spoke but to the man in the chair.

"You must not treat her so, Mr Andrews, not in her condition. You could harm the child." Her voice was severe, scolding, ludicrous really, she knew it herself, in the bitter, menacing atmosphere which charged the cottage, but it was all she could think of. The man might have broken Katy's arm, or her neck and here was Chloe Hutchinson lecturing him as though he were a big, naughty boy, one who had been caught bullying a smaller. He needed horsewhipping for the way he had handled her cousin, and her so close to her time, she thought, idiotically, she realised later. Taken outside and bent over a rail like one did with naughty boys, or so she had heard, and . . .

It was then that her eyes dropped to his hands which were clenched furiously in his lap as though in the deepest frustration, and from there moved down to his legs . . . to his one . . . one leg which ended in a bare and dirty foot, and to the other which didn't. A half a leg then, not even that, for the stump of it finished obscenely about six inches above his knee. It was wrapped about in what looked to be a bit of soiled cloth. His trousers were filthy, crumpled rags which looked as though they were never removed and his torn shirt was the same. It was evident that he had shaved, or someone had shaved him, but not for the last week.

He was still smiling as she lifted her appalled gaze to his face, his mouth cruel over his even white teeth which were the only thing about him which still remained attractive.

"Norra pretty sight, is it, Mrs Hutchinson, but my Coppertop still loves me, don't tha', Coppertop? Well, she did once since she's to 'ave me bairn, or so she ses. That it's mine, I mean. But she likes it, if tha' know what I mean, Mrs Hutchinson, an' wi' me like I am it occurs ter me she's gerrin' it elsewhere. Dost tha' tekk me meanin'?" He winked roguishly as though he and Chloe were kindred spirits in matters of the flesh.

"Be quiet, Paddy, you're making a fool of yourself." Katy began to move ponderously towards Chloe, her enormous belly swaying before her, her eyes glittering in her bone white face and, despite her determination to be heard, Chloe found herself moving back before her, almost tripping on the step, though she kept both hands resolutely on the frame of the door in order to prevent Katy from slamming it to.

"Katy . . ." she ventured tentatively. "Won't you . . .?"

"I thought I told you to get out of my house. You and I were never friends and why in hell's name you've come here I don't know, nor do I want to know, so get off my doorstep now before . . ."

"Katy, let me help you . . . please." She released her frantic grip of the door frame for a moment, using it to indicate the grinning man who would plainly be of no help to a labouring woman, the dog which could be heard throwing itself against a door upstairs, still clamouring to be let out and the awful, awful sense of hatred and fear which permeated the place.

"I don't want, nor need your help and why you should imagine I do is beyond me."

"But you are to have a child . . . I didn't know."

"Well, I did," Katy sneered, "and so does everyone else in this valley except you."

"Jamie didn't or he would have told me."

Chloe knew she had made a grave mistake as soon as the words were out of her mouth.

Katy's face twisted and the clamped-down, tightly held emotions within her, despair, hopelessness, fear, were beginning to surface despite her bitter struggle not to let this hated woman see them. No one was allowed to see what festered inside Katy Andrews. The deep, yearning, living love for this woman's husband which just would not die, the misery, the grief which had altered her until she was just not the same person any more as she struggled to come to terms with her appalling sense of loss. And then there was the remorse, yes, she who had not known the meaning of the word, when she heard from Annie Lennox of the slow deterioration of her mother's health and her father's devastation over it. The compassion she did not want to feel for the big, once handsome man in the chair who had been crippled by Katy's brothers for what she had done. Not shame, no, never shame, though she didn't know why, for surely she should feel some and now detestation for this . . . this thing which grew and jostled for space inside her. Paddy's child. The child which the gross man in the wheelchair had given her before he was crippled. Dear God, with what hot joy her body had welcomed his then and with what disgust it contemplated it now.

She could actually feel the tears welling up within her like some pool which slowly fills up with rainwater in a storm and, when it is full, overflows, but she would not weep in front of Jamie's wife, who was looking at her with such sorrow, such gentle compassionate sorrow Katy wanted – to her own amazement and horror – nothing more than to be gathered into the arms which were stretched across her doorway.

Dear God . . . dear sweet God! She opened her eyes wide, then blinked rapidly but Chloe had seen the moisture which was forming. It encouraged her and her face softened into a smile.

"Please, Katy, can we not . . .?" She could not quite bring herself to say "be friends", not yet, but surely, surely now they were both facing motherhood . . .?

As though reading her thoughts Katy stiffened in what appeared to be deep offence and her face, which had been wavering into tears, hardened. Her lip lifted in contempt and she bared her teeth for a savage moment.

"Don't start prattling on to me about babies or as God is my witness I'll knock you to the ground. I heard about you when I was at . . . at Cloudberry End but let me tell you I have no interest in, nor concern for this," placing a hand on the mound of her belly, "and I would be obliged if you would give me the same consideration. It is nothing to do with you and I don't need . . ."

"But you do, Katy, you do. You'll need a woman's help." Her eyes went over Katy's shoulder to the bloated carcase of the man behind her. "You can't manage . . ."

"I can certainly manage without you, madame."

"No . . . no, Matty says— "

"What Matty says is again nothing to me. And how dare she gossip?"

"She didn't. I was only going to say she has told me what will happen . . . explained it to me so that I would not be afraid and I believe you should have someone . . ."

"You? D'you mean you? Are you saying that I should have you in my home to help me with the birth of this . . . this child?" Her eyes blazed with incandescent fury and her lips curled. She placed her hands on her hips in a stance which would have been glorious but for the shape and size of her. Instead she looked pathetic and Chloe felt the tears flood to her eyes.

"Please, can we not put what has gone . . . behind us? I

have come to ask you . . . to see if I can . . . well, in the circumstances . . ."

Again her eyes went beyond Katy to the man at her back but it was no use. She was no use to Katy Andrews who reviled the very ground on which Chloe Hutchinson walked.

Katy laughed. "Oh, you mean Paddy? Now don't you worry about me and Paddy." Her voice was mocking. "We're just like a couple of love-birds, aren't we, Paddy?" turning to smile brilliantly, heartbreakingly in his direction. "Him and me will manage just fine, won't we, lad? He'll act as midwife and then there's always Josh and Jake."

"Please, oh please, don't joke."

Katy's face hardened. "Who's joking? Now get out of my sight, you unspeakable trash. Get out of my house and don't come back here, ever. I detest the very thought of you and your . . . your . . . what you are carrying almost as much as what is inside me. If you don't take your hands from my door frame I shall trap them without the slightest compunction."

To prove she meant it Katy crashed the door to and Chloe had time only to leap backwards, sitting down in a graceless heap on the track.

Inside the house the man began to laugh.

It had never once occurred to her to turn him out. She lay in the dark that night listening to him as he and his cousins sloshed down their throats the whisky the twins had brought over to "cheer him up" and for which she would be expected to pay. There was laughter and something crashed to the ground. The dog barked furiously and through her open bedroom window she heard Jinty Pickles's husband, who must have come to his door, complain bitterly that it wasn't fitting and they had no right to be disturbing decent folk who were trying to sleep. It was a bad day indeed when Madge Andrews had passed on and left her pleasant, peaceful little home to the bad lot who occupied it now. He wouldn't say it to Paddy's face, of course, for though Paddy was no longer capable of felling a chap, not unless he came and knelt in front of him, Josh and Jake were and Barty Pickles valued his hide too much to chance it.

Though she did her best to fight it, the face of the woman who had knocked on her door this morning imprinted itself on the inside of her closed eyelids. At once she opened them, staring at the silent shapes of the things which had once known the calm presence of her beloved grandmother, praying – though not in the true sense of the word – that her grandmother's memory would disperse that of Chloe Hutchinson but she could still see her, distressed, afraid even, but determined, nevertheless, to have her say.

Help her . . . Help her . . . Help Katy Andrews! That's what she had offered to do and dear God, the temptation to accept had been so great it had almost had her over. But what action could Chloe Hutchinson possibly take, had Katy herself wanted her to, that would rescue her from this impenetrable greyness, this perilous dread she was slowly sinking under? The naïvety of the woman was laughable had it not been so infuriating, but at the same time, though she hated the thought, she could not help but admire the bloody nerve of the woman. Of course, everyone knew there was nothing to be done with, or for Katy Andrews now. Her own family never came near her, though she knew in her heart where truth lay that if she asked for help it would be given. Every week Jimmy or Dicken rode up, their faces averted, to deliver the envelope which contained enough money for her to live comfortably and even feed Paddy's increasing appetite for alcohol. As long as she kept out of his reach and those cruel hands of his which, now that he was incapable of giving her pleasure, loved to pinch and bruise, not as once they had but simply for cruelty's sake, she could go on.

Annie – Mrs Lennox – came in every day while Paddy lay insensible in his bed to clean up after him and put the small cottage to rights, but she was another one who kept her face averted and had it not been for the generous wage Katy paid her would not have set foot inside the place. They were polite with one another, that was all and it would have been . . . pleasant to have another woman, a young woman . . .

God Almighty, what was she thinking of? What had put that preposterous thought in her head? What preposterous thought? her bewildered mind asked, for it had never been completed, and never would, for there was nothing more certain in her life than the truth that she would consider Chloe Hutchinson with loathing until the day she died. Chloe Hutchinson, the woman who had stolen Katy Andrews's life.

18

She was up on Great Crowden Intake when the first pang struck her. Low down in her back it was, more like the start of the dull cramps which came to plague her each month, moving dully to the pit of her belly. Well, if that was all it was going to be she'd manage it fine, she told herself. Up here with no one to see but a hawk which floated on the flickering wind, a skylark or two doing acrobats against the grey sky and some sheep who called fretfully to one another across the dense carpet of purple heather above the intake.

Though the day was dull it had not been cold when she lumbered down the stairs. Paddy had been snoring on his bed where his drinking partners had flung him the night before, his face slack and puffy, his mouth open, his lips coated with some nasty white substance which made her stomach heave. The dog lay next to him. He raised his head and watched her as she began to move things about haphazardly, an empty whisky bottle, a plate on which a half-eaten meat pie congealed, Paddy's shirt which, unusually, he had removed. After a moment or two, knowing she was no threat either to him or his master, the animal lowered his muzzle, resting it on the stump of Paddy's leg, not at all revolted by it as she was.

Moving back into the kitchen she began to fidget with

dirty cups and plates and cutlery, finding, to her surprise, she felt a great need to have them washed and set to rights, to tidy the place up. Even, God forbid, to fetch a pail of water and scrub the table top which was stained with whatever the men had eaten and drunk the night before. What in blazes was the matter with her? Katy Andrews who had never willingly washed a plate in her life and certainly had barely noticed the state of the table top, let alone felt the need to scrub it.

The fire had still been in, for despite their negligent attention towards anything which smacked of cleanliness, and their drunken state of the night before, all three men had been brought up with the ingrained principle that a kitchen fire, once lit, must never be allowed to go out. It was the centre of cottage life, the focal point, its heart. It kept them warm and it fed them, for all the cooking was done in the ovens on either side of it and in its slumbering coals which one of the twins had replenished. The kettle whispered softly above it and her grandmother's chair rocked before it. Peace was total and Katy savoured it while she drank a cup of tea and ate an enormous dish of porridge Mrs Lennox had made and left in a pan to the side of the fire. With syrup trickled into it it made a satisfying breakfast. Mrs Lennox, though she had nothing to say on the matter, or indeed on any matter, often left some culinary offering. A dumpling stew, a steak and kidney pudding, a slab of boiled bacon with pickles, bread on most days, the extra few shillings Katy put in her hand for payment going completely unremarked. It was as though Annie Lennox could only manage the dreadful state of affairs in Madge Andrews's cottage and her own financial need to be involved in it if she did not speak of it, or to its present occupants. A nod, sometimes a muttered reminder that his bed needed changing, which meant Katy was to have him out of it while Annie tackled the slovenly mess it was in.

Katy was aware that without Annie Lennox's reluctant help she would have gone under.

She was restless, wandering from the scullery where, again to her astonishment, she found herself with a passionate desire to clean the windows, for heaven's sake, which naturally she resisted. Back to the glowing hearth, then over to the front door, flinging it open to stare down the track towards the reservoir, where the water rippled in a gentle, aimless way, eddying this way and that as the wind caught it. Grey clouds, their undersides lined with dark blue, sat almost motionless above distant Bleaklow Hill and from the railway track which ran on the far side of the water came the shriek of an engine's whistle.

It had rained in the night and the hedgerows were spattered with moisture. Wild flowers bloomed, bright and unruly. The trees, product of the abundant rainfall which predominated in this high peak land, were garbed in lush green foliage, dripping somewhat disconsolately to soak into the already sodden ground. Barty Pickles's gnarled, mossy trees were laden with apples and plums and Katy smiled, for at this very moment a plum pie resided in her cupboard, baked by Annie, the plums, though he was not aware of it and would have been highly indignant if he had known, from Barty's trees.

She sighed, leaning her shoulder against the door frame, her hands linked beneath the awkward, hated burden of her distended stomach, then, turning clumsily, she reached for her warm, lined cloak. She threw it round her shoulders and, closing the door quietly behind her, she left the cottage, going not down the track but crossing it behind Enter Clough. The clough itself was not deep and neither was the water which chuckled down it and she was able to reach the other side without getting her feet wet.

Working her way steadily across the horizontal waves of gritstone which lay above the farmland she felt her spirits lift. She breathed deeply, filling her lungs with the pure, heady air which had in it the scent of heather and gorse, of rich soil and rough grass, of all the things she had known and taken for granted all her pampered childhood.

A lark, despite the cut-throat and buffeting wind which had sprung up as Katy climbed higher, rose straight up in front of her into the whirling air and poured out its bubbling song. She stopped to watch it and to catch her breath, bending over a little to ease the stitch which pierced her side.

She stood for several minutes, wishing she was on Storm's back with Muffy racing along at the mare's heels. What with one thing and another, she thought grimly, Paddy Andrews had a lot to answer for, though she supposed she could not blame him entirely. First there was this blasted infant which surely must come soon and when it did a home had to be found for it since she knew nothing about babies and had no intention of learning. Second, because of her condition she had been unable to ride Storm for weeks and third there was the loss of her constant, devoted companion, her scruffy little dog whom she had been forced to leave at Cloudberry End. How she missed her and she knew Muffy fretted but there was nothing to be done about it, not with that ugly brute which never left Paddy's side taking up residence in what he evidently believed to be his rightful place on Katy's hearth. Now and again, when his furious barking at every damn thing which annoyed it, annoyed *him*, Paddy begged her to lure him up into the spare bedroom so that he could have a bit of peace, but even there he was forever whining and howling and throwing himself against the closed door. Damned dog! She hated the thing.

The deep gully down which Little Crowden stream ran had her panting badly by the time she had traversed it. It was more of a climb than she had bargained for, since she had never done it on foot. Still, she managed it, her breath heaving triumphantly as she rested for a moment, looking down the steep slope towards Woodhead Chapel. The trees surrounding it hid it from her view and it seemed to her the bunched clouds which had begun to tumble across the sky were lower than when she had left home.

Great Crowden Breck, the largest of the waters which ran down to the reservoirs, was easier to get across. There were numerous scattered rocks in the smoothly flowing, white-dashed water and holding the awkward weight of her unborn child with both hands as though for balance, she managed to flounder from stone to stone, clambering up the bank through the vivid yellow gorse bushes which lined it to flop on her back with relief.

It was then that the first pain nudged her. The rough grass of the intake was damp but soft. Her cloak was thick, warmly lined and would provide her with a comfortable bed, especially if she could reach an outcrop of dizzily balanced rocks higher up the intake which would give her some shelter from the wind and what appeared to be a coming rainstorm.

She had almost reached them when another pain rippled through the small of her back, down her loins and up to the pit of her belly, this time stronger than the twinge she had first suffered and she had to pause, panting a little, waiting until it had passed but it didn't. Instead it lingered, a persistent nagging backache which, no matter how she stood, would not ease.

She was not frightened. "Oh damn and blast," she muttered, vaguely annoyed somehow for she had never been ill or known pain of any sort beyond a skinned knee in childhood since her birth seventeen years ago.

The rain was falling more steadily now, droplets catching in her hair and beginning to run uncomfortably down her face. They clung to her eyelashes, making her blink and she knew that if she didn't get into the shelter of the rocks, even with her sturdy cloak about her, she would soon be wet through.

She was still not frightened. "Damn you to hell, Paddy Andrews," she snarled savagely as she struggled up the incline, slipping on the wet grass, until she reached the grateful, if not entirely waterproof shelter of the rocks. She knew nothing of childbirth, only that it could take a while and that there was not much to be done about it until the end when, presumably, you wrapped the result up in a shawl and handed it to someone who would know what to do with it. In the meanwhile she'd lie here and wait.

Wrapping her cloak about her, glad of the warmth, she huddled against the biggest stone, doing her best to keep out of the drizzle which the wind would persist on flinging against her. No matter which side of the stone she crawled to, it still found her and she began to shiver.

She was alarmed several minutes later when she suddenly found her lower body, her thighs and legs, her drawers and petticoats, soaked with something which gushed from between her legs in the most undignified manner. It was warm and for a dreadful moment she thought it might be blood but as the pain began to attack her with a vengeance she found it no longer mattered. Blood, or perhaps she had wet herself in this disgusting thing which was happening to her, but did she care? Not at all! She only cared about the increasingly agonising crescendo of pain which knifed into her body at shorter and shorter intervals and her need to get it over and done with so that she might be returned to the person she had been before Paddy Andrews had got her with child. She'd known him and his body and this was the outcome and as God was her witness it would never, *never* happen again. Not any of it.

Jamie heard the scream, well, a succession of what sounded like screams, from where he was just starting the descent between Rakes Rock and Black Tor. He had gone to search for one of his flock. All sheep were stupid in his opinion, following one another blindly, even over the gritstone edge of Oakin Clough, which he knew to his cost, for three of his had done just that. But this particular beast did not seem to have the flock instinct, wandering off by itself as though in search of something, though God alone knew what. What would a ewe look for? he asked his wife, shaking his head in wonderment but there seemed to be no answer and every now and again he was forced to search for the bloody thing. He had not found it today.

The driving rain slanted almost horizontally into his face and the wind lashed the bracken to frenzy. Already, though it had been raining for no more than two hours, a fast-moving swathe of water was flowing across the sodden grass and over his stout boots and the track was almost invisible. It was slippery and he had gone down more than once on to his behind. The rain was coming down faster, or rather across faster, hurtling directly into his face, almost with the ferocity of hailstones, it was so hard and cutting.

He hesitated as the sound was repeated. At first he had been inclined to put it down to the keening of the driving wind, cursing the bloody weather which could turn from the warmth of summer to the raw chill of winter in a couple of hours. Jesus, it was July but it might have been January it was so bitter and he wouldn't have been surprised to see the rain turn to snow.

There it was again. He saw Captain prick his ears and turn his head in the direction of Great Crowden Intake which was away to his left, then look up at him as though seeking a command. The animal was becoming a well-behaved and competent sheepdog, alert and obedient, mindful of his job as the keeper of his master's flock and though his sharp ears were well aware the sound was not that of a sheep it was one which needed investigating, surely?

"What is it, Captain? You can hear it too, can't you?"

The dog almost nodded his head. He was poised, one foot raised, ready to dart off when his master said he might and when Jamie's hand waved him on he was off like a greyhound from the slips, a fast-moving blur blending into the soaked, mud-coloured ground and the slanting rain before vanishing from Jamie's sight.

"Captain?" Jamie called, his hands cupped round his mouth and when the dog answered with a short, yipping bark which meant "over here", he moved as fast as he could go across the sloping, greasy grass in his direction.

She had fallen into a light doze between the tail end of one slash of the knife and the beginning of the next. She had been writhing and screaming for hours, days, weeks, up here with no one to see her, or hear her, which is what she had wanted, she remembered thinking dazedly. To get this over by herself without any other woman fussing about her and by God, she'd got her wish and now look what a bloody mess she was in. As far as she could tell, and how was she to know, the child showed no sign of making an appearance and not only was there a claw scrabbling at her back and her belly, and every other part of her racked body, her throat was on fire with her own screams. Several times she had turned her face up to the pelting rain, opening her bitten mouth wide and allowing the icy water to fill it up and then slide down her throat but she was so tired now, so battered, so dazed and uncaring, she no longer had the strength. At the beginning she had stood up and walked about, holding on to the rough stones among which she sheltered and she had found some benefit, but that was a long time ago and so now she would lie here and let this thing continue to tear her to pieces, when, presumably, she would die. And the child, which would concern no one. In fact there most certainly would be more than one who would be glad to see the back of her, and Paddy Andrews's bastard. Chris, for one, and who could blame him, although it had been his initial attack on Paddy which had brought about this maelstrom of events.

Oh God . . . Oh sweet Jesus . . . it was here again, that agony which was slowly tearing her apart.

Her head was jerked back and her throat became taut, the tendons in it straining and rigid, her voice no more than a thin wail, when something wet and warm and rough moved across her face. Her eyes were tight closed, her mouth opened wide but the tongue, for that was what it was, continued to lap at her with the cheerful abandonment of a young dog.

Muffy? Was it Muffy? Was she at home then in the kitchen at Cloudberry End, her own little dog in her lap, her ecstatic tongue licking at every bit of bare flesh it could reach? Her face and neck and now her hand which she lifted weakly to ward it off. But she was so cold, so cold and tired and hurting and someone was sawing at her with a blunt knife and she really ought to raise her voice in protest but the thing was she was just too exhausted to care any more.

"Muffy . . . good girl," she said hoarsely, glad to have her, for if she were to be alone up here . . . up here . . . aah, she wasn't in the kitchen at Cloudberry End then . . . of course . . . too cold . . . then in what better company to die than Muffy's who loved her?

But she must be dead already . . . and gone to some heavenly place, for here was Jamie, her love, her joy . . . the reason she lived . . . for Jamie . . . for the only man she had ever wanted . . . needed . . . Jamie . . .

"Katy!" His voice sounded strange, hoarse, and in it was something odd which she could not recognise. His eyes, blue as the sky on a midsummer day, blue as turquoise in candlelight, were glittering, wide.

"Jamie . . . Jamie . . . have you . . . come to . . .?"

"Dear sweet Christ, Katy . . . what in heaven's name . . .?"

She smiled and her hand gripped his sleeve with a strength which surprised her, for she had been fighting this thing for so long and she was burned out, finished, but there was something she must say before the end.

"I love you, Jamie. This . . . with Paddy . . . is nothing. I love you . . . and I always will." She wanted to tell him that. She wanted him to understand about her and Paddy . . . it was most important before she died. She could feel the claw beginning to rip at her again but when he put his arms about her and lifted her contorted, contorting body against his strong one she didn't mind so much.

"Put your arms round my neck, sweetheart."

Sweetheart! He had called her sweetheart, so what else mattered in this bad, mad world, this agony, this bitter, joyless day on which . . . she couldn't quite remember what it was . . . on which something awful was happening to her.

Her arms felt so heavy though, so lifeless, boneless, useless.

"I don't think . . . I can, Jamie."

"Never mind . . . never mind, my love. Just rest . . . I've got you. Just rest until I get you home."

"Are we to . . . go home then, Jamie?"

"Yes, sweetheart."

It took him over two hours to negotiate the steep track which led down from Great Crowden Intake to Valley Bottom Farm. Again and again he was forced to kneel and put her on the ground, her labouring body too much for him to hold and with each contraction she threw herself about, screaming and begging him not to let her go. She was off her head, her eyes deep pools of dull brown amber in her putty-coloured face. She was as wet as if she had dragged herself through the rapidly filling breck which he followed, and so was he, doing his best to stay on his feet in the headlong race of rainwater which was on its way to the storm-tossed fury of the reservoir in the valley. It was growing dark and several times he was convinced that he and Katy, her unborn child and the brave dog who never left his side, were to go too.

Chloe had a dozen candles lit in the kitchen, making sure he would not miss the farmhouse in the black fury of the storm which had come upon them so suddenly and as he staggered through the gate and round the corner of the building into the yard, sheltered from the shrieking wind at last, she was there, the door standing wide, a shawl about her head, for she had been up to the drystone wall at the back of the farm a dozen times to peer up the track from which he would come.

For a moment she thought he had a sheep across his arms, grey, sodden, senseless, perhaps injured in some way and was alarmed when he moved towards the kitchen door with, it seemed, every intention of bringing the animal inside.

"Jamie . . .?" she questioned.

"Quick, for Christ's sake get out of the way."

"Jamie!" He had never, as long as she had known him, spoken to her in other than the gentle tones of a lover and her mouth dropped open in astonishment.

Then she recognised what it was he carried.

"Blessed Lord," she gasped, rearing back from him and his burden, her eyes wide and frightened, her hand going to her mouth. "What . . . who . . .?"

"Quickly, it's Katy and she's in labour, and in trouble by the look of her. God knows how long she's been up there. We've got to strip her off, Chloe, and get her warm or she'll die."

Yes, Chloe could see who it was now, the woman who had put that anguished look on Jamie's face and made his voice so hoarse and afraid. She already looked dead to her, her arms and head lolling back across Jamie's arms, her hair streaming like tangled seaweed towards the floor, dripping and limp, its vital colour completely gone. Her eyes were closed and her wet face was carved as though from stone and Chloe was about to put out a tentative hand to her cheek, for surely it would be cold and lifeless, when Katy suddenly stiffened, then arched her body in some dreadful spasm and began to scream, a high-pitched scream of pure, undiluted agony.

"Oh sweet God," Chloe whispered. She could feel the blood freeze in her veins but Jamie would have none of it.

"Chloe, pull yourself together or they'll both die."

"Both?"

His voice was harsh as though he was angry with her and she wanted him to put down Katy Andrews and take her in his arms. To put to one side the woman he held who was nothing to do with Chloe and Jamie Hutchinson and their life. To take hold of his wife who was – dear God, forgive her – jealous of his attention to the woman who was her cousin.

She had no time to examine this astonishing thought, for Jamie was becoming increasingly impatient.

"Chloe, she's in labour, for God's sake. You know what that means. Now move. Clear a space in front of the fire and spread that rug. Yes . . . yes, that will do. Then we must take off these wet clothes," and all the time he spoke Katy's voice rose higher and higher in a wail of white-hot agony.

"I'm not sure I can manage her on my own, Jamie," Chloe heard herself whisper, clutching at her own belly where her child slept.

"I'm not proposing that you should, my dove. Now run upstairs and bring down the blankets from our bed and some clean sheets . . . quickly . . . quickly."

For perhaps the last time in her life Chloe's early training at her mama's knee rose to the fore.

"But surely you cannot mean that *you* are to help?"

"For Christ's sake, woman, stop dithering about and do as I say."

She became calm then. His concern for Katy was only natural and this was not the time to be studying her own sudden and strange feeling for this man who loved her and who had been her husband for nine contented months. She became the woman she really was beneath the veneer her mama had painted over her. The woman who was now a wife, a true wife. A farmer's wife who would shortly go through herself what her cousin suffered and she did not intend to flinch from it.

They stripped her while she mumbled and screamed and writhed and bucked beneath their hands. Chloe was strong now, soothing her, stroking her face and her sweat-streaked hair, unembarrassed to have this naked woman straining on her kitchen rug beneath the pitying gaze of her own husband, for that was what was in his face for Katy Andrews, his wife saw it plainly.

Even like this Katy was beautiful, earthy, a female labouring to bring forth life. Her fine white skin stretched dangerously tight over the distended mound of her belly. Already her swollen breasts leaked some milky fluid, Chloe noticed, as she eased Katy gently into one of the capacious nightgowns she had already made in preparation for her own pregnancy.

"Oh God . . . God help me . . ." Katy Andrews, as though her body knew that it must take an active part in this last stage of her labour, came to her senses to find the compassionate face of the woman she hated more than any other bending over her. Her heart, which was already banging away inside her chest as her body strained to rid itself of its burden, gave a sickening lurch and though she scarce had breath to breathe let alone speak, she heard her own voice rasp in her inflamed throat.

"What in hell's name d'you think you're doing?" she snarled. "Take your filthy hands off me and bugger off before . . ."

"I have no intention of buggering off, as you so engagingly put it, Katy Andrews," Chloe answered serenely. "This is my house we are in. That is my nightgown you are wearing and my rug you are staining with your blood, so kindly lie back and allow Jamie and me to deliver your child."

Katy's mouth popped open even wider, then stayed that way as she began to bellow.

"Oh Jesus . . ." She was up on her elbows. Her head fell back and her heels dug into the bright rug as her splayed legs moved instinctively wider to allow passage for the child she was pushing out of her.

"Where the bloody hell is Jamie?" she screeched, panting like a dog on a hot day.

"Here, at the working end" – his voice smiled – "and you're not to worry. Chloe and I have done this before, you know, so we're quite experienced."

"Who . . . who with?" she managed to ask as she bore down relentlessly, unable to do anything else.

"Oh, several calves and at least half a dozen sheep."

"Calves . . . sheep! God help me . . ."

"No, lass, just me and Chloe."

It took no more than fifteen minutes, minutes through which Katy roared and raged, for Jamie kept telling her to stop, to rest a moment, to slow down then to bear down, to stop . . . stop, until she said she had had enough and was off to old Dr Highcroft who wouldn't keep her hanging about like this.

A final heave, a sort of plopping noise like a landed fish coming to rest on a river bank and then, with a bellow which had Captain leaping to his feet and barking furiously, Katy Andrews's son was born into the hands of the man she loved.

The woman she loathed held her hands and cried and Katy allowed her to kiss her brow and cheek before being taken into her strong and slender arms, glad to be there at the last.

19

She walked up the gravelled driveway, her skirts swinging, her ankles bare, her son tied to her breast in a shawl, just like a gypsy woman selling pegs at the back door, Mrs Tiplady moaned to Freda, though of course, Miss Katy didn't use the back door but marched boldly in at the front.

"Is my father at home, Freda?" she asked the flustered parlourmaid. "I've come to introduce him to his grandson."

And there he was, Freda reported later to the open-mouthed servants who clustered round her, undeterred by the presence of Mrs Tiplady, who was not as commanding as usual in her astonishment. Paddy Andrews's son, lying sweetly in his mother's arms, plump and brown and with eyes and hair exactly the colour of hers. They said she took him up on the moors, striding out like a man, though she no longer wore her breeches, nor did she ride her sorrel mare. Saul Gibbon said he had seen her as high as the Black Hill itself, sitting on a rock, the wind in her hair, the child suckling at her breast.

"Good day to you, Saul," she had called out, bold as brass. "A lovely day, is it not?" and Saul had no choice but to answer that it was. Well, he was that taken aback he'd had no time to remember that she was the scarlet woman of Crossclough, with her crippled lover and her bastard child and that no one had a good word to say for her except that cousin of hers who was herself suspect. She looked so . . . well, Saul was not familiar with words such as "tranquil" or "serene" but that was what Katy Andrews was now, despite what had happened to Paddy Andrews and Chris Andrews, for which she was surely to blame, the wildness gone from her with the birth of her boy.

Jack, she'd called him, though naturally he'd not been baptised, not with him being illegitimate, but perhaps if Jack Andrews, his grandfather, were to get a look at him, things might be different.

He was sitting in a leather chair drawn up to the fire in his study and he did not get up when she entered. Neither did he turn round. He was smoking a cigar, his head wreathed in the fragrant smoke from it and Katy breathed it in deeply, realising how she had missed it. It brought back memories of her childhood, of her father coming home from his travels laden with presents, big, strong, handsome, his smile wide as he swept her up into his arms. Not for long, of course, for her mother would detach him from his children and carry him off to the private world she and he lived in and it would perhaps be twenty-four hours before they saw him again.

"Father," she said quietly, for Katy Andrews had learned to be quiet now she had a child. "Father."

He turned then, sighing deeply as his eyes lifted to hers and she was shocked to see the change in him. She had not seen him since he had come to the cottage to try and take her home, and she had thought him to be ageing then but he looked ten years older now. He was no longer big and strong, though she supposed he could still be called handsome in a lean and furrowed way. Where his face had been smooth, well shaven, amber-tinted, it was now lined and sallow, the flesh dwindled somehow, his dark brown eyes, so like hers, so like Paddy's, sunk deep in dusty shadows. He had grown so thin, his well-cut jacket standing away from his neck where once it had fitted snugly and when he stood at last she could see his waistcoat hang away from his stomach.

"Katherine," he answered courteously, as though she were no more than an unexpected guest. His eyes strayed briefly to the child but he showed no particular interest, not even when her son awoke, blinking his eyes slowly like a baby owl. After a lingering contemplation of her own face, which the baby always seemed to find of immense interest, especially when she talked to him, he looked about him, turning his well-shaped head on which russet curls had begun to spring until his gaze came to rest on his grandfather. He smiled briefly, a sort of bobbing half smile which seemed to take him by surprise, then he turned his face to her breast in search of nourishment. His mouth nuzzled against the cotton of her bodice, open and demanding and Katy knew she would either have to feed him or be quick in what she had to say to her father.

She smiled hesitantly. He was so distant, so unconcerned, not only with her but with her son whom he surely could not resist. This was his grandchild, his first grandchild and though circumstances were . . . well, she could only call them disastrous, surely her parents would recognise that things were different now. She was different since Jack's birth. This was her family home and in it was her family and she wanted Jack to be welcome in it, to have a family, a grandmother and grandfather, uncles and . . . well, a proper place in the way of things. Paddy treated him like a plaything, something to divert him when he was bored, wanting to dandle him on his good knee, tossing him about roughly, making a man of him, as he put it, boasting to his cousins on how brave and handsome his son was. His son who was the dead spit of him except for his hair, he said, and that, of course, came from his Coppertop, leering in her direction, giving the impression to the grinning twins that he and Katy still shared a physical relationship. Not that she ever left Jack alone with him, not for a second and when Paddy had him in his rough embrace she hung about no more than an arm's length away in case Paddy got too boisterous. Truth to tell she didn't like him to touch her son at all, even though Jack was his as well. Paddy was so gross now, eating and drinking from daybreak until he fell into his bed at night, the fat hanging in folds down his once arrow-straight, fighter's body. What had once been hard muscle was now creeping obesity, flabby and disgusting and to see her sweet baby on his knee, her son whom she loved with all the passion she had once lavished only on Jamie Hutchinson, was something she could not bear.

She was not sure, even as she stood before her father, what she expected of him, what could be done to put right the wrongs she had committed but she had to start somewhere. This child was the catalyst. Already he had shown her that love was never-ending, ever-growing; that it took many forms. That it could not be divided, or subtracted from. That no matter how many there were to share it it was always the same size. She loved Jamie. That was a fact and was unalterable. That love would never wither but now her son took her love for himself, for did she not have an everlasting abundance of it, stealing nothing from Jamie since love was indivisible.

Her father waited patiently for her to begin. She felt a tremor of apprehension for she had not expected this indifference, this complete lack of concern for anything she might have to say. She was his daughter and so he had agreed to see her but it was no more than a gesture, his attitude said, as if he were waiting civilly for her to get on with it and then leave him in peace.

"Is Mother well?" she asked for want of something to fill the dreadful emptiness while the baby, whom she had hoisted to her shoulder in order to divert him from the smell of her milk, did his best to turn his head. He was almost three months old now and beginning to take a great deal of interest in what went on around him and she patted his back pacifyingly.

Her father looked at her for a long time before breaking the silence. His face could not be said to have come alive but there was an expression on it which she did not recognise.

"I was going to write to you," he said at last, his voice quiet, "since you have a right to know but as you are here now I may as well tell you."

The apprehension began to grow in her, to become something more than apprehension and she felt her heartbeat quicken. The clock at the back of the room sounded the quarter hour with a solid clunk and it made her jump. She held the baby more tightly to her and he began to struggle strongly. She patted his back feverishly and began to sway to and fro, doing her best to avert the full-throated roar of his demand for the breast.

"Father, you're beginning to frighten me. I came to— "

"Really, lass, d'you think it matters to me now? What you came here for? I'm sure whatever it is will be to your advantage as has every action you have ever taken since you were a child. At least what you imagined to be to your advantage— "

"No, Father . . . no," she interrupted him. "I came not for myself but to show you your grandson." She turned the baby to face Jack Andrews, holding his back against her breast, but her father, after a casual glance into the child's appealing face, looked back to his daughter.

"See, Father, is he not a lovely boy? Please, don't look away. I named him Jack . . ." After you, of course, though without the conscious intention of pleasing you. "Father, he is your flesh and blood . . . please . . ."

"Aye, an' Paddy Andrews's." Her father's face became animated for a moment and his voice was harsh. A flush of blood ran under his skin making him look more like his old self, then it died away and so did his show of animosity.

"Father, I know it has not been . . . pleasant," she mumbled, "but Jack is your grandson, and Mother's, so may I not go up and show him to her?" Her voice had became pleading, desolate but her father cut it off, his own sharp and positive.

"No, you may not. That is what I must talk to you about. Your mother . . . is not well." His voice broke and he passed a trembling hand over his face. "She has not been strong, not for years, but I dare say with a peaceful, trouble-free life she might have remained in good health. But of course that is just what she has not had. None should know better than you. It has broken her heart, Katherine. You have been a trial to me and to your mother, lass, you must know that?"

"Father, I did not mean to— "

He cut off her wail of protest with a dismissive movement of his hand.

"Maybe you did not mean to, Katherine. Nevertheless you did, so I am taking your mother away. I have bought a house in Scarborough. It stands on a cliff overlooking the sea. The air and a life of tranquillity free from the pressures her family have forced on her in the past will, Dr Highcroft assures me, be beneficial to her and she may, to some extent, recover. She is to lead a quiet life with only those people about her who care for her."

"Father, I love her," and it was true though she had not been consciously aware of it.

"You have a strange way of showing it, lass. You have broken her health and her heart. Your wildness, your flouting of every rule her society believes in has become more than she can bear. She has been forced to listen to tales of your . . . your depravity. Yes, that is the word I would use, and I mean to see she is protected from it from now on. We leave at the end of the week and— "

"But, Father, please . . . please don't shut me out."

"Shut you out! Girl, you did that to yourself when you took up with Paddy Andrews."

"I know, I know I was to blame, for Paddy and his feud with Chris which is . . . Oh, please, Father, now that I have a son, won't you . . .?"

Her father looked at her sadly, then, putting out a trembling hand, laid it for a moment on his grandson's head.

"Now you know, Katy. Now you are a mother yourself you will realise what you have done to yours."

She scarcely heard the rest of his words which explained to her the arrangements he had made for his children, which, presumably, included her, and for his property. Mrs Tiplady, Ivy and Freda were to go to Scarborough with their mistress since they were used to her ways and she to theirs. Lottie and Janet would remain at Cloudberry End with the remainder of the kitchen staff to take care of the house and of Christopher who was to be in charge of the paper mill.

He would need a home and there were his brothers, Richard and David, who would require some place to come back to from their travels.

The outside staff would remain, since Jack Andrews did not wish to see his property go to rack and ruin. Jimmy and Dicken would continue to see to the stables and the horses,

Storm included, if she so wished and he himself would travel back now and then from Scarborough to check on things. Cloudberry End was to remain as it was and, if she needed it, he added distantly, doing his duty, no more, and, not wishing either himself or his beloved wife to be concerned with it, there would always be a home for her here.

"A home?" she repeated dully.

"Yes, I really cannot see you living your life out with that . . . that . . ."

"Cripple? Is that the word you're searching for, Father?"

"If you wish."

"Have you never wondered why I stay with him?"

"No, I can't say I have, Katherine. Not lately, at any rate."

"He is a cripple because of me, Father. Chris and the others gave him a beating."

"Richly deserved, my lass. Had I been young enough I would have helped them. For a man to . . . to violate an innocent girl— " He stopped abruptly and the glow of madness which coloured his face faded. "Well, what's done is done, Katy, and we are left with the results. We must make of them what we can. My concern is for your mother now. No one else. Now I must go, if you'll excuse me. I have things to do."

"Yes . . ." She stood up, the child in her arms, not thrown out, oh no, far from that, but abandoned just the same, by the man and woman she herself had abandoned so carelessly.

They watched her go, Janet and Lottie, from the upstairs window where they were packing their mistress's clothes. They had no idea why she had come, apart from what she had said to Freda about showing her boy to her father, but even now, when she surely must have been told of her parents' departure for Scarborough, she did not droop nor falter. Her head was up, brilliant and glowing in the "back-end" sunshine, her back straight, her skirt swinging, her stride long and graceful as she turned into the woodland just before she reached the gate. Now where was she going? they asked one another. Taking a short cut beneath the brown and copper and tawny orange of the autumn trees and then on through the fields where the crops were being harvested, perhaps.

Well, wherever she was off to it was none of their business, though they did admit to one another they would have liked to get a look at Miss Katy's little lad.

It was a mellow, sunny day and Katy could hear through the misted jumble of her thoughts the voices of children blackberrying on the other side of the hedge and the sweet, solitary singing of a robin. A mist was gathering in the hollows and the sky was turning to the pearly blue of the coming evening. Her child was beginning to clamour with more persistence for her breast which was full and doing some clamouring of its own. She felt dazed, a sense of disorientation which was foreign to her, she who had always known her own mind, her own needs and her own ruthless determination to follow them.

The sun was sinking in a blaze of crimson glory at the back of the peaks towards Black Hill but there was still a patch of warm sunlight on a bit of drystone walling facing the west. Just below her lay Valley Bottom Farm. She could hear the constant cackle of the hens in the yard, quietening slowly as the day drew towards its ending and the voice of young Tommy shouting goodbye to Chloe. Soon Jamie would be home, his eyes darkening with love for his wife. Katy had seen them do so, his arms reaching out for her with a hunger which spoke, as words could not, of his need. She had seen that, too, in those few days she lay in their house after Jack was born and she had also seen Chloe's answering ardour, her eagerness to be in the arms he held out to her. She had lain on the truckle bed in the warm kitchen, her new son snuffling beside her, for three long and endless days and nights until she could stand it no longer and Thomas had come to take her back to Woodhead in the gig.

The baby nuzzled contentedly at her breast, his eyes beginning to glaze with sleep and the fullness of his small, distended stomach. His mouth relaxed and released her nipple which was moist and shining with milk and she rested him across her lap, studying the perfection of his face. The fluff of red curls just over the pulsing fontanelle, the honey tint of his silken flesh where the sun had touched it, the length of his curling auburn lashes, his rosy, pouting mouth which still sucked even in sleep. His hand rested peacefully against his own cheek and she bent her head to it, lifting it gently, kissing the plump palm.

She did not hear his boots on the tufted grass and her breasts were still exposed, rich and ripe with motherhood, heavy and yet not drooping, for Katy Andrews was not yet eighteen. Young, proud breasts with peaked, almond-tinted nipples in the perfect circle of the areola. Her head was bent to her child, her glossy, burnished hair pulled back and tied on the crown with a knot of bright green ribbons and her face was so unutterably sad Jamie Hutchinson felt his heart move for her. She looked quite startlingly beautiful, her skin honey smooth with a rose flush on her cheekbones. Her wide, passionate mouth, a vivid poppy red, began to curve in a smile as she studied her son and he found himself unable to move. She was the perfect woman, the personification of motherhood, everything female which a man dreams of and yet there was a sensuality about her, an earthiness which awoke a stirring in the pit of his belly. He was scarcely aware of who he was, or who she was as he allowed his eyes to roam dreamily over her shadowed face, the strong column of her throat, her half-bared shoulders, the glory of her breasts and thrusting nipples on which milk still glistened.

She looked up then, suddenly aware of his presence. For a split second she recognised what was in him, the shock he was experiencing, the flare of awareness of her as a woman. Not Katy Andrews who had tagged along at his heels as a child and young girl. Not Katy Andrews the wild, defiant creature who had become embroiled with her own cousin, nor Katy Andrews the mother, but herself, a beautiful sensuous woman in whose eyes glowed her deep love for Jamie Hutchinson.

Neither of them moved or spoke. She made no attempt to cover her nakedness and the moment stretched on endlessly as the blood ran hot and rich in her veins. He was seeing her, really seeing her, she knew, for the very first time and she gloried in it, wanting the moment never to end.

A cloud shifted across his face and his mouth moved and lifted as he tried to smile, to be casual, for had he not seen her suckle her child in his own kitchen. But this was not the same and they both knew it. Her breasts were uncovered but she was no longer suckling her baby. They were alone up here but for her son who was peacefully sleeping and for several long, throat-catching moments she allowed Jamie's gaze to flicker about her then, with deliberate slowness, she pulled her bodice together.

At once he became brisk, clearing his throat, doing his best to pretend that nothing unusual had happened between them, that her exotic beauty had not disturbed him. She was Katy, for God's sake, his wife's cousin, his wife whom he loved so tenderly, so deeply, so endlessly he would die for her.

"You're a long way from home, Katy," he managed to say.

"Yes, I walked over to Cloudberry End. I had something I wished to discuss with my father. I left in rather a hurry and . . . well, Jack was hungry so I sat down here in the sunshine to feed him but I suppose I had best be off."

She made no attempt to stand though, continuing to smile up at him, her eyes narrowed with a message he had no wish to read. There was a silence between them overlaid with the call of sheep up on the intake, the song of a thrush nearby and the panting of Jamie's dog which had flopped down in the shade of the wall.

Jamie did his best to avoid Katy's eyes for there was nothing more certain in this world than the love he had for his wife, but some invisible cord, some signal from Katy to himself, from her deep brown eyes to his, was drawing him to her as though she had him on the end of a rope and he knew he must put an end to this madness before it was too late. Before this sudden fascination with Katy Andrews's ripe and lovely body, which she seemed to be telling him was his for the taking, overcame him and ruined not only his life but hers and Chloe's.

"Your father?" he managed to croak and was relieved when the expression in her eyes altered, becoming vague as though she were looking inwards, or backwards to something which gave her no pleasure. Her gaze left his to wander up towards the peat moorland at his back and he felt as though he had been released from some possession which had him in its tenacious grip.

He edged backwards, wary, ready, should she scorch him with those hot, burning eyes again, to have plenty of space between them but it was as though she had moved from one dimension to another, from this time to another.

Her voice was soft and weary, pain-filled, her expression one which asked was Katy Andrews never to know the simple, day-to-day content other women had? Like Chloe, for instance.

"Yes, I . . . well, I suppose I wanted to mend the rift between us. Between my family and me. Because of Jack, you see."

"Not while you live openly with Paddy, sweetheart." The endearment seemed to come naturally. As her sadness had grown so had his compassion and he momentarily forgot the bizarre emotions he had felt only seconds ago.

"Yes, I realise that but as it happens, it doesn't matter."

"No?" Despite himself he moved closer to her, leaning over her seated form.

"No. He and my mother are to go and live in Scarborough. She says she can take no more of my . . . the word he used was . . . depravity."

"Aah, no."

"And so he is to take her where it will no longer weaken her. He is to leave the house and some of the servants to look after Chris."

"My mother has not spoken of it."

"Perhaps she is not to go. She is very . . . attached to Chloe and with the child coming she will not want to leave. Her family, her life is here and she has already given so much to Mother."

"Yes." Jamie sighed and lowered himself into the patch of sunshine where Katy sat, leaning his back against the wall, his shoulder no more than six inches from hers. The sun was almost gone. Shadow crept down the slope of Round Hill towards them. Soon they would be in it and the warmth and light would be gone and she had several miles still to trudge to Woodhead but neither seemed to care about it.

"And then there is Tommy."

"Yes," he said again.

"But I am, if I wish it, to move back to Cloudberry End." Her hold on her baby tightened. She lifted him up to her face, resting her cheek on his downy curls, then kissed him in a passion of love. "I want what's best for him, Jamie. I didn't know I would . . . love him so, you see, and what kind of a life will he have with me and Paddy in Grandmother's cottage? Even if we married . . ."

"Aah, no . . . no, you cannot be thinking of that, Katy?"

She turned to look at him in surprise, clearly startled.

"Why not, Jamie? It would be the proper thing to do. For Jack, I mean."

"But not right, Katy. Not you and that . . . that . . ." Though he had not seen Paddy Andrews, indeed no one had bar Josh and Jake and Annie Lennox since his leg was removed, Jamie could imagine what he had become and the idea of this fine and lovely young woman who seemed bent on making reparation for what she had damaged in her wildness, tied for ever to what was left of Paddy Andrews revolted him beyond measure.

"Move back home, Katy. Now that you have the chance bring up your child among your own people. In the way he should be brought up. As your brothers were. A decent education, all the things he should have."

"And what about Paddy? Who is to look after him?"

"Surely Mrs Lennox . . .?"

"Annie? She loathes the sight of both of us."

"Not from what I heard."

She turned to look sharply at him. "What have you heard?"

"She talks to my mother . . . not gossip, you understand," he added hastily, "but my mother is concerned for you and Annie knows it. She admires you enormously for what . . ."

Katy snorted disbelievingly and the baby stirred. At once her hand cupped his rosy, rounded cheek and, comforted, he settled again.

"She can barely bring herself to take my money, Jamie. Had she not been so desperate . . ."

"Oh no, you're wrong. Annie Lennox would scrub floors until her knees bled rather than work for someone she despised. She disapproves of you, lass, but at the same time she respects what you have done since Jack was born. And though she has no time for Paddy she recognises the way you have stuck to him, cared for him since his . . . his . . ."

"Since the beating my brothers gave him. *That* is why I stayed, Jamie. Not for some high-falutin' sense of honour but because it was my bloody fault."

"Katy, Katy, don't blame yourself for everything that has happened."

"Oh please, Jamie, don't be nice to me or I shall cry. All that has happened in the last year is because . . . because . . ."

She turned her head to look at him. Everything except their faces was in shadow now but the last of the sun's rays lit her eyes to deep molten copper and his to the brilliance of sapphire. Brown looked into blue, the message again shining brilliantly for him to see. The message which said, "Because I loved you, Jamie, because I love you still and you don't love me."

Jamie was often to wonder what might have happened had his wife, now in her fifth month of pregnancy, not taken it into her head to wander up the gentle slope at the back of the house to meet him.

The dog heard her first, springing up rapturously, leaping the drystone wall and charging down the field to greet her.

The sun was in her eyes, the dog bouncing joyously about her skirt and when her husband and her cousin rose she saw nothing confused or furtive or guilty in either of them.

"Katy . . . oh, Katy," she cried out, her pleasure genuine at the sight of her cousin who, despite Chloe's pressing invitations, had not been back since the birth of her son in Chloe's kitchen ten weeks ago.

"Jamie, darling, bring her down, and the baby. Oh, will you look at him . . . so big now. Let me hold him. May I, Katy? I promise to be careful. Oh Lord, oh dear Lord, is he not perfect, Jamie? Katy, he's beautiful. Look at him, Jamie. Oh please, come down to the farm, Katy."

A mother will love anyone who loves her baby, it is said and Katy Andrews was no exception. Chloe's genuine admiration for Katy's son eased another fraction the animosity she still could not help but feel towards the woman who had married Jamie.

"Well . . ." she answered awkwardly, watching anxiously as Chloe held her sleeping child in careful arms.

"Please, Katy, say you will, please. I have a steak and kidney pudding big enough for six. Stay, we would love to have you and then Jamie will take you home."

And all the way down the field and for the two hours Katy remained in his wife's kitchen Jamie's eyes did not once meet hers. If Chloe was aware of the constraint, the tension, the attempt on Katy's part to be polite since, after all, but for Chloe and Jamie, Jack might not have survived, and neither might she, she showed no sign of it. She made the teatime small talk her mother had taught her, effortlessly filling in awkward gaps with details of her own, often laughable attempts to be a farmer's wife, bringing a grudging smile to Katy's face. This was a different Katy to the one she had known a year ago. Quieter, calmer but still not inclined to be a friend to Chloe Hutchinson with whose husband she was in love.

Only when the child woke and began to display his cleverness, which at ten weeks consisted of a wide, lopsided smile, a deep, infectious chuckle, a vigorous kicking of his sun-tinted, sturdy legs and a sudden intense interest in his own hands, did the two women form that link, that smiling delight which is part of the female nature when an infant is present.

They bade one another goodnight, Katy polite but non-committal as Chloe begged her to come again and when Jamie walked her home in the dark, endeavouring to make obliging conversation, his manner told her irrefutably that Jamie Hutchinson loved his wife and no one else.

Only as he stood at the bottom of the track which led up to her grandmother's cottage did he allow himself to escape the restraints he had put on himself, admitting only to himself that they were needed.

"Go home, Katy. Go home to Cloudberry End. My mother will help you, and so will Chloe, if you would let her. She has become . . . fond of you."

"I know." Her voice was low and sad.

"And you have a friend in me, Katy," but only a friend his voice and manner seemed to add.

"I know that, too, Jamie."

She bowed her head over her baby then lifted it resolutely as she started the climb to the cottage.

20

Paddy Andrews was still in his bed when the crash woke him. It sounded as though someone had dropped a heavy object from a great height and he winced as the noise collided painfully about like cannonballs inside his head. The dog who lay stretched out beside him leapt frantically to his feet and jumped from the bed, making for the closed door which led from the parlour, where Paddy slept, to the kitchen, growling ominously. Something was happening on the other side of it and the dog didn't like it. To prove it he began to bark, a deep-throated, gasping bark which showed, like his master, he was not in the condition he once had been.

"Shurrup, yer daft sod," Paddy snarled, putting his hands to his splitting head. Last night he and the lads had put away . . . well, he'd lost count of how many bottles they'd seen off, but however many it was it had done neither his constitution nor his temper any good. And who could blame him for drinking himself into an unconscious state? he asked himself peevishly, after what that bitch had told him she meant to do. Not that he had any intention of letting her get away with it, naturally, and he'd said so to the lads when they arrived and they'd promised to back him to the hilt. Good lads they were, vowing that no man should be treated as she was threatening to treat Paddy, since he was an Andrews and Andrews men were used to ruling their womenfolk with a rod of iron. Who the hell did she think she was? And after all Paddy had done for her, an' all. What that was specifically none of them could have said by then, being far gone in their cups, maudlin and sorry for themselves, as men are at such times, though why Josh and Jake, who both had two good legs, should include themselves in Paddy's ill-fortune, again none of them could have said.

"What the bloody 'ell's goin' on?" he roared now, then clutched his head in agony. God, he could do with a drink and where was that bloody woman, either of them bloody women, meaning Annie and Katy who were supposed to have the looking after of Paddy's needs. His mouth felt as though the cat had shat in it and he could barely see through the slits of his eyes. His stomach rolled and churned and heaved and with a muttered oath he leaned over the bed and vomited in great waves all over his gran's colourful rug. The stink was appalling but what did he care? He hadn't the cleaning up of it, had he? It'd give that bitch something to do and serve her right for upsetting him so.

"Katy, will yer get yersen in 'ere an' on't double," he bellowed, beyond caring about his head but there was no answer except for more strange noises, bumps and footsteps across the flags, a soft voice instantly hushed and what could have been the whinny of a horse from somewhere beyond the closed window.

The baby began to wail for no more than a second or two, then became silent as if something had been shoved hastily in its mouth. That'd be Katy's titty no doubt, and by God, he wished he could get it in his mouth now and again.

At first, after his leg had gone he had felt a great reluctance to expose what was left of him to Katy. Afraid of what she'd do, or say. Afraid to see her recoil in horror which, while the rest of him was still in a reasonable condition, attractive to women, he'd say, he'd been terrified to attempt. Now he didn't give a fart. He was in a bit of a mess, he knew that. He'd seen himself in that mirror over the mantelshelf which Annie Lennox had lifted down to clean. Gave him a shock, it did, and for several weeks he'd felt like getting shut of himself but that'd worn off, especially with the help of the whisky or the brandy, and so had his consideration for how Katy might act if he tried to lay a hand on her. Give him half a chance and he'd have her skirts up over her head, her bum on his knee, his cock inside her and bugger her feelings.

The door opened and there she was, the subject of his lustful thoughts, his son in her arms, her flaming copper hair brushed smoothly back into an enormous bun at the crown of her head. She was dressed in a plain, pearl grey gown of soft wool with white at the collar and cuffs and a knot of ribbons in her hair to match. On her face was an expression of steely determination which quickly changed to one of revulsion when she saw the mess he had made on the floor. She drew her skirt to one side as the dog lumbered past her on his way outside to relieve himself and Paddy began to smile in satisfaction. She looked bloody marvellous, there was no doubt about it. A real lady in her elegant gown. He wondered where it had come from, since he had never seen her in anything like it in all the time he had known her. Mind you, you'd have to go a long way to beat the sight of her in those tight breeches she had worn and the sheer silk shirt which had showed off every peak and curve, including those tasty nipples of hers.

Never mind, he'd take a great deal of satisfaction in seeing her clean up after him in what she had on, since the nasty task would soon spoil its immaculate stylishness.

"Where in 'ell 'ave you bin?" he snarled, prey once more

to the cannonballs in his head. "I've bin yellin' me bloody 'ead off fer 'alf an 'our but could you or that old 'arridan come an' see what I wanted? Oh no, too busy bangin' about the place ter bother wi' the likes o' me. Can't a man gerra bit 'o peace of a mornin' in 'is own 'ouse?"

"It's afternoon, Paddy. Half past one to be precise."

"Oh, be precise, do, my lady, but not fer my benefit. Time means nowt ter me." His snarl had turned to a whine of self-pity but Katy ignored it, wrinkling her nose and making some movement with her hand to indicate her distaste and indifference.

"I came to remind you that I'm leaving, Paddy, as I said I would. I am going now so I . . ."

His head, which he had been about to lay wearily back on his pillow, shot up and he reared into a sitting position. The sheets fell away to reveal the fleshy folds of his naked, sagging body, the pendulous breasts which were as big as a woman's, the enormous paunch of his belly, the sagging, dough-like remains of what had once been the well-proportioned and masculine beauty of Paddy Andrews. For a moment he saw the pity in her eyes and his face became engorged with the blood of his fury.

"Oh no, madame . . . oh no. I told yer last night tha' were goin' nowhere, an' neither is my lad. This is 'is 'ome, an' thine, an' this is where tha' stays. I'm master in this 'ouse an'— "

"Oh, Paddy, don't. There is nothing you can do to stop me leaving you, nothing. We are tied together by no more than . . . what we once were and those two people are gone."

"What yer talkin' about, yer daft cow? I'm still 'ere an' so are thi' an' that's our lad tha're 'oldin' an' tha's tekkin 'im nowhere."

Her voice was low and sad. The baby's eyes were round and alarmed in his rosy face and his lip was ready to tremble, but she held him close, pressing his face into the curve of her neck as though to prevent him from seeing the hateful state, not only of the room, but of the man who was his father.

"You can't stop me, Paddy, and it's my fault that you can't. But then if you'd not lost your leg we would none of us . . . I know he – Chris, I mean – was at fault as much as me but I cannot . . . I have tried for the past . . . since it happened to forgive both of you, and myself, but . . . well, there's no good dwelling on what might have been." She shook herself, like a dog coming from water and her voice became steely. "I'm going home to Cloudberry End as I told you. I can't bring my son up in this . . ."

"*My son*," he howled.

"No, not any more. If you had . . . well, accepted what had happened and tried to make something of yourself I would have helped you, Paddy, but you didn't. You have drunk yourself— "

"Because of you . . . *because of you.*"

"I know and I will look after you, financially. My father is not without means and has been generous. This cottage will be yours. Annie, and anyone you want to employ to help you, I'll pay for but I must get my son— "

"Never . . . never, d'yer 'ear? Tha'll not gerr away wi' it. Josh an' Jake'll 'elp me. Good lads they be an'll do 'owt I tell 'em. So you just watch out, my lass. They'll do fer thi' if I say so an' that brother o' thine, fer I've not forgot it were 'im what took me leg. 'E gor away wi' it last time but I've not forgot, Katy Andrews. Tell 'im when tha' sees 'im. 'Im an' thee'll live ter regret what tha've done ter me, lady. An' watch out fer't bairn an' all. Don't tekk yer eyes off 'im fer I'll 'ave 'im back. As God is me witness I'll 'ave 'im back."

* * *

The excitement was intense. Janet who, now that Freda and Ivy were gone, had stepped into the role of head parlourmaid, kept saying she was sure she could hear the doorbell, running up the hall a dozen times to check. Lottie and Mabel, though Mabel was, strictly speaking, only the kitchenmaid and therefore did not go beyond the green baize door into the house, had cleaned and polished every room from the top of the house to the bottom, as Mrs Tiplady had trained them, and though she had been gone a fortnight and standards had slipped slightly, since a servant needs a firm hand and a firm voice of command, they had felt a compulsion to prove their reliability. The place looked grand, all clean and shining and smelling of the polish Lottie had made from a mixture of common beeswax, white wax, curd soap, turpentine and water. She and Mabel had applied it to every piece of furniture in the house, using a piece of flannel, then polished the surfaces up with a duster and finished off with a buffing with an old silk rubber. It had brought everything up a treat, Lottie informed the others in the kitchen, Janet and Dilly and Chuckie who had recently been taken on as odd-job boy and was busy polishing the cutlery.

They had cleaned the marble of the drawing room fireplace with a blend of soap, turpentine, pipe clay and bullock's gall, applied with a soft brush, leaving it to dry before polishing it with a duster. The gilt frames round Mrs Andrews's lovely pictures had been brightened with sulphur, water and garlic and honestly, Lottie said to Mabel, Mrs Tiplady would have been proud of them. They had neglected nothing, dusting the books in Mr Andrews's library, polishing the deep leather chairs, cleaning the long windows with vinegar, brushing as best they could the green baize top of the table in the billiard room which Master Chris and his wild friends had damaged, beyond repair in Lottie's disapproving opinion.

They made up Miss Katy's bed with snowy linen, the high, old-fashioned bed smelling of honeysuckle and lavender from the sachets of pot-pourri beneath the mattress and tucked into the pillows, and for half an hour argued on the best place to put the cradle which had been brought down from the attic.

They did not stop to question why they should be taking so much trouble to please Miss Katy, for knowing her as they did, and her complete disregard for anything of a domestic nature, would she even notice? It was just that it was all so dramatic, the return, not of the prodigal son, but the prodigal daughter and what would their lives, which had been turned upside down by the events of the past month, be like from now on? No Mrs Tiplady to tell them the way of things. No Mrs Andrews who was, after all, their mistress. No Freda or Ivy who were trained up to be efficient servants, to give a hand or a direction. Just Miss Katy who had set the valley aflame with her doings and Master Chris who was scarcely ever in evidence before two o'clock in the afternoon.

And Miss Katy's illegitimate child, son of Paddy Andrews who, it was said, was drinking himself to death since they cut off his leg. How were they to manage, they asked one another, since they really did need a hand to guide them, to steady them and was Miss Katy's hand, once so unsteady, the one to do it?

"Will she be tekkin' on another cook, d'yer think, Janet?" Lottie asked anxiously. They had been making do, all of them, trying their best to produce something for Master Chris to eat of a night when he came home from the mill, which was not often but none of them, except Janet, knew anything about the culinary arts and Janet's talents lay more in the baking of scones and biscuits and perhaps a custard tart. She was a housemaid and Mrs Tiplady had only been letting her try her hand because Janet was walking out with Dicken and was eager to learn a bit of baking for when she and the groom were wed. She could make a decent vegetable stew, of course, and a suet pudding but that was not the sort of thing one served a gentleman amongst his crystal and silver. They had mackled up a slice or two of bacon, some mushrooms and such for Master Chris's breakfast, which had proved to be a complete waste of time since, with his pa gone, he was hardly ever out of his bed before noon.

"Nay, don't ask me, Lottie. I'm as much in the dark as you. We'll need someone ter take the place of Mrs Tiplady, if such a person exists," Janet added sadly, for they all missed the cook's firm but kindly hand, "an' we'll need a kitchenmaid if Mabel's to be housemaid with you. Anyroad, let's wait an' see, shall we? I suppose there'll be a nursery maid needed an' all. Eeh, it'll be grand ter see that there nursery bein' used again. You made a right good job of it, both of you. Dear God, there's the bell. Now, is me cap on straight?"

They were all there except Chuckie who said if you'd seen one baby you'd seen 'em all, even Dilly peeping round the green baize door for a sight of the young woman and her child, who, Dilly was aware, had committed a dreadful sin, or so Dilly's mam had told her. In fact her mam had been in two minds whether to fetch her away from Cloudberry End for she did not want her girl associating with such a person, she said. But then Dilly was not likely to have much, if anything, to do with the infamous Katy Andrews, was she? Not in her humble capacity of scullery maid and good jobs were not easy to find, especially if you were a bit undersized and childlike as Dilly was.

Muffy was barking frantically with joy, doing her best to climb up Katy's skirt, the one the new dressmaker in Crossclough, not knowing Katy's past at that time, had made for her, and for several minutes pandemonium reigned.

"Good morning, Janet. What a simply lovely day," Miss Katy remarked as the maidservant held open the front door and bobbed a curtsey. Behind her mistress on the drive, Thomas and Dicken were busy with the unloading of her boxes. It was October and pale amber sunlight fell through the reddening trees. Leaves were beginning to fall, yellow and gold and tawny brown and rooks were clamouring about the empty nests which had been their homes in the spring. Smoke rose on the still air, drifting lazily from the side of the house where Angus and Billy were burning leaves. The aromatic fragrance mingled with the smell of the withering leaves and dying flowers and suddenly a great burst of joyousness rose in Katy and she smiled at Lottie and Mabel who had come to help with the luggage.

It was good to be home. She said so.

"Eeh, 'tis grand to have thi', miss," Lottie cried, so carried away with the singularity of it all she was ready to gallop about and shout it to the four winds. And her a maidservant in this house for six years and should know better! Anyone'd think she was as young and daft as Dilly. She quite forgot what Miss Katy had been up to this past year, which by rights she should deplore, and of course, being a decent girl, she did, but could you resist the results of it who peeped boldly from his mam's arms, his toothless smile and bobbing head which he could now hold up unaided enchanting her until she longed to hold out her arms for him.

It must have shown in her rosy-cheeked, freckled face and her smiling, shining eyes. Katy recognised it at once.

"Here, hold him for me, will you, Lottie, while I sort out what is to go where. Aah, Dilly, isn't it?" dashing Dilly's mam's hopes that her innocent daughter would not be contaminated by her mistress whose own innocence was long gone. "Come and help Janet, will you?" for Katy Andrews cared naught for the nuances in the ranks of the servants. Janet was supposed to be head parlourmaid now and Dilly was only a scullery maid and that they should be asked to share the carrying, one to each end, of one of Miss Katy's boxes was quite irregular. It was very evident that Mrs Tiplady was no longer there to guide them all, including the young mistress, in the way a house should be run.

Thomas and Dicken were shouldering a box between them, both of them directing orders at the other when a voice from the path leading to Thomas and Matty's cottage hailed them cheerfully. Thomas recognised it and breathed out thankfully, for with his wife in charge all would soon be in good order.

"Mornin', Katy," Matty called, the only one of the servants, if you could call her that, who did not preface the young mistress's name with the title of Miss. Matty held a special position here at Cloudberry End, due, no doubt, to her long friendship with Mrs Andrews. "I've come ter see if yer need a hand, lass. P'raps wi't baby, seein' as how this lot's had nowt ter do wi' one."

"Well, Lottie seems to be managing nicely, Matty," Katy remarked smoothly, earning a gratified and triumphant smile from the parlourmaid, "but if you could direct where these boxes are to go I would be grateful."

"Rightio, lass, glad to 'elp. Now then, what's in that there box them lads is chucking about?"

"Grandmother's china."

"Dear God above, will yer tekk more care, Thomas Jenkins or yer'll 'ave it all smashed ter smithereens, and don't go jerkin' it about like that, Dicken. Them's valuable ornaments in there."

Katy had been determined not to leave any of her grandmother's precious things, precious to her at least, if not in value, and each piece had been reverently wrapped and carefully packed by her and Annie. She had been desolate that she could not fetch the chiffonier from the parlour, the one which had belonged to her great-grandmother, but during the night as she and Annie tiptoed about, quietly putting all they could manage into boxes, she had been reluctant to enter Paddy's room and manhandle the lovely piece of furniture from directly under his snoring nose.

It was like bedlam with everyone running hither and thither, all giving orders and none taking them – Mrs Tiplady would have been appalled – as the last box was heaved up the steps and into the hall. Janet and Dilly were falling over their own feet as they dithered over who should take the lead up the stairs. Dilly was so excited she could barely restrain herself from bursting into hysterical laughter and she swayed to and fro as she waited for Janet to tell her which end to get hold of. Mabel was already struggling up the stairs with a box containing Jack's baby clothes, while at the bottom Lottie was performing a little jig to amuse the child in her arms. Matty was still berating her long-suffering husband on the correct way to handle a box of china and Dicken had his arms full of what looked like old Mrs Andrews's exquisite patchwork quilt, the last one she had made before she died.

"Where d'you want this put, Miss Katy?" he asked fretfully, for he was a groom and this was really not his job. "Where'd she want this?" he demanded of Matty but Matty had turned her attentions to what she considered she was best at and that was getting her hands on Sara Andrews's little grandson. She and Lottie were both becoming red in the face, ready, or so it seemed, to tear the lad apart and

Jack looked as though he were about to howl for his mother.

"Well, I might have known that when Katy Andrews walked through that door she'd bring nothing but chaos with her," a male voice drawled from the study doorway.

It brought them all to a faltering standstill. Even the baby turned his head to stare at the man who had spoken.

Katy, who was a third of the way up the stairs, following close on Mabel's heels with the intention of supervising the unpacking of her son's tiny clothes, many of them made and sent over with Tommy by Chloe, paused, causing serious confusion to Janet and Dilly who were directly behind her. She turned slowly, then, doing her best to avoid the unsteady servants, moved slowly down the stairs.

Standing at the foot, she faced her brother who was leaning indolently, hands in pockets, a cigar between his teeth, one of his father's best she was sure, in the study doorway.

"Chris, good afternoon. I had not thought to see you here." She lifted her neatly coiffed head and smiled, a tight smile which had no warmth in it. She had known he would be here, of course. Well, not at this precise moment which was half past three in the afternoon when a man of business might be expected to be performing it, but here at Cloudberry End where at some point they would be forced to face one another.

She had not seen him since Christmas Day and though there was no visible change in him she sensed a restlessness, a rawness, a snapping tension which made the very air about him uncomfortable.

"I live here, Katy, or were you not aware of that when you made your arrangements with Father?" His own smile was no more than a rearrangement of his mouth and facial muscles and did not reach his eyes. It was very evident she was not welcome.

"I meant at this time of the day, brother." Her voice was soft but with a slight touch of menace in it which said, "Do nothing to endanger me or mine. Stay out of my way and I'll stay out of yours." "I imagined, for some reason," she went on, "that since Father left you in charge at the mill that was where you would be."

"To what purpose when I have a perfectly capable manager to see to it all for me? What is the saying? Don't keep a dog and bark yourself."

"I believe it is, but surely a dog needs a master to keep it in check. To give it orders and— "

"Really, sister, you have, through your own choice, lived apart from this family for a year and yet you have the gall to come back the moment Mother and Father are gone and presume to tell me— "

"I am here because Father told me I might. This house belongs to him and it is up to him who lives in it. I and my son . . ."

"Your son!" Chris's mouth curled in an ugly sneer and his moss green eyes grew diamond-bright with venom. "Paddy Andrews's get! A bastard who has my name and you expect me calmly to accept him, and you, into this house where decent members of society— "

"You mean Johnny Ashwell, I suppose, by decent society, and Tim Warren and all the other wild-riding, wild-gambling rakes you associate with?"

"Of which you yourself were a part not so long ago, remember?"

"Oh for God's sake, Chris, stop it." Katy put a weary hand to her head, conscious suddenly of the paralysed figures of the servants hovering, for want of a word of command, about the hall and staircase. "We are to live in this house together but if, as it seems, we cannot do it in some sort of peace then I suggest we avoid one another as much as we can. I should perhaps warn you that I mean to run this place as it should be run. I have nothing else to occupy me but my son so I shall make a career of . . . of being a competent mistress."

"I thought you had been that for some time."

"If I have I did it well."

"Is that so?" There was a sneer in his voice but she lifted her head and squared her shoulders.

"Yes, but that is over and as I must fill my life with something then I shall embark on this . . . this new vocation. I am fully aware that I shall never be a hostess, as Mother was, for there are none in this valley who will call on Katy Andrews but I am a mother and intend to make a decent home for my son."

"Oh, spare me," he groaned, putting a hand to his brow with a theatrical gesture.

"There will be proper meals at the proper time and you are welcome to join me."

"Jesus Christ, what bloody game is this you're playing, Katy? Surely you don't imagine that you and I can . . .? He tried to kill me, your lover, you know that, don't you?"

Ignoring the horrified gasps which whispered about the hall and up the stairs, Katy took a step closer to her brother.

"You were not without blame, Chris."

"And neither were you."

"True. And I cannot tell you, except for my son, how much I regret it. Because of him I intend to put it behind me and try to make a respectable life in a respectable home for both of us."

"Is it not too late for that?"

"Whether it is or whether it isn't, I mean to try. He is all I have. Now, if you'll excuse me, I have things to do."

As though she had given a signal the servants snapped to attention and began to move about in a somewhat aimless way, for the encounter between Miss Katy and Master Chris had unnerved them. They none of them, for a moment, could quite remember what it was they had been doing, or where they were going and it seemed Dilly might break out into hysterical tears this time since, for the life of her she couldn't recall whether Janet had told her to go first or last up the stairs.

Katy pulled them all together. It was as though the confrontation with her brother had put a heartener in her. Stiffened her backbone which was already perfectly stiff and straight and strong.

Before the day was out she and Jack were comfortably settled in her old room, her boxes unpacked, her things put away for now in the empty drawers, since she did not intend to remain in this room which was smaller than she required now she had Jack. She and Lottie and Janet had gone through all the gowns in her wardrobe, those she had left behind when she went to live in Woodhead last year, searching for something she might wear in this new life of hers, at least until she had a chance to see her dressmaker and order some more.

They had all three been disconcerted to find they were too small for her, especially in the bodice.

"Tha've put weight on wi't baby," Lottie told her sagely. "It allus happens."

"Mrs Jenkins can alter them for thi', miss," Janet added. "Yer know how clever she is with a needle."

"Yes, there's no hurry. It's not as if I am to be overwhelmed with callers, is it?"

It was said without bitterness, just a simple statement of fact and the maids exchanged glances, for what she said was true. How was she to manage, this young girl, only just eighteen last week, this wicked girl, as everyone knew she was and yet somehow, as they watched her quietly going about the business of settling herself and her son back in her old home, they could not quite bring themselves to believe it. She had her boy, a lovely little chap, to prove how wicked she had been, a boy of whom they would all grow fond, they were sure, but what was she to do with the rest of her life? What she had said in the hall about running the house would have to be seen to be believed, for if there was one young woman who was totally and irrevocably undomesticated it was their new mistress. They all knew her and were used to her wild ways which surely could not vanish overnight even if she were a mother now. She'd be off on that there animal of hers in those breeches she had once worn as soon as someone could be found to care for Master Jack, for leopards don't change their spots overnight, now do they, Lottie told Janet. They were all prepared to overlook what she had done in the past since this was a good place to work in and fond as they had been of Mrs Tiplady, without her eagle eye about them they could relax a bit and you couldn't say the wages weren't fair, could you?

So, they'd all see how things went, they told one another complacently. With a young woman who in the past had cared not a tinker's toss for things of a "housewifely" nature and a man who was scarcely ever at home, life could be very pleasant at Cloudberry End.

21

Katy Andrews was wrong. There was one woman in the Longdendale Valley who was only too happy to call on her as she had been taught by her mama.

Katy was in the drawing room. She was down on her knees playing with her son on the rug before the brightly glowing fire. She had removed his nappy and flannel pilch and pushed up the skirt of his long petticoat, allowing his rounded, sun-tinted legs freedom to kick vigorously. His tiny penis bobbed merrily, his heels rose and fell, his legs stretched and bent and his hands clutched at one another, then reached for her as she leaned over him. She blew a raspberry, her mouth warm on his bare stomach and he chortled with laughter.

"Do you like that, my darling?" She smiled. "You do, don't you?" repeating the action several times then, sighing with pleasure, bent closer to study the handsome, irresistible face of the child while he gave her the same careful scrutiny.

The dog, who was sprawled as close to the fire as she could get, lifted one eyelid and lazily moved her short, stubby tail, then resumed her doze, for she knew the words were directed, not at her but at the strange creature on the rug who had come to intrude on her space. She sighed heavily, hitching closer to the fire.

The warmth and glow of it fell about mother and child

and painted the delicate furniture which Sara Andrews had chosen, glinting on silver and crystal and delicate porcelain. On Sèvres and Meissen and Wedgwood and Coalport. On the chandeliers, two of them, each with eighty gently shimmering candles apiece. On the French ormulu clock which sat above the mantelshelf. On wide peach-coloured velvet sofas and matching balloon-backed cabriole-legged chairs. It warmed the ivory carpet to a rich cream and turned Katy Andrews's coppery hair to a fiery red. It flushed her cheeks and put dancing reflections of flame in her warm brown eyes. She was in a gown of tawny silk, the one she had worn long ago in another time when she and her mother and brother had gone to the railway station to meet her cousin, unaware that the day was to alter her life. It had fitted her then, as it did now, but not until Matty had let out the seams in the bodice. The gown suited her, its colour catching the fire's glow in its folds, shading the richness of the silk from palest amber to the deepest burgundy.

There was a light tap on the door and the astonished face of Janet appeared, her eyes wide, her cap somewhat askew as though she had come in a great hurry from whatever it was had caused such consternation.

She had been in the kitchen, sprawled in Mrs Tiplady's chair, her feet up on Mrs Tiplady's stool when the doorbell rang, discussing with an equally lethargic Lottie what they might put together for Miss Katy's and, if he should put in an appearance, Master Chris's dinner that evening. Mabel was peeling the spuds and Dilly, who had dropped a jar of Mrs Tiplady's raspberry preserve which they had fancied with the sponge cake Janet had made, and a bit of custard, of course, shattering it all over the flags, was on her knees scrubbing half-heartedly at the stains it had left. Chuckie had been given some vague instructions to sharpen the knives an hour ago and had gone to fetch the knife sharpener but as yet he had not returned.

It was two weeks since Miss Katy had come home and in that time the two maidservants had sent in a menu of endless chicken broth, dubious soggy vegetables and tough meat with bread and butter pudding to follow, which was not exactly up to the standard of Mrs Tiplady, was it, but Miss Katy had not complained. And neither had Master Chris for the simple reason he was never there to eat them. Should they try a bit of haddock tonight for a change? The fish man had been that morning, telling them it was straight off the boats but how were they to know? Perhaps a custard tart might be a welcome change, which Janet could manage but as Miss Katy seemed quite content with what they had served, so far, despite what she had said to Master Chris, should they let well alone and stick to what they knew?

"What is it, Janet?" Katy looked up from her absolute contemplation of her son, something she did a lot of, Janet thought, wondering if it was right. Of course the women in her class had no time for such nonsense and those who were not of her class, like Mrs Andrews for instance, had not the inclination, but then Miss Katy was like no mother Janet had ever known, falling into neither category.

"A visitor, miss, an' are you at home?"

"A visitor? For me? Are you sure they don't want Mother, or perhaps my father?"

"Oh no, miss. Asked fer you particular."

"Who is it, Janet?" beginning to look a shade apprehensive, for though she had talked of living the life her mother had led, which included, if they came, the receiving of calls, she had not really expected them.

"Well, she give me this, Miss Katy. In the absence of a card, she says, an' would you forgive 'er."

Janet held out the silver tray on which Sara Andrews had been used to receiving the calling cards of Mrs Ashwell and Mrs Warren and other ladies of a similar background. On it lay a neat square of paper, perfectly clean but plain with nothing on it except a name inscribed in exquisite copperplate. It said, "Mrs James Hutchinson".

Katy studied it carefully, reading and rereading the beautiful writing, aware that Janet was watching her with intense interest. She was also aware, wondering why she had not noticed it before, perhaps seeing her head parlourmaid with the eyes of the caller, that there was a dirty mark on the maid's apron and that her normally immaculately ironed, frilled cap with its long streamers down her back to her waist was crumpled. She was in the correct black which was usual for afternoon wear but somehow she did not appear to be in the proper state of immaculacy Mrs Tiplady had insisted upon.

Janet waited. None knew better than the servants in this house how Miss Katy felt about Mrs James Hutchinson, her own cousin, Chloe, and Janet held her breath, wondering what her young mistress would do. Mrs Hutchinson sat where Janet had put her on a hall chair, in view of her condition, the gig in which presumably her father-in-law, the Andrews' own coachman, had brought her, waiting on the gravelled driveway to see if she were to be received. Talk about cheek, her coming here after all this time. The master and mistress scarcely over the doorstep and in their carriage on the way to the railway station and the young woman neither of them had seemed able to stand handing in her card as if she had every right to be calling on her cousin, their daughter. Perhaps she had. Miss Katy had given birth to her baby on her cousin's kitchen floor, rumour had it, and happen she and Miss Katy had become friends over it but if they had the servants at Cloudberry End hadn't heard about it and Matty Jenkins would have been the first to tell them of it, wouldn't she?

"Shall I send her in, Miss Katy?" she asked somewhat impatiently for she was dying to get back to the kitchen and spread the news.

Katy sighed deeply. Her son crowed on the rug before the fire and as she watched him he urinated in a delicate filmy arc almost into the fireplace. Janet gasped then laughed and at once Katy relaxed, beginning to smile. It was as though the child had intentionally performed his little trick to remind her that nothing really mattered but him. He held in contempt her mother's expensive rug, the maidservant's avid curiosity, even the visitor who would have to take him just as he was.

"Show her in, Janet," Katy said coolly, just as though she were quite accustomed to "morning callers", who came, as was socially correct, directly after lunch, and indeed would not be surprised if another dozen arrived in the next hour. She reached for the baby, lifting him to her shoulder, her forearm under his plump, bare behind, her left hand holding his right to her mouth.

Chloe Hutchinson was in her sixth month of pregnancy, her figure thickening about the waist but with a carriage so straight and graceful it was barely noticeable. She looked quite glorious with that peach bloom some women acquire when bearing a child. A sort of sheen, a polish, a tawny look of good health which glowed through her fine creamy skin like a candle behind gauze. Her eyes were a clear blue-green, steady and unafraid, looking first at Katy then going, with obvious pleasure, to the half-clothed boy.

She began to smile, the hesitancy with which she had come into the room slipping away and again her very evident approval of her son had its effect on Katy, who felt her heart move gently then relax. The dog rose to her feet, stretched, first one back leg then the other, yawned and padded over to Chloe while the baby watched with great interest.

"Katy . . . and Jack! I had not expected to see him so this is a lovely surprise. Oh my dear, what a handsome boy and so sturdy. And Muffy," bending to pat the dog. "She must be pleased you are home. I know how she missed you."

"Yes." Katy's voice was gruff. She still knelt on the rug, holding her son somewhat in the manner of a shield but her eyes had lost that guarded look of wariness.

"May I hold him?" Chloe asked softly.

"He has nothing . . . no pilch."

"I don't mind. I see he has already relieved himself," nodding at the small puddle in the hearth.

"Yes." Both women began to smile at the rudeness of the young male who is able to perform his bodily functions wherever and whenever he pleased. The boy was passed to Chloe and he didn't seem to mind. He settled himself in a companionable way in her arms, watching her face and when she smiled so did he.

"May I sit down?"

"Oh, sorry." Katy indicated the sofa beside the fire, waiting until Chloe was seated, the boy held gently on her lap before she sat down on the matching sofa opposite. They were very conscious of one another, the two cousins, wary even, though there seemed to be no actual antagonism, both wondering what they were to talk about, since not only did they have nothing in common, not in their nature nor their outlook on life, they were both sharply aware that they loved the same man. It was past, that savage time when their lives had been devastated by a love so passionate and destructive it had mangled many lives. That devastation had been forced by Chloe's marriage to Jamie and the irrefutable fact that it must be accepted, unacceptable as it was to Katy. So much had happened in the past year. Doors had been opened, passed through and closed again, leaving behind them pain and sorrow, hatred and bitterness, but it was over with. They were both to make new lives with their children, one of whom, as he gurgled unknowingly on Chloe's lap, seemed to be destined to draw them slowly closer together. He had been born to Katy on Chloe's kitchen floor and even now his mother could still feel that strange and unbelievable feeling of comfort which had sighed thankfully through her after her labour in Chloe's arms.

"I never thanked you properly," she said abruptly, surprising not only Chloe but herself. Chloe's eyebrows lifted questioningly, though she still allowed her fingers to be firmly gripped by the baby who seemed intent on getting them into his mouth.

"Thank me? For what?"

"For what you and Jamie did last July. If Jamie had not found me and brought me down I don't suppose either of us would have survived. I thought, in my naïvety and stubbornness, I could manage the whole damn thing on my own. Have the child then tramp down to Woodhead where I meant to . . . well" – she shook her head dismissively – "never mind. Anyway, thanks to you both . . ." Her voice trailed off. Her eyes strayed to her child and a rosy flush of embarrassment stained her cheeks.

"Don't be silly," Chloe protested. "We only did what anyone would have done, Katy, you must surely know that."

"Not for me, they wouldn't. The people of the valley would have stepped over me sooner than be associated with the hussy Katy Andrews."

"I can't believe that, Katy."

"Oh, come on, Chloe, just because you're a bloody saint doesn't mean everyone is."

For a moment there was a breathless silence then Katy grinned. "Go on, you know it's true."

"I am not a bloody saint, Katy Andrews," Chloe said indignantly, "and don't you dare call me one. Dear God, not only do you insult me, you provoke me to swear in the most unladylike way. You are a bad influence," but she was smiling as she spoke. "As for Jack, I only did my duty."

"Rubbish, you're too good by half and it'll get you into trouble one day."

"Katy!"

Katy began to laugh then, throwing her head back and opening her mouth wide to reveal her perfect white teeth while her son watched her with startled bewilderment, for though his mother smiled and talked to him for hours on end he had never once seen her shout out loud in joyful laughter.

"Katy, you are startling your son. And can I take it you are poking fun at me?" Chloe smiled ruefully.

"Yes, cousin, I'm poking fun at you but only because I'm not used to being polite."

"I can see that. I have been here for fifteen minutes and have not yet been offered tea."

"Dear God." Katy clapped her hand to her brow. "Is that what I'm supposed to do?"

"Of course. Did your mama not teach you?"

"Don't be daft. When was I ever at home to serve tea to Mama's callers? I suppose I'd best do something about it." She rose to her feet with the evident intention of going to the door and shouting down the hall for a servant.

"Katy, what are you doing?"

"You wanted tea, didn't you?"

"Yes, but there's a bell beside the fireplace. Don't tell me you did not know of its existence. If you ring it one of the housemaids will come. You tell her what you want and she will fetch it."

"Aah, now I remember seeing Mother doing that." She grinned to let Chloe see she had known all along. "Of course, it's just that in the past year I have forgotten everything I was ever taught. Not that that was much, I can tell you, but she did try, poor Mother, to make me into a lady."

Katy pulled the bell and when a flushed and excited Janet had gone off full-tilt to tell the others that the visitor was to take tea, sat down to face her cousin, inclined to smile as though at some foolish memory.

"How is your mother?" Chloe asked courteously, remembering the cool woman who had barely allowed her niece a brief "Good morning", never mind a friendly smile.

Katy's face became shadowed. "Not well," she answered abruptly, "though I did not see her. Father wouldn't allow it."

"Not allow it?"

"No. He said I had broken her heart."

"Oh no, Katy . . . no, surely he did not mean it."

"He did, cousin, and I suppose it was true. I was a . . . well . . ." She sighed deeply, her face pensive, her eyes deep brown pools of sadness. "I was a bad girl. I haven't changed, you know. Not really. It's just that I'm afraid I have damaged irretrievably Jack's chances of a decent life. I didn't want it particularly for myself but I do for him. I was going to give him away, you know."

"Give who away?"

"Jack. Of course, he wasn't Jack then, he was . . ."

"Katy! Katy Andrews, how can you sit there and tell

me . . . how could you even contemplate such a wicked, wicked . . ."

"Oh, for goodness sake, cousin." Katy's voice was irritable. "That was then. Before I met him and by the way he has fallen asleep so I'd best put him on his sheet. He's inclined to widdle in his sleep."

"Widdle?"

"Yes, relieve himself as you so politely put it."

The sleeping baby was placed beside the dozing dog. The tea was brought and sipped, though when Katy asked for biscuits or cakes, those which Mrs Tiplady had once made for her, she was astonished when Janet said there were none, besides which it was not the correct thing to do to serve cake and biscuits to a caller, morning or afternoon, though naturally Janet did not say so.

"No, miss, I'm sorry but neither me nor Lottie is really a cook, yer see."

"Yes, I had noticed."

"We was wonderin' like . . ."

"Yes?"

"Whether yer meant to employ one, miss. A cook, I mean." Janet twisted her hands in her apron while her young mistress stared at her in bewilderment as though the idea had never once occurred to her. Chloe watched her with breathless fascination, for this was a side of her wilful cousin she had never seen before. Indeed, had never expected to see. It was hard to visualise Katy managing this household, in fact it was downright impossible and yet from what she had just said it seemed she was to make a stab at it if only for the sake of her baby son. He would have no chance at all of mixing with the children of decent society if he were to be brought up in a cottage in Woodhead with Paddy Andrews to influence him, to fill his childhood days with the brutality she herself had seen Paddy employ against Katy. Katy's child would be coarsened, knowing nothing but the boorish manners and attitudes of his uneducated Andrews cousins. A child of working-class parentage with an education to match and though it was how his grandfather had started it was just not appropriate for a generation to revert back to the humble origins of its predecessors.

But what of young Jack Andrews? Even living and being reared at Cloudberry End, which was a gentleman's residence, as the grandson of Jack and Sara Andrews, as a child born out of wedlock he would have a hard enough time of it for how many of the Ashwells and the Warrens and others of the local gentry would allow their offspring to be tainted by the slur of illegitimacy? Katy was being very optimistic if she thought she had only to return with her son to her old home and they would both be accepted again.

Chloe herself was married to a farmer, the son of a servant and, like Jack, illegitimate but Jamie had pulled himself up by his bootstraps, taking advantage of the education Jack Andrews had given him, travelled the world, even if it was only as a common sailor, saved his money, learned things, bettered himself and through sheer hard work and a resolute determination was making a success of his life. Their child would have the best they could give him. She was what was known as a lady, or so her mama had told her, with a great-uncle, or was it a great-great-uncle? who was titled and she meant to claw every advantage she could from her birthright for her child. She was well educated, for Mama had believed in it and she would bring up her and Jamie's child in the ways of a gentleman. He would be a farmer, but he would be a gentleman as well. Katy wanted, no, *demanded* the same for her son. Not to be a farmer, of course, but to be accepted into the class of society of which her mama and papa, her brothers and herself were a part. It would be a hard, grinding task, the sheer immensity taking Chloe's breath away. Katy had offended Crossclough and Crossclough would not forget it. She had laughed in their faces, snapped her fingers at their horrified disapproval, swaggered about the valley in her silk shirts, her tall top hat and her mocking smile and they would not take kindly to her expectations that now she was repentant they must forgive her and take her, or at least her son, to their hearts.

"What d'you think, cousin?" she heard Katy say, her voice impatient since, though she was determined to do it, it was hard to be serious about playing the role of mistress of Cloudberry End.

"I'm sorry?"

"Really, cousin. I am trying my best to take up the reins of running this house and what are you doing? Daydreaming! I am asking your opinion since I suppose you will know more about such things than me, on whether I should employ a cook and perhaps a housekeeper, and if so where on earth might such a person be found? What d'you think?"

Chloe lifted her head decisively, squaring her shoulders and straightening her back which, despite the dull ache in it, she did not allow to touch the cushions on the sofa. Her memory took her back to the tall house in Liverpool and her mama's cool and ladylike control of the few servants they had. She could recall the way Mama had spoken when she was interviewing their last cook, one of many, unfortunately, for Mama had a way of getting the back up of every servant she employed and none stayed longer than six months. Still, it had given Chloe an insight into what was required in a servant and how not to treat one.

"Neither Janet nor Lottie can cook a meal, Katy, so it seems only sensible to get someone who can. If you are to do any entertaining you will need a good cook."

"Entertaining! You are joking."

"No, I am not. The time will come" – determined to be positive for Katy's sake – "when you will invite perhaps not friends of your mama but friends you yourself will make."

"Where, for heaven's sake?" Katy hooted.

"I don't know." Chloe's expression became stubborn. "If you make up your mind to it you will do it, I know you will, but you'll need a decent woman in your kitchen. Someone who can cook well and also manage the household as Mrs Tiplady did. You must interview."

"Interview! Oh, God, I wouldn't know where the devil to start. How does one go about such a thing? Do you know? Would you help me?"

"Well, I suppose one would advertise, or perhaps Matty might know of . . ."

"Perhaps Matty might even be persuaded to do it, cousin. What d'you think? She knows the house and . . ."

"She is not a cook, Katy, but perhaps, if she were willing, she might agree to be housekeeper."

"D'you think so?"

"You could ask her, I suppose, and then, of course, a lady in your position will need a nursemaid to look after— "

"Oh no, no one will have the caring of Jack but myself. I have done so for the past three months and can see no reason to stop now."

"Katy, are you to bring him up as the son of a lady as your mama would have done?"

"No, not as Mama did." Katy's voice was brusque.

"I know what you mean and I can understand your reluctance to put him in another woman's care but there is surely a way to . . . to rear and nurture a child so that even if he has a nursemaid, you are involved in it and the centre of his universe. You will have . . . well, I don't know, things to do that will require attention and you cannot walk about with a child on your hip as women do in certain classes."

"Jesus, oh Jesus, this is going to be harder than I thought," Katy moaned while Janet's eyes moved in a mesmerised fashion from one face to another, wondering on the strangeness of seeing these two young women so involved with one another, and, even more amazing, Miss Katy's evident intention of whipping this household into some sort of shape. Not that it had slid far since Mrs Tiplady had gone but even she was aware that things weren't quite what they should be. Wait until she told them in the kitchen that Matty Jenkins was being considered for housekeeper!

Matty refused. She was too old, she said, and besides, would the maidservants take kindly to being ordered about by a woman with whom they had all been on familiar terms? And then there was the expected birth of Chloe's child, looking fondly at her daughter-in-law, so all in all she'd have no time for it, she said apologetically to Katy. She'd help out in any way she could. She might even know of a good woman who had once worked for Mrs Ashwell until the Ashwells had gone in for fancy chefs and such like. Though she didn't say anything to Katy Jess Kelsall was getting on a bit which was another reason why Mrs Ashwell had got shut of her, but Jess, having found no other work, might be persuaded to work for the "scarlet woman of Crossclough" as Matty had heard Katy described. She wondered as she spoke what on earth this girl, the daughter of the woman Matty had loved dearly for thirty years and missed more than she could say, imagined she was up to! Did she honestly think she could move back to this house and live the life she had known before she left? The daughter of Jack and Sara

Andrews and, therefore, despite her wild ways and shocking behaviour, recognised as a young lady of class. She'd taken on a heavy load, poor lass, but then most mothers fought tooth and nail for what they thought best for their child and that was just what Katy Andrews was doing.

She sipped her tea and, like Janet, marvelled at the tentative show of cordiality which seemed to be budding between her daughter-in-law and Sara's lass. Katy kept addressing Chloe as "cousin" but it was a vast improvement to some of the names she had laid about her last year when Chloe had moved in with Jamie. Matty sympathised no end with Katy since she herself had borne a child out of wedlock and but for Katy's mother would have finished up in the gutter, or a brothel. Aye, she'd not forgotten that and she'd like to see Katy Andrews claw her way back to respectability as Matty had done.

The gig jolted sickeningly on the rutted road back to the farm and though it was only a few miles it seemed interminable to Chloe. It was a glorious day, a vivid blue sky streaked with hurrying clouds above the deep reds and gold of October but Chloe didn't notice as she concentrated on keeping down the tea she had drunk at Katy's and the infuriating pain in her back.

Jamie was up at the back of the farm, he and Tommy busy with the last of the harvesting as Chloe, after saying goodbye to her father-in-law and thanking him for driving her up to Cloudberry End, moved slowly into her kitchen. Adah-May had been put to scouring the setting dishes and butter churns in the dairy, a task she was capable of performing without supervision and Chloe could hear her intoning the words of one of her favourite songs as she clattered the churns in the sink.

"Early one morning,
Just as the sun was rising,
I heard a maiden sing in the valley below,
Oh, don't deceive me . . ."

The tune bore no relation to the words but Adah-May did not seem to notice as she warbled on.

It was warm. The fire glowed in the grate, its embers spitting a little in flames of orange and yellow and fierce crimson. Everywhere sparkled and gleamed, for only yesterday Adah-May had declared her intention of giving the place a bit of a spring clean, despite the autumnal nip in the air. The dark lustre of the polished furniture reflected the glow from the fire. The little chair which Chloe knew her child would not be able to use until it was at least a year old had been furnished with a new, brightly embroidered cushion and set before the fire and she smiled at her own insistence that it should be ready. Jamie humoured her, his eyes gentle, his hands gentle as they curved about her belly, since he was as eager as she to see their first child seated in it. There was a lovely aroma, for she and Adah-May had baked a fresh batch of bread this morning before Chloe left for Katy's.

Not wanting to call Adah-May, moving slowly, she made herself a pot of tea, more for something to do than for any need or desire for it, drank a sip or two then moved outside again into the crisp amber day, shivering a little as the wind, coming straight from the moor, struck a blow at her.

The dairy was on the far side of the farmhouse and Adah-May had not seen her return. Breathing deeply, her hand protectively about her unborn child, she strolled up to the wall at the back of the house, shading her eyes for a sight of Jamie, wondering why it was such an enormous effort to move one leg after the other, of keeping her aching back erect and forcing her uneasy stomach to remain calm.

She clenched her teeth as a brief pain bit into her and suddenly she was afraid, deathly afraid, for it seemed to her that something inside her body appeared to be breaking. She must get into the house, find a corner in which to crouch and mend the damage which her woman's mind knew was happening to her woman's body. She must find safety, shelter. Oh, sweet God, where was Jamie? She needed Jamie . . . where . . .?

Slowly, like an old, old woman she moved in a half crouch down the gentle field, her hands to her belly as though, in this strange position she might protect the treasured burden inside her. She must not miss her footing, nor must she jar herself. It was as though she were a vessel carrying a precious liquid which if it tipped would run away. The more carefully she walked that endless distance from the wall to the house the less likelihood there would be of spilling it, and it must not be spilled.

She reached the kitchen doorway and stumbled inside. Everything seemed to have come to a stop, the clucking of the hens, the tuneless singing of Adah-May, the hissing of the fire, the ticking of the clock and the absolute silence enveloped her in a frightening cocoon. She put out a hand to the table, first to steady herself but more importantly to convince herself that it was still there, but as she reached for it her hand found nothing but empty space which she went headlong into.

She felt it then, the bleeding, and understood she had started to lose her child.

22

She couldn't summon the strength or inclination to be concerned about anything in those next few months and certainly could find nothing to interest her in her cousin Katy's efforts to take over the running of Cloudberry End. It had been weeks before she had allowed Matty to coax her from her bed where she had lain, hour after hour, her head turned to the window, watching the seasons slowly move from autumn to winter. The skies had changed from the sun-warmed, sun-tinted blues and golds of the fading year to the hazy, opalescent hue of the coming winter, matching the feelings in her heart. She could hear the sheep cough in the meadow where Jamie had brought them down for wintering. A bright fire sang cheerfully in the bedroom grate and mixed with the fragrance of the burning wood she could smell the frost which had begun to crisp about the window frame and coat the rough grass of the slope where her child had begun to die.

She vaguely expected, for so it was said, that time would diminish the pain of her loss. Matty had repeated it gently again and again. Time soothes the raw pain of wounds, she said, and perhaps she was right. If it was so Chloe longed to go to sleep and wake a year from now, or even two, when, presumably, she would have recovered. She had carried her child for six short months. Their time together had been brief but she had loved her and now she mourned her, though her daughter had never breathed. She allowed herself to imagine now and again, as she lay in her bed, how it might have been, dreamed of it until reality returned and her child was dead.

She had felt nothing at first, huddling in the grey wrappings of her grief through which no pain could reach. Her mind drifted but she allowed no thought or memory to assault her by the simple process of falling asleep whenever her mind's eye recaptured the happiness she had known. Her body had been bruised and tender, as though she had been severely beaten, but Matty, who had suffered a miscarriage herself, told her this would wear off.

For five days she had been troubled with a fever, neither knowing nor caring whether she lived or died and at the fringes of her semi-conscious mind she had been aware of Jamie. Jamie weeping and begging her not to leave him and, knowing how he loved her, and how, at last, she had come to love him, she made a great effort not to follow the tiny girl who had been born dead into Matty's hands. She had seen her, held her, a perfect child whose head had fitted in the palm of her hand and whose skin had the glow of the pearls her own mama had once worn. She had no eyelashes, no finger- or toenails but her beauty was so fragile, so delicate Matty had wept bitterly and so had Jamie as they put her in her tiny, satin-lined coffin.

But Chloe couldn't. She hadn't shed a tear, not even when Katy, quite distraught since she could imagine exactly how she would feel if her own precious child were lost to her, flung herself on Chloe's bed, weeping in that dramatic way she still retained. With the compassionate, headlong warmth that, despite her wildness, had always bloomed in her, she let her emotions flow from her like a bursting stream. Poor

Adah-May had given way to hysterics before collapsing in such a storm of grief they had been forced to send for her mother to fetch her home, though she had returned the next day and been a tower of strength in her own simple way to Matty and Jamie. They had all wept, even Thomas and Tommy, her mother-in-law told her, but somehow it didn't seem to matter to her inside the bubble she was trapped in. Nothing did.

She watched snow fall in early December, sitting in her chair by her kitchen fire, just a few scattered flakes at first which grew in size and ferocity until it was a dancing white wall beyond the kitchen window, a few flakes finding their way down the chimney to hiss on the coals.

"I'd best gerr 'ome, chuck," Matty said uneasily, "or I'm likely to get snowed in. Thomas'll be worried."

"Of course," she answered politely, since she was unfailingly polite with them all, not turning her eyes away from the window.

"Will yer be all right till our Jamie comes 'ome?"

"Oh, yes."

"I don't reckon 'e'll be long. Not with this lot," nodding her head towards the window. "It'll be dark soon, anyroad."

"I'll be fine, Matty. You go. I'll just sit here and wait for Jamie."

And that is just what she would do, Matty brooded, biting her lip and sighing. Her son would come home to a warm house and a steak and kidney pudding in the oven because Matty herself had provided them. But for her, God only knew what poor Jamie would have to put up with and if Chloe didn't snap out of it soon she'd tell her so an' all. Every woman who lost a child must grieve, must suffer the bereavement, the loss, the pain, but she must also share her sorrow with, and comfort the man who had given her that child. It would be Christmas soon and dearly as she loved her son's wife Matty couldn't keep running up here every day to see to her. Chloe had her physical health back. It was just her mind which seemed to have withdrawn itself to some despairing corner where it hid and suffered and would let no one, not even Jamie who suffered too, get close enough to comfort her. Oh, she allowed him to put his arms out and draw her slender body against his but she could not be said to be responding in any way. She merely allowed it.

"I'll be off then," she murmured, placing a gentle hand on her daughter-in-law's soft cloud of curls.

"Righto, Matty, and thank you."

"Can I get you a cup of tea before I go, lass?"

"No, thank you, Matty. I'll just . . ." Her voice trailed away and Matty sighed as she turned towards the door.

It could have been no more than ten minutes later, both Katy and Matty agreed, laughing and marvelling on how they could have missed one another, that the kitchen door was flung open and the room came alive with the exuberance of Katy Andrews, wrapped around in a mantle of snow, her son in her arms, peeping and blinking from his multiple wrappings, both of them glowing with the simple, joyful excitement of arriving through the snowstorm.

"For goodness sake, cousin, do come and take this heavy boy from me and let's get the door closed before we have a snowdrift halfway across your kitchen floor. Now I can see it in your face," as Chloe remained where she was, staring in open-mouthed astonishment, "that you are about to say I shouldn't have come but I couldn't resist it. You know me. A challenge cannot be ignored, besides which, I'd promised Jack I'd bring him up to see you today and one can't let a child down, don't you agree? He would have been so disappointed."

Katy pushed the door to with her behind, leaning on it as she caught her breath, fully believing what she had just told Chloe. She credited Jack with an understanding well beyond his five months, talking to him endlessly on any subject which at that moment concerned her, from what Mrs Kelsall should serve for dinner that evening to the undeniable fact that Jack Andrews was the centre of Katy Andrews's world. She never tired of telling him so and he seemed to find what she said to him fascinating, smiling and reaching for her as though he knew he and his mother were special to one another, for were they not two against the world?

Despite Chloe's advice she had not yet employed a nursemaid for him and had totally rejected the idea that her son should sleep in the nursery on the top floor, declaring that the room was too far away for her to hear him should he wake in the night.

"That's what a nursemaid's for, Katy," Matty had admonished her. "She an't little lad'd sleep up there an' . . ."

"But I feed him in the night, Matty, and so it seems to me that it is much more convenient to have him close to me. He's not yet old enough to be weaned. I have plenty of milk and he is thriving," which was true. You had only to look at him, Matty agreed, to see what a bonny lad he was and what a bonny man he'd make. The dead spit of the Andrews lads with none of Sara's side in him except the colour of his hair which was turning to a rich, fiery copper.

And he was sunny-natured too, so God only knew where that came from, though Sara had been merry as a girl. He got it from neither of his parents, that was for sure. Jack, the lad's grandfather, had once been an even-tempered, good-humoured sort of a man so perhaps young Jack had inherited his disposition from his grandparents. Anyroad, he was the apple of his ma's eye, any fool could see that and who'd have believed that undisciplined, untamed Katy Andrews would turn out to be such a gentle, loving mother?

Katy, with an air of making a great concession to the woman whom she was finding more and more of a friend, a support and an adviser, had moved into the bedroom which had once been shared by her mother and father. It was the biggest room in the house with two large bow windows and an area about the fireplace where a sofa and deep velvet chairs stood, with several small, pie-crust tables scattered between them. The room was quite exquisite, as Sara herself was, decorated in a shade of dove grey, duck egg blue and white. There was a vast double bed with a pleated silk canopy drawn up to the ceiling like an Arabian tent. A great deal of white in cushions and floor rugs. A white lace counterpane over duck egg blue silk, white muslin curtains, a muted shade of dove grey for the plain, rich carpet. A serene room which had the effect of soothing Katy's often troubled thoughts into a state of such tranquillity she was often reluctant to leave it to struggle with her self-imposed problems.

But its main advantage apart from its size was the modern bathroom her father had had installed which led off it and a room, once her father's dressing room, which Katy had converted into a nursery for Jack. There was a fireplace tiled in cheerful shades of yellow in which a fire burned behind a burnished brass fireguard, a deep bow window with a wide window seat. Once her father's things had been removed there was plenty of space for a crib with polished, turned rails, since young Master Jack had already outgrown his bassinet. There was a chest of drawers in which his baby garments were stored and a great many soft toys and books. Mechanical clockwork clowns and mice were scattered about the deep-piled carpet which was the same shade of pale grey as that in his mother's bedroom. The walls were painted yellow, the curtains were a bright shade to match and though the servants all deplored her carelessness in allowing an infant who would soon be crawling to lie on the dove grey elegance of Mrs Andrews's carpet, Katy Andrews took no notice.

When had she ever?

As the door clicked to behind her the snow was beginning to melt and drip from the rich, russet curls which tumbled over Katy's forehead. The drops of moisture made her blink and her smile deepened.

"I know you will be angry with me for coming through the blizzard, cousin, but I swear it wasn't a blizzard when I set off. Here, take Jack, will you?" since her cousin had still made no move towards her or her son, and without waiting for her approval she placed him on Chloe's lap where the snow on his wrappings immediately began to slide on to Chloe's pale grey gown.

"Take his things off, will you, there's a dear, while I get out of this cloak. I should have put up my hood but with Jack to carry and this," indicating the basket she had flung carelessly on to the table, "I hadn't a hand to spare."

She shook her head energetically and her hair swirled about her in a burnished mantle, the pins in it scattering everywhere. Her baby watched her in great admiration as if he could scarcely believe his luck in having such a splendid mother, then turned to Chloe, his wondering smile asking didn't she agree as he displayed the pearls of his new teeth which were also much to be admired.

Chloe seemed unable to move. Her hands had automatically gone to steady the child as Katy arranged him on her lap, but the depression which clouded her mind by day and by night appeared to have stolen her ability to think coherently. She had dwelled in near-oblivion for so long, transformed by her loss into an empty chalice which nothing could fill, she could not quite understand what it was she was being asked to do. This was Katy's child on her lap, she knew that. He was warm, solid, heavy as he turned again to look trustingly into her face and she supposed . . . what was it she was supposed to do?

"Do get his things off, Chloe, or he will take a chill."

There was a sharp, anxious note in Katy's voice which she did her best to hide. Her child was hanging about in wet clothes which must be got off him as soon as possible but she wanted Chloe to be the one to do it. It was an experiment and one she was sure was as cock-eyed as many of the other ideas she had had in her life, but something must be done to drag her cousin from the treacle-like morass of despair which the loss of her child had tumbled her in. She had thought of it this morning and with her usual impetuosity had dashed up here to try it out, but as she watched Chloe's look of blind panic and the way her hands trembled, letting Katy know that she was longing to be free of the baby on her knee, Katy could see she had made another error of judgment.

It did not once occur to her that not many months ago she would have been gratified to see her cousin, her enemy, adrift in this sea of senselessness. Before Jack was born she would have looked for some advantage to Katy Andrews in this tragedy of Chloe's, some edge which might have driven Jamie into her own arms but Jack was her guiding star, her conscience now and she found she could not contemplate any action which might shame her in his eyes. She had done enough of that in the past and to entangle herself with Chloe's husband, with Jamie whom she loved still, would certainly do Jack no good in the community. She must be circumspect now, for her son's sake and besides, there was something . . . something vulnerable, something defenceless about Chloe, something which awoke a strong feeling of protectiveness in Katy. Chloe who was so frail. Katy who was so strong. She had come to . . . she found her . . . Goddammit, she seemed to . . . to *like* her! This young woman had always done her best to support Katy, even if Katy hadn't wanted that support. Like the time she had come down to the cottage and stood up to Paddy, a fragile kitten squaring up to a battered, evil-tempered bulldog which if it could have got its jaws about her would have snapped off her dainty head. When Jack was born she had been magnificent in her strength and then, the moment Katy moved back to Cloudberry End she had come to call in the formal manner which was meant to say this was how Katy Andrews should be treated.

She had removed her own cloak, hanging it to dry over a chair, pretending an air of unconcern with what Chloe was doing to her child. She crashed cups and saucers about on the table and made a great display of interest in the kettle and teapot and when timidly and with great care Chloe began to unbutton Jack's little jacket Katy let out a slow and triumphant sigh of relief.

"I've brought an enormous batch of biscuits and cakes and scones and God knows what else for you to try, cousin. Mrs Kelsall seems bent on showing me she's a better cook than old Tippy and I must admit she's not bad. We had a splendid leg of lamb last night, the best I have ever tasted, with mint sauce and roast potatoes. Very simple but cooked superbly. Mind, when I say 'we', of course you will know I mean just myself. That brother of mine might just as well have gone to Scarborough with Mother and Father for all I see of him. Not that I mind, you understand, for we only argue and upset the servants. Lord knows where he spends his time for Chris doesn't tell me, but there have been nights when the place is alive with drunken young men and – now don't be shocked, cousin, though I swear I was – I have heard women's voices too. I am in bed, naturally, with my door bolted, I don't mind admitting it, and in the morning when I see the havoc they have caused in Mother's drawing room I could cheerfully wring his neck."

She turned abruptly, her exercise with the tea caddy and sugar swept to one side, her heart beating faster, then slowing again, dreading that she might find Chloe sitting like a frozen mannikin with Jack awkwardly on her lap, but she was easing his arms out of his coat, bending to smile into his face, chafing his little pink hands to warmth. Jack was watching her in that intent way young children display, vastly interested in her, ready, should she seem inclined, to be friends.

Katy felt her body relax into boneless relief. She took a quiet step or two across the kitchen, reluctant to intrude on this special moment, this healing moment between her son and her cousin, but drawn by something unique which had begun to flower.

"There," Chloe was murmuring softly, "there, that's better. Were your hands cold, darling? There, let Chloe warm them for you," and Jack watched her with big, unquestioning eyes, giggling as she pretended to nibble his fingers.

Katy quietly took his coat and the shawls she had closely wrapped about him before she left home, spreading them out to dry before the fire, then, sighing, sank down to kneel beside the woman and child in the rocker.

They were all considerably startled by the sudden appearance of Adah-May who had been bottoming the bedrooms, a task she had been set by Matty and, since no one had told her otherwise, she had continued until the light failed. She was like that, was Adah-May. Although she was certainly not quiet about it you often found you had completely forgotten her presence, Matty often said, and for the next few minutes it was pandemonium as Katy got her into her coat and boots and scarf for her journey home to her mam's.

When she had gone with Katy's exhortations to "Go straight home and keep to the path" ringing in her ears, Katy resumed her position at the feet of her cousin.

There was silence for several minutes, then, "I want to take him to Scarborough, cousin," she said abruptly. "What d'you think?"

It was the first time anyone had asked Chloe Hutchinson what she thought for a long time. She turned her gaze, which had become soft and tremulous for the boy, to Katy and in her eyes was a cloud, an indecision, or was it a reluctance to return to the world where decisions must be made, to the reality of everyday living? Let me, for just this moment, stay in my corner, it pleaded, where, if I know not content, at least it is not pain. It did not last long.

Almost without knowing she did it she drew Katy's child to her breast, resting her chin on his bright fluff of curls. She gazed into the fire, her eyes still clouded and pensive, her teeth unconsciously nibbling at her bottom lip.

"I think . . ." she said hesitantly, not quite sure of herself in this devastation which had shattered her. She would not have vacillated before. Before the death of her daughter she would have known exactly what to say, for there was no one more loving, more dedicated to the concept of family than she was. She had been unloved for most of her life. Now she knew she was the soul, the heart of her husband. She knew that Matty loved her and, she suspected, deep in her heart, so did Katy Andrews, her awkward, forthright, unconformable cousin. Surely, where love was there should be no doubt, no reluctance, absolutely no prevarication.

"Go," she said huskily. "Take their grandson to them, Katy, or you will never forgive yourself."

"They might not accept me."

"You must try." Chloe's voice was throaty with something which seemed to stick there, clogging it so that she could barely speak. "Don't ever miss the chance to make amends, Katy."

"No, you're right. It's been so long since I saw Mother. I didn't care much once. I'm sure you're aware of the . . . the great passion between my parents?"

"Yes."

"We, my brothers and I, were shut out, but now I have Jack I realise how much I must have hurt her."

"Go, Katy, and take Jack to meet them." Her voice became even lower. "I would have taken my . . ."

"Chloe . . . oh, darling . . ." Katy put her arms about her cousin, hugging her to her, knowing exactly what she suffered since she had a child too and could imagine the agony of his loss. The baby, owl-like, blinked between them, then decided he did not care for this close confinement, struggled and let out a howl of protest.

Instantly Katy let them go, reaching for the baby with hungry, suddenly empty arms, but Chloe looked up at her, on her face written her appeal though she said nothing. Her eyes were wide and bright with the tears she had never shed but which, Katy suspected, would come soon.

"Hold him for me, will you, cousin," she said, doing her best to be casual, "while I make this pot of tea I promised us. And we must sample some of Mrs Kelsall's fancies. She will be most offended if I don't report back the moment I get home on your opinion."

"Why should my opinion matter, Katy?" There might have been a glint of a smile on Chloe's face.

"Don't ask me, cousin, but it does. Now me, I count for nothing. Oh yes, she made it very plain when Matty brought her over that it was she who was conducting the interview, not me and that she was doing me a great favour in even considering gracing my kitchen with her presence. You must come over soon. When this damn snow has gone and Thomas can get the gig through I shall beg Mrs Kelsall to make us lunch. I want you to see Jack's nursery . . . Aah, I'm sorry."

"Katy, please, Matty and Jamie walk round me as though they were treading on eggshells and I know they mean to be kind. They love me and don't wish to hurt me but this . . . with Jack . . . though it grieves me that it is not my child I am holding . . . God, you cannot realise . . . but this is real. I long to nurse my own child, Katy, but until I do I should be glad to borrow yours now and again."

She had fallen asleep and so had Jack when Jamie came home. Katy stood up, the chair in which she had been sitting opposite Chloe rocking gently. She had been watching over them, her son and her cousin, while they slept but her eyes could not help themselves as they hungered across Jamie Hutchinson's face. He seemed thinner, older, his lean cheeks gaunt with worry, but when his gaze fell on his wife and the child in her arms Katy saw quite distinctly the relief sag through him.

He smiled briefly in her direction, going at once to kneel at Chloe's feet. He placed a big, gentle hand about her cheek, his eyes dreaming, then moving to Jack who had his rosy face pressed against the swell of her breast. His hand moved to push back a tendril of hair from Chloe's forehead, lingering in an agony of possessive and compassionate love and Katy watched, the knife in her heart twisting cruelly though she was aware he did not mean to cause her pain. He was simply demonstrating his love for his wife who had lost her child, his child, but was now sleeping peacefully with Katy's son in her loving arms.

Katy loved him. She loved his quietness, his strength, his air of knowing exactly who he was and, though it was ready to destroy her, who it was he loved. She loved the set of his chin, the way his dark hair curled into the nape of his smooth, amber neck, the quizzical tilt to his eyebrows, even in seriousness, the way his mouth turned up at the corners. She was aware that her love for him had changed. It had grown steadier, deeper, coming as naturally to her as her milk flowed for her son. Whatever she might have told herself earlier he had only to turn, hold out his hand and she would go with him in an act of complete surrender.

Had he not loved his wife.

At last he rose, turning thankful eyes to her, inclined to be embarrassed, for this thing, this strange unwanted feeling begun when he had found her suckling her child behind the wall, or perhaps, if he were truthful, even before that, would always be between them.

"Thank you, Katy," he said simply, putting out a hand to her then dropping it hastily before she could respond.

"She didn't want to hold him. I made her."

"Your instincts are sure and you have a good heart, Katy Andrews."

"Jamie . . ." Her eyes were as clear and golden as amber. Her love for him shone from them like a beacon. She could not hide it and it lit up the dim room, illuminating every corner, but he turned away from it lest he be burned, or blinded, or both.

"It's stopped snowing," he said, addressing the clock.

"There was only a thin fall though it seemed a lot and it's frozen hard so we should be able to walk on it. Stay and have some of Ma's steak and kidney pudding which I can smell in the oven and then I'll walk you and Jack home."

"Thank you, Jamie," she answered gravely, knowing how it was between them. "Let Chloe sleep a while though. She seems to find comfort in Jack. He'll wake up as soon as his belly commands him."

She smiled, wanting to talk of anything but her child, Paddy Andrews's child, but conscious of the relief on Jamie's face. He was afraid of her, she knew that, wondering why since his love for Chloe was incontestable. Perhaps it was because he knew she loved him. That even after all that had happened, Paddy, and then Jack, her love for Jamie had never wavered. It glowed like a candle in a dark room, lighting her heart, warming her. Perhaps, when she turned her gaze on him he could see it, that candle which would never go out, never flicker and die until the day she did. He was uneasy with it. Whenever she called he was courteous, hospitable, begging her to make herself at home, inviting her friendship with his wife but she had noticed that he had always found some excuse never to be alone with her.

She sat down again while behind her Jamie moved about the kitchen, setting the table for their meal. It would be Christmas in a week or two and she intended, if Chloe was recovered, to invite them to dine with her at Cloudberry End. Now that she had a decent cook. A proper affair with herself and Chloe in evening gowns though she doubted if Jamie had an evening suit. It didn't matter. She would have candles and a Christmas tree with presents under it and it would be her first attempt at entertaining.

The dog, Captain, who had come in with Jamie, nudged her hand with his muzzle and she fondled him, smoothing his rough coat. She felt strangely at peace. She was not a part of this household, merely, she was aware, a welcomed guest, at least by Chloe, but she was also aware that there was something here that – what was the word? – gentled her. Moved her imperceptibly away from the wildness which had caused so much pain and desolation to so many people in the past. It was all her fault, the whole dreadful débâcle. Paddy, Chris, her parents' escape from her to Scarborough. Yes, her fault and yet, could she choose where she loved? Could anybody? It was her love for Jamie and his inability to return it, and then, to exacerbate the situation further, his love for Chloe which had set them all on the devastating path which, strangely, had led to this peaceful room.

She turned her head to look about her, sighing for what might have been and gazed directly into Jamie's troubled eyes. He looked away at once, his eyes dragging from hers, his hands going to the cutlery he was placing on the table and as it rattled Chloe awoke. Her sudden movement disturbed Jack and he turned, still half asleep, his mouth seeking sustenance from her breast.

It did not seem to trouble her. She smiled, then looked at Katy and in her smile was a lessening of her pain.

"Thank you," she said simply and they knew she would be all right now.

Katy and Jamie studiously avoided one another's eyes.

23

She took the train to Scarborough, accompanied by Matty, determined to do this thing properly since she knew it would mean a lot to her mother. Ladies did not travel alone, especially with an infant. Katy, who had never listened to Sara Andrews's remonstrances, knew that. Remembered it from somewhere or some other time when her mother had still hoped to make a lady out of her.

She had not told them she was coming, she confided to Chloe, who had looked at her with some misgivings, dwelling perhaps on the possibility of the front door being slammed in her face. No, they would not do that, she was certain, but Katy might find that her parents might see her impetuous journey as just another example of her heedless irresponsibility and close ranks on her. They were not to know of their daughter's new, gentler approach to others now that she had a child to consider, a part of herself, another human being who depended on her, not only for his life but for what his life would be as he grew.

It was a long journey necessitating a change at Sheffield and Leeds. Jack was fretful, for with her usual hasty need to be at whatever it was that challenged her and her disregard for what might be described as setbacks, she had made no provision to feed him, blithely assuming, if she assumed anything at all, that she would find some secluded corner in the ladies waiting room in which to do it. The ladies who waited there, of the same social class as her mother, looked quite scandalised as she sat down, Jack squalling on her knee, with what seemed to them the obvious intention of baring her bosom like any low and common woman and nursing her child, and she had fled in confusion, hoping the journey to Scarborough would not take too long. Her breasts were dangerously full and tender when the hansom cab they had hired at the railway station finally delivered them, the baby wailing miserably, on to the front step of the house in Scarborough, the address of which had been given her by her father in case of an emergency.

The town itself was situated in the recess of a bay, rising to the summit of a cliff or "scar" from which it had got its name. It combined the advantage of sea bathing with mineral baths and had a beach of the finest sand, or so Katy had heard, though she had no great hopes of ever sampling any of it.

But she was concerned with none of these things as she and Matty climbed stiffly from the cab, the grizzling baby protesting so loudly the horse which pulled the cab almost dragged the driver off his seat in its alarm.

Katy was elegantly dressed in a travelling outfit made for her by the new Miss Johnson who, having set up in competition with Miss Mason in Crossclough, saw no reason to cease sewing for Miss Andrews, even though she now knew her story. She could not afford to turn customers away, even one as infamous as Miss Andrews, in fact, she was of the opinion that her other clients found the possibility that they might come across the "scarlet woman of Crossclough" in her smart little salon and whom of course they would cut dead, quite exhilarating. The pale sand-coloured pleated skirt and Norfolk jacket, the very latest fashion imitating the male garment, the dashing hat, so-called because its ribbons tied beneath the chignon and not the chin as did the bonnet, were a testament to Miss Johnson's considerable talent.

"Ring the bell, Matty," Katy said autocratically, her nervousness so great it made her sound rude. The house, set high on the clifftop if the climb up to it was anything to go by, was surrounded by trees, dark, moaning winter trees, for dusk had already fallen and she was vastly relieved when the door opened and an oblong of bright golden light fell across them.

"Mr Andrews, if you please," she told the astonished housemaid who opened the door. "We will come inside and wait in the hall since the child is cold. Oh, and would you send someone to fetch our luggage?"

"Beg pardon," the housemaid piped, quite overwhelmed by this patronising young woman, by the protesting child who stank of something unpleasant, though the second woman, older, sensible and unruffled, seemed well enough.

"I would like to see my father as soon as possible," Katy went on, her voice imperious and it was only when Matty dug her in the back, shaking her head warningly when Katy turned towards her, that she was made aware that she must not take the high-handed attitude that had been hers in the past. She was doing this for Jack and, she admitted, if only to herself, because of a strangely uncomfortable need to see her mother. It was over a year, a year last October on the day of her grandmother's funeral when they had last met so how would they greet one another? Would they greet one another or would Jack Andrews, his face turned against her, simply ask her to be on her way?

He walked down the wide, shallow staircase, his usual cigar held between his fingers and her heart leaped with gladness for he looked so much better. In the four months he had been at Scarborough he had regained some weight and his usual sun-tinted colour had come back, no doubt due to walks along the beautiful sandy beach Katy had heard about.

"Father?" She could say no more. The yearning in her voice was very evident and Matty could see Jack Andrews was affected by it.

"Katherine. You're a long way from home, lass. I hope there's nowt wrong. Is Chris all right?"

Katy felt a great need to tell the truth. To say, "As far as I am aware for I never see him and only hear the sound of his wild parties from behind my locked bedroom door," but she smiled instead.

"Yes, but I have come to ask about you and Mother, not to talk of Chris. How is she?"

"Better. We both are. The sea air is very bracing and we are comfortable here." He turned to smile at Matty. "Go on up, lass. She's waiting for you. When the maid said it was my daughter and an older woman we thought it would be you."

"Which way, Jack?"

"Up the stairs and the first door on your right."

The sound of Matty's pounding feet followed by the banging of a door died away. There was a small but very tense silence as Katy studied this deliberate – or so it appeared – slap in the face aimed at her. Her father was at ease, waiting for her to declare her purpose in coming here, unbending, not unfriendly, cool, but despite himself his eyes strayed to the grizzling, somewhat unsavoury child in her arms.

"Perhaps I might beg the use of a room, Father?" she ventured. "The boy is hungry and . . . and needs changing." She grinned suddenly, her old challenging grin that said that though she was no longer the hellion he had once known she still had spirit in her. "Your nose has probably noticed it."

"Er . . . yes." He smiled somewhat uncertainly.

"Perhaps . . . afterwards we might talk?"

"Well . . ."

"Please, Father. I have travelled a long way to see you."

They put her in a small parlour at the back of the house. There was a good fire, a comfortable chair, tea on a dainty tray which she drank as she nursed Jack. He had been changed and washed and now, warm and dry, with a full belly, he lay heavily in her arms, his head lolling back in a deep sleep.

She rang the bell and when the housemaid, who must have been hanging about outside she came so quickly, bobbed her smiling, eager face round the door, asked if she might beg a blanket or two and perhaps someone could be spared to watch her son.

"Eeh, raight gladly, miss," the housemaid said in her broad Yorkshire accent, obviously claiming the privilege for herself, though when Katy left the room there were two or three of them, Freda and Mrs Tiplady among them exclaiming how he had grown, hanging over the sleeping child. It was always the same. Put a woman, or several women in the vicinity of a young child and they would become as clucking as the hens in Chloe's yard. They took no notice of her, even Mrs Tiplady and Freda, considering as the daughter of their master she could go anywhere she pleased.

"Up the stairs and first door on the right."

She knocked hesitantly and when her mother's voice bade her to enter she did so. She closed the door behind her, standing with her back to it, noticing the way her father stood up at once, placing himself between her and her mother and it was perhaps at that moment that she recognised precisely what she had done to her parents and the reason for her father's subsequent removal of his wife from her daughter's excesses. Roughshod she had ridden over their hopes for her, their ideals and belief in what they considered proper, what everyone in their social circle considered proper. She had cared naught if they were damaged, concerned only with her own pain, her own needs.

Now they no longer trusted her and could you blame them and certainly her father was about to make sure that his wife, her mother, would not suffer again.

"Katy . . ." he said warningly.

She held up her hands placatingly. "I know, Father, and I understand. I promise, on the life of my child who, everyone knows, is the most precious thing in the world to me, that I have not come here to upset Mother. Matty here will tell you I have . . . changed . . . since Jack was born."

"'Tis true, Jack," Matty murmured.

"I am living an exemplary life at Cloudberry End and though I am aware that nothing will ever change what I did, that Jack will always be . . . illegitimate, I have come to try and make peace. To become . . . friends, if you will let me. I don't intend to make a nuisance of myself, to pester you and Mother but now and again, if you will allow it, I should like to bring him to visit his grandparents. He is a lovely boy— " her voice was thick with tears— "and does not deserve what I have done to him but . . ."

"Sit down, darling," her mother said to her father. "I think we may safely assume that our daughter would not plead her case so eloquently if she did not mean it. That was one thing you could always rely on, you know. Her total honesty. Her passion for the truth no matter who it hurt."

"Mother . . ."

Her mother sighed as Jack Andrews moved slowly towards her. She and Matty were seated hand in hand on an elegant little sofa in front of an enormous fire. The curtain had not yet been drawn and through the bay window the lights of the little grey town climbing down to the bay twinkled in the darkness. Katy could hear the pounding of the sea on the beach below and smell the tang of sea spray and sensed suddenly the lovely peace which her parents had found here away from their troublesome children.

"Bring him up, Katy. How can a woman refuse the sight of her first grandchild?"

"Sara . . ." her husband said warningly.

"She is a mother now, Jack, and knows how I feel."

It had been surprisingly easy, helped by the engaging charm and copper-haired good looks of her son, and by Matty who eased them all through three days of careful attention to one another's needs and fears and hopes.

How strange it was, Katy was to think later, that this child about whom Crossclough had thrown up its hands in horror, a child born of sin, they said, in his short, sweet life had, unknowingly, begun the healing process in Chloe and now was perhaps to do the same with the raw wound between her parents and herself.

"Yer ma an' pa do care about thi', Katy," Matty adjured her, "yer know they do, but, well, yer know 'ow they are about one another. Yer ma 'ad a poor sort of a life until she married yer pa. Get 'er ter tell you about it sometime, an' then you an' Chris were never easy. With yer pa away so much when you were little, an' now with this last – you an' Paddy Andrews – it were more than she could take, burrif yer mean what yer say about bein' different, towards 'er an' yer pa, I mean, actin' proper an' such, they'll stand by yer. They've tekken a shine ter't little lad an' can yer blame 'em but . . . well, my lass, I've this ter say. If yer let 'em down again yer'll 'ave Matty Jenkins to answer to."

Though the farewell they gave her was not exactly fulsome, for they could not quite hide their satisfaction at being alone together again, it was at least affectionate. Their manner seemed to say they were glad the rift between them was on the way to being healed but they could not at once put behind them all the years and all the anguish she had inflicted on them in those years. Not on the basis of one visit. But they were willing to give her a chance, for was that not what parents always did? Give a child a second chance. She would know now what that meant. They stood together on the wide steps, her mother leaning slightly on her father's shoulder, a handsome, well-dressed couple of middle years, smiling, waving, her mother's eyes turning more to her grandson than to her daughter.

A start had been made and Katy leaned back in the cab well satisfied.

It had been the practice of Annie Lennox to walk up to Cloudberry End from Woodhead once a week to collect her wages. She would have a cup of tea in the kitchen of Matty Jenkins with whom she had grown increasingly friendly in the past few months, before being shown into the drawing room of the big house where Miss Katy waited for her. Ever since those days when Annie and Matty had bumped into one another in Crossclough and had sadly discussed the awful predicament Miss Katy Andrews had got herself into they had recognised one another in each other. They were both decently wed women, Annie, sadly, a widow now, with an interest in Katy Andrews which was not one of ghoulish curiosity, which could not be said of most folk in Crossclough. They were genuinely concerned for her, pitying the wild streak in her which had brought her to her present deplorable position. Approve of her? No! Admire her spirit? Yes, for had she not dragged herself from a situation which, had it happened to almost any other woman, would have extinguished the life from her.

They enjoyed the transference of these amicable chats in Crossclough to Matty's cosy kitchen at the lodge of Cloudberry End, spending an hour or so exchanging recipes for almond macaroons and Aunt Nelly's pudding which Matty had brought with her from Liverpool; the best way to make old crape look new again and the worry of growing sons since they were both blessed – or tormented – with one. Thanks to Katy Andrews, Annie Lennox had no need to worry where her next shilling was to come from and all through the winter she had fed her well-clothed, well-shod children on nourishing broths with the best cut of stewing steak in them, custards with milk and eggs, thick soups brimming with vegetables and the improvement in them had been remarkable. Poor old Frank, she often thought. He had done his best, working himself literally to death, but he had never had the joy of seeing his children thrive as they did now.

Of course there was a price to pay as there was for anything in this life. A cross to bear, a fly in the ointment and Annie's was Paddy Andrews. It had taken her nearly ten days after Katy left him last back end even to get inside the front door of what had once been Madge Andrews's spotless little cottage to do the job she was paid to do and Annie Lennox was not one to take money she had not earned. When she did finally gain access it was only on account of them Andrews twins who had no desire to clean up the foul mess Paddy had got himself into. Knocked on her door, they had, muttering that he was dead to the world, drunk as a stoat, lying unconscious in his own body wastes – though they had used a coarser expression – and if she would come in and give the place a bit of a clean they'd guarantee he'd not bother her, should he come to. Even their strong stomachs could stand it no longer, they had implied, hanging their unkempt heads and shuffling their enormous feet like two overgrown lads who have been up to no good.

It must have been a bit of a shock to his system, she often smiled to herself, to fall into a stupor one evening in a state of such filth even a pig would have been ashamed, and wake up the next morning with the place like a new pin about him. She'd not touch him, she vowed to his ham-fisted, red-faced cousins, but if they would attend to that part she thought she might see her way to buying them a pint or two in the Queen's Head in Crossclough.

It all worked out a treat. Between the three of them they kept Paddy Andrews in some sort of state halfway between cleanliness and beastliness, the lads glad of a bob or two, which, of course, Miss Katy supplied and Annie was made up with her family's new standard of living. With that and several other little jobs Annie managed, her life was free from the dreadful ogre of poverty which had always hung over her and Frank.

It was no fun living next door to him, mind, she told Matty, with his drunken shouts in the dead of night, his obscenities flung at her when she ventured into the cottage, his threats and abuse directed at his cousins who only grinned and leaped out of the way of his lethal fists. He was a devil and so was that dreadful dog of his which regularly butchered Barty Pickles's chickens. Again it was Miss Katy who patiently replaced them and any other damage or loss that was reported to her and which could be laid at Paddy Andrews's door.

But all that had ended four weeks ago and Annie was not

sure which was worse, the squalid drunken chaos in which Paddy had lived or his sudden transformation into what she could only call "a new man".

It was quite nerve-racking. He had stopped drinking. Just like that he had stopped drinking and how could a man who had put away at least two bottles of brandy a day – she knew, for didn't she have the clearing away of them – stop drinking overnight? she asked Matty wonderingly. His temper, of course, was absolutely foul, terrifying in fact, and she had refused quite positively even to take his food in unless the twins were there with him. They were not very bright, she confided to Matty, but they were both like young bulls and between them they held him down until he had roared himself out.

And then there was this chap. What chap? Matty wanted to know, for the shenanigans that went on in the cottage of Katy Andrews's erstwhile lover sickened and fascinated her at the same time.

Well, Annie didn't rightly know. He came up on a horse, an old mangy thing with a basket over its rump and left half an hour later, in which time there had been absolute silence in the cottage. Four times he'd been now and when Annie had found out why she had raced up to tell Matty and now if Matty would excuse her she'd best go and warn Miss Katy.

But Matty could no more contain her curiosity than she could her own good nature. "What? What is it, for goodness sake?"

Annie paused in the doorway, her hand dramatically to her bosom. She was not a woman taken to dramatics but this was enough to alarm the most imperturbable of women.

"I went in not an hour since, Mrs Jenkins," for she and Matty recognised the proprieties and still addressed one another by their surnames, "an' I nearly fainted. Honest to God, I thought me heart'd stop beatin'. There he was as large as life an' twice as ugly . . . standin' up."

"Standin' up!" Matty put her hands to her mouth in much the same dramatic fashion as Annie.

"Aye, as God is my witness he was standin' on his own two legs."

"Never!"

"It's the truth, Mrs Jenkins. At least it were one real leg an' one wooden leg which stuck out of the end of his trousers like . . . eeh, like I don't know what. He was wobblin' all over't place but he laughed when he saw me, laughed an' laughed an' I tell thi' this, it scared the livin' daylights outer me."

Which was saying something since it took a lot to frighten Annie Lennox. During his long sojourn in his wheelchair in the cottage next to hers, though he swore and bellowed and flung himself about in order to get at her, he had never scared her, not once, but now he did and Miss Katy must be warned.

"'Aye,' he says, 'I'm up on me pins, Annie. Not walkin' yet but I will be. By God, I will. I've 'ad enough sittin' on me bum, lass, so I decided ter get messen a new leg. So yer can tell them what might be interested that Paddy Andrews is back in business.'"

It was the talk not only of the small hamlet of Woodhead which he and his cousins had terrorised as he floundered up and down the narrow, sloping track which ran through it, but of Crossclough where the news reached by the end of the week. Paddy Andrews was up on his legs again, even if one was made of wood. Josh and Jake supported him at first, one on either side until he had regained his balance and then, when they were elsewhere, he wobbled about on the crutches, presumably fashioned by the same man who had made his "peg-leg". They watched him from their cottage windows, not even the children daring to laugh at his comical hop-step-jump. "Peg-leg" they would have chanted after him, or "Hoppy" if he had been anyone but Paddy Andrews. "Fatty" or "Lumpy", "Dumpling" or "Tub o' Lard", from a safe distance, of course, for his girth was enormous with folds of flesh hanging about him and his wicked eyes sunk in the unhealthy pallor of his bloated face.

After a while they got used to him stumping up and down, keeping out of his way, naturally. Hop-step-jump he would go, his bull-like neck folded down, his chin on his chest, his eyes on the cobbles which threatened to catch the end of his crutches. Soon he no longer needed Josh and Jake and neither did he need Annie Lennox, he told her two months later, since he would get about the cottage on his own now. In one way it was a relief to Annie who had not felt safe with him on the move, though she had to admit he made no attempt to threaten her as he once had, but how was she to manage without the wage Miss Katy had paid her all this time?

"You're not to worry, Annie." For by this time the animosity shown by Annie Lennox towards Katy Andrews had vanished. "I am in need of a daily . . . what d'you call them?"

Annie bridled, on her high horse at once. "Nay, there's no call ter mekk a job fer me, Miss Katy. I'll manage well enough," though the prospect of being returned to "managing" after all this time was daunting.

"Rubbish," Miss Katy said in that high-handed way she had. "A good woman, in any capacity, is hard to find and if you think I am going to dispense with you over this then you are very much mistaken. Besides, I need to see you every day so that you can let me know what . . . what he's up to. You do see that, don't you? I know you're not afraid of hard work and not too proud to earn an honest shilling doing it. There is the washing and the ironing which, I'll be honest with you, Mabel cannot make a decent fist of. She is heavy-handed with the goffering iron and . . . well, you will know what I mean. Will you not come up to Cloudberry End each day as . . . as . . . general cleaner and factotum. I will pay you the same wage and it will be a great relief to me to know exactly how much progress that devil makes."

Katy was glad, of course she was, that Paddy was taking his life and putting it back together again. In a way it took away some of the heavy sense of guilt she had known ever since the doctor had cut off his leg, and also reduced the responsibility which she had expected to carry until the day of his death. Perhaps, if he could get about he might find life worthwhile again although, a small voice whispered inside her where she had cherished a certain peace of mind knowing he was tied to the cottage at Woodhead, if he can get about what mischief might he get up to?

Annie hadn't the faintest idea what a factotum might be but she was so thankful she didn't care. If it involved the heaviest cleaning or the mucking out of the damned horses in the stable, she would do it.

She wouldn't show it though. She was a decent woman who had earned her own living and paid her own way since she was a little lass. She bleached and scoured her kitchen table every day no matter how tired she was. Her stone floor was as meticulously scrubbed and her washing, hung out in the stiff wind which cut down from the moors, smelled of strong soap and lye. She was used to carrying heavy burdens, and she'd had plenty to carry in her time so she'd not bend her head to this slip of a girl, no matter how . . . fond . . . yes, fond she had become of her, nor how grateful she felt towards her.

"Right," she said, as though she was doing Katy a favour. "I'll start termorrer. Six o'clock do thi'?"

"Well." Katy was not at all sure what time her kitchen staff began work. "Perhaps we'd best go and see Mrs Kelsall," who, by now, ran the kitchen, the servants, the house and even the grooms in the stable like a general in charge of an army.

When she had anything to report, anything unusual that is, Annie would knock on Katy's drawing room door, stepping inside with no sign of the overwhelming awe she always felt at the sight of so many beautiful things. Shining, glittering, polished things that winked and shimmered at her from every corner of the room. Lovely colours and lovely pictures, flowers and even, in an enormous glass room she had heard Janet call the conservatory, birds singing in cages. If for nothing else it was worth the tramp twice a day to see this lovely room.

"He 'asn't half lost weight, Miss Katy," she reported several weeks later. "'Appen it's all them exercises he's doin'."

"Exercises? What sort of exercises?"

"Nay, I don't see 'im do them but I 'ear him sometimes, thump, thump, thump, an' Jinty Pickles ses he can get up that track as fast as you an' me. Sticks, he 'as now but he don't hop no more. He walks proper, one foot in front of t'other, like. It give 'er quite a turn, she said. It were like Lazarus come back from't dead, seein' him up an' about an' chirpy as a bird in a tree. 'Mornin', Jinty,' he ses to 'er. 'Fine mornin' fer a walk,' grinnin' like he used to," for there was no denying Paddy Andrews had been a fine, handsome, laughing man before he lost his leg.

"What . . . what d'you think he means to do, Annie?" Katy's

voice trembled for though she had not taken his threat seriously at the time, for what harm could wheelchair-bound Paddy Andrews do to her and her son, Paddy Andrews up on two legs, even if one was made of wood, was a different matter altogether.

"Lass, I don't know, but I'd tekk care if I were thi'."

24

The man was admitted to Cloudberry End just as Katy and Chloe were about to sit down to lunch. Katy wanted Chloe to judge her once again on her skills as a hostess, though God only knew when she would have a chance to show them off, she laughed, not, Chloe understood, particularly concerned. No one had called on her since her return to Cloudberry End, which was only to be expected and had it not been for Chloe and Jamie she would have had no visitors at all. Truth to tell she was becoming slightly bored with being mistress of Cloudberry End, since Mrs Kelsall was excellent at her job and though she consulted Katy – tongue in cheek, Katy was inclined to think – on every household matter, there was no need for Katy to be involved apart from the accounts which Mrs Kelsall kept meticulously.

Katy saw Chris every now and then, sometimes at dinner, sometimes passing one another in a hallway like guests in a hotel but they had little to say to one another, speaking only to argue.

"Do your . . . er . . . friends have to make such an infernal row at two o'clock in the morning, Chris? Half the servants were out of their beds and Angus is quite incensed by the state of his lawn after someone galloped a horse across it."

"Really, and what is it to do with you, or Angus what I do in my own home? Besides, that brat of yours is for ever caterwauling. Sounds like a bloody cat on the tiles. I was quite mortified when I had to explain to my . . . well, a lady guest I was entertaining that it was not a cat but your— "

"That's enough, Chris. And I'd be obliged if you would not bring your loose women into Mother's house."

"You mean besides yourself."

"You bastard . . ."

"No, it is your son who is the bastard, Katy, and the sooner you remove him from a decent household the happier I will be. Why do you not return to your lover now that he is back on his feet? I'm sure a man with two legs must be infinitely more appetising than the wreck he was purported to be."

"Chris, I'm warning you . . ."

"Oh go to hell, Katy, and take your bastard with you."

On the whole they made a point of avoiding one another.

The dinner at Christmas to which she had invited Chloe and Jamie had been somewhat strained and also on the several occasions in the past few months when they had driven over to Cloudberry End, borrowing the gig which spent most of its time in the barn at Valley Bottom Farm. Chloe must have some sort of transport, Katy declared, since she did not ride and Katy had no need of it since she did ride and besides, she had the use of her mother's carriage so it seemed only sensible to have the gig and the horse that pulled it stabled at the farm. Call it a Christmas present, she had pronounced carelessly. Yes, she knew she had given them both some trifling thing or two from under her Christmas tree but it was a waste to have it and the animal where no one used them. The horse could pasture in Jamie's meadow and would cost nothing much to feed and as it appeared she was to entertain no one but her cousin and her cousin's husband in her home, she said cheerfully, and was invited nowhere, what would she need with a gig?

She had taken up riding again now that Jack was old enough, or so she said, to be taken up before her on Storm's back. It did no harm to start them young, she argued when Matty protested, and Jack was nine months old now. He loved it, sitting up before her on the gentle slopes she took him on, wrapped in a warm shawl, the ends of which were tied firmly about his mother's waist so that there was no danger of his falling off. His face glowed as the wind touched it and his bright eyes roamed across the burgeoning moors just beyond Cloudberry End. Not far, since he was still young but he seemed to have the same empathy with its broad and sculpted emptiness as his mother. Bracken, its tall fronds rising to greet the spring, green and restless above the heather moor. The broken ground exploding with cotton grass, with bilberry which formed a continuous fringe above the gritstone, a wildness, a lonely wilderness to which the heart and soul of Katy Andrews responded. She loved it. The vastness which stretched on into infinity. The rolling moorlands, the steep-sided cliff faces, the sighing trees, the whisper of the wind through the undergrowth. It had never frightened her because it was her land and she loved it. There was nothing up here but sheep sheltering behind the cobweb of drystone walls which criss-crossed the peaks, a solitary shepherd who raised a hand in surprised greeting, a hawk hanging on the wind, rabbits showing off their little white scuts as they darted out of her way. She was never lonely. Just she and Jack, Storm and Muffy and if, sometimes, when her son slept in her arms after his feed she wept for her lost love there was no one to see or hear it.

"Now let us see what miracle Mrs Kelsall has prepared

for us today," she was saying laughingly as she and Chloe entered the dining room followed by Janet who was to serve. They were all three considerably startled when the doorbell rang. In fact they looked at one another as though to ask who on earth this could be at Miss Katy Andrews's door. Janet, who had been heard to remark, not by Miss Katy, of course, that she was sick of sitting on her bum all day since it was her job as housemaid to answer the door, ventured a step in its direction.

"See who it is, Janet," Katy said firmly, noting that her heart was missing every other beat at the prospect of seeing Paddy Andrews on her front doorstep. Surely he could not have walked all this way from Woodhead, despite the progress Annie reported he was making on his new leg. She found she was hovering at Janet's back and behind her, Chloe, who seemed to be beset with the same fear, did a bit of hovering herself.

Jack was in his nursery having an after-lunch nap with Lottie sitting beside him, for Katy had still not got around to hiring a nursemaid for her son and the housemaid appeared to find the occasional hour she spent watching over him something to enjoy. Indeed the maidservants argued over whose turn it was to do it.

The gentleman at the door seemed vaguely familiar, though Katy could not quite place him. He was, she supposed, in his late forties or early fifties, a stocky, well-dressed gentleman who, at the sight of her behind her maid, whipped off his low bowler hat and held it politely against his plain waistcoat. He wore a sombre grey frock-coat which was not buttoned and trousers to match. He was decently dressed, neat and immaculate but he was not a "gentleman" and both young women, and indeed Janet who had been housemaid for enough years to recognise one, instinctively knew it.

"Aah, Miss Andrews," he said at once and somewhat breathlessly as though he had been running. Though he inclined his head at Chloe, his manner was brusque, businesslike, with no time to spare for polite conversation.

"I am Miss Andrews," Katy said, stepping forward and, though as usual she did not mean it to be, her attitude was imperious.

"Aye, I know, but it's actually Mr Andrews I'm after, Miss Andrews. Is he at home?"

"Mr Andrews?" Her voice rose on a questioning note and she arched her delicate copper eyebrows. She was looking quite magnificent. If she had been a lovely girl before the birth of her son, motherhood had matured her to a womanly beauty, a shining, glossy beauty which most men, had she met any, would have found hard to ignore. She was tall, her back straight but graceful, her posture and bearing that of a young queen. Her breasts were full, high and rounded and though she had almost weaned Jack there was no droop or sag to them. Her waist was slender, her hips curving, her legs long and in perfect proportion to her body. She wore her hair in an enchanting tumble of long, floating curls, thick and springing, fastened carelessly to the crown of her head with a knot of silver and cream ribbons to match her gown, which today was of a rich, creamy silk. Her skin was lustrous, smooth as honey, her cheekbone touched with rose as was her mouth, and her warm, golden eyes snapped and gleamed with good health and at that moment with keen interest, for she had just recognised the gentleman on her doorstep.

"It's Mr Harrop, isn't it?" she exclaimed, smiling at him with such brilliance he blinked. He had heard of her comeliness, as who had not in Crossclough; of her association with her cousin and the illegitimate boy who had been the result of it and like them all he had been shocked, appalled even at her behaviour, sorry for Mr Andrews and his wife who had so much to bear with their two youngest children. He had seen her about Crossclough in that shameless get-up of hers, averting his eyes, which was hard to do for how was a hot-blooded male to resist those bobbing breasts and hard-peaked nipples, those spread thighs which opened across her horse's back. Even a respectable man such as himself was not immune and he was glad to see she was modestly dressed today.

"Yes, miss, but I'm somewhat pushed for time, if you'll forgive me. I'm after Mr Andrews . . ."

"Do you mean my father, Mr Harrop?"

"Eeh no, Miss Andrews. He's away to Scarborough or so he told me last back end and a sorry day it was when . . . well . . ." He interrupted himself hastily, the expression on his face telling her quite plainly he really had no time to be chitter-chattering with a woman and certainly not a woman such as her, pretty as she was.

"Well, do come in, Mr Harrop," she entreated, opening the door wider, smiling again in a way which did nothing for Mr Harrop's pulse.

"Nay, lass . . ." getting irritated, with himself and her but trying not to show it.

"I insist, but first let me introduce my cousin, Mrs James Hutchinson."

"Ma'am."

"And this is Mr Harrop, Chloe, who is, I believe, manager at my father's paper mill. Have I got that right, Mr Harrop? You are manager, are you not?"

"Aye, I am that, Miss Andrews, but I'd take it very kindly if . . ."

"Oh, do come in, Mr Harrop. We can hardly continue to

chat on the doorstep like this. My cousin and I were about to sit down to lunch. Will you not join us?"

"Nay!" Mr Harrop was deeply shocked. In his social group you just did not associate with a woman, no matter how well bred, who had done what Katherine Andrews had done, and besides, he had come here on urgent business and certainly had no time for socialising.

He stood firmly on the doorstep, refusing stolidly to put one foot over the threshold, just as though the three women who stood in the hall were sirens who might lure him to some dreadful bacchanalian orgy he might possibly regret.

"It's Master Chris I'm after, Miss Andrews," he declared firmly. "There's a problem at the mill which needs his attention so I'd be obliged if you wouldn't mind asking him . . ."

"My brother isn't here, Mr Harrop, and . . ."

"Perhaps you could tell me where I might find him then, Miss Andrews. I really must— "

"But I thought he was at the mill, Mr Harrop. I must admit our paths don't cross much. He lives his life and I live mine."

So Mr Harrop had heard, his grim expression said, but that was nothing to do with him, he just wanted to get his hands on the young wretch whom Mr Andrews had, much against Mr Harrop's advice, put in charge of the bloody mill when he took flight to Scarborough. He'd begged him and begged him, if he didn't want John Harrop to do it for him, to get in a decent engineering manager to help run the paperworks but Mr Andrews had seemed unwilling or unable to make a decision about anything at the time, for ever dashing off, so Mr Harrop had heard, to see that wife of his as though all those servants up at Cloudberry End couldn't manage without him. Daft he was about her, any fool would agree, and to go gallivanting off to Scarborough and leave a good business in the hands of a bone-idle young pup who cared for nothing but drinking and wenching and gambling was, in his opinion, nothing short of criminal.

"So he's not at home, Miss Andrews?"

"I have just said so, Mr Harrop."

"I must find him, Miss Andrews. I will be frank with you," though she could tell he didn't want to. "Perhaps a moment of your time?"

"Of course. Come into the small parlour. Chloe, do you mind? Janet, tell Mrs Kelsall lunch will be a little late, oh, and bring the brandy. I'm sure Mr Harrop would not refuse."

The tale was short, simple and so characteristic of her brother she wondered why Mr Harrop should be surprised not to find him here.

"It's over three months, Miss Andrews, since he was last down at Waterway which, pardon me if I speak bluntly . . ."

"Please do, Mr Harrop."

"Well, it was no loss, for I am quite well able to run it without him. Your father left ample funds, for the men's wages and any other need which might arise and, of course, any profit made has been paid into the account. Your father gave me and Master Chris power to draw on that account. Today, when I went to the bank to withdraw cash for the wages, tomorrow being pay day, the bank manager tells me the account is empty. That Mr Andrews, meaning Master Chris, had taken every last farthing from it a week ago. Unless I can lay my hands on a considerable sum, Miss Andrews, the men will not be paid and no man is willing to give his labour free. In other words there will be trouble, Miss Andrews, and your father would not like that."

"Of course not, Mr Harrop, I quite see that, but surely you could telegraph my father."

"Where, Miss Andrews? He was so adamant about keeping his whereabouts secret he gave his address to no one. For some inexplicable reason he decided that Master Chris was capable, and willing, to run the paper mill. He put his trust in him and now see where that trust has landed him."

"I don't think that was in his mind when he went, Mr Harrop? He and my mother were . . . well, let us say they were not themselves; family problems, if you take my meaning, and my father was concerned only with my mother's health. Truthfully, I do believe he did not really care what happened to his mill, but that is not the problem now. I know where he is, Mr Harrop, and I'm sure if I telegraphed him he could do the same to the bank manager, transferring funds from . . . I know he has a private account since I draw on it for the household— "

She stopped speaking abruptly, biting off her words, her narrowed eyes so vivid and startling a colour, so excited, so lit up with energy and force, Mr Harrop nearly choked on his welcome brandy.

"I could get the money for you, Mr Harrop," she said softly, "providing there is enough in the account. I dare say Mr What's-his-name at the bank will kick up a fuss but he cannot stop me. My father signed a legal document and so did I, giving me – what's the word? – power of something or other and I know he could only agree that, in this emergency, I might use this power."

She sat back in triumph and Mr Harrop could see quite clearly what it was Miss Katherine Andrews had which allowed her to get her own way as, it was said, she had done all her life.

"Happen you'd best telegraph your father, Miss Andrews,"

he said a little uncertainly. "Mr Wainwright's a bit of a . . . well, he likes things done the right way."

And so do you, Katy thought. They were all the same, of course, men! They thought they were the only ones with a brain in their head and that a woman was incapable of making any decision except what colour her drawing room curtains were to be and now look where that opinion had landed them. Now that she recalled, she had neither seen nor heard her brother about the house for over a week which was unusual, for though they rarely met he never failed to make his presence felt in some explosive way or other. She must ask the maids if his bed had been slept in and the grooms should be questioned on the whereabouts and movements of Chris's grey, Zack. In fact there were several questions which must be asked before she contacted her father but in the meanwhile she must put into some sort of order this dilemma into which it seemed her brother had tipped poor Mr Harrop.

She stood up so joyfully, so suddenly, Mr Harrop jumped and sloshed his brandy over his plain grey waistcoat but she did not appear to notice. He was struggling to his feet but she shook her head, her red-gold curls bobbing vigorously, indicating that he was to remain seated.

"No, no, Mr Harrop. Finish your brandy. Indeed help yourself to another. I won't be long. I must see to the care of my son and tell my cousin what I am about and then I will be with you directly."

"But Miss Andrews, what are you to do?"

"Now you are not to worry, Mr Harrop. We'll have this situation sorted out in no time. I will just go and speak to my cousin and the servants, then I shall put on my hat and return at once. I think we had best go in my carriage so I must ask Janet to tell my coachman to fetch it to the front door."

She smiled brilliantly. "Is it not a splendid day, Mr Harrop? I always think April is one of the loveliest months of the year, don't you?" Then she was gone with a graceful dipping of her cream silk skirt to reveal the inch or two of scarlet ruffles on her petticoat which made Mr Harrop gasp. Wait until he told Mrs Harrop that Miss Katherine Andrews wore a scarlet petticoat! No, on second thoughts, best not. Women were funny creatures and his wife might put some connotation on it that could cause no end of trouble and he was in enough of that already.

Though he protested volubly that all it needed was a note from herself, in the absence of her father, to Mr Wainwright, instructing him to transfer enough funds from the private account to the business account, she wouldn't hear of it, telling him it was no trouble, none at all, as she sat beside him on the journey to Crossclough. He could distinctly see, wherever he looked, the slack-jawed amazement of passers-by, many, of course, with whom he was acquainted, for Crossclough was a small town. Jesus Christ, what had that bloody little whippersnapper Andrews brought him to when he, John Harrop, a respected member of the community and a sidesman at the local church in Pilkington Way, should be seen riding in the same carriage as a woman who had not only lived with a man without benefit of marriage but had borne him a child.

Mr Wainwright was considerably taken aback by the unprecedented sight of Jack Andrews's harlot daughter sweeping into his office, her wide skirt held up to reveal the scarlet frills on her petticoat which matched exactly the scarlet feather on her jaunty hat. His clerks, like the good folk John Harrop had passed in the street, were open-mouthed with wonder. Strangely, it was then that John Harrop began quite to enjoy the situation, for after all there was nothing he could do but sit back and, hopefully, at the end of the day have the necessary cash put into his hands. She was a beautiful young woman and on the drive from Cloudberry End to Crossclough had chatted to him pleasantly in a way he would not have thought possible from what he had heard of her. She was bright, intelligent, even witty, and he found himself regretting the circumstances which had driven her to a point where no decent folk would so much as speak to her, let alone receive her in their homes. Her own fault, of course, but still, she would have made a fine wife for some man of business, charming them in that way a man in business needs in a wife.

"Now then, Mr Wainwright," she said briskly after they had been introduced, though naturally Mr Wainwright knew exactly who she was. He had not dealt with her himself when she came into his bank to withdraw funds for her household, leaving that to his head clerk, but he certainly knew her, as who didn't in Crossclough. "I have come here today," she went on, "to transfer enough funds from my father's private account into his business account which, Mr Harrop informs me, has been emptied. May I sit down?" For Mr Wainwright in his consternation had omitted to ask her, or Mr Harrop, to be seated.

"Oh, please do, Miss Andrews, but I'm afraid— "

"There is nothing to be afraid of, Mr Wainwright." She smiled, showing him her strong white teeth and sitting down with a flourish which allowed him another peep at her scarlet frills. "I'm sure it is a simple enough procedure which needs only my signature on a bit of paper and then Mr Harrop here" – smiling vividly in Mr Harrop's direction, a smile he found he was returning with a beaming nod of his own – "can pay my father's workers."

"Miss Andrews, you surely cannot expect me to transfer

. . . how much?" – turning to Mr Harrop who mentioned a sum – "from one of your father's accounts to another without his permission?"

"Why not, Mr Wainwright? He gave me the legal power to withdraw cash."

"For household expenses and your own allowance, Miss . . . er . . . Andrews," clearly finding it distasteful discussing with a woman, and a woman such as this one, the affairs of a client, even if the client was her father. True, she came in every week and signed her name to the papers her father had had drawn up but that was for funds which a woman, a mistress of a household, would ordinarily deal with. Not this! Not this large amount which, to his amazed disapproval, Mr Harrop seemed to connive at.

"Mr Wainwright, tell me this. Does it specify on those documents how much cash I may withdraw at one time?"

"No, but— "

"And would you agree, as a man of business, that those who are in your employ must be paid the wage they have earned?"

"Of course, but— "

"And that my father, who is a wealthy man, has put his trust in you to manage his financial affairs in his absence in a manner which is beneficial to him?"

"That is precisely why— "

"And do you think that, having given the same trust to myself as he has to my brother who, it appears, has run off with a considerable sum of money belonging to my father, which you allowed, my father will be pleased to hear that his men have refused to work until they are paid and his mill has come to a standstill because of it? Surely you, who have done business with him for so long, must know that my father would beggar himself rather than withhold the wages they have earned from his men?"

She sat upright in her chair in a way which would have gratified her mother and waited, exuding authority in a way which astonished both men.

"Miss Andrews, what you say is true. There was nothing I could do to prevent your brother from emptying the account though I protested vigorously. But your father had given him authority to do so and I had to allow it." Mr Wainwright sat back in his chair and caressed his side whiskers in a way which told this young madam there was nothing more to say on the matter.

The young madam did not agree.

"Because he is a man."

"I beg your pardon?"

"We share exactly the same right where withdrawals of cash are concerned, my brother and I, albeit from different accounts, and yet what you allowed him you will not allow me. I can only presume it is because I am a woman."

"Miss Andrews, you go too far."

"Do I indeed, but it is the truth, is it not? So all I ask of you is to show me where in my father's document it says that his daughter does not have the same entitlement to draw out cash as his son."

She lifted her head regally and Mr Harrop felt like applauding. She was a rarity indeed, was Miss Katherine Andrews, with a square set to her chin and a firmness about her full mouth which spoke of a resolve so obstinate, so bright and positive, Mr Harrop had a great deal of difficulty in restraining himself from showing the same enthusiasm. He felt himself to be magnetised by her absolute certainty that she was right and of course, she *was* right, a fact Mr Wainwright finally conceded.

"Very well, but I shall expect to have your father's written authority in my hand by the week's end, Miss Andrews, and I shall impress it upon him when I write to him," he pontificated, as he watched his clerk count out the required money into Mr Harrop's bag.

"Tell me, Mr Wainwright, when my brother emptied the business account did you not think it worth writing to my father at the time?"

She smiled in triumph, then, giving the bank manager no time to answer, swept from the bank, bestowing on each clerk at his tall desk a smile of such shimmering brightness they fell back from it, blinded by it and by something in her which looked surprisingly like intoxication.

"Well done, Miss Andrews," Mr Harrop murmured as he handed her into her carriage, smiling broadly as Mr Wilson, the hatter, walked smack into Mr Garfield, the chemist, both of them so intent on staring at himself and Miss Andrews they neither of them saw the other until it was too late.

"I am most grateful for your help," he continued, "but I think I will take a cab back to the mill. There is no need to trouble you any further."

"It is no trouble, Mr Harrop, none at all, and I insist I drive you there. I find I have a curiosity to see what goes on in that paper mill of my father's and so if you will hop up we will be on our way."

Hop up! "Miss Andrews, I cannot allow it, really I cannot. Your father would never forgive me if I were to expose you to the rough atmosphere of a working mill. There are sights to which you are not accustomed."

"Mr Harrop, you have no idea what sights I am accustomed to, really you haven't." She positively twinkled in his direction as she said it and Mr Harrop could feel the hot blood rush beneath his skin in the most appalling way as his imagination ran riot with pictures of her and Paddy Andrews. Dear God . . .

He argued with her all the way back along the road from Crossclough. When they reached the gate which led up to Cloudberry End he begged her to allow him to get down and walk the rest of the way but she merely ordered her coachman to "Drive on, Thomas", adding that, now that she had retrieved the men's wages for him she had a fancy to see, not only the men who were to be paid, but the place in which they worked.

"Have you women working there, Mr Harrop?" she asked him civilly.

"Yes, we have, but— "

"What do they do?"

"Miss Andrews . . ."

"Never mind, Mr Harrop, I shall see for myself."

When she got home Chloe was still there, sitting with Jack on her lap while she played some clapping game she was trying to teach him.

"Pat a cake, pat a cake, baker's man," she was chanting, "bake me a cake as fast as you can," holding his small, plump hands between hers, then bending her head to drop a kiss in each palm. She had recovered from the loss of her child, outwardly at least, regaining that tranquil look of composure which her husband loved and which her cousin unknowingly leaned on more and more. She was often quiet, dreaming off into some distance, but inclined now and again, particularly with Jack, into bubbling laughter. Katy knew she wanted another child. Chloe had confided as much but she had intimated that Jamie was not yet prepared to chance it.

And could she help but be glad, Katy brooded in the tossing restlessness of the dark night, that it appeared that Jamie Hutchinson was not yet making love to his wife.

But these thoughts were far from her mind as she tossed her red feathered hat on to the nursery table and began to dance round it in a lively polka, her arms about an imaginary partner. They were both laughing, Jack and Chloe, their smooth cheeks pressed together as she spoke.

"Chloe, you are not going to believe this but I have just spent the most exhilarating afternoon I can remember. It was quite wonderful and I do believe I have found exactly what I want to do with the rest of my days."

25

It appeared that young Chris Andrews was in Baden-Baden, where, it was reported in Crossclough, though they could not swear to the authenticity of it for what did they know of such things, the nobility and even royalty did their gambling.

"He's in debt, Katy. He's lost the money he withdrew from the business fund and has telegraphed begging me to let him have a draft to cover the debt. He'll never gamble again, he swears to me, if I will only help him out of this mess and I suppose, for your mother's sake, I cannot refuse but I know what I'd like to do to the young bugger."

Jack Andrews sighed heavily, doing his best to restrain his grandson from clambering up on to the table in his study and playing havoc with his inkstand and pens. The boy was sitting on Jack's lap, diverted for the past five minutes, which was the span of his baby attention, by his grandfather's solid gold watch and chain, listening with awed delight to its repeating chime and solemn tick. It was a calendar railway watch with three dials showing the date, the day and the seconds and had been bought for Jack by his wife on the occasion of their twenty-fifth wedding anniversary. It was very precious to him and his reluctance to allow young Jack to grind at it with his sharp new teeth had frustrated the baby who was now intent on targeting his lively curiosity in another direction.

"Put him on the floor, Father," Katy told him.

"And have him remove the coal from the scuttle as he did yesterday?"

"I know, he's very lively," his mother said fondly. "Never mind, I'll ring for one of your maids. Perhaps Ivy will amuse him for half an hour."

The child, who was already pulling himself up on to his brown and sturdy legs, objected at first when Ivy swooped down on him but his baby mind remembered where this smiling person came from and he was carried off to the kitchen where he would, his mother knew quite well, be completely spoiled, played with and sung to and fed Mrs Tiplady's biscuits until he was sick.

"You have heard from Mr Wainwright then?" she went on mildly, though her eyes gleamed the colour of pure malt whisky between her long, coppery eyelashes.

Jack smiled, a smile which lit up his face and made him look like the dashing young navvieman Sara Andrews had fallen in love with over thirty years ago. His grin was wide and his teeth, which were still white and sound, gleamed in the dim, wood-lined shadows of the room. His eyes narrowed and Katy felt her heart lift to see her father, on whom she had inflicted so much distress, evidently enjoying a moment of humour.

"By God, lass, you must have made an impression on the old buffer, and no mistake. Anyone'd think you'd stolen the money from him, or got it under false pretences and not only that but it was his money you'd wheedled out of him! Hell's teeth, I'd've liked to have been there, Katy." He grew serious. "You did well though and I'm grateful to you. Harrop wrote and said he couldn't have managed if you'd not stepped in like you did. And of course, you did the only thing you could in the circumstances. The men had to be paid from somewhere, surely the old fool could see that. I'm . . . grateful, Katy."

"And surprised, Father?"

"Aye, I'll not argue with that. You've not shown a great deal of sense in the past, my lass, but . . ."

"But?"

"You've . . . you seem to have made some effort to control that wild streak. Well, you'll know what I mean." His voice was gruff and he fiddled with the watch he had allowed his grandson to play with, not meeting her eyes, not wanting, she was well aware, to allow her to get under the guard he had erected around himself and her mother lest she inflict further damage on their hard-won peace of mind.

She had arrived in Scarborough earlier in the day to find her parents were out, Freda told her, and when they came home hand in hand from a walk on the long, sandy beach, her mother's uncovered hair tangled with sea-wind and sea-mist, her cheeks poppy flushed, she was glad when they showed a degree of pleasure at her arrival. Jack was kissed and admired and taken on to her mother's lap for a moment and they both agreed he was a handsome, taking little chap, though Paddy Andrews, whom he definitely favoured, was not mentioned.

It was four months since she had first come to Scarborough. She had not been back and she knew they were grateful that she had not become troublesome to them in their hard-won struggle for the peace and harmony they sought in their declining years. Knowing her impetuous, demanding nature, she was aware they were afraid she might intrude on them, constantly harangue them to forgive her, as she might once have done. Overwhelmed them with her guilt and shame, but she had gone away quietly and got on with whatever she did at Cloudberry End, causing no trouble, nor gossip, making no ripples and, surprisingly, being a big help to her father over the worrying matter of Chris and the missing money.

Now she had come again, giving Mr Wainwright time to put his "two pennorth" in, as her father said wryly, travelling with Matty as a decent woman should, to discuss it with him, though what was there to discuss now it was all over? Jack wondered.

"Have you heard from Mr Harrop again?" she went on diffidently, beginning to fiddle with the sash at her waist. She had changed into a gown of the palest yellow, soft and elegant and very feminine. She wore kid slippers dyed to match and ribbons in her hair of the same colour. She knew she looked as her mother and father had always wanted her to look, as she herself needed to look now that she was the mother of a son whom she was determined not to let suffer because of her wickedness.

She glanced up to find her father watching her with a slight air of apprehension, as though he had caught some whisper of why she was here and she was suddenly aware of how difficult this was going to be.

"No. I wrote to him and gave him this address, since I realised, after what had happened with Chris, it was foolish to allow him no contact except through you or the bank, but it seems, now that the emergency has been resolved, he has nothing further to say on the matter. Why do you ask?"

She took a deep breath.

"I . . . well, I know you will not like it, Father, but I went to the mill with him," she answered in a rush as though she must get it out before she took fright. "I wanted to see what went on there and I'm afraid I rode roughshod over his wishes so please don't blame him, but . . . well . . ." Her smile broke free, a smile like a sunburst, an explosion of light, of fireworks against a dark sky, stars glittering and flashing and her father's heart sank like a rock in deep water. Dear, dear God . . .

"I was interested, Father, and so, though I know you will not care for it, I go there for an hour or two on most days. I sit with Mr Harrop in his office and study the accounts and, well, I find it absolutely fascinating. I realise I have a lot to learn but as Chris is not in the least bit interested I thought . . . Oh, Father, unless you give your permission Mr Harrop says he cannot countenance, that is the word he used, having a woman intruding in a man's world. I took him by surprise, I think, with my curiosity and so he did not try to stop me at first, thinking, I suppose, that I would quickly lose interest but now he can see I am serious he has dug his heels in and insists that you . . . advise him on your wishes."

She was doing her best not to break out into the turmoil of excitement her visits to the Waterway Paper Mill had induced in her. The excitement the Katy Andrews she had been before the birth of her son would have engaged in but it was very hard. Her stomach was lurching in the most violent way and she could feel every breath catch like a barbed fish-hook in her chest but she did her best to remain composed. Her father was staring at her with growing horror as though he could not believe what she was asking of him and even as she watched, his head began to shake in violent denial.

"There is no one else but me, Father," she added desperately. "The boys don't care and it is hopeless with Chris, surely you know that after what has just happened. Mr Harrop says it is three months since he even showed his face at the mill."

"Are you daring to ask me if you can take his place?" her father thundered. He hit the flat of his hand violently on the desk and the inkstand jumped several inches into the air, spilling the ink.

"Yes. Yes, I am." Her voice was defiant. "It is a sound business and it would be a shame to let it run down, for it cannot be left under the leadership of a manager for ever, Father, diligent as Mr Harrop is. I would go there perhaps no more than two or three times a week, since there is Jack whom I would not like to neglect. Besides, I think it is time to face the truth which is that no matter what I do, no matter how respectable I have become, it is too late. When I go into Crossclough faces are still averted. I am a leper in their eyes, not worth a moment of their time. As for calling on me or inviting me to their homes I must face the fact it will never happen. So, I must make a life in another direction. As I said, none of the boys are concerned with 'trade' as Chris so scathingly calls it, but I mean to be. If I can find something worthwhile to do with my life and Jack's life, for it will be there for him when he is a man, then that is all I ask. I shall never marry, we both know that so I will devote myself to creating a life, a purpose for my son. I want to do it, Father. I can do it. Mr Harrop said he had never met anyone who had grasped— "

"Bugger Harrop! He had no right to take a woman into— "

"He didn't, he didn't! I forced my way in."

"Just like you have always done, Katherine. Force! You know of no other way. And just when your mother and I were beginning to think you might . . ."

"Might what? Become respectable?" Her voice was filled with painful self-mockery. "I've tried. For over six months I've tried to be what a daughter of yours should be but I find I cannot fill my days with nothing but counting the linen and discussing menus."

"You have a son. Is he not enough? Don't you realise that if you do this thing you will further jeopardise any chance he may have of a decent life among decent people?"

"Why, for God's sake, why?" she demanded passionately. "What is wrong in honest, honourable work? And don't tell me it's not for women. There are women in business. Only the other day I read of two, years ago now, who ran the North Wick Mill in Somerset, a paper mill like yours."

Suddenly, with a savage movement of his hand he capitulated, turning away from her with great bitterness.

"Very well, then, further humiliate and degrade yourself by mixing with men who are the roughest, most uncouth you will ever meet, who use language you have never before heard. But I tell you this, expect no quarter from Harrop because he will be humiliated himself when he finds he is forced to work alongside my daughter. He will take it as an insult and so will the men. They won't like it and they won't hesitate to let you know. They will make your life such a bloody misery you'll be glad to get back to your menus, believe me."

"No . . . oh, no, all I want is a chance to prove I can— "

"As you always have done, you mean? You haven't really changed, have you, Katherine? You still have that stubbornness which demands what you think you should have, no matter how it might affect those who care about you. Well, do as you like, lass. Just leave your mother in peace, that's all I ask. If Harrop will put up with it then I shan't argue. I find I care less and less about business matters. I'm a wealthy man and I have no need to work. I have a fancy to spend the years I have left in peace with your mother. We are going to travel. Through France and Germany, Switzerland and on to Italy. Did she not tell you?"

He was informing her that they were escaping again. Distancing themselves even further from the turbulence their youngest son, and now their daughter, it appeared, was again to fling them into. They had allowed themselves to believe that everything was going to be all right. That Chris was knuckling down to his position, as the owner's son, of running the small family firm of Waterway Paper Mill and that their daughter, though she would never be the proper young lady they had hoped for as she grew, and whose past would always haunt them, was at least giving the community of Crossclough no further chance to point the finger, nor to gossip about her. The dust was settling, not as neatly as they had hoped it would, but enough to be able to breathe deeply without choking on it and now, within the space of a week or two, it had all blown up again into a gigantic storm which it seemed would never be stable.

"Father . . ." Katy's voice trembled but she held herself stiffly erect. "What are you to do about Chris?"

"Fetch him back, of course. For some reason he has run off to Baden-Baden, taking a considerable sum of money with him, money which did not belong to him and which he has lost in the gambling casino . . ."

Her father's voice began to grow fainter, fading away until she could hear no more than a murmur, a murmur which needed no concentration on her part but allowed her mind to travel back to the day she had left the cottage in Woodhead and moved back to Cloudberry End. She could hear another voice, not soft and filled with resignation as her father's was, but coarse, harsh with fury and frustration.

"I'll get thi', my lass, an' that brother o' thine. I'll not forget . . ."

And they had tried, hadn't they, she was convinced of that, Josh and Jake, under Paddy's direction. They had waylaid Chris, knocking him from his mount, abandoning him at the bottom of Deep End Clough where he had almost perished in the freezing January night. He had been drunk and had fallen from his grey, or so it was said. His animal had found its way home and Saul Gibbon had discovered Chris who, though Deep End Clough was faced with jagged, bone-breaking, flesh-tearing rocks, had been found without a mark on him. The mystery of it had kept the gossips at it for weeks but no one was ever to hear the true story.

Which was what? Katy had her own opinion but Chris had had nothing to say about it, probably because he had been too drunk to know what had been done to him, or by whom, but Katy had been troubled with thoughts of the revenge Paddy had sworn he would exact, against Chris who had beaten him, against her who had caused the beating and then stolen his son.

And was it just coincidence that Paddy, who had suddenly risen from the dead, or from what must have seemed like a living death to a man such as he, could now walk upright again, could even clamber up the rough sheep tracks and trails of the moorland, and that, at the very moment Paddy was mobile again, Chris Andrews should take it into his head to steal his own father's cash and slip quietly abroad?

Was she being unbalanced? she asked herself, as her father's voice continued to rise and fall in the far reaches of her mind, or had some threat been made against her brother, one that had caused him to bolt in panic? Dear God in heaven, where was it to end? Where was the sweet and enduring strength of her love for Jamie Hutchinson, which had set off this explosive chain of events, to bring them, all of them, since it affected so many people? One event had led to another and now there was this last. Of course, Chris was a weak, wilful man, much given to self-indulgence, with an ability to avoid anything which smacked of hard work, of trade, which he despised. Even without the threat of Paddy

Andrews, which had been no real threat at all to him, he had believed, until Paddy had risen to his feet again, he would never have settled to this function, this role, this job to which she herself was so eminently suited and which had suddenly become such a fascination to her. Which she must have, even if it meant defying not only her father, but Mr Harrop, Mr Wainwright and every other damned fool man of business who got in her way.

". . . is not very far from Strasbourg," her father was saying, "and the Rhine where we mean to spend a week or two, so when I have got your mother settled I'll go and see him. Inform the young limb of Satan that unless he returns home and settles down to his work I'll not put my hand in my pocket for him again. I made an error in trusting him with the business, thinking a bit of responsibility might do him good, but I'll not do it again. Perhaps if he can't lay his hand on some cash he'll buckle down and face up to where his duty lies."

Aye, if he promises to be good and turn over a new leaf you'll give him another chance, but what about me? she thought bitterly. And it was this that hardened her resolve perhaps, or was it the thought that her father was willing to do almost anything to oblige his son, even if that son had proved a bitter disappointment, but was unwilling to give her, his daughter, a chance to do what should have been done by Chris?

"So Chris is to come home and take over again, is that it?" she asked sharply.

"I can see no other option. He'll be under Harrop's control, of course."

"I see, but what would be the point of that, Father? He will only do the same again. Go galloping off here and there with his wild, hell-raising, pedigreed friends whom he so earnestly desires to emulate. Getting up to mischief with women, gambling his money away or stealing what he can lay his hands on. The petty cash, no doubt, from Mr Harrop's desk drawer."

"Katherine." Her father stood up abruptly, pushing his chair away and striding to the window, his feet heavy on the carpet in his anger. He glared out of the window and the young gardening boy who was about to plant some bulbs in the wide bed picked up his tray and scuttled off, thinking it best to leave this part of the garden until later.

Jack Andrews gripped the windowsill until his knuckles showed white, fighting his inclination to strike out at this recalcitrant daughter of his, wondering why, since she spoke only the truth.

"It's true, Father. He stole that money. It did not belong to him and at the rate he was going, and who is to say it would ever slow down, he would bankrupt Waterway by the end of the year. With no one to care about it the mill will close down since you will be travelling with Mother and have no concern for it. Now I realise that it is only a fraction of the income you receive from the fortune you have invested and that you will still live in luxury, you and Mother."

"And you, Katy Andrews."

"Yes, and me, but what of the hundred or so men and women the mill employs? When Chris has beggared it, or Mr Harrop finds he no longer cares to accept the responsibility you have forced on him, with none of the benefits an owner might expect, what then, Father? What is to happen to them all then, Father?"

"Katy, you cannot do it, lass." Her father turned from the window, his face still flushed with his anger. His voice was pleading but already in its tone was a note of uncertainty, for he could suddenly see in her what had been in him at her age. A raw youth working on the railways; a rough navvie but with already in him the ambitious, aye, ruthless businessman he had become. He had met and loved Sara and she had become his star, leading him on to want more and more, and now his grandson, his daughter's child, was her star, her guiding light. She wanted something for him and perhaps with that inspiration to draw her on, to keep her steady, to keep her level and strong and bold, she might just achieve it.

What had he to lose? he asked himself, for he knew in his heart that his son would let it all slip through his fingers. He watched the expressions play across the lovely face of his daughter. Hope, eager hope, need, a hungry need to have some worthwhile goal in her life, excitement, anticipation in her glowing eyes, her cheeks flushed, her bright lips parted in a determined smile to let him know she would not accept defeat easily. So much in her. Such goodness and sweetness, such wild rebellion and defiance, such honesty and strength and yet a vulnerability which would make her prey to every predatory man who did business with her.

And yet . . . Dear God, dear sweet Jesus, what was he doing to her? What was he thinking of even to consider it for one moment? How would she and Chris exist together on the battleground which the mill would become? What profits would there be? And was Katy not already a pariah in her home town and would not this madness only make things worse for her?

"Father, please," she whispered, seeing the indecision in his face. "I have nothing to lose . . . please."

The men in the yard had grown accustomed in the last few weeks to seeing her canter through the open gateway and swing down from her mare. She would turn and beckon to one of the watchful small boys who hung about and who should have been at school. It was seven years since the Education Act had ordained that a school should be placed within the reach of every child in England, but until such schools were built the Act could not be made compulsory and it would be several more years before this was accomplished. Consequently, children from a young age still did work which was within their strength and one such work was running errands for the "maister" at Waterway Paper Mill. They would race one another, barefoot, cheerful ragamuffins, to hold a visitor's horse, or, in the case of the pretty young miss who had come to sit mysteriously in the maister's office, to lead her mare away to the stable at the back of the rectangular mill building. There was a man there whose job it was to look after the giant work horses which pulled the waggons carrying rolls of finished paper to customers, or brought the cotton waste, sent from the mills of Lancashire by train, from the railway station. The man would unsaddle the little mare, rub her down, give her tit-bits, petting her until her mistress called for her again.

Today Miss Andrews was dressed in an outfit of a beautiful rich shade of russet red. The material was barathea, a mixture of twilled hopsack, silk and worsted, consisting of a wide divided skirt over tight trousers and high boots and a neat little jacket which nipped her waist and clung smoothly to her high young breasts. She wore a cream stock tied about her neck, like a man's, and a wicked little cap with a peak, like a jockey's, in a velvet which exactly matched the colour of her outfit. She looked neat, businesslike, modest and yet there was something about her and her outfit that was certainly not the latter. Perhaps it was the way she walked, or held her head and her graceful back, the thrust of her full breasts or her brilliant smile as she thanked the boy who took her mare.

But whatever it was it brought the whole yard to a complete standstill until she vanished from their sight up a flight of steps which led to Mr Harrop's office. The men would sigh, not knowing they did so, some winking, or nudging one another in the way men did, as though to suggest how much better she might be employed if they had the keeping of her; then they would get on with their work, for what the maister's daughter did was nowt to do with them. It'd not last long, they told one another, just like the young master had not lasted long. Give her a week or two breathing in the reek of rotted rags, of chloride of lime; the stink of the boiling, pasting and mingling houses and all the other throat-catching aromas which hung about inside the mill like some almost visible miasma. She would soon be offended by the fine, cloying dust of the china clay, the sulphate of lime which coated her fine gown and choked her breath in her lungs and throat so that she could barely speak, gritting behind her eyelids until they were red raw. Let her get her splendid boots ruined at the "wet end" of the machine where the operatives worked barefoot and she'd soon run back to her baby and her sewing and whatever else fine ladies like her did all day long.

"Good morning, Mr Hardacre," she called out to the clerk who sat at his desk by the window of the outer office. "A fine morning, is it not? The sort of morning when one should be galloping up Spond Moor and not crouched over a desk in a stuffy office, don't you agree?"

Mr Hardacre, who had never been on a horse in his life and could think of nothing he would like less than dashing about the dangerous moorland on one, bobbed his head and thinned his already thin and disapproving lips. If that was what she would rather be doing, then why didn't she, his grim expression said, for he, at least, had no time to pander to the whims and fancies of Mr Andrews's spoiled – in more ways than one – daughter.

With another backward smile at the clerk, she knocked on Mr Harrop's door and without waiting for an answer, opened it and went inside. Mr Harrop, who had just lifted his coat tails to warm his buttocks at the glowing fire in the grate, let them drop hastily, moving to his desk, so flustered by her appearance, since he had been convinced her father would put a stop to this nonsense once and for all, he almost sat down behind it while she was still on her feet.

"Mr Harrop, good morning. No, please, do sit down. I just thought I would let you know I was here. I'm sorry I'm somewhat late but my son held me back. You know how it is." She smiled engagingly.

No, Mr Harrop didn't know how it was, for though he had three sons and four daughters of his own not one of them, at any stage of their growth, had ever held him up from his true purpose in life. His work.

He had been patient with her, prepared to put up with her for an hour or two, since she had got him out of a hole over the men's wages. He had been quite amazed at the strength of her perception, her sharp grasp, and at once, of everything he had explained to her but it would not do, not at all and surely with this visit to her father in Scarborough she would have been made to see it.

"Good morning, Miss Andrews," he answered as patiently as he could, "how pleasant to see you," treating her as though she were a casual visitor who had ridden over for the exercise. "But really, there is no need for you to abandon your son, you know. I'm sure he— "

"Oh, I have not abandoned him, Mr Harrop. I have left

him in the charge of his new nursemaid. A fine young woman who is the niece of my cook and absolutely to be trusted. They are devoted to one another already which is just as well."

"Oh, and why is that, Miss Andrews?" Beginning already to feel the first trickle of dread ice through his veins. If this young woman thought . . .

"If I am to spend part of my day here, Mr Harrop, I must have a woman I can trust implicitly to look after my child, would you not agree?"

"Miss Andrews . . ." Mr Harrop stood up as though to display his male authority, his face becoming as red as a brick, but even standing he was still shorter than she was. "Miss Andrews, I really think you should be aware that I cannot approve of your apparent determination to work in my office and I'm sure your father must agree. You have shown an aptitude, I admit, for figures and— "

"As it happens my father does not agree, Mr Harrop," she interrupted him smilingly. "I intend to do more than just work here; much, much more, with your help, of course," she added hastily. "I could not do it without you, Mr Harrop, I am well aware of that, but all mill owners have to start somewhere, don't they?"

"Mill owners?" he said faintly.

"Yes, I have the documents here, Mr Harrop. My father has made me a gift of Waterway Paper Mill, you see. I am the millmaster. In fact, the new owner. 'Sink or swim,' he said, and I have no intention of sinking."

26

Jamie Hutchinson laid a gentle hand on his wife's naked breast, cupping it, rubbing his hard palm across the almond nub of her nipple, before bending his head to take it delicately between his lips. His tongue teased it, circling the little pink bud while his hand moved to stroke her neck and shoulder, the tips of his fingers tracing her fragile collarbone. His mouth moved from one breast to the other, slowly, lingeringly, tasting, making no rough or violent gestures, his hands exploring the surface of her skin with a touch which was almost featherlike, fingers trailing from her throat between her breasts, across her concave belly to the copper fluff of curls which flowered between her legs. Inquiringly they stroked and parted the soft lips they veiled and obediently her legs opened to allow a tender finger to enter her. Jamie sighed, for instead of the moist welcome he had hoped for she was painfully dry.

Removing his hand he brought it up to cup her face and with infinite patience began again, kissing her closed eyes, the high bone of her cheek, smoothing his warm, moist lips along her hairline and down to the small shells of her ears. His tongue probed delicately and his teeth nibbled her earlobe then his mouth moved to follow the line of her jaw. He was careful to touch no part of her body which could be considered erotic or sensual, sliding his mouth and his fingers along the inside of her slender arms, the backs of her tapering legs, the arch and instep of her foot, then up her body to the nape of her neck. He loved her body with all the sweet tenderness he had in him which was endless, beginning to caress her breasts again, biting them a little, moving down from them to her belly and finally between her thighs.

"Please, oh please, go on, Jamie," she whispered. "I don't mind, really . . . please . . ." just as though she could take no more of his patient attempt to kindle her body to the flame which was consuming his. His penis was a hard rod against her thigh, painful with need and with a muttered oath he plunged it into her, his body welding itself shudderingly to hers, his head thrown back, his voice erupting into a groan which seemed to speak of deep pain.

When it was over he turned abruptly and lay with his back to her, tense and dissatisfied, she was well aware, then slowly, with a deep sigh which could have been compassion, turned back to her. He put his arms about her and she tucked her head in the hollow of his shoulder, her body curving, fitting itself against his, sighing too, for she knew she had not pleased him.

"I love you so much, Jamie," she ventured hesitantly. "You know that, don't you?"

"Yes, my little dove, I know that." His voice was infinitely tender. He pulled her closer, beginning to stroke the tangled mass of her curls which were spread across her pillow, cupping her cheek, lifting her chin so that he could kiss her but at once he sensed her withdrawal. Not distaste, never that, for she willingly nestled against him, in their bed at night, on his lap in the big rocker before the kitchen fire. There were times when he unbuttoned her bodice and fondled her naked breasts, even undressing her completely to lay her across his knee in the firelight and she made no objection, but somehow those exciting, sensual days before the loss of their child could not be recaptured. She allowed him to make love to her. She did her best to respond, he knew that, sometimes dragging her nails across the skin of his back until he flinched, in her determination to be as once she had been to him but somehow she was no longer with him, part of him, riding him to glory as he did his best to ride her.

"I'm sorry, Jamie."

"It doesn't matter, my dove. It will come back."

"You are so patient with me and yet I fail you . . ."

"No, no. Chloe, you don't fail me, never. You are my life, my heart. I live for you, you must know that." His voice was hoarse with urgency and he lifted himself on to his elbow to look down into her face. "I have loved you from that first moment on the train, remember? Your face so pale and anxious. Your eyes quite haunted with something."

"I was afraid."

"I know and I wanted to protect you from it whatever it was. I felt a great desire to make you smile, to see you free of what troubled you. To lift you up in my arms and carry you away to some safe place where I would pamper and pet you."

"Jamie, you didn't." She began to laugh, reaching with her hand to smooth back the rough shock of dark hair which fell across his forehead. Her hand lingered at his fiercely dipping eyebrows then moved down to touch a finger to his mouth. He took it between his lips, biting it gently, then bent to kiss her. Her mouth was warm, moist, parted, but she closed her eyes so that he would not see the shadow which came to muddy the clear, blue-green depths of them. She longed to be able to cling to him, her legs wrapped about his body as he plunged into her, her voice crying out in joy as once it had, but inside her that small, secret place where her baby had been shrivelled and shrank and withdrew from his male penetration, not wanting to suffer again the loss she had known.

He, who loved her, sensed it, lying back and drawing her against him, soothing her to sleep with gentle hands. For a long time after her quiet breathing told him she was deep in dreams he lay, one hand behind his head, staring at the pattern of light and dark on the ceiling, listening to the patter of the leaves of the hawthorn tree against the window and the sighing murmur of the moorland wind in the grasses. Downstairs Captain moved restlessly, padding across the flags to sniff at the bottom of the kitchen door, growling a little in his throat as a dog fox barked somewhere over the brow of the hill. There was a moon, full and white-faced, slipping in and out of cloud so thin it was like gauze, lighting the bedroom at intervals, since the curtains were undrawn and the familiar, well-polished shapes of the wardrobe and chest of drawers made shadows against the whitewashed wall. There was a pleasing scent of wild flowers, poppies, speedwell and white bryony, arranged in a plain glass jug by Chloe and placed in the low, wide, window bottom, and from downstairs the aroma of woodsmoke from the damped-down fire.

It was eight months since Chloe had lost their daughter and he wondered despairingly when she was going to recover from it. She was well, and seemed happy, singing about the place, laughing with Adah-May whom she was teaching to read, going about her household and farm work with every sign of strength and enjoyment. The same, but not the same and he could not put his finger on what it was that was wrong. She spent a couple of afternoons a week over at Cloudberry End, with Katy's approval, driving herself in the gig which

Thomas had taught her to use, then walking with Jack in his fine new perambulator in the grounds of the house, taking him up into the woodland and playing with him on the mossy floor beneath the wide canopy of summer trees. The nursemaid, Biddy, was none too pleased about it, Matty had told her son, since Jack was her charge and she resented what she saw as Mrs Hutchinson's interference, and though Matty dearly loved the sweet-faced woman who was her daughter-in-law, she really did agree with Biddy, she said. Oh no, Katy didn't mind, she knew that, hoping, as they all did, that perhaps the companionship of Jack would help to assuage the pain of her loss. And, of course, wasn't Katy consumed with her new passion to become a businessman, for God's sake, and as long as Jack was happy she didn't mind who had him. Down at the mill with her brother Chris – who put in an appearance now and then in order to give credence to his claim to be working – the pair of them locked in deadly combat, it was said, and providing her son was at the door to greet her when she came home what did it matter whose arms he was in.

Jamie shifted slightly in the bed, easing Chloe from his chest, then, when he was satisfied she was still asleep, slipping from the bed. He moved towards the window, stepping lightly, his tall, lean, naked body quite beautiful in the luminous wash of the moonlight. The fine covering of hair on his chest and belly was dark against the strange pallor of his skin, thickening into a springing bush between his thighs. His penis was not completely flaccid, indicating his lack of complete sexual fulfilment and he felt an irritated need to attend to himself as men were forced to do during long weeks at sea. Irritated and shamed, for what he had just done with Chloe was the act of a man who gratifies himself with little thought for his partner's needs. That was not true, of course, he told himself, for he had done his best to awaken desire in her but was that not because her desire pleased him?

Seating himself on the sill, his back against the frame, his knees drawn up to his chin, his arms loosely clasped about them, he stared out blindly over the deserted farmyard to the slope of the hill beyond the gate. He should be asleep. He was a farmer who must be up and about with the dawn, which came early at this time of the year, and yet he was restless and edgy, tired and yet not ready to sleep. He had made love to his wife, his beautiful, loving wife who meant all the world to him, who was his world and yet he could not quiet the turmoil which still churned at the pit of his belly. What was the matter with him? Most men would consider themselves lucky beyond words to have a lovely, compliant wife in their bed, a wife who gave herself gladly whenever she was asked, so what the bloody hell was the matter with him? What was it he sought? What was it he missed in Chloe? She was as loving, as welcoming, as affectionate, as agreeable in all matters as she had ever been but there was some unique thing lacking which he knew had been there before the child's death.

He sat for perhaps ten minutes, breathing in the scent of summer bracken and fern, of the heather and gorse which climbed the hill, the distant spice of bilberry and cloudberry which grew in the rich peat moorland. He thought he could detect the scent of his early potato crop and the ripening acres of corn he had planted in the spring. Up on the rough grazing of the moor his sheep were fattening and his first two years as a small, mixed farmer had proved successful beyond even his own hopeful dreams. He had a tiny herd of cows, Fresians, bought with the proceeds of his first year's profit which Chloe and Adah-May milked with Tommy's help, and if he sat down and compared his good fortune with a hundred other men in the valley he could only give thanks for what he had. He had been the luckiest man in the world, he told himself, on that day he had stepped down from the train at Crossclough, with Chloe beside him, his future, though he had not known it then, stretching out like a scented carpet for him to walk on, so why was he so . . . so restless, so unquiet, so jumpy about nothing? Of course the loss of their child had been a sorrow, a blow to his heart as well as Chloe's but they would survive it. They had survived it. There would be other children. It did not need passion to make a child.

Now why had he said that? he asked himself painfully, glancing across at the bed where his wife slept. She had pushed back the bedclothes and her white body gleamed like pearl against the sheet, the darkness between her parted legs a deeper shadow and he found himself drawn towards her, yearning to put his hand on her, on the secret, hidden part of her woman's body and find it wet and waiting.

With a half-strangled cry he reached for his breeches and without waiting to put on his boots ran noiselessly down the stairs and out of the cottage.

"No, not you," he snarled at the surprised dog, shutting him in the kitchen, then, pulling on his breeches, he began to run. Across the yard he went, vaulting the gate and then the wall on the other side of the track, running on his bare, calloused feet, the result of his years of going barefoot on the deck of a ship, across the rough-textured grass of the field where his herd rested. They lumbered to their feet, stumbling away from him in panic into the moon-streaked darkness. Another wall and then he was out on the open moorland, going higher and higher until his heart thundered in his chest, threatening to burst out of its cavity. Up and up, leaping small cloughs down which the everlasting water ran until he reached the top of Round Hill.

He stopped, leaning forward, his hands on his knees, his head hanging down and when she spoke his name he was not surprised, for it seemed quite natural that she should be there. As his breath quietened he could hear the quiet chomp of the mare's teeth as she tore the grass from the ground, and the chink of her bridle.

"Dear God in heaven . . . oh, dear sweet Jesus," he groaned as he tore his breeches down across his lean buttocks, delivering himself into Katy Andrews's hands with a great moan of relief.

Her body was a rich, creamy white in the strange moonshine as she divested herself of her own breeches and shirt and boots, all she had on and when he knelt over her, breathing in the warm, flowery scent of her, lost in the exciting beauty of her turbulent body, he wondered who it was who was groaning in what seemed to be agony. Her lips opened like a thirsty flower to his, her warm tongue greeting his and from both of them escaped a long, shuddering sigh as their bodies fused together, breast to breast, belly to belly, thigh to thigh. His body pierced hers at once with no attempt to woo or prepare the way, both of them mad for it, tearing and biting and scratching at one another as he sank himself so deep inside her she moaned with the pain of it. Deeper and deeper her body swallowed his, taking away his desperation, his restless and wild longings, serving him, holding, drawing him in until he thought he would die of it. It was like being flung on a wave, one of those which thundered, a wild and vivid turquoise, on to the golden beaches of the Indies where he had once sailed. He felt he was standing on the edge of a dangerous precipice, or carried away on an uncontrollable runaway horse, going faster and faster until his body was pounded beneath the wave, dived like a bird over the precipice, galloped to the edge of no world he had ever known on the horse's back. Until he had emptied into her all that seethed in him. Passion and grief and love, yes, love for this woman, he admitted it now, and guilt for his wife who lay sleeping innocently in his bed at Valley Bottom Farm.

Afterwards he held her in his arms smoothing her trembling body, for it seemed she could not control the storm of her weeping. He kissed her forehead and eyebrows and, helpless again to withstand the supple, willing loveliness of her body, cupped her breasts, his breath quickening again, feeling the rock hardness of her nipples between his fingers as she came up against him, slipping his hands to span her neat waist, the full curve of her hips, holding her buttocks, straining her to him. Her arms were tight about his neck, her mouth as hot as flame upon his and though deep somewhere in his swirling, colour-filled mind he thought he heard a soft, familiar voice cry out to him, when her hand found his penis, hard and jutting in masculine arrogance, he was lost, without sight, or hearing, or thought. She moved over every curve and crease of him, exploring his groaning flesh, tasting it, every one of her senses satisfied, every one of his answering her need, calling out his name again and again. She lay under him and upon him, rolling with him in her arms, limpet-like, across the dark, upland, tufted grass, carrying him on and on until his body was nothing but an exploding jangle of feeling, every inch of him a sensation, a tingling, a joy.

"I love you, Jamie," she breathed into his open mouth, "I love you, I love you," echoing the words his wife had said to him no more than an hour ago.

"Katy . . ."

"Please, Jamie, you cannot, must not ask me to stop. I

must say it. I have loved you, wanted you, waited for you for years and this is mine. This and this," her hand smoothing his muscled shoulders, his long hard back, his chest and his flat belly, moving to the crisp hair in which his maleness grew, feeling him tremble as she took it in her hand. "Now, here, it is mine. I know you love Chloe."

"Yes."

"And so do I."

"Katy . . ."

"No, my darling, allow me to speak. I ask nothing of you. I will take nothing of Chloe's, but please, if you care for me, about me, tell me . . . tell me so that I can treasure it. Stay with me a while, please."

"Katy . . ."

It seemed he could say nothing more, could say nothing of how he felt, about her, about this, about the singing joy which surged through him, a joy he had never before known, indeed had been unaware existed, and yet a languorous melting of his bones beckoned him to sleep, to sleep with his head on her full, ripe breast.

"What in hell's name were you doing up here?" he managed at last, feeling her beginning to shiver in his arms now that the fire of their lovemaking was burning low. He drew her close, wrapping them both in her warm cloak which was slung across the rock at their back. He knew he should leave, walk away from the temptation of her long, lithe body which was clasped tight against his, but she was glorious, her breasts big and full and tipped with rose, pressed against his chest, one long leg wrapped across his body, her hair drifting in scented disarray about his throat and mouth. He did not want to lose the feel of her, the warmth of her, the passion of her, not yet, not yet. Just another moment was all he asked for.

"I might ask you the same," she answered, her breath warm on his chest, hardening his nipples and causing his own breath to flutter in his throat. God, he was ready for her again, this wonderful, sensuous woman who had been, not very long ago, the wilful young girl whom he had thought of as nothing but a bloody nuisance.

"I couldn't sleep. I thought a run, but you haven't answered my question." His hand took her breast and he heard the indrawn gasp of her breath.

"Which was?" she managed to say.

"What are you doing up here at this time of night?"

"I often come up here."

"Well, you shouldn't. You don't know who you might come across."

"That's true." He felt her smile against his chest and his arms tightened about her. She was brave and bold was Katy Andrews, funny and bright and she caused a pain in him he found hard to describe.

"I'll take you home," he said gruffly.

"Oh, don't be so bloody silly, Jamie. I ride these moors day and night on my own and will come to no harm. This is my favourite place. It's sheltered from the wind and on a summer's day, or evening, is as warm and secluded as one's own bedroom. I ride up almost every night when Jack's in bed."

She was telling him that this, if he wanted it, would always be here for him. There was no need for words now. He knew her, knew of her love for him, her passion which would never end and which, always, before and after this, belonged to no other man but him. She was his, if he wanted her. She belonged to Jamie Hutchinson. She was his woman.

She sat up and the cloak slipped away from her. His eyes dropped to the soft weight of her breasts as they fell forward.

The clouds raced across the blue-black night, leaving the moon unclothed, like the woman, filling the hollow in which they lay with a milky white radiance, coating her body in a silvery pearl which was quite breathtaking. He reached out, mesmerised, laying his hands on her throat, sliding them down to cup her breasts, leaning to take first one into his mouth and then the other until she purred like a cat. Her back arched, her legs fell open and he took her again, covering her mouth with his, gagging her cries as she called out his name to the lustrous moon.

The dawn was breaking, a sliver of apricot showing above the line of Bleaklow Hill when he slipped, shivering a little, into the warm space beside his wife. She murmured in her sleep, uttering what seemed to be a gurgling laugh, then turned to him, throwing an arm across his familiar chest. Her breath was sweet and soft and so was her cheek as she pressed it against his shoulder and his heart was filled to bursting point with his love for her. He lifted his arm, drawing her gently against him and with a little sigh she settled. He held her, this precious woman, this vulnerable precious woman and he felt the pain tear at him, split him, rip him apart, for could a man love two women at once? He had not meant to make love to Katy, nor to dishonour her, if that was the word, for she was a woman worthy of any man's love. A woman not to be taken lightly to satisfy a man's appetite and it was not like that. They had come together like two stars on a converging course, bound to collide, not planning what they had done but bewitched by it just the same. For that, he supposed, they could be forgiven since they had not intentionally set out to hurt Chloe.

But if he went again! If he slipped from his bed on another night when his restless, dissatisfied body took him from his wife's side. If, knowing she was up there waiting for him, he sought out Katy Andrews, then he, and Katy, would do his wife a wrong which could never be pardoned. By Chloe, or by himself.

For three weeks he made love to his wife with an urgency, a frequency which alarmed her. She did not question it, or his almost feverish need to have her constantly near him, coming down the hill to the farmhouse at any time of the day on any pretext, putting his arms about her, clinging to her, kissing her even in front of Adah-May who was horribly embarrassed by it all. Chloe did not know what it was that troubled him unless it was a desperate need to get her pregnant again and though she herself shrank from it since she did not think she could bear the pain of loss again, should it happen, she submitted to it as lovingly and as willingly as she could.

"Is our Jamie all right?" his mother asked diffidently on the day she came over to Valley Bottom Farm to help Chloe preserve the plums which had multipled on the tree growing on the sunny side of the farmhouse. Its branches hung low with rich, ripe fruit which Adah-May had picked and washed and in the dairy the clean stone jars stood waiting. Water was boiling in the kitchen range and rounds of paper over which they would pour melted mutton suet were cut in readiness for sealing the jars. The plums would make a welcome change throughout the winter when fresh fruit was impossible to come by. They had already preserved pears and apricots, bought cheaply in the market at Crossclough and Chloe's preserve cupboard stood neat and almost full, waiting for this last batch.

"Yes, why do you ask?" Chloe blushed deeply, her breath catching in her throat, for how could she reveal to her husband's mother Jamie's passionate need of her these last few weeks? How could any woman say to another that her husband's attentions, dearly as she loved him, were . . . well, not becoming tiresome, for that smacked of some rift in their marriage, but were performed in the manner of an automaton. It was as though he were using his skills as a lover to coax her to act in a certain way which apparently was lacking. There was an almost desperate appeal in him which demanded something of her she could not, as yet, give him. She needed time. How much? a voice inside her asked, for it was August now and her miscarriage had taken place last October.

Only think, that voice which whispered in her head, whispered now. If she had lived, that sweet, small girl, she would have been ten months . . . No, no, *no*, she would not let it in, that thought. She would welcome Jamie's body into hers and soon she would have another child, a little girl like the tightly furled bud who had not been allowed to flower, who had never breathed, or smiled, or clasped her hand as young Jack Andrews did.

He loved her that night and she took him into her with love, closing her eyes as his body pounded out some message hers could not understand.

She woke in the night and he was not there, probably gone to the privy at the far end of the yard. She sighed a little as she turned her face to the open window. He would return soon, she told herself and she would make love to him as once she had done, but when he came she had fallen asleep again.

27

Even above the din of the beating room you could hear them arguing. The huge, oval tubs in which all the ingredients for the making of paper were mixed, the revolving horizontal roll set with knives so that it resembled a paddle wheel; the constant clack of wheels and pulleys, straps and wires, all made a stridency which assaulted the brain and deafened the ears, but the men were used to it, cheerfully shouting to one another above the tumult, and they had also become used to the constant bickering which went on between the new maister and her brother.

They were standing face to face, almost nose to nose beside the pile of bulging sacks containing china clay, two of which were open, spilling their pure white contents on to the stone-flagged floor. It was as though a light flurry of fine snow had fallen, powdering the area about the sacks, clinging to Chris Andrews's highly polished black boots and to the expensive, well-fitting, dark grey trousers he wore. It drifted as some vagrant draught caught it, floating to settle on the fine cut of his matching grey frock-coat and pale lemon waistcoat and the men about the vats nudged one another, grinning as the young dandy fastidiously brushed the china clay from his sleeve.

The men could not hear the actual words of the exchange above the clatter of the machines but at one point they were convinced that young Master Andrews was about to strike his sister and they all held their breath in delighted fascination. They looked very much alike in their fury, the red-hot flush of temper beneath their fine, creamy, pale skins, their eyes, though of a different colour, narrowed and dangerous, like two cats who have met in an alley. They almost appeared to be arching their backs and spitting, as alley cats do, their hands turned into claws, ready to do one another a mischief and, as Ned Coleman said to Bert Garvey, he almost fell into his bloody vat he was so intent on watching the pair of them squaring up to one another. The new owner stamped her foot and a little puff of china clay rose to eddy about the already liberally coated hem of her plain, coffee-coloured skirt.

Lately, as though to parallel her new position as mill owner, Miss Andrews had taken to driving to the mill in her father's carriage. She often took papers, files, ledgers home with her to study in the evening and it was awkward carrying them on her mare. Consequently she was dressed in the fashion of a young lady of position, smart and up to the minute in her sheath-like skirt, discarding the small train which would have made it unsuitable for the exigencies of her working day. The skirt was short by the standards of the day, the hem two inches from the ground, revealing the fine bones of her slim ankle and her shoes, coloured to match her skirt, worn with matching stockings and laced over with a tongue. She wore a jacket bodice and under that a tight, buttoned waistcoat of a shade several shades deeper than her skirt and top. At her neck was a creamy stock, tied like a man's. She looked businesslike but still decidedly female, for the outfit clung to her full breasts, her neat waist and curving hips, and everywhere she went heads turned to look at her.

And she went everywhere. It was five months since

the explosion of incredulous outrage that had rocked the community of Crossclough, rippling out from her father's paper mill, sweeping the length of the Longdendale Valley, up to the small town then on west into Lancashire and east into Yorkshire. Men who bought her father's fine writing paper and bond paper, wrapping paper and the paper on which newspapers were printed were aghast, for how were they to deal with a woman, a young and beautiful woman, they had heard, with a reputation which did not bear thinking about? Perhaps, they asked one another, it would be possible to ignore her, despite her ownership of the mill, for Mr Harrop was still manager, they had been told, and all they had to do was to state that they would much prefer to conduct their business with him.

But it was the actual inhabitants of the town itself and its outlying districts who were turned on their collective ears when the news reached them that the Waterway Paper Mill was now in the hands of the disgraced "scarlet woman" of Crossclough, a gift from her poor father who must surely be off his head. The whisper that his son had run off with the firm's funds had gone from house to house, farm to farm and cottage to cottage and they were not unduly surprised, since the lad had owed money to every wine merchant and tailor and bootmaker in Crossclough and was it not just like him to take to his heels across the Channel when they began to press him?

But still, a son was a son and though he would rather be a young squireen, riding to hounds and shooting grouse and pheasant at the right season, his father, as manufacturing fathers did with their sons, would have soon licked him into shape, surely?

The tales about Katy Andrews and her absolute determination to run the paper mill exactly to her own requirements, which were many and varied, it seemed, flowed into Crossclough like the myriad, fast-moving streams which sparkled down the cloughs to the reservoir. She had taken over her father's old office which he had furnished in the style of his study at home. It had gas lights on the wall, since the windows were small but there was an oil lamp with an independent cylindrical reservoir feeding the wick on the big, leather-topped desk, providing a good light for studying the numerous accounts, ledgers and invoices which Mr Harrop reluctantly thumped in front of her.

The walls of the office were lined with softly glowing wood. There were several pictures of stern, bewhiskered gentlemen hung on them, presumably of the previous owners, a deep and comfortable leather chair in which Mr Harrop often found her with her feet curled up beneath her, and a good fire burning in the black-leaded grate. Her father, having a fancy for the small luxuries to which he was accustomed in his own home, had arranged a glass domed clock on the mantelshelf, a couple of Dresden vases and a globe set in brass on a table beneath the window. There was a decent carpet patterned in rich shades of red and green and, on the desk, a matching pair of silver and brass cheroot and match holders with distinctive eagle claw feet. A handsome military chest, the drawers of which were stuffed with papers relating to his business, stood against the wall.

She loved it. She would enter her office at just after nine in the morning, later than Mr Harrop since she liked to organise her son's day before she left. She would smile and incline her head towards the grim-faced Mr Hardacre, telling him what a lovely day it was, what a wet day it was, what a cold day it was, though he could see it for himself, he brooded sourly, cursing the day Mr Andrews had put his good, sound business into the hands of this silly female.

She would take off her hat then move slowly round her desk, savouring it, letting her senses enjoy the anticipation of sitting down behind it, of placing her hands on the soft, dark green leather of its top, before ringing the bell to summon Mr Harrop and all the papers necessary for the day's business. He would sit opposite her, his face surly, doing his best to be polite since she was the owner. He was inclined to be patronising as he opened the company's books, or handed her the weekly reports, the audits compiled by Mr Hardacre, who knew a great deal more about paper-making than she did, the accounts and wages books.

"This letter came from Birkenshaws," he would say, letting her make of it what she would, no longer the tolerant, grateful gentleman who had been willing to indulge her whim in the weeks following Chris's disappearance with the firm's cash. He knew the letter would make no sense to her, for how was she to differentiate between "long elephants", "small hands" and "grocery papers"? But Katy was not too proud or foolish to ask, and once he had explained what their size and purpose was, she did not need telling again, he'd give her that. Her mind clung like a terrier's to the facts and figures he poured into it, a sponge which would never be saturated, a jug which would never be full, but when she made it clear she meant to speak to every man and woman in her employ since she paid their wages; that she intended scrutinising every job, every small cog that made up the machine which was the manufacture of paper; that she wanted to see it, hear it and understand it, he was mortified, insulted as her father had told her he would be. It was bad enough having her poking her nose into every damned drawer and every paper that drawer contained in the office, where at least she was out of sight, but to contemplate striding about the bleaching room, the beating room and along the path of the great white ribbon on the paper-making machine, the drying room and on to the cutting room was quite out of the question, he told her bluntly.

She took no notice, of course, since Katy Andrews meant to burrow into the mind of every man and woman who worked at the Waterway Paper Mill, including Mr Hardacre's for it was only in this way, since Mr Harrop was so reluctant to part with information, that she would learn the running of the business. And, she told herself bravely, if he refused to fit in with her, and not the other way around, then she would fire him and employ another manager.

The thought of the power she had took her breath away in much the same fashion it had done when she had her first sight of the magnificent Fourdrinier paper-making machine, various modifications of which produced different papers. It was a miracle of man's inventive mind, her father had told her and now that she had seen it she knew the reason why.

Her only problem, she told herself, since she was confident that she would soon become an accepted and familiar figure in the mill, was her brother Chris. He had swaggered home a week or two after her father had paid his debts, leaving him only the necessary cash for his journey, yelling at the front door of Cloudberry End to Janet to get someone to carry his bags in and fetch him some hot water, since he was to change and be off out within the hour.

Katy, since it was a Sunday, had been in the nursery with Jack and at the impatient sound of her brother's voice she moved along the upstairs hallway to his room.

"Aah, so Father persuaded you home then?" she enquired casually, leaning on the door frame, her arms crossed over her breasts.

"Oh, you're still in residence, are you?" he answered shortly. "And yes, it seems he did for I am here," not looking at her as he threw open his portmanteau and shook out a jacket. "Where's that bloody girl?" he went on, more to himself than her. "This jacket needs pressing before I can wear it."

"You're off again, I take it? May one ask where?"

"No, one bloody well may not, since what I do is none of your concern."

"Is that so?" the anger snapping through her. "Well, perhaps when you come home drunk at three o'clock in the morning and cannot get out of your bed the next day I shall make it my concern since I employ you."

He turned then and began to laugh. "Dear God, girl, do you honestly believe I intend to work for you in that God-forsaken place of Father's?"

"Mine, brother, and you have no say in the matter. It is my mill and I am the master there, a fact you had best get used to. You had your chance and you threw it away and so you are answerable to me."

"Oh please, let us keep this within the realms of sanity. If Father wishes to play his little games then that is up to him but as I couldn't work there, or chose not to work there when I had nobody but old Harrop to nag at me, are you such a fool as to imagine I would do it for you? Sweet Jesus, even I know more than you do about making paper and that's not saying much. Oh, I'll show my face often enough to placate Father and make sure of my allowance but as for working there, forget it. Now, if you don't mind, I've things to do before I go and meet my friends."

"Would those be the friends who helped you beat Paddy Andrews to a bloody pulp?"

He hesitated then, his face set, turning a little paler, she thought.

"What if they are?"

"And are you to make further plans to deal with him as you did before, now that he's up on his feet again and you can no longer run away with the firm's money?"

"Really, Katy, you talk a load of drivel."

"Is it? Is it drivel, or has Paddy made threats against you?"

"What could that cripple do to me, for God's sake?" His voice was contemptuous but he appeared uneasy.

"Nothing, if you keep out of his way but he's a devil when he's crossed, Chris."

"Well, you should know, my pet, since there's no one more intimate with him than you."

"You're a bastard, Chris Andrews," she said, smiling pleasantly, "but you are a bastard who is now working for me and unless I get my money's worth I shall fire you and we'll see if Father feels like paying you your allowance then."

He turned up on most days and on others simply vanished, slipping off, she supposed, with his friends on a bit of shooting, and once, when the hunting season began, vanishing for a whole week. He was often pale and tense and she knew he was suffering from the effects of a night's drinking but she turned a blind eye, unconcerned with his absences since it meant an avoidance of the inevitable arguments and she had enough of those with Mr Harrop.

The business flourished, still run by Mr Harrop while Katy moved quietly about, picking every man's brains who would speak to her, which was most of them for they could hardly turn their back on the one who paid their wages. They let her see, many of them, that they thought she should be at home with her child and her sewing. They had no need of her, for it had all gone smoothly under Mr Harrop's guidance.

They were not to know that though the mill did not need her, she needed the mill.

Mr Harrop blocked her way at every turn. There was this foolish idea of hers that they should begin to import timber and adapt their machines to the making of wood pulp, and he was against it, for what was wrong with esparto grass, or even rags and cotton waste for that matter?

"It's out of date or will be soon, that's why, and it is costly to process, owing to the large quantities of chemicals that are needed for treatment purposes," she answered tartly.

If he was surprised at the amount of knowledge she had stored in her brain in five short months he did not show it.

"And the grass has to be brought all the way from Tunisia so why not fetch timber instead?" she continued. "Now I want you to go to Liverpool and find out what is being brought in."

"Liverpool! You mean I am to stroll about the docks and buttonhole every docker I meet as to the whereabouts of— "

"Of course not. There will be timber merchants, importers, and you have only to find out who they are. Believe me, if I could go myself, I would."

"Aah, so you admit it is no place for a woman?"

"I admit to nothing, Mr Harrop and I will do it if I have to. It seems to me that if we can find out who is importing timber, or more importantly turning it into wood pulp, or even if the wood pulp is being introduced directly into the country, then we should be halfway towards our goal."

"It is too soon," Mr Harrop said stubbornly.

"It is over thirty years since that chap in Germany, I forget his name, patented a method of preparing pulp from wood, Mr Harrop. He ground it by mechanical means, I believe, and six years later paper was made from ground wood on a commercial scale. Thirty years, Mr Harrop, and you are telling me it is too soon."

Again, if he was surprised by her grasp of the paper-making industry, he did not let her see it, his irritation at being told his business by this damned headstrong girl almost too much for him.

"Miss Andrews, I cannot— "

But her enthusiasm for this new method of manufacturing paper, which as yet was in its infancy, fired her on and she would not let him continue.

"And what about those two fellows in America? In 1854 they patented a method of making pulp from wood by treatment with caustic soda and there are other treatments."

"I have heard of them, Miss Andrews, but— "

"Chemical treatments in use right now for producing good-quality cellulose from wood. The sulphite process, it is called. Oh yes, I have read about it quite extensively. My father was interested, you see, being a forward-looking man," implying that Mr Harrop was not, "and his papers on the subject are in those drawers. We cannot be left behind, Mr Harrop. Think of the vast resources of timber in the world."

"Aye, and the difficulties which still exist in turning it into pulp."

"Oh please, Mr Harrop, don't be such a fuddy-duddy. We must keep up with the times."

She did not mean to be rude but Mr Harrop took instant offence. A slip of a girl in the business no more than five minutes telling him, who had worked in it all his life, what he should be doing! It was intolerable.

His head snapped sharply and his face became a bright, beetroot red, his expression one which his wife and children would have recognised at once. His hand went to his collar as though it were choking him and he stood up with a movement which would have had his family cowering in their chairs.

It did not frighten Katy Andrews who in the past months had begun to grow in confidence, in her control of herself, in her knowledge of her own clever mind, which was as sharp, as quick, quicker, than this man's and many of the men with whom they did business. All she required was experience. She had the rest.

She needed him though. She needed him until those very men had become accustomed to the brutal fact that she was the master here, the decision-maker and that business was to be done with her.

"I'm sorry, Mr Harrop," she told him gently. "That was unpardonably rude of me."

Mr Harrop sat down abruptly since this was his office they were in and slowly his dangerous colour died away. He was not at all sure what to make of this lovely, self-possessed young woman who had risen, phoenix-like, from the ashes of the wild hoyden who had once been Jack Andrews's daughter. Still was, of course, but something, presumably her fascination with her father's mill, *her* mill, damn it, had altered her, but surely it could not only be that?

She rose to her feet and smiled, murmuring that she would speak to him later. He watched her swaying back as she moved towards his office door then let out his breath on an explosive sigh which he was not sure was relief, anger, or a male's admiration for a beautiful woman.

The men in the beating room watched her come from Mr Harrop's office, eyeing her splendid figure as she strode between the enormous vats, wondering, like the man whose office she had just left, what it was that was different about her lately. It couldn't be all down to the satisfaction she seemed to find in her new career as millmaster, surely, for what was there about it to put that sheen of glowing burned honey and polished amber in her skin, of rosy, bursting vitality in her long-striding, straight-backed figure? Her hips and buttocks in her tight, sheath-like skirt rolled boisterously and her breasts moved enticingly as though they were unfettered beneath her jacket. Her hair seemed to be lit with fire and her eyes, narrowed and slumbrous, were deep with some apparently golden secret she was keeping to herself.

She smiled a lot and was often heard to laugh outright, usually when she was in the room where the women sorted the rags and flax and hemp, the linen and cotton waste which Mr Harrop was determined to continue using and which came every day in great waggon-loads from the cotton towns of Lancashire. She seemed to find some affinity with the women and, against Mr Harrop's wishes, since it could only cut their profit, he snapped at her, had devised ways to make their days easier. She employed one of them, an older "sorter" who was "none too clever on her pins" though the woman would have admitted it to no one, for jobs were hard to come by, particularly at her age. A small room was furnished where the women, on a rota basis, might stop work for ten minutes morning and afternoon and drink a cup of the decent tea the woman provided.

The men had been astounded, and affronted, but when she had offered them the same service they had refused her as she had known they would. What did they want with a bloody cup of tea and a gossip, they muttered, but at least it had been offered. Her wages were good, that's all that mattered and, as many of the women in the rag sorting room were their own wives, they were mollified.

Aye, the talk of the valley was Katy Andrews with her

new ideas, which soon got round as these things do, and her liberal fancies for the comfort of her female workers, who were mothers, many of them, but, unlike her who had servants to wait on her hand and foot at the end of the day, went home to scrubbing and washing and ironing and the care of perhaps half a dozen young children.

She was happy. She had never been so happy, so gloriously alive and glowing with an inner fulfilment which had begun two months ago on Round Hill when Jamie had come to her one silvered moonlit night. She had ridden up there each night after that, leaning her patient back against one of the outcropping rocks which grew out of the rough turf and which had sheltered them on that first night, waiting, her face quite expressionless, her eyes unblinking as they tried to part the veil of darkness which hid him, the darkness which would, she knew without doubt, bring him back to her. There had been something more between them than mere physical need, her body knew that at once. It was wrong, completely wrong, with no good in it for anyone, no justification for what they had done. She was aware that no matter how much she loved him he could, in the end, only do her harm. And Chloe. She should not be here, waiting in the secret hollow on the top of the hill. It was madness but she was possessed by her own need and capacity to love only this one man and she would wait here until he came.

It was three weeks before he did, tearing at her clothing with no tender gestures, no gentleness and she did not require it. There was an urgency in them that nailed their naked bodies together, an urgent need to possess and be possessed, her body wanting his, wanting to be crushed and hurt as he claimed her. Gasping and clutching and biting and then a fierce penetration that split her asunder, invaded her, enraptured her, terrified and thrilled her at the same time, leaving her docile and bemused. His!

Two months, and in that time he had come to her four times and on the fourth time his voice had called out her name as he came shudderingly to the climax of his endeavour.

"Katy . . . aah, Katy, I love you, girl."

It was enough. It was everything, and only on the days when she came face to face with her cousin Chloe, which was several times a week, did her heart die a little. This was adultery, which seemed a silly word, for what she was doing to Chloe was nothing short of murder but how could she stop? Only the night before she had cradled Jamie's dark head against her breast, holding it there with strong, possessive arms, kissing his tumbled hair with a fierceness which was ready to fight and kick and scream to protect what was hers, which was little enough. And when she smiled at Chloe who had come to ask if she might take Katy's son down to the station to see the trains, with Thomas driving the gig, naturally, since Chloe would have her hands full with the active little boy, how could she refuse? Jack was fifteen months old now, a tumble-legged, darting, inquisitive handful who must be watched over every minute of the day, for his fertile mind encouraged him to investigate everything in this fascinating world, from the taste of soil to the lethal clippers Angus used on the hedges. Chloe adored him and though sometimes Katy felt a small, guilty dart of jealousy when she saw the way her son ran into Chloe's arms she put it from her in the knowledge that what Chloe took from her, she took a hundredfold from Chloe.

"Of course you may," she had answered, turning a false smile into a genuine one, since she felt a great deal of affection for her cousin. "It will give me a chance for a good gallop up on Spond Moor."

She sighed, then shook her head as Chloe looked at her questioningly. She had been wondering what she and Jamie would do when the dark cold of winter came to the peaks, which would not be long now but she could not allow her thoughts to be voiced to Jamie's wife. Already it was bitter when they lay naked together under the warm lined cloaks they took up with them and soon their meetings would be impossible. She had not spoken to Jamie about it for it was too new, too fragile, too precious, this loveliness between them and she hardly dared to press him on how it was to continue during the winter months.

"Oh, it's the approach of winter that makes me despondent, cousin, nothing more. At this time of year, for an hour, I can ride out when Jack is in bed but it will soon be possible on Sunday only and I'm keen to get Jack started on his first pony."

"Oh, darling, not yet. He is so small."

"I began at eighteen months or so, cousin," doing her best not to be irritated by Chloe's protective attitude towards the boy who was Katy's son after all.

It was a glorious autumn day when Storm picked her way delicately up the rocky track leading towards Luds Leap and the great sweep of wildly rolling moorland beyond. There was a wind blowing, beginning to have an edge to it and the leaves beneath the trees she had passed through were thick and crisp, richly golden and tawny on the ground. There were fir cones and pine cones and windblown branches to be jumped, but when she reached the top of the track Katy reined in the mare to look down to the neat pattern of green and brown fields in the valley. She could see men, tiny and slow-moving, working on the harvested corn and one of them, she knew, was Jamie.

She sat for a long moment, her leg in its tight breeches bent across the pommel, her elbow on her knee, then with a click of her tongue and a nudge with her heels she moved Storm on, into a trot, a canter, a gallop, on and on into the teeth of the wind across the tufted upland grass of Spond Moor.

There was a clump of gorse, waist high and thick, ahead of her. She slowed down, to a canter, a trot, then a walk and when Paddy Andrews rose up from behind it, grinning broadly, she allowed him to catch the mare's bridle in her heart-stopping terror.

28

Storm reared and bucked, rolling her eyes and flaring her nostrils. Her ears flattened in terror and she whickered shrilly in the back of her throat. Katy did her best to control her, to drag her out of Paddy's strong hands, to hang on herself but Paddy kept on laughing and hauling on the reins and, as the mare's fear grew and she plunged more and more frantically Katy felt the strength go from her hands, and from her thighs which did their best to grip the mare and with a despairing cry she fell from Storm's back.

At once Paddy let the animal go, laughing exultantly with no need of the shooing gestures he aimed at her with his hands as she raced off in the direction of Rakes Moss.

Katy had landed on her back, sprawling awkwardly with her legs flung apart, completely winded, white-faced and blinded by her hair which had torn loose. She was dazed. The sky at the back of Paddy's head was whirling round and round and she thought she might be sick, but Paddy's mocking face and air of triumph, which seemed to be telling her that he had always known he would win, stiffened her spine and brought her to a sitting position where she remained for a moment. She thought it might be a good idea not to be too eager to get to her feet just yet, since there was every possibility she might fall down, or be knocked down again by the man who grinned at her derisively, so she sat quite still, her arms round her bent knees, doing, she realised, what an animal which is cornered will do, which was to remain as quiet as possible.

"Well, well, well, will yer look what's fallen inter Paddy's little trap?" he said softly. "I bin watchin' thi' fer weeks now, girl, just waiting fer thi' ter ride my way. They do say as 'ow if tha're patient enough tha'll get what tha' wants in't th'end, an' by God, it's true. I've thought o' nowt else ever since last January when I medd up me mind ter walk again, did tha' know that, lass? I've dreamed o' this moment, times, an' now it's 'ere an' I mean ter enjoy every bloody minute. I don't rightly know what I mean ter do wi' thi', after I've 'ad me cock in thee, that is. I'll 'ave ter decide then, won't I, but in't meanwhile we'll 'ave them britches off thi' sharpish. Let's see if thee an' me're as good as we were together afore our Jack were born, shall we?"

She felt able to get to her feet now. She was in terrible danger here, certainly of rape, possibly of murder, for Paddy would never forgive her for her desertion of him and her abduction of his son. He was strong again, and mobile, it seemed, for it was miles from Woodhead and he could only have walked up here. All she had was her cunning mind, her wit which was sharper, clearer than his, and her two good legs. Storm had vanished, not, she prayed, into Rakes Moss, please God, which was nothing but a quaking, spongy bog which would swallow her in a moment, but gone just the same and it was up to Katy Andrews to get herself out of this perilous situation.

With one part of her mind she could hear the calling of sheep from higher up the moor and across the sky at Paddy's back lapwings floated like large snowflakes and peewits wheeled and tumbled. Why, she wondered, again with that layer of her brain which seemed another part of her, is our attention captured by small, inconsequential things when all we should be considering is the danger in which we are trapped? The spicy aroma of the dying gorse bushes in which Paddy had hidden was sharp and pleasant in her nostrils and yet she was convinced she could smell her own desperate fear. She was not going to let Paddy Andrews see it though. She dusted her hands on the seat of her breeches and attempted a careless smile. Paddy was no more than three feet away from her, his eyes narrowed and gleaming, alert, balanced as he used to be balanced when he fought in the ring, ready to dart in any direction which was to his advantage, his hands formed into loose fists.

"You look well, Paddy," she told him, her tone conversational as though they were two acquaintances who had bumped into one another on the pavement in Crossclough. But for the short peg of wood which emerged from the bottom of his left trouser leg he was exactly as she remembered him two years ago. It was quite incredible that this lithe and handsome man had been hidden for so long in the bloated tub of lard which had sprawled in a wheelchair drinking himself to death in the cottage at Woodhead. He was bronzed, his skin firm and freshly shaved. His hair was a tumble of dark, glossy curls over his eyebrows and his eyes were a deep, untroubled copper brown, the whites clear and healthy.

He grinned amiably, pleased with what he thought was her admiration, his teeth which had started to rot the only part of him he had been unable to restore, those and his leg, of course. She marvelled as her eyes ran over him how he had managed to bring himself back to this.

As though he read her thoughts he squared his shoulders and arrogantly threw out his chest. He preened, almost like a girl in her first ballgown, prepared to let her get a good look at him before he threw her down and did what he had come to do. He'll flex his muscles next, she thought, ready to be hysterical, fighting her need to laugh in his face, longing to make a dash for it but knowing his reflexes were – had been – like lightning. His hand would shoot out, grasping her wrist before she had barely moved and she must keep these three feet between them for as long as she could.

She was helped by his own need to play cat and mouse with her and that was all to the good for she wanted to lull his senses, keep him talking, playing for time until the right moment came.

"I know 'ow ter train fer a fight, Coppertop," he said, "an' though it were bloody 'ard, once I medd me mind up to it I wouldn't be beaten. Just like I wouldn't be beaten in't ring. I cut out the drink an' set messen on a diet what an old trainer once told me about. Them fancy pugilists up in London an' such don't keep fit on batter puddin's an' suet dumplin's. Meat an' veg, and stuff what don't fill thi' but don't put no weight on neither. An' I exercised. Jesus, it were 'ard at first."

A thoughtful look of remembered pain crossed his face and had it not been for the purpose of his endeavours she had it in her to admire him. A strong will and a strong constitution Paddy Andrews had which, in nine months, had changed him from a grossly overweight cripple in a wheelchair into this well-muscled, well-proportioned and handsome man who looked like a gypsy with his brown skin and eyes, his dark hair and audacious grin.

"Oh aye, I got messen back ter condition, Coppertop. Me an' me alone, fer them cousins o' mine don't like movin' their fat arses unless it's ter't Queen's Head in Crossclough. I walk fer miles an' I swim in't reservoir an' it were all fer one thing an' I reckon tha' knows what that is. I medd a mistake wi' that soft prick of a brother o' thine. I left it ter Josh an' Jake the first time. Chuck 'im in Deep End Clough, I ses, but they'd no stomach fer it, them two, so what they do?" He went on contemptuously, "They only bloody leave 'im at bottom, thinkin' he'd turn up 'is toes quite nicely wi' no blood on their 'ands. Second time it were my fault an' I should've known better. Me what's trapped rabbits ever since I were a nipper. I were on't track up by Saltersbrook when he come ridin' by on that there grey of 'is an' instead o' lyin' low I tried ter catch 'im. Course, I couldn't . . ." His face twisted at the bitter memory. "An' he were warned then, weren't he? Took off like some frightened lass ter France or somewhere, they said, but he's back now an' I'll 'ave 'im one day, tell 'im. He'll turn 'is back fer a minute when he's on't road ter them grand friends of 'is, an' I'll 'ave 'im."

"Paddy, surely now that you are yourself again, could you not leave it all behind?" She was talking nonsense, she knew it. Talking for talking's sake and she was not surprised when he began to laugh.

"Yer what? Leave it all be'ind? Like I left me bloody leg, yer mean? Coppertop, I might look all right ter thee, aye, an' to other women an' all, 'cause I can tekk me pick again now, but I'm not. Not in 'ere."

He thumped his teeth with what seemed like despair and his teeth bared in a snarl.

"I can't fight no more, tha' see. I'm twenty-two years old an' I can do nowt what I used ter. Oh, I can tekk a woman an' I'll show thi' 'ow in a minnit, an' father another brat but I can't do what were in me blood. I were good, a bloody good fighter an' I'd 'ave gone far. 'Ad a go at championship, but that's all finished. So, I've ter find summat else ter fill me days an' I've a fancy to 'ave thi' an't lad wi' me again, Coppertop. Thee an' me were good together so 'ow about it?"

She did her best not to let her revulsion show, arranging her face into what she hoped was a pleasant smile.

"Look, Paddy, if I were to give you some money, enough to set you up in a business, perhaps in America where your brothers are, would you not consider it? You could make a decent life, marry, have children."

It was a mistake to mention children. His face darkened and became suffused with red rage.

"That's another bloody thing, an' all. I seen that woman, that cousin o' thine an' if tha' want ter work at that bloody mill, well, suit thissen, but I mean to 'ave my lad wi' me."

"Over my dead body," she hissed. She lifted her lips in a snarl of pure female rage, the rage of a mother in defence of her young, ready to leap for him, for his eyes, for any part of him which might hurt, preferably in his trousers, for any part of him which might disarm him for a minute, but some instinct, some primeval instinct inherited from the women who had gone before, surfaced to her inflamed mind, calming it, telling her to keep away from him for it was only thus could she escape him.

"That could be arranged, Coppertop," he said softly, dropping into the stance she had seen him take up in the prize fighting ring. It was the moment. He had had enough of talking, of boasting, of showing off to her the marvel of his recovery and was ready for action.

Katy glared at him, but he began to grin even more broadly as anticipation flooded his body and swelled the crotch of his trousers into a bulge of enormous proportions.

She tried not to let him see which way she was going to move, feinting a little, first one way then the other but he was too quick for her, too experienced. His hard, calloused hand shot out and gripped her wrist, a vice-like grip which no power on earth could loosen. He dragged her to him, his other arm going about her waist and his mouth fastened on hers before she had time to turn her head away. His teeth sank into her bottom lip and she tasted blood, then, letting her mouth go for a second, he slapped her hard across the face, ordering her in an icy voice to be still. Her cheek burned and her eyes watered. She could feel the blood trickle down her chin and terror trickle through her veins. He would not just rape her, she knew that. She had scorned him, hurt him in a way a man such as he could not cope with and it would be so easy to throw her body, when he had finished with it, naturally, into some quaking morass where it would vanish for ever. Storm might get home. They would search for her but would not be surprised when they could not find her, for more than one careless wayfarer had vanished in these bog-ridden uplands.

His free hand fastened in the front of her shirt and with a grunt of pleasure he tore it open, freeing her breasts which swelled into his cruel hand.

"By Christ, tha're better than ever, Coppertop," he muttered hoarsely. "That's right, lass, struggle. I like it when tha' struggle, and now them britches."

His hand left her breasts and he hooked his thumb in the waistband of her tight breeches, forcing them down over her hips and buttocks. His fingers dug into her thighs, doing his best to wrench them apart, then fumbled between her bared legs.

"That's it . . . that's it," he kept saying as they swayed together in a ridiculous dance of lust, but he had made the mistake of not laying her down before removing her breeches, of being too sure of himself on his wooden leg, and before he could steady himself again she forced her own strong leg between his, twisting it out and round his peg, wrenching it from under him and pushing him violently at the same time.

Caught off balance he did what she had prayed he would do. It is instinct to put out a hand when you overbalance and are about to fall and Paddy did just that. He put out both hands, for a man with one leg does not have the same automatic manoeuvrability as a man with two. He crashed on to his back and in a second Katy had lurched away from him, her breeches still about her knees, four, six, ten feet away from him until there was enough of a gap to prevent him reaching her, pulling at her breeches, struggling to get them up again, using both hands now, for what did it matter that her breasts were still exposed.

"You bitch," he screamed, lifting every bird for miles around. "I'll kill you for this, I'll kill you."

"You'll have to catch me first, Paddy Andrews," she taunted him, her fear gone, hopping about from foot to foot, widening the distance between them until her breeches were up round her waist.

"And don't think I won't. Tha'll not be shut o' me, my girl, never. Wherever tha' go . . . up 'ere . . . I'll find thi' an' when I do I'll 'urt thi' in a way tha've not dreamed of."

He was on his feet now, staggering towards her, surprisingly nimble but she danced further away, light as a feather, free and exhilarated with it, for she knew he could never hope to reach her now. He was shaking with rage and frustration as she moved backwards, her hair a living flame about her face, her eyes glaring from beneath it.

"No, I don't think so, Paddy, for I'll have every man in the valley looking for you before nightfall when I tell them what you tried to do to me."

"Give over! Who the 'ell cares what 'appens to a piece like thee, Katy Andrews. Tha' were my woman once an tha've a bairn ter prove it."

"The police will be called."

"Oh aye, an' 'ow are they ter search the whole of the bloody moor, tell me that."

"Don't go back to the cottage, Paddy, I'm warning you. I'll have it boarded up and though, as you point out, I may be nothing in this community, my father is a respected man and has influence. You've threatened my son, his grandson and you'll not be safe in this valley if you show your face again. I'll have you hounded."

She was beginning to shake now, for though she had managed to outwit him she had been badly frightened. He had stopped moving towards her, standing quietly with a menace which was even more terrifying than his livid fury. He made no attempt to follow her as she turned in the direction of her home, watching her go. She could feel his eyes in the middle of her back, like a knife, and she wanted to keep turning round all the way down the track just to convince herself that he wasn't there, behind her, but she resisted it, holding her head high, holding her torn shirt across her breasts, though there was no one to see her except some sad-faced sheep.

She began to cry when she reached Luds Leap, the tears blinding her so that she could barely see the shifting stones of the clough which led down from it. She floundered through the tumbling water, careless of her boots, ricking her ankle, hardly noticing the pain but by the time she had reached the stable yard at Cloudberry End she was in control of herself.

"Miss Katy . . . Dear Lord, what's 'appened to yer?" Dicken was aghast, dropping the tangle of harness in his hands and running across the yard towards her. Jimmy appeared from the tack room, his pipe drooping from his slack lips and old Noah heaved himself to his feet from where he had been enjoying the last bit of warm sunshine trapped against the stable block wall. They all three eyed the tattered remains of her shirt which was gaping immodestly despite her attempts to hold it together, then hastily averted their eyes from the inordinate amount of naked flesh that was revealed. What in the name of God had she been up to now? their combined expressions asked, for no matter how she seemed to have settled down to motherhood, to the running of the mill, which she was making a decent fist of, they'd heard, and her determined effort to be a worthwhile mistress of Cloudberry End, they could never quite believe she would not suddenly revert to the wild, uncontrollable girl they remembered only too well.

"I'm all right, really I am, Dicken, so don't fuss." She pushed her way through them, for they were inclined to crowd about her, continuing to stride towards the gate which led to the kitchen yard and the back door. Her breeches were stained. Her hair was flung about like that of a mad woman and she had what Dicken was convinced was the beginning of a corker of a black eye but she managed a smile somehow.

"Wheer's Storm, Miss Katy?" hardly liking to bother her, the state she was in but his concern, not only for her but for her handsome little mare, could not be suppressed.

"I don't know, Dicken. I . . . I came off her on Spond Moor and she . . . galloped off."

"Galloped off!" Dicken was clearly astonished for if there was one thing Storm could be relied on not to do that was to bolt like some wild, untried animal. Highly strung she might be, expensively bred but he had taught her himself to be as obedient as a well-brought-up child, to stand like a rock, and he had often said, fondly, that you could lead her on a bit of thread she was so sweet-natured. Unless she was frightened!

"What 'appened, Miss Katy?" he asked, almost accusingly. "Did she tekk fright or summat?"

"Yes, yes that was it. She took fright, threw me and raced off towards . . ."

"Aye?"

"Towards Rakes Moss."

"Jesus." The three men exchanged horrified glances, for everyone who lived in these parts knew the menace of Rakes Moss.

"She'll come home, Dicken. She won't get into the bog. She knows the moors as well as I do and she'll find her way home."

"Aye." The men sighed, relieved, for what Miss Katy said was true. Dicken had taught Miss Katy, and the mare, the ways of the bleak, inhospitable uplands and Storm would find her way home.

"I must go and tidy myself," their young mistress said vaguely, moving, now she was home and safe, in a somewhat erratic fashion towards the kitchen door. The men watched her go, then, without a word, wandered across to the gate, leaning on it side by side, shading their eyes to gaze up at the peaks where one of their "flock", one of their own, was lost.

"Shall us go an' look fer 'er?" Jimmy ventured anxiously.

"Give 'er 'alf an 'our, lad, then if she's not back thee an' me'll tekk Hal an' Jenny an' go an' fetch 'er 'ome."

The servants in the kitchen, as women do, were more inclined to shriek and drop things when their young mistress walked in on them in her wild and dishevelled state, but Mrs Kelsall, who had controlled three times as many as this lot in her day with no more than the raising of her hand, soon restored order. Like the grooms she knew something . . . well, unusual had happened to Miss Katy but the girl was in a shocked state and did not need histrionics.

"I came off my mare, Mrs Kelsall," she said, her eyes

wavering in the most odd way, "but I'm not hurt at all. Now I'd be obliged if one of you," turning appealingly to the circle of sympathetic faces, "would run up to the nursery and check on my son. At once please."

"Master Jack?" Mrs Kelsall was perplexed.

"Yes, who else, and at once." Her voice rose to a pitch Mrs Kelsall thought might be hysteria but she did her best to get her young mistress to sit down and drink the nice cup of tea Lottie was fetching her. Master Jack was out in the garden with Mrs Hutchinson, she said and—

"Oh, Jesus . . . Jesus . . ." They cowered back, Lottie dropping the nice cup of tea with a crash which made Dilly squeal like a stuck pig. Even Mrs Kelsall recoiled from the shrieking, shaking, leaping dervish their mistress had turned into, their hands to their mouths in horror, their kind faces appalled and bewildered, for what could be wrong? Mrs Hutchinson regularly took young Master Jack for a walk in the grounds and on up into the woods which surrounded the house. Biddy had just gone back up to the nursery, grumbling that she had nothing to do half the time with the little lad off somewhere with Mrs Hutchinson, but expecting him back any minute for his midday meal and afternoon nap, she said.

"Miss Katy, dear God in heaven, what?"

"Run, Lottie, Janet, and you, Mabel." They were trained to obey an order instantly and they began to mill about, making little runs here and there but not knowing where they were suppose to run to, or what they were to do when they got there. "Quick, tell Mrs Hutchinson to bring him back."

"Back, Miss Katy?"

"Find him, for Christ's sake, find him. I'll go up to the wood while you look in the . . . in the garden and shrubbery.

Oh, for God's sake, split up, don't all go together and look everywhere."

"Oh, my Lord, Miss Katy, lass, don't get upset. Mrs Hutchinson will be back soon. There's no need to . . ." Mrs Kelsall nearly said "go off at half cock" but it was not the kind of remark one made to one's employer, was it? Really, what was up with the lass? How had she got herself into this deranged state? Her bosom was practically on view for anyone to look at and young Chuckie's eyes were out on stalks. The sooner they got her out of the kitchen and in her own room the better. Lottie and Janet would see to her. Get her undressed and into a hot bath, perhaps even a little sip of brandy to calm her, though Jess Kelsall was aware that ladies did not normally drink spirits. Just this once wouldn't harm her, would it? she asked herself as she tried to catch the whirlwind which was her young mistress. Tearing across the kitchen she was, dragging the bewildered Janet with her, screaming at the open-mouthed Chuckie to run to the stables and get the grooms and what the hell did Mabel, who had come to a full stop in her confusion, think she was doing standing there like a bloody brick wall when she had been specifically told to run out and look for Jack.

"Katy. Katy, darling, what is it? What's the matter? Oh, dear Lord, what has happened to you? Here, Janet, hold Jack, will you? Oh, Katy, what has been done to you?"

Chloe was there in the doorway which led into the hall, advancing towards her, her face creased with concern, her arms, now that she had safely deposited a wide-eyed Jack into Janet's care, outstretched to Katy, but Katy ignored her. Her face broke up and tears seemed to come from every pore and crease of her flesh, simply flooding it as her distraught arms reached out for her son, seizing him from Janet with a force which nearly knocked the girl to the floor. The child began to wail, for this demented woman who crushed him to her, though she looked like his mama, did not seem like his mama. He struggled and all the women about the room longed to snatch him away, soothe him, pet him, tell him his mama was not well, but she held him to her, her arms wrapped tight about him, her face buried in his neck as he strained away from her.

"Katy, don't . . . he's frightened."

"Don't touch him, he's mine, all I care about."

"I know, darling, but you must not alarm him so. Give him to Janet who will take him to the nursery and you and I will go to your room and you shall tell me what happened."

"Nothing . . . nothing happened. I fell off my mare . . ." for somehow, she didn't know why, she could not bring herself to mention Paddy Andrews's name in front of all these gawping maidservants. She felt dirty . . . perhaps when she had had a bath . . .

As though she had caught her thoughts Chloe said, "Then you need a bath, a change of clothing."

"Oh, Chloe . . . Chloe."

"I know, sweetheart, I know." Chloe sensed the utter terror in her cousin and though she had no idea what had caused it she was prepared to let Katy tell her when she was ready. "You are tired and hurt but you are safe now and so is Jack."

Safe from what? the expressions on the faces of the astonished servants had time to register as their mistress became calmer.

"I'm sorry . . . oh, I'm sorry, baby." She let the fear, the pain, the rigid tension slip completely away from her, turning the child in her arms, kissing him gently, smiling, smoothing his hair from his face, kissing him again until he recognised his real mama. "There, that's better. Silly Mama, getting so upset. I must have bumped my head when I fell from my horse. Silly Mama fell from Storm's back, darling . . . silly Mama."

They all began to smile and sag with relief, still not knowing what the fuss had all been about, but recognising that there had been some dreadful demon inside their young mistress. A demon which had terrified her, and them and her son but it was gone now, whatever it was. Mrs Hutchinson would see to her in that tranquil way she had. Biddy would tend to the boy and Mrs Hutchinson, who was the sweetest, most tender-hearted woman any of them had ever known, bless her, would see to Miss Katy. She would bring peace and serenity to this house which was often so sadly short of it.

29

It was one of the hardest winters anyone could remember in the Longdendale Valley. Snow began to fall just after Christmas, a violent maelstrom of air sweeping across the dark uplands and peaks, throwing up great drifts of banked snow against walls and gates and the sides of unprotected cottages and farmhouses, gathering and growing until it reached the eaves of some roofs and at its lowest was no less than four feet.

"It'll not be the last," Mabel, who had been born in a cottage up Barmings way, retorted darkly. "It'll get worse afore it gets better."

"Don't talk daft, girl," Mrs Kelsall said firmly. Mrs Kelsall had lived on the Lancashire side of the Pennines most of her life, the west Lancashire side where the air was somewhat gentler and had not yet been privy to a blizzard such as the one which blew vigorously down the backbone of England, from the Lake District to the Derbyshire Peaks. She had seen snow, naturally, but nothing like the stuff which, overnight, isolated not only Cloudberry End from Crossclough where Mrs Kelsall ordered all her provisions, but her kitchen from the stable block which was no more than a hundred yards away. When she opened her kitchen door she was vastly put out to find a wall, waist high, barring her progress, stretching in a featureless white expanse as far as her eye could see, which was to the gate which led into the stable yard. Young Chuckie, though, had thought it was marvellous, offering to make her a path through the yard to the stables.

"Lad, what do I want to get to the stables for, tell me that, and if they want to get here," which of course they did since her kitchen was where the food was, "they must dig their own path. Now, get on with them potatoes, if you please, for the mistress'll want dinner on the table just the same, snow or no snow."

Of course Miss Katy, like them all, was snowbound for several days, unable to get down the driveway, let alone struggle along the bottom road to the mill. It snowed again, and then again, blinding snow which obliterated the peaks in a white, ferociously moving curtain and everyone who was forced to go out in it came back with the stuff frozen on to their clothes and eyelashes, floundering about like blank-faced snowmen at the kitchen door, needing the giggling help of the maidservants and the implements with which they beat the carpets to remove it.

Katy fretted about the house, wondering out loud how she was to get that order to Birkenshaws by the weekend as she had promised and what shape her waggon horses were in, for if she could not get down to the mill, could Harry Ellison whose job it was to stable and feed them?

And where in hell's name had her brother got to since before Christmas? Not a word, not a message, but then had she expected anything else? she asked herself. As he had said he would, he showed his face at the mill enough times to support his claim that he worked there and for the rest she supposed he went about with Johnny Ashwell and Tim Warren, doing with them what young gentlemen of their class did. Presumably he had spent Christmas at Ashwell Hall, riding to hounds on Boxing Day, shooting and gambling and raising hell and would drift back when the snow had melted.

Nothing had been seen or heard of Paddy Andrews since the day he had caught her up on Spond Moor last October. He had simply vanished, taking his dog with him, and though the constable in Crossclough had assured Miss Andrews and her cousin Mrs Hutchinson when they made the complaint, respectfully, of course, since they were related to one of the most powerful men in the community, that he would certainly keep a look out for him, would even pass it on to other divisions of the police force since a man with one leg would not be hard to spot, there was not a lot more he could do. The man had not hurt her, had he? the constable had asked delicately, believing in his own private thoughts that a woman such as this one could not be hurt. Yes, a threat was a serious thing and if she had a witness . . . yes, he knew it had happened up on the moor but . . . well. Of course, he agreed it would be a good idea to board up her grandmother's cottage in Woodhead and he'd certainly keep an eye on it and she must be sure to let him know at once if her cousin, Paddy Andrews, her attacker, was sighted anywhere near her home.

Storm had returned later that day, whinnying her delight to be safe home, petted and cossetted and treated like a lost child who has returned by the three grooms and by Katy herself, who by then was calm, bathed, brushed and had been cossetted herself.

She had not seen Jamie alone for weeks. Once they had managed an hour in a crumbling sheepfold up through Pasture Wood by Rollick Stones but it had not been satisfactory since the cold had penetrated the very bones of them and all they could do was huddle together and try to keep warm. Without the feverish passion of their lovemaking to take away their senses, they had both been aware that their guilt at what they did to Chloe was ready to overwhelm them and it would not take much to persuade Jamie that the enormity of the crime they committed against her cousin, his wife, could not be continued.

"I love her, you know," he told Katy abruptly, not wanting to hurt her in any way but compelled to ensure that she knew the truth.

"Yes, I know, my love, I know," her own voice heavy with sadness, for he was telling her that there would never be anything but this for them. That Chloe was his wife, the woman he had chosen and that he would never abandon her. Katy knew it but it made no difference to her need for him. She was famished, thirsty, in pain without him, her heart beating, or so it seemed, more sluggishly in the hours which did not contain him. His image was the first one she saw each morning and her last thought was of him at night before she slept. To get through the winter was all she could think about and then, with the long days, the mellow nights ahead of them when spring came, they would recapture the enchantment of those first weeks on Round Hill. Perhaps, in the meanwhile, they could find somewhere. If she could manage it, holding the thought of it tenderly like some precious child, they might use some sheltered, private corner of the mill in which to have an hour or two alone. It would at least be out of the bitter winter weather and, after all, she had the keys.

Not yet, though, since she was not certain Jamie would agree to it. He was still in the first, guilt-ridden torment of longing for her, bewitched by her body and what it did to his but was not yet ready to speak of the future, of future meetings and where they might be and she was afraid to seem too eager for fear he would recoil from it. The meeting on the moor had been spontaneous, unplanned, but to slip down to the mill, unlock doors furtively, smacked somehow of deceit, intrigue, degrading, and though she was prepared to do anything to keep him, did he feel the same way? She was not sure she wanted to put it to the test.

The snow lasted for a week and in the first few days of January began to melt in the sudden milder weather. Clouds were thin, streaking the pale blue sky and the hurrying tumble of water could be heard once more. The sun shone and the far carrying, musical whistle of the teal fluted across the valley. It would come again, the snow. Again and probably again before spring arrived but it was grand to be able to step outside your own kitchen door again, Mrs Kelsall told Chuckie as she set him to sweeping the yard and the last remnants of the slush which hung about at the base of the walls.

"That there Biddy's got an awful cold, Mrs Kelsall," Janet was heard to say, indiscreetly Mrs Kelsall was inclined to think, for Miss Katy and Mrs Hutchinson were in the hall and heard the housemaid say it as she closed the green baize door which separated it from the kitchen.

"That's got nothing to do with you, Janet," Mrs Kelsall said sharply, but of course the pair of them were up the stairs like two birds in flight but with only one nestling between them. Mrs Kelsall often wondered which of them loved that little chap the most and was often surprised at the way Miss Katy let Mrs Hutchinson remove the boy, whisking him away to play in the garden as though he were her own. You'd think Mrs Hutchinson, who was, after all, a farmer's wife, would have enough to do about her own kitchen and dairy, wouldn't you? She had that girl to help her but even so all the farmers' wives Mrs Kelsall had known had been at it from cockcrow to sunset. Her husband spoiled her, and so did that mother-in-law of hers, but as she'd said before and would say again, it was nobody's business but theirs. Still the little mite should be with his nursemaid, or his mama, in her opinion, though you couldn't fault Mrs Hutchinson in the way she cared for him, but a child needed stability, a bit of discipline which he didn't get in this household of women. Miss Katy kept saying she was going to put Master Jack up on his first pony since he was eighteen months old now but she'd not done so yet.

Biddy sniffled and snuffled her way up to her room on the top floor, protesting volubly since it was only a head cold and Master Jack was a strong, healthy little chap who never ailed a day. Nevertheless she promised to stay in bed if Mrs Hutchinson insisted, wondering, like Mrs Kelsall, why Miss Katy allowed her cousin such free rein in what was, after all, Miss Katy's house and with Miss Katy's son. Still, they were cousins, so perhaps that was why, watching from her dormer window as her mistress and her mistress's cousin, with Master Jack on her lap, set off down the drive in the little gig with Miss Katy at the reins.

The man watched as the two women drove up the track, keeping in the shadows, his hand on the dog's head to ensure he would not make a noise. He had seen the brothers set off an hour ago, their own young dog at their heels, both of them carrying a shepherd's crook, both of them warmly wrapped up as though they meant to go above the snow line which still lay at a thousand feet, about halfway up the Black Hill. They would be searching for sheep that might have wandered off the safer pastures and would not be back for hours.

The girl, big lump of a thing an' all, was tied up securely in the dairy with one of her own dishclouts stuffed in her mouth and would cause no trouble for a while. He'd be away in half an hour, anyroad.

"I'll be back before dark, Chloe," he heard Katy say. "Thomas will fetch me in the carriage. Now are you absolutely sure you can manage? You won't be able to get far without his perambulator and you know how active he is."

"Oh, go on, Katy. You know we'll be fine. I'll take him for a walk round the farm and he can come to no harm."

"I know. I've put his boots in his bag."

"Good, and then he can have his lunch and a nap, can't you, sweetheart? Now give Mama a kiss and then you and I will go and see the chickens. Oh, Lord, he's off already and he hasn't got his boots on."

There was the sound of laughter and the high, delighted squeal of the child and the dog pricked his ears and snuffled a bit, wanting to growl a warning, but his master kept a hand across his broad muzzle, muffling the sound.

"Where's Adah-May, Chloe?" Katy called as she carefully manoeuvred the horse and gig to face in the other direction, a difficult task on the narrow track.

"She'll be in the dairy. No, darling, don't stamp in that puddle until Aunty Chloe has put your boots on. Now wave to Mama."

The child did so, then turned obediently towards the farmhouse, holding Chloe's hand with perfect trust.

"We'll have a warm drink first, I think, darling, and you shall have one of Aunty Chloe's gingerbread men. I made them especially for you, did you know that?" she was saying as she opened the door, guiding the child's feet across the threshold, smiling down at him as she closed the door behind them.

The boy saw the man first, his eyes round and dark in his rosy face and he pointed his plump finger as though to draw her attention to the visitor.

"What . . .?" That was the only word she got out, then he was upon her, shoving her fiercely to one side so that she fell heavily between the chair and the table. He was snarling a little in his haste as he picked up the startled child.

"I'll 'ave that an' all," he said, grabbing at the bag in her hand, since the conversation he had overheard in the gig had led him to believe that there were spare duds for the boy in it and he'd be needing them where he was going. He'd have to be quick, for the boat left Liverpool tomorrow.

"Right," he went on, "I'll be off wi' me son, then. Tell that bitch I've gorrim, will tha', an' that 'e'll 'ave a good 'ome wi' me."

She was stunned. Her head had hit the table as she went down. It had all happened so quickly she couldn't seem to get her bearings or drag her dazed wits about her, but the last words brought her round as though a bucket of ice-cold water had been dashed over her.

She leaped to her feet with the speed and grace of a cat, a she-cat defending her young, for mixed inextricably in Chloe Hutchinson's mind was the confusing belief that Jack was *her* child and not Katy's. Not all the time, of course, but when he was with her, when she had him all to herself she had begun to pretend that he was hers.

She began to scream and in the dairy Adah-May's eyes bulged and her face sweated a beetroot red as she strained against the washing line with which the man had tied her up.

"No . . . no . . . put him down," Chloe shrieked, leaping at Paddy Andrews's back and fastening her slender arms about his throat like the paralysing tendrils of ivy which grew up the wall outside. Enraged by the attack on his master the dog sank his teeth into her ankle, drawing blood, but she merely shook him off and the dog, old now and past such things and having done his duty, slunk to Paddy's side.

The boy began to wail, struggling in the strong grip of his father, his face crimson, his mouth opened wide to reveal his little baby teeth, his eyes spurting tears of terror.

Paddy quivered, amazed that this fragile-looking woman could be so strong, but of course she was no match for him, nobody was. The dog had given her a fair nip an' all but it didn't seem as though it was going to stop her, the silly cow. He didn't want to hurt her. She was nothing to him. She'd done him no harm, though he remembered she'd given him a bit of lip on that day she'd come down to Woodhead. Spirited little thing she was, and Paddy admired spirit.

He reached up and prised her arms loose, shaking her off much as she had done with his dog, flinging her back towards the rocking chair where she sat down heavily, but like a rubber ball she bounced out of it, hurling towards him at the speed and with the same ferocity as one of them bloody trains which roared through Crossclough Station.

"Give . . . him . . . to . . . me . . ." she panted, doing her best to snatch the screaming, terrified boy from his arms, kicking and biting and scratching and all the while his bloody dog would keep barking and it was all beginning to get on Paddy's overstretched nerves. He'd have to shut her up, get her off him or he'd never get away before her husband got back. He was sorry, really he was, because he didn't want to hurt anyone, only Katy. That was where his bitter rancour was directed. Not even at Chris Andrews who had crippled him, but at her who had humiliated him. It was she he was punishing by taking the boy. Besides, he was his son and he'd a right to him, hadn't he? As much right as her. A handsome lad, he'd thought proudly as he'd watched him toddle across the yard, a proper lad an' all, stamping in them puddles, and he'd fetch him up right in America.

First the woman though.

"Look," he said, his voice reasonable. "I don't want to 'ave ter tie thi' up but I will. I'm tekkin 'im . . ."

"No . . . oh, no . . . no, I won't let you. Please give him to me."

"Yer can't stop me, lass. He's mine."

"No, no, he's not. He's mine."

"Yourn?" Paddy looked puzzled for a moment but he had no time to be arguing.

"Yes. Oh please, don't hurt him."

"Nay, I don't mean to 'urt 'im, lass. Not me own son, but tha've got ter stop interferin' wi' me or I'll 'urt thi'."

"No, give him to me," and she launched herself against him with such force he almost fell over.

"Oh, fer Christ's sake, woman." He'd tried to be patient, to explain to her what he was doing and why he was doing it, but she'd not heed him and so he did the only thing left to him. Lifting his hand, he hit her with the back of it, snapping her head on her neck with such force her hair fell in a wildly flying swirl about her face. The blow split her cheek to the bone, knocking her across the room and she lay where she had fallen.

He waited a moment to see if she would get up again then, when she remained where his hard fist had flung her, he called to his frantically barking dog and, shouldering the bag, he hitched the crying child closer to his chest, opened the door and set off towards the small stand of trees which bordered the bottom road by the reservoir.

He avoided the track, keeping out of sight of the road until he reached a point where it zigzagged between Torside and Rhodeswood reservoirs. He crossed it hurriedly, intending to make his way across Peak Naze Moor to Hadfield where he would catch the train to Manchester, changing there for Liverpool. He'd get lost there in those crowds, as he had done for the past three months. He'd have to dirty the boy up a bit, for he'd stand out like a sore thumb in his fancy outfit but that was no problem.

There was a small sound behind him. A chink of stone on stone and when he turned round she was there. There was blood pouring down her face on to her cloak which was still tied about her shoulders. Her hair was drifting in a great coppery cloud about her head and down her back. The ground was heavy with the thawed snow and her little feet, clad only in thin kid shoes since she had travelled in the gig, sank into it, already as wet as though she had waded through a stream. Her ankle, where the dog had mauled her, was torn and bloody.

She stopped when he did, making no attempt to go for him as she had done before, merely standing, like a pale wounded animal, her eyes unblinking and fastened on the child who was hiccupping in deep distress on Paddy's shoulder. He had gone past the stage of frightened weeping, retreating, as children do, into the quiet, shocked state that is nature's protection.

"Give him to me, please," she said softly, holding out her arms. The boy saw her and raised his in a gesture which was heart-rending.

Paddy felt his temper flare and race through him like a flame through dry wood.

"Now look 'ere, tha' daft cow, if yer don't leave me alone I'll 'ave ter give thi' a clout that'll knock thi' out, see. I can do it, believe me."

"If you can reach me," she answered, in much the same tone Katy Andrews had used to him three months ago. Her eyes dropped to his wooden peg and Paddy was incensed, since he knew what she said was true. He could manage well enough on the often steep and craggy tracks he walked and clambered over, providing he could go at his own speed, pick the spot where he placed his right foot and, more carefully, his wooden peg. His left leg had been removed above the knee and the well-crafted but unjointed piece of wood on which he balanced so adroitly was stiff and awkward. There was no possible way he could reach anyone who was determined to keep out of his way and this lass knew it.

He'd not be bested though!

"Why, yer bloody fool, d'yer think I'd let this stop me?" he roared, hitting his left leg. "If I catch 'old o' thi' I'll kill thi', I'm warnin' thi'."

"I know that, Mr Andrews. That's why I'm keeping away from you but I mean to follow wherever you go and you can't stop me, so won't you put Jack down and just go? I won't tell anyone about this, I promise you, but please, give me my boy."

"My boy, yer daft sow, an' yer can go ter buggery. I'm off, an' if yer keep after me I'll set me dog on yer again."

"I'll take that chance, Mr Andrews, for I'll not leave that baby in your care. Wherever you go so shall I."

"Damn thi' ter hell, woman." His voice was hoarse with his frustrated fury, for how the devil was he to get across the moor with her on his heels and, more to the point, when he reached Hadfield how was he to get himself and the lad on to a train to Manchester? Once they had reached a town, anywhere where there were people, she'd only to scream out that he was pinching her bairn, not even that, for with a face on her like she had every able-bodied man in sight would rush to help her.

Well, he'd just have to lose her, that's all. His threat to set his dog on her was no more than that really for the poor old bugger could hardly walk, let alone charge at anyone with a pair of nimble legs on them and had only got her last time because she was hanging on to himself. There was something wrong with his rear end which manifested itself in a most disgusting way and Paddy was doubtful he would get him across Pike Naze Moor, never mind the train to Liverpool and the boat to America. He'd have left him with Josh and Jake but they'd only neglect the poor old sod and he'd been a loyal and trusted . . . well, friend to Paddy, the only one he'd ever had really.

"Suit thissen," he said curtly, calling up his dog and turning in the direction of the moor. It was just two thirty but the midwinter darkness was already beginning to fall.

"Take me up to the farm, Thomas, will you? Chloe has Jack and I promised I'd pick him up before dark."

"We'd best look sharp then, lass. I doubt I'll get carriage up that track, an' if I'm not mistaken theer's goner be a heavy frost ternight. It'll already be slippy up theer."

"Yes, then let's get on, shall we? You can wait for me on the road at the bottom of the track. It won't take me long to walk up there and get Jack."

The journey to Valley Bottom Farm did not take long. It was half past four but already the clear, frosted night was upon them and the winter stars were rising. They were bright for they had not yet reached their aloof suspension in mid-heaven, resembling a scattering of pin-heads on the purple-blue velvet of a pincushion. Though Katy was wrapped about with warm rugs and even a hot brick at her feet provided by the grateful little woman in the "tea room", as the equally grateful women rag sorters called it, she could feel the cold penetrate her bones and catch her lungs and her breath was a thick vapour about her head. The ground was iron hard, the horses straining up the hill, the panting of their chests and the creaking of their harness the only sound in the icy air.

As she struggled up the frozen track, slipping a time or two, refusing Thomas's offer to go for her, since Jamie might be there and just a glimpse, a word, a smile would be a crumb to feed the hunger of her longing, she was surprised to see the windows of the farmhouse were not lit. What was Chloe up to? Had she fallen asleep by her own hearth, Katy's child in her arms, the pair of them warm and dreaming in the peace of her kitchen? If that was so it meant Jamie was not yet home from wherever he had spent his day, probably up in the pasture checking on his small flock, or searching for a lost ewe which had not the sense to stay where it was safe.

Realising sadly that she was not to see Jamie, Katy felt a heavy pang of disappointment as she struggled with the gate to the yard which had become frozen to its hinges. She cursed fluently, ready to swear at whoever had left it closed, but as she turned from it she was brought to a paralysed halt and her heart was squeezed by a grip so strong she thought she might fall over.

The farmhouse door stood wide open, just as though someone had gone through it at great speed with no thought of closing it behind them to contain its warmth. The icy hand gripped her even more agonisingly and she wanted to scream out to Chloe but she could force no sound to her frozen throat.

But even though her heart already knew what had happened her mind refused to function and she stood for ten long seconds staring stupidly at the open door. What? . . . what? . . . what? her brain kept repeating, though of course her mother's heart knew.

"Chloe . . . Chloe . . . Jack?" she began to babble, tripping over the hem of her gown, despite its shortness, as she flung herself towards the open doorway.

"Chloe . . . Chloe, for God's sake, cousin, don't tease me, don't do this to me . . . please, oh please." She knew she was gibbering like one of those monkeys she had seen in the zoo as a child, for one part of her brain which still operated coolly at some basic level knew quite well that Chloe was incapable of playing such a cruel trick. The kitchen fire was still in, though it was obvious no one had replenished it for many hours and its sluggish light revealed no unusual disturbance, nothing out of place but . . . oh Jesus . . . oh sweet Jesus . . . where?

She began to scream then, knowing . . . knowing!

"Chloe . . . Jack . . . oh, please, where are you . . . where?" She pounded upstairs, swirling wildly round Chloe's neat bedroom, then down again, falling heavily at the bottom, catching the small of her back on the last tread, springing up again much as her cousin had done when Paddy Andrews had knocked her into the chair, and again, as it had done up on the moor with Paddy, a small part of her brain told her she would have a nice bruise there tomorrow and all the time her screams echoed about the kitchen and up to the very rafters of the farm roof then out in the yard where she blundered in her blind terror. They carried shrilly to the man waiting by the carriage, to the half-frozen girl in the dairy and to the brothers who were striding down the dark field at the back of the farm towards warmth and food and shelter on this bitter, bitter night.

When they reached her she was about to clamber over the drystone wall and stumble off into the dark peril of the moor in search of her son. She had found Adah-May gobbling senselessly in the dairy but Katy was out of her mind by now and since Jack was not there she whirled out again and on to the barn, the henhouse, the stable where the little horse which pulled the gig snorted in fright.

"Chloe . . . Chloe . . . Chloe . . ." she was screaming, "where's Jack? Where's my baby? What have you done with my baby?" beating her fists on Jamie's broad chest while Thomas and Tommy, white-faced and trembling, stared in growing horror at the half-demented maid, trussed up like one of Chloe's own chickens bound for market and at Katy Andrews who seemed ready to kill anyone who stood in her way, and at Jamie, whose own face had crumpled to the texture and colour of suet.

"Where is she, Jamie? Where's my boy? Oh please . . . please . . ."

"Katy, Katy, calm down, darling. Tell me . . ."

"He's got her . . . and Jack, Jamie. No, I haven't time to be sitting about the kitchen, dammit, let me go . . . let me go . . ."

They lit lamps and stoked up the fire and all the while Katy Andrews screamed and fought like some mad woman escaped from bedlam and Adah-May huddled in a chair by the fire, repeating time and time again, "'E tied me up . . . 'e tied me up," which, since they already knew that was no help to them at all.

They found the blood, a small pool of it on the far side of the fireplace, a scattering of it across the kitchen floor and out into the dark yard and for five minutes, all of them in such a state of shock and disbelief, they milled about, calling her name, calling Jack's name as though the pair of them were hiding in some childish game beyond the wall.

It was Thomas who was the first to collect himself. His stepson was having a hard time, not only with Katy but with his own mortal terror and Tommy, who was only a lad, was waiting for someone to tell him what to do.

"Can thi' drive carriage, lad?" his father asked him.

"Aye, I reckon so, Pa." Tommy could not help but feel a thrill of excitement.

"Then go hell for leather fer tha' ma, an' fetch Dicken an' Jimmy. Quick, lad, but mind them 'orse's legs on the ice."

30

They had climbed up the steep slope to Bramah Edge then dropped down again on to Peak Naze Moor itself, slipping and slithering on the black reefs of gritstone. Its frozen waves were perilous, for a fall could scrape the flesh from your bones, or shatter a limb and Chloe's feet were already bleeding inside her shoes. She marvelled at the agility of the man ahead of her who somehow, despite his wooden leg and the child in his arms, managed to keep his balance. Her heart was in her mouth, for if he should drop Jack the boy would be seriously injured.

From a distance they might have been taken for man and wife, the man carrying the burden of their child while the woman struggled wearily at his back some way behind, but they met no one in this vast wilderness of moorland and gritstone and wet, boggy peatland. This was murderous country, the gritstone hacked through by ice when glaciers made the deep valleys, and the summit of the Dark Peak was a peat-mantled tableland where it could snow for almost a quarter of the year. When it did so, or when it rained, the bogs became quaking pools and the becks were treacherous with flash floods scouring the cloughs, tearing everything down as they went.

The recent snow, thawed only a day or two ago, had

caused such a saturation and every step they took their feet sank almost ankle deep into the sodden ground.

He turned on her again and again, his face a distorted mask of red fury, threatening her that if she did not bugger off and leave him alone he would do for her, but even in his rage knowing he must reach her first which made his fury greater. When he did she merely stopped, patient as a dove, saying nothing, her eyes on the boy in his arms. She was exhausted, for every step in the boggy ground required an enormous effort. Her ankle was on fire where the dog had sunk his teeth and her cheek still bled. She had no idea where they were, only that she must keep up and she believed the pain she was in helped in some strange way. She must not let Jack out of her sight. She didn't know what was to happen, what she was to do at some point in this nightmare, she only knew she must keep up, keep steady, keep her wits about her, for this man was not only powerful but he was deadly. He had had his chance in the kitchen and rejected it, thinking she was no threat to him but if he could reach her now he would kill her, she knew that. He dare not put the boy down to try, since he knew she would evade him, dart forward and scoop Jack up and run like the wind to where Paddy Andrews could not go.

They had lost the dog on the far side of Bramah Edge. He had done his best to scramble up the steep, slippery tumble of moving stones, heaving and panting, encouraged by the man but always falling back and for a while she had thought Paddy meant to pick the thing up and carry him along with the boy, wondering at the depth of his feeling for the ugly animal.

He had cursed, obscenities Chloe had never heard before, torn between his child and his dog and the child had won, not, she was aware, because of any fondness he might have for his son but because Jack was the only weapon he had to use against Katy.

"Let me have him, Mr Andrews," she pleaded, as Paddy knelt by the dog, his hand tender on his broad head.

"Sod off," was all he said, his mind not on her but the animal, then rising to his feet he turned, stumbling away, moving his head this way and that as though in an effort to shut out the piteous cries of the abandoned creature.

"Where are you going, Mr Andrews?" she called out to him as he lumbered up the steep, stony track used by sheep to reach the sweeter grass towards the summit of Peak Naze Moor. A thousand feet up it was and the snow fringed it, but Paddy Andrews had trained himself for this, planned every step of the way and it did not seem to concern him unduly. He was making for the rutted track which lay on the far side of the stretch of moorland and which, earlier in the century, had served a quarry. From there it was down to the main road which would be deserted as night fell and which would take him to Hadfield and the railway station there.

"Mind yer own bloody business," he snarled, twitching the child, who had fallen into a deep, death-like sleep, from one shoulder to the other. Blasted kid was heavy and Paddy was feeling bad, still inclined to grieve over his poor old dog left to perish on the moor all alone and he didn't deserve it, poor old sod. He was in no mood to chat to this persistent bitch who, before long, must be got rid of. They would reach the track in an hour and by then it would be completely dark and safe to venture on to it but not with this bloody woman at his back. Christ, he hadn't bargained for this but it made no difference, he'd still get his revenge on the bitch who had brought him to such a bitter end.

His peg sank suddenly into a dark patch of oozing, quaking ground which sucked at it greedily and he had a moment as he frantically pressed down on the firm ground with his good foot to thank God it was his peg which had gone in. Using his own foot he was quite easily able to apply the pressure needed to free himself, sweating a little at the closeness of his escape. Get stuck in there and you'd be a goner! A mate of their Walter's had lost a whole bloody horse and cart in a bog up Featherbed Moss way when he blundered off the path and any man who was careless, as Walter's mate had been, did not live long to regret it.

He stood for a minute or two, getting his breath back, for the long walk on his wooden leg, a walk he would have eaten up in the old days, was taking it out of him and he realised it was because he was hurrying, hurrying to get away from the woman at his back.

But there, out of the blue, was his answer. There was always a solid path across these patches of deadly bogs, or so his pa had told him and Paddy Andrews, born and bred in these parts as his pa had been, knew how to find them. If he could lure her after him – and what need did he have to lure her since she followed him like a bloody shadow – he had only to get her into the middle of the bloody thing, perhaps no more than a step or two for that would be enough, then, leaving her helpless, sinking, for she'd not know how to tread, the silly cow, he could make his way down to Hadfield in nice time for the train.

He was smiling as he turned, smiling as he had never done before, a wide grin of evil intent which warned Chloe at once that he was up to something. He was not cunning enough to hide it and her heart began to thud and she felt a great desire to turn and run. But he couldn't get her, could he? All these miles they had walked, she following him at a safe distance and he had not been able to get to her, had he, so what devilment was in his mind now? There was something. His eyes had narrowed speculatively as though he was weighing something up and despite herself she took a step backwards.

There was barely enough daylight left to see the misted outlines of the peaks which rose up about them. The coarse, tufted green of the grass and the rusty brown of the short winter bracken were becoming indistinct, blurred into an indistinguishable contour of dips and hollows, cut here and there by narrow tumbling water. It was intensely cold and the water which lay inches deep about her feet had a thin crackle of ice on it. She shivered, dragging her cloak about her, and waited.

"Well, I'm goin' across 'ere, seein' as 'ow it's a short cut," he told her, taking a cautious step forward on to a patch of ground which had a slightly different colour to it than the rest, but it was his voice, his words, for why should he tell her where he was going, that warned her more than the curious colour and texture of the ground he was stepping carefully across. He seemed to put his foot, his good foot forward first, gently, tentatively, as though he was testing the ground before bringing up his peg leg to join it.

He stopped for a moment. "'Ave thi' 'ad enough, then?" he threw over his shoulder, not turning. "Are thi' ter give up or . . ." and as he spoke, his voice mocking, he seemed to lose his balance. He threw out his wooden leg to steady himself and immediately it sank twelve inches into the ground and in an effort to draw it out his good foot went in too and in thirty seconds Paddy Andrews was up to his knees in the clutching, sucking, clawing embrace of the morass. A morass just as lethal as the one which had taken the horse and cart of his brother Walter's mate.

He began to scream in panic, for a man with one leg has not the strength or dexterity of a man with two who might have struggled out, threshing about like some earth monster which has been caught in the primeval swamp from which it crawled. He let go of the bag containing Jack's duds and it disappeared with a nasty squelch, gone in a moment and Paddy's efforts to free himself became more frantic.

For ten seconds Chloe stood there, her eyes wide with shock, convinced that in a minute Paddy would claw his way to the safer ground, for he was caught only to the knees, then Jack began to whimper, his own mind catching the despairing fear of the man who held him, the man who knew better than Chloe Hutchinson what desperate peril he was in and at once life and movement and thought returned to the woman who watched.

"Jack!" she screamed as she sprang forward, racing across the last bit of firm ground towards the bog, but even as her icy feet reached it and prepared themselves to run lightly across it to get Jack, some instinct made her hesitate. Paddy was going down, faster and faster as his struggles became more frenzied, and if she didn't do something quickly he would be gone, taking the child with him. She was here, on firm ground, no more than six feet from him and surely it would serve no purpose to fling herself into the same brown slime which had Paddy in its deathly grip. She needed something, something to throw across the quaking mass for Paddy to grab hold of. But what? She looked about her desperately for a piece of wood, something, anything, but there were no trees up here, no handy branches to lay across the morass which was taking Paddy, and Jack into its stinking embrace.

Someone was moaning, crying piteously, calling out for help, a voice rising to a piercing shriek of despair and she knew it was herself. Herself, for there was no one else here. Chloe Hutchinson was the only one standing between death and the child she loved.

She steadied and so did her voice.

"Paddy, listen to me . . ."

"Oh Jesus, Jesus save me."

"No, there's only me, Paddy, only me. I can take off my cloak and throw it to you. You can crawl across it. I'll help you, pull you out."

"Do it, fer Christ's sake, do it, yer bitch. I'm goin' . . ." and it was true for already the ooze had reached his chest and Jack's little feet were beneath its viciously clutching surface.

"I will, but first you must throw me the baby."

"Fer pity's sake . . . oh lass, fer pity's sake . . ."

"Throw me the baby, Paddy and I swear I'll throw you my cloak. A fair exchange, I think, don't you, but be quick about it before it's too late."

How can you be so calm? a voice was shrieking inside her head, a voice which was telling her to forget caution and fling herself across the bog, to grab at Jack and pull him from Paddy Andrews's arms and if she couldn't, then she'd go down with him for how was she to live if Jack died?

"Paddy?" He could barely hear her over his own demented screams. The ooze had reached his shoulders but incredibly, perhaps an instinct which is inherent in a father, even the worst, to protect his own, he was holding Jack above it, both hands about his waist, the child slack with shock, almost unconscious.

"Here," Paddy roared and with one tremendous effort he threw the boy, like a man chucking a ball into a football match, a perfect arc which took Jack across the stretch of bog and into Chloe's frantic arms.

But that last movement was his undoing and without another sound, his eyes still open, his gaze on his son's face for the last time, Paddy Andrews slipped beneath the oozing slime of the bog.

They almost had to tie Katy Andrews to her cousin's rocking chair to keep her in the kitchen and only Jamie Hutchinson's arms about her, which seemed a bit queer to those Cloudberry End servants gathered there, appeared to keep her steady as she fought to be allowed to go and search for her boy. Deep liver-coloured hollows in which her haunted eyes were sunk, her cheekbones standing out where the flesh of her face appeared to have been burned away, and him no better, really, the pair of them clinging together like each was a life raft to the other.

It did no good, said Saul Gibbon, who knew the area as no other man did and who had been called on to help them in the search, blundering about in the dark, even if it was a clear night. Starlight, like moonlight, was queer, casting shadows that looked solid enough to walk on and giving the illusion there was firm ground where none existed and a man could smash his ankle on a rock, or blunder into one of the stretches of bog which waited up there to trap the unwary. He was sorry to have to say it, as Katy Andrews moaned and Jamie Hutchinson bowed his head, but they had to be warned.

And they didn't know which way they'd gone, did they? Aye, tomorrow morning at first light there'd be a score, fifty men up here to set off in search of the little lad and Mrs Hutchinson but no good would come of rushing about like headless chickens in the dark. That blood which led out from the kitchen, bobbing his head apologetically in the direction of the distraught mother of the missing child and the equally distraught husband of the missing woman, might give them a clue as to the direction to take and in the meanwhile Miss Andrews'd be better served by getting a good night's sleep.

It was just like that time Miss Katy herself went missing, did they remember it, they asked one another as they gathered at dawn in the farmyard where chickens squawked their displeasure. She was a right beggar for causing trouble, that one, they murmured, as they watched her mount her little mare, her cloak flung about her shameful breeches and a warm jacket one of the women from Cloudberry End had been instructed to bring over. She and the grooms from her stable were to ride up towards Spond Moor, fanning out, going north and west, while Ned Garvey and Harry Ellison, both decent riders and provided with a mount by Katy Andrews, were to go east. The rest of them were on foot, moving off from the farm in an ever-widening circle, calling and beating the bushes which, after the night's heavy hoar frost were white and frozen, ready to snap off if treated roughly. There was a bit of a mist which could hamper them to start with but Saul was of the opinion that it would soon clear and a cold, bright day would follow.

Matty and Adah-May were to remain in the farmhouse in case Chloe returned, Matty said, though her expression revealed she did not really expect it to happen. She would be here to make hot drinks and good nourishing soups in case of need, she added brightly, though her eyes said she was dying inside.

They covered every square inch of the moorland within a ten-mile radius of Valley Bottom Farm, looking behind and under each shrub and gorse bush, every rock, every stretch of frozen bracken and heather, every hole and gully and clough, even bloody rabbit holes, Arnie Bagshaw reported, close to tears as anyone could see, when the men came in exhausted, blank-eyed and almost furtive, for they found it difficult to meet the despairing gaze of Katy Andrews and Jamie Hutchinson. Saul Gibbon had not come in yet, having gone off towards Pike Naze Moor for some reason of his own, taking Barty Pickles and Barty's brother, Joseph, who were shepherds like him and good trackers.

It was just as dusk fell that they found them, Saul and Barty and Joseph. They had been no more than half a mile from the road which led from the moor down to Hadfield, the bairn and the woman, and had Mrs Hutchinson known of it she could have walked it in ten minutes.

But the poor lass was in a bad way, anyone could see that, with blood frozen solid to her face and tears frozen solid to the end of her long silken eyelashes. She'd taken off her good, warm cloak and wrapped the little lad in it, then lain down against the base of a rock, afraid to move, she had managed to whisper, in case she fell into the bog. She'd curled her body about the boy, her back to the vicious cold, the bairn tucked snug between her and the rock. All night and the best part of the next day she had been there when they found her, babbling through the alarming crackle in her chest which heralds pneumonia, of dark slime, of Paddy Andrews and cloaks and such and they knew her to be delirious.

They wrapped her up and brought her home to her husband, the little lad crying for his mam, who snatched him out of Barty's arms and held him to her with a great deal of crying of her own.

They put Mrs Hutchinson in her warm bed, her weeping mother-in-law and her frantic husband, but for some reason the men, even though it had all ended happily, could not quite bring themselves to leave, hanging about the farmyard, smoking their pipes and talking quietly. They glanced up at the lighted window where the lass was, they all knew it, fighting for her life. Brave lass, sweet-natured and kind, many of them and their wives knew it first hand. She'd saved that little lad's life and if there was anything they could do for her they'd do it, so if no one minded, bobbing their heads at Katy Andrews who came to the door to hand out cups of steaming tea, they'd just hang about a bit.

They were still there a week later, not all of them and not all at once but there was always someone there, a working man, or perhaps his wife, keeping a vigil for the lass who, they knew now, was not to recover.

Her face on the pillow was little more than a pale smooth oval, fragile as a snowflake, or the snowdrops which push through the greening land Chloe Hutchinson would never see again. Gone was the pink of rose in her cheeks, that sheen of good health which had lain about her since her marriage to Jamie Hutchinson. The scar on her cheek was a livid reminder of what had been done to her, of what had killed her. Only her hair was alive, rich and coppery, a smoothly brushed halo of curls which glowed in the candlelight, or in a stray beam of sunlight which came to lie across her pillow. Her breast rose and fell on her light, painful breathing, the drugs the doctor had given her making her drowsy though she did not sleep much. The harsh crepitation of the pneumonia seemed to fill the room and Matty, who had barely left the chair by the fireside, wept silently.

Just before dawn on the seventh day she awoke and spoke quite clearly.

"He saved . . . his life . . . in the end."

It was no more than a whisper, a sigh, a breath of softness in the warm room and at once Jamie bent over her, smoothing back her hair in an agony of love.

"Don't talk, little dove . . . save your strength."

"Katy?"

"Is downstairs."

"Must see her."

"Rest, darling, rest."

Chloe opened her eyes. They were a clouded blue-green, glowing with her love for him but already beginning to haze a little as death touched her and his tears dripped on to her hands which were as light and frail as a bit of swansdown.

"No, Jamie . . . you must . . . not weep . . . I love Jack. I could not have . . . borne it . . . if he . . . had died."

"I know, my lovely girl."

"Tell Katy . . . to come."

They brought her up, though she knew quite simply she could not bear it, for how was she to manage without the serenity and sweetness of Chloe whom she had known for less than three short years in her life? But she must not cry. She must not add to the burden of Chloe's going, as Jamie was, with tears.

"Katy . . ." It was the merest whisper.

"Yes, darling, I'm here. What is it?" She took one of Chloe's hands and held it to her cheek, smiling a little. "Tell me."

"Paddy . . ."

"I know about him, darling."

"He died in the . . . bog."

"Yes, they told me."

"But you must . . . he . . . redeemed himself, Katy. He threw . . . Jack to me . . . saved him."

She closed her eyes and for a long aching time was quiet. Katy watched her, scarcely aware of what Chloe had told her in her own painful grief. She thought she would not wake again and what did the revelation about Paddy Andrews, who had caused all this, matter to her now?

Chloe's breathing became sharp and shallow as the night wore on and the doctor shook his head. Katy rested her head beside Chloe's, sleeping a little but a light touch on her hair roused her and she lifted her head and looked into Chloe's eyes.

"Yes, darling, I'm here." Sliding her own strong arm about her cousin's shoulders she drew her gently into her arms. Chloe was no more than a bit of thistledown but she seemed to gain a little strength from the force of Katy's love.

They clung together, watched by the man who loved them both, the wild, forceful vigour of Katy Andrews holding back the dying spirit of Chloe Hutchinson for a brief moment. It was too late now to tell Chloe how she felt, how she loved her, for already the white, waxy face cradled against her shoulder had taken on the sunken look of death, but Chloe saw it in her eyes and a small tender smile tugged at her mouth.

Kissing her brow, smiling into her cousin's fading eyes Katy passed her into the arms of her husband and went downstairs.

Those gathered in the yard saw the curtains being drawn across her window. They bowed their heads, standing for a long moment in respectful silence and a woman, Archie Bagshaw's wife, threw her pinny over her head and wept, then, without speaking, they quietly left for their homes.

It was the same in the churchyard on the day of her funeral. The little chapel at Woodhead was like a ship floating in a sea, a great sea of silent people, all of them mourning the woman who had gone. Katy was astonished, filled with a wondering sorrow that she had not known of the esteem in which her cousin had been held. Archie Bagshaw, who had delivered her letters, held a handkerchief to his eyes and sobbed visibly, to his wife's distress, and Fred Beardsall, who collected the tickets at the station and who, it appeared, had a sickly wife whom Chloe had regularly visited, was quite shattered, leaning against the stone wall as the coffin was lowered into the ground.

Katy had brooded on whether she should write to Chloe's father to let him know she was dead, for after all she was his daughter and he had a right to know. But did he? To the best of her knowledge he had not written one line to Chloe in the years she had lived here so it had seemed inappropriate, not something Chloe herself would have wanted. All the people who loved her, and whom she had loved were here at her graveside, every one of them, and surely that was all that mattered?

"Crossclough must be empty," Tommy was heard to remark brokenly to his father, the pair of them clinging to Matty. Mrs Kelsall and her "girls" were there, all of them silently weeping, for a loud outburst, which was what they felt like showing, would not have been seemly. Not for Miss Chloe. She had been so ladylike, so gracious and serene in all she did, surely at her funeral they must behave in the same tranquil, respectful manner in which she herself would have acted.

Only Adah-May made a show of herself and she was no more than a child in a woman's body, poor soul. She was led away by her mother to weep inconsolably at the back of the chapel among the first snowdrops. She'd picked some, it was said, when the grave had been filled in and put them with the wreaths and dozens of simple bunches of flowers which covered it.

The biggest surprise was the appearance of Jack and Sara Andrews who had been known to hold their niece in some disfavour, something to do with Mrs Andrews's past relationship with her own sister who had been Mrs Hutchinson's mother. They had come to support their daughter and to check up on that grandson of theirs, no doubt, for the bairn had had a nasty experience and clung to his mother more than he once had.

They had all gone at last, drifting sadly away along the bottom road, most walking, for they were ordinary folk, towards their homes in Crossclough or Saltersbrook or Woodhead, some to climb into their carriages and make their way to Valley Bottom Farm where Mrs Jenkins had provided refreshments.

"Will you come with us in the carriage, darling?" Sara asked her daughter, touching her hand gently, only realising now how much her cousin had meant to Katy, bewildered by it in a way, for the enmity between them had once been ferocious.

"No, Mother, I'll be up directly."

"Very well, darling." Her mother followed Katy's gaze up the gently sloping ground of the churchyard to where the bowed and lonely figure of Jamie Hutchinson stood by his wife's grave. "But don't . . ."

"I won't, Mother. I do have some sensitivity."

"Of course," though once Katy Andrews had not been known for it.

She made no move to join him. She remained out of sight at the gate, watching over him to see he did not falter, in much the same way she watched over her son. The day was grey, sharp with a hint of the snow to come and she saw him shiver but he did not move and neither did she. She would leave him soon when she was convinced he was steady. She would let him grieve as a man should for the woman he had loved, but not for long. Soon she would go to him and they would speak of farms and paper mills and his child which grew inside her and soon, before too long, she would ask him to marry her.

There would be talk, of course, but when hadn't there been talk in the valley about Katy Andrews?